Adriano Exists

Written by Lisa Sa

© 2019 Lisa Sa

All rights reserved. No part of this publication may be reproduced, stored in a retrieval system, or transmitted, in any form or by any means, electronic, mechanical, photocopying, recording or otherwise, except as permitted by the UK Copyright, Designs and Patents Act 1988, without the prior permission of the publisher.

To everyone close to me who puts up with my terribly anti-social tendencies.

I'll go sit in the corner now and listen to Nirvana.

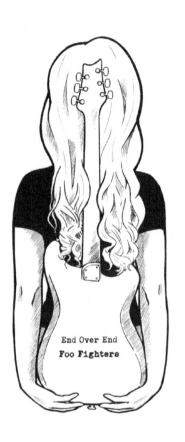

1

"You'll be fine," the bathroom assistant tells me.

"Sure. I'll be fine," I reply, as I stare back at my reflection in the eerily clean mirror; my twenty-two-year-old self in all her glory. I look over the cherry red hair and the roots that need re-dying. The curious, terrified eyes looking back at me, and the pale lips after my throwing up fest.

And I proceed to tell myself what I always tell myself:

I can and I will.

I put a stop to the hiccups (drinking upside down is always the trick, I recommend trying it, though maybe not in front of the bathroom assistant, who, when I spill some water on the collar of my shirt, takes whatever was left of my self-esteem and obliterates it when she kindly helps dry me off).

Once I've been thoroughly judged by the two very beautiful and ferociously bitchy women behind the reception desk, I get told to take one of the lifts to floor sixteen.

Everything in the TK Records building is insanely intimidating, from every platinum and gold record you eye twice, to every shiny chandelier you look up at in fascination. Even pressing the lift button feels like you're gate crashing a party you were never invited to.

When I arrive at floor sixteen, this time I'm greeted by a sixteen year-old looking hipster with a man bun, who is sitting behind the desk and listening to Blur.

Blur! Must be a slow day – usually at companies such as TK Records they'll be playing the latest, unheard of, next big thing, to remind potential clients waiting in reception that they know the good stuff, the bands that make shit tons of money from that music that they discover way, *way* before you. It completely screams *you will never make it without us*.

"Hi, I'm here for a 5pm job interview with Stephen Sandal," I tell the hipster, who looks at me with far less judgemental eyes than the two hyena downstairs. In fact, he rises, walks around the desk and gives me a genuine smile.

"Hey there! What's your name?"

"Alexis Brunetti," I tell him, praying my hiccups don't make a comeback in time for the main event.

"Right! Hi Alexis, I'm Joe. Welcome to TK Records. If you'd just like to take a seat, Stephen should be finished soon. Would you like anything – tea, water?"

A new body that doesn't throw up and hiccup when extremely nervous would be lovely, thanks.

"No thank you, I'm fine."

He nods with a friendly smile, and makes his way back to behind the desk, scrolling away on the computer in front of him. I look around at the empty waiting room, spotting the music magazines on the table. With my poor eyesight long distance and my refusal to get glasses, I squint at the cover of one of them, just about making out David Bowie.

All hail the Music King. Bring me some good luck won't you, oh Bowie?

It's a good twenty minutes before Joe calls my name. I get up a bit too quickly and the blood rushes to my head. He tells me to take the third door on the left down a long corridor. He then wishes me luck, and goes back to bopping his head to Song 2.

When I knock and enter, there is a man sitting at his desk with very expensive-looking shoes, lying back on his chair with his phone pressed to his ear. His suit is Dolce & Gabbana, his hair is pristine, and his eyes, though not on me yet, are already something to fear.

This, is Stephen Sandal. He may look like the CFO of TK Records, or, hell, he may even look like the founder, but he's neither of those things. He's simply one of the managers. But he's the one seeing me today, and he's the one that will be deciding if I will work at TK Records.

He spots me and signals for me to come forth and take a seat, motioning his free hand like an over enthusiastic lollipop man. I awkwardly smile and take a seat in one of the two leather chairs opposite his desk. "I'll call you later, okay Benjamin? Don't sweat it, it's in the bag. It's in the bag, I got this! Okay, gotta go, my 5pm is here. Yeah, okay, bye." When he hangs up, he looks at me a few seconds before taking his feet off the desk and standing up. I do the same. "Hi...Alexis?" he searches his desk for my CV as he shakes my hand – his palms are clammy and semi stick to mine as I pull away.

"Yes – I'm Alexis, lovely to meet you," I tell him. "Thank you for seeing me."

"Oh, no worries, Jess is a good friend of mine from university. When he said his little brother's friend wanted to work for TK, I said *come on in and meet us!*"

Stephen Sandal's accent is Californian – he's been living in London for fifteen years but still maintains the accent as if he inhabits a desire to remain loyal to his upbringing. He's worked for TK for eighteen years, starting off in the Californian office before eventually moving to London. He likes hiking, photography and renaissance art.

I know all of this because I obviously stalked all of his credentials before the interview. Outlining a person's career before a job interview is extremely important; they want you to stalk them, to know them, to do your research – and you never want to be caught off guard. "Great! It's wonderful to be here."

He motions for me to sit down and we both do so at the same time. "So, Alexis, tell me a bit about yourself. I see you've interned in radio, you did a bit of music journalism, you even had an Internet show that went viral…this is all very impressive! And how old are you?!"

"Thank you, I'm twenty-two," I tell him, "yes, I've worked in various fields in the music business."

"You started at sixteen! Jesus. And with your own music magazine at college – wow, you seem to be a real outside thinker, always coming up with ideas."

"Yes, I like to always think of new ways to interact with music lovers."

"And, what are you doing right now?"

I gulp, and he sees me gulp. "I'm looking for the position that's right for me in the music business."

"Do you have any ideas?"

"Well, I believe I'd be perfect as an A&R scout at TK Records. I've been scouting since I was sixteen, when I launched Music Mayhem, then I continued to do so when I worked in radio, at various PR companies, and really, I've never stopped scouting since. That's the beauty of London; there's always music to discover."

"Uh huh," he looks down at my CV, licking his upper lip and deep in thought. "From what I can tell here, you've never had an actual paying job in music, is that right?"

Shit. Shit. Shit.

"Yes, that is correct. I've interned at a lot of companies whilst at university getting my degree and since I graduated last year I've continued to do so-"

"I understand, this business is very tough for people just starting out. And the music business is one mean son of a bitch, I know this." There's silence and I'm not sure how to respond.

Quick Alex, save this!
Save this, damn it!
You wanna work here – it's TK Records, for goodness sake!
This is the UK's biggest record label.
They have their fingers in every single pie imaginable.
This is where you belong!

"It is, but I believe that being in the environment for as long as I have, I've picked up the various skills needed to progress, to get a paying job and work hard to go far. I'm willing to do whatever it takes to push through, to get my foot in the door."

Stephen lies back in his chair, and throws my CV on the desk. He's smiling at me now and I feel like this may be the turning point I've been waiting for. This may just be it. The start of my career in the music business. It's happening.

It's happening…

"I'm glad to hear that, Alexis. Because we are actually looking for a scout at the moment."

My heart somersaults.

"Our boy Tommy is moving on, he's going to work for Black Rose. So we need a new scout, and I think you may just be the one, Alexis."

"Oh, that's fantastic to hear!"

He rests a hand on his belt, as he looks at me. "Yes, though there are many candidates that have applied for the role, you understand," he tells me as he fiddles with his belt. "All very young, very talented…"

"Yes, I understand, however, with proof of my ability to think outside the box, I believe I can bring-"

"Yes, it's always good to work in different sectors of music, get a feel for the different environments, how they work, the politics…"

His belt is making a lot of noise now and so my eyes drop down to his waist. As they do so, I notice that he is not fiddling with his belt – he is taking it off.

I freeze, as I watch him undo the buckle as he continues to talk.

"…there's plenty of kids out there, all just as keen and eager as you to join a monopoly of the music business. We're the industry everyone wants to work in."

I'm finding it hard to concentrate now, as I watch him slowly pull his unbuckled belt out of his trousers.

What the fuck is he doing?

"You understand, this is a very competitive role."

This cannot be happening?

I am trembling pretty hard at this point, completely shocked and not understanding what is going on, but knowing that this is wrong, that this is very wrong.

"We had two thousand applicants for this job," he tells me, as he successfully pulls out his belt, and wraps it around his knuckles. "We shortlisted a hundred to the first round."

He's looking me in the eye, I can feel it, but I can't seem to be able to take my eyes off of his belt. I am afraid that if I do so, I will miss something. As if, in a blink of an eye, I could miss something important.

"Fifty made it to the second round," he pauses, as he holds his belt within his clutches. "And only ten made it to the third round. But you, Alexis…"

I look up now, meeting his eyes as soon as he says my name. This is, after all, a job interview. I have been trained again and again in life to be courteous, polite, and always maintain eye contact in job interviews.

Though no one ever tells you what to do if something like this were to happen.

Why is that?

Why is it so hush-hush?

Something so critical in life, something every woman and girl should know how to handle at the drop of a hat.

And no one ever speaks of it.

Though we all know, it exists.

7

His eyes have a malevolence in them that is terrifying me, and yet, I do not move. I maintain eye contact.

"You are our lucky eleventh and final candidate. Straight to the third round you go. And you are very lucky to be here."

He slowly puts his belt on the desk in front of us. It makes a loud *clunk* noise as it hits the wooden table. There is a brief moment where both of our pair of eyes are fixated on it in silence, and I am trying to understand how this can possibly be reality.

"The question I guess is, how can we make this job yours?" he slowly unzips his flies, and I can see that he is wearing grey boxers. He is looking up at me now, waiting for me to get up, to walk over.

To get on with it.

"I really need to be smart about who I choose to represent A&R at TK, Alexis. You understand?"

Again I gulp, but this time it's as if I'm swallowing a hard rock. I jump out of the leather chair, bolt out of the room, and run down the spiral staircase three steps at a time.

Once outside, and without any say in the matter whatsoever, I throw up again in the nearest bin.

After buying some mouth wash and re-doing my make-up, I jump on a train to Kentish Town. I've stopped trembling now, but it's the first time this sort of thing has happened to me so I'm still reeling. I've heard stories, rumours, myths in the past, of course – of what it's like to be a girl in the music business. But never have I lived it myself.

Until just now.

I'm not a throw-up-when-nervous type of girl, I'm not. So to throw up *before* the interview and also *after*, for completely different triggers of anxiety, is making me a little dizzy.

But I'm okay. This is a minor setback. It doesn't matter that I graduated from university over a year ago, it doesn't matter that I've been unsuccessful in securing a job in the music business in that time, despite my many years' experience, and it doesn't matter because I'm going to find a way. Some other way. A way that doesn't require me giving blow jobs to low lives like scumbag Stephen Sandal.

He wanted a blow job.
The man interviewing me wanted a blow job.
In order to work at TK Records.
Stephen fucking Sandal.

For a split second I imagine a scenario where I unleash the sexual predator in me, walking over to him with a certain charm.

And…
Well…
I get on with it.

He comes after three seconds because, well, he looks like one of *those* people. If he's asking interviewees for blow jobs he's definitely one of *those*.

Stop it, Alex.
You would never have gone through with it.
Ever.
You are not that girl.
Nor will you ever be.

But despite my thoughts, I let my mind go ahead and create a scenario where I am head of A&R at TK Records, strolling into the office arm-in-arm with Dave Grohl. "Oh *Alex*, we would love to have you jam in the studio with us on Friday!"

All it would have taken was one blow job.
And five-ten seconds of my dignity.
I open my eyes and look around the busy carriage.

You are going to find a different way to make that scenario come true, Alex. You are.

My phone buzzes in my pocket and I get it out.

Blake:
Don't be late please, I'm here already and everyone's Italian! Help!

Seeing Blake's message brightens my mood slightly, and I remember that I have an evening of entertainment ahead. I'm en route to a gig – Paolo Petrinelli is playing at the Forum tonight, and I'm a relatively big fan of his music, have been since I was little. My parents are Italian, and though I was born in London I speak both languages fluently. This means that I grew up with two countries' ideas, morals, and perceptions of what makes great art. I consider myself very lucky.

When I arrive at the Forum I'm reminded of just how small a venue it really is, with a capacity of only two thousand people. It has two levels and a standing area. When I enter the place is swarming with people.

I have to say, the Forum is probably my favourite venue in London. It's intimate enough to be close to the band, yet not too small that you're likely to get squashed, and there's a bar at the back that is convenient to get to. I'm not really a huge fan of those massive venues where you pay £200 to see the band a mile away, being careful not to drop down to your death as you try to mosh in the sitting area. Who the hell buys a seated ticket to a gig, anyway?

I notice Blake near the front of the stage in second row, and I begin to make my way through the crowd to get to him. The key to pushing through a crowd without someone trying to start a fight or push you back is *not* to give them puppy dog eyes; it's to give them your meanest look. It has taken a few years to master but my Mean Look is now pretty convincing. It consists of lowered eyebrows, squinting eyes and a tightened jaw.

As I push through, I recognise Blake's dark blue Reebok jacket and floppy light brown hair instantly, and tap him on the shoulder. Even from the back of his head I can tell that he is uncomfortable. He turns and grins at the sight of me.

"Alex-y, bab-y!" he yells over the support act.

"Hi!" we hug briefly and he pulls me next to him, forcing a young, cute Italian in his twenties to move.

"Alex, all I can hear is 'mamma mia!' every two seconds…why am I here?!"

I cackle. "To accompany me to a gig 'cause you're a good friend. And to be blown away by Paolo Petrinelli."

"He better be good," he tells me, suddenly grinning, "hey, you're on time!"

Blake and I have been friends for as long as I can remember. He loves gigs more than anyone else I know, even more than me, and he's the type of person that will show up to one even if the world is coming to an end. He is funny, and kind; that type of awkward kind that you can feel is genuine. This is one of the reasons I really like Blake and keep him close. Genuine people give you a part of their heart every time you interact with them; it's up to you then what you do with it. I, for example, keep every part of Blake's heart with me. It keeps me warm.

"So, how did the job interview go?!"

I gulp, but try very hard to hide the trauma. "Uh, don't think I'll be getting a call back."

But even as I say the words, there is not a speckle of surprise in them.

Maybe I should introduce myself. My name is Alexis, and where I begin this story I am twenty-two years old. I work part-time in a chicken shop, and I live at home with my parents. Wow, in a single sentence I realise how pathetic my life sounds. This is not the full extent of my life goals, I promise you.

I live this life because there is only one thing I want to do: work in the music business. It's all I've ever wanted, but I'll resist going off track with some bullshit cheesy malarkey about how it's always been my dream and that I know it's my calling, blah blah blah. I'll save that shit for the unimaginative twats of this world.

You already know all of that. You've already heard all of that, a *thousand* times over. So what makes me different from the rest of them, I hear you ask?

I have no clue.

All I know is that I'm applying everywhere, but getting nowhere. I've been looking for a job on the London music scene since graduating last year: record labels, music PR, radio stations – nobody is hiring, or at least, nobody is hiring *me*. I'm applying for everything – assistant jobs, internships, apprenticeships, even work experience designed for spotty fifteen-year old clueless kids – but nada.

Every second that is going by, every single second, feels like I'm missing something I'm supposed to be experiencing as a twenty-something in the music industry.

Every morning I wake up lost and unhappy; I think about what I could be doing in this moment to help my career, and I get pulled into what I call Unemployment Oblivion.

Even though I am technically employed by a chicken shop on Enfield high street, I am failing to get into the industry and career I dream to have. This, for me, qualifies me for membership to Unemployment Oblivion. Here all you have is self-loathe and sadness. You wake up without purpose, and without purpose, what the fuck is there in life?

"You'll get the next one," Blake tells me and I force an appreciative smile.

But will I? What if I never get one? What if the only ones who will be willing to interview me will be the Stephan Sandals of this world?

I don't say any of this to Blake though, I don't mention what happened or how I am still pretty traumatised by the experience. I am pretty private, even with my closest friends. I trust no one, and assume that *anyone* can fuck you over at any given moment. Even the most genuine.

And so I instead smile, and turn the tables back on him, demanding an update on things since I last saw him two days ago.

The time in-between the support act and the main act is always the most painful. It seems like you are stuck there hours, just waiting, listening involuntarily to the crap playlist they put on in the background. You can't move to get a drink or go to the bathroom because when you come back nobody is going to let you through again.

Blake and I discuss our goals and the usual 'no I haven't found anything yet' routine from me, every time the shame and frustration mounting even more, and the conversation goes dead for a minute as the other person wonders how the *hell* I haven't managed to find a job in music yet. Is it time to give up? Am I deluding myself? I'm terrified of answering those questions, but I know that one day I will have to.

Just not tonight.

Tonight I'm at a gig, and it's Friday night. Don't I get a pass on Friday night?

Suddenly the crowd starts screaming in my ears as the venue goes dark, my heart pounding, and my eyes fixed on the stage.

A man in his early forties jogs onto the stage and sits himself down at the drums, the bassist follows, and then the two guitarists, keyboardist, and finally, Paolo Petrinelli. The crowds' screams only get louder and I join in, Blake too, screaming purposely like a girl.

He's wearing a tight, white t-shirt that highlights his semi-toned body, and casual blue jeans with brown boots. He looks younger than his forty-five years, but perhaps it's more his long brown hair, because if you look closely at his face, he has a few wrinkles now. His eyes are big and blue, full of wisdom, and he has the most beautiful smile that assures me it's going to be a night to remember.

"Buona sera, London!" the sound of his deep, raspy voice sends shivers down my spine and I join in with the *woo*ing from the crowd.

We have a really good view; he is only metres from us, and thankfully, there is nobody taller than me in front of us, something that happens way too often for a girl of average height. It always makes me feel short.

"Are you ready for some rock?!"

Again more *woo*ing and I put my arms in the air, like everyone else, already lost in the magic when the music hasn't even started yet. A heat wave hits my face and I'm glad I'm wearing a sleeveless top.

We're standing right in the middle of second row, Paolo Petrinelli directly in front of us with the mic. I look around the stage at the other members as an upbeat, happy rock song I know well starts playing and Paolo begins singing. Blake and I join in jumping up and down with the crowd and I look at the guitarist on the left – Mauro Fontana.

Mauro Fontana had previously been an Italian singer songwriter before he joined the Petrinelli band, but after a few years of success he had hit a downward spiral of drugs and alcohol. He reappeared five years later as Paolo's lead guitarist, and has since remained clean in this role for a good ten years now, releasing new stuff on the side that never gets more than five thousand hits on the Internet, and never even getting close to selling out a solo tour.

Every other member in the band looks unfamiliar to me, and since I play a little guitar I like to watch the guitarists in particular at gigs and see who is playing which riff. My eyes fixate firstly on Mauro, and I watch him intensely, waiting to be impressed. But he disappoints pretty quickly, playing a simple riff, and nodding his head with his eyes closed as if it's a really difficult song.

Poser.

He's wearing a black top hat, only further highlighting his bleached white-blonde hair underneath, which looks ridiculous with his thick, black eyebrows. He has a gold chain round his neck and I can just about make out a guitar tattoo on his upper arm.

Argh, poser, poser, poser!

I switch over to the right to watch the rhythm guitarist. The man on the right of Petrinelli is a surprisingly young guy, no more than twenty-eight, with fairly dark brown hair, big brown eyes and a nice, toned build. His muscles flex underneath his black buttoned shirt as he plays.

Wow, he's attractive. But he's so young. How come I don't know this guy?

Just then he smiles at Petrinelli.

Damn, that is a nice smile.

He looks casual and down-to-earth, and I'm intrigued. I'd like to tell you how the hell I can tell he's a down-to-earth guy just by looking at him but I can't – it's just that look in his eyes, as if he's there because he loves to play, that the girls in first row screaming at him doesn't affect him at all. It's drawing me in instantly.

Who the hell is he? How can Petrinelli have such a young guitarist in his band? Isn't he worried that some of the attention will shift to him? Everyone else in the band is in their mid-thirties at the very youngest!

I watch him play some easy chords on rhythm, and suddenly it all becomes clear to me.

He must not be a very guitarist, that's why. He's just there to look pretty.

Disappointed, I turn my attention back to Petrinelli.

"His accent is pretty good!" Blake wails over the music.

"Of course it is!"

I've always known that Paolo Petrinelli would be an amazing artist to see live; watching him interact with the crowd it takes all of three seconds to witness his abilities as an artist. More than anything, he is able to set the crowd alight with passion through his voice alone – one single voice box. He has the power to make you feel like you are alone in the room with him, like he's singing only to you, and whatever feeling he is evoking in his song radiates off of him and you take it all in like a sponge.

Not only does his songs hold this supremacy over you, but his lyrics are always poetic and creative metaphors that you love to sing along to and think about late at night.

Blake and I jump around, drowning in a sea of sweat and beer and screams, one woman near us even taking off her top at one point, waving it around in the air, all eyes on her double D red bra.

Blake and I occasionally look at one another to give each other our 'this is awesome!' looks.

Two hours whiz by, and I know it's nearly the end of the gig when Petrinelli slows it down with one of his classics – a sad song about a man haunted by his own demons. I glance at the young guitarist – he has barely done anything the entire evening – always on rhythm, always following Mauro's lead.

See. I knew it. Just a pretty face, I gloat to myself, shaking my head a little. *He does not even deserve that guitar. Look at it! A J5 Triple Tele Deluxe edition, what a beauty.*

And just as I stare at the guitar within his clutches, the young guitarist steps forward, the limelight shining onto him, and he begins playing a solo; an amazing and aggressive solo.

Petrinelli looks on, smiling, and Mauro, having had all the other solos of the past two hours, looks bored and slightly jealous. The crowd screams and a girl near us yells, "ti amo, Riccardo!" looking as if she is about to faint. I glare in disbelief, as the solo goes around and around, sending shivers down my spine, I have goose bumps, and then it's over.

A guitar orgasm, that was.

The limelight disappears and he steps back, grinning like mad, and he looks so damn sexy. I smile, both amazed and embarrassed at the thought that he was unworthy of the Fender in his hands. I glance at Blake, who looks just as stunned as me, his eyes big and shocked. There's uproar from the crowd, and as I stare at the young guitarist, he catches my glance as he looks around the crowd. I smile at him and join in with the *woo*ing.

I did what everyone else does and judged a book by its cover. Just because he's young he can't be good?

I'm feeling especially bad because this is exactly the sort of judgement I get from others and detest. '*She's just a girl, what the hell does **she** know about rock music? She looks like a groupie.*'

Learn your lesson, Alex. Do not judge people.

"Hey!" says a familiar voice, as the crowd begins dispersing the second Petrinelli disappears offstage, followed by the band. Is it just me or at the end of a gig it seems appropriate to say a mental 'goodbye' or 'see you next time' to the empty stage?

Blake and I turn around to find Enrico standing there, grinning from ear-to-ear so that you can see his buck teeth perfectly in the still dimly lit venue.

"Hey, Enrico."

"How's it going?!" he wails, as if we are best friends that haven't seen each other in years, and not two people that briefly dated years ago. Oh, how I do love to remember my teenage years, when my taste in men was about as sharp as play dough.

Before I can reply, a girl approaches him yelling 'Enrico!' and throws her arms around him before he even has a chance to react.

"Susy! Ciao!" as they speak in Italian to one another, both of them ignoring us, Blake moves in closer to my ear.

"Douche," we glance at each other and smile, just as the girl suddenly disappears with the moving crowd. He turns back to me, pretending Blake isn't there, and continues grinning.

Man, he has such a big mouth. What the hell did I see in him?

"Fancy seeing you here!"

Enrico is the Italian-American ex-guitarist of a mildly famous singer, but he thinks he's God's Gift to the music industry. Okay, for five seconds I had believed him. But in my defence, at seventeen I didn't know enough about guitars and music to really be able to tell the difference between great musicians and phonies. Enrico, as I know now, is a phoney. Sure, he can play mildly well, but not half as well as he *thinks* he can play.

All my life I had wanted to meet a musician untouched by the superficial elements of the music industry, but Enrico turned out to be the most fake, cloned sheep of them all. Now we sometimes bump into each other at gigs, he pretends he's super pleased to see me and we exchange pleasantries. He's been with his girlfriend, Bianca, for five years – Bianca likes black and white photography and Coldplay, according to her social media page. Of course I checked out her profile – I'm a girl.

"Yeah, love Petrinelli," I tell him.

"I remember you liked him."

Okay he doesn't usually bring up remembering anything about me.

He stares, almost nostalgically, and I become uncomfortable as I remember the conversations we used to have late at night.

I used to tell him about my arguments with my mum. How weird.

"Where's Bianca tonight?" I ask.

Why doesn't he ever bring her? Not that I want to meet her.

"Uh, she's at home."

"Ah, right. So you like him, too?"

"Yeah, yeah! Remember, I know the guitarist!?"

"Oh, yeah!" I say, vaguely remembering something. He had talked an awful lot about himself when we had been seeing each other. "Which one? The young one?" I ask, hoping he says yes.

"Riccardo? No, no…the other one, Mauro Fontana."

*Oh. The **poser.***

"I'm going backstage now in fact, y'wanna come?"

He's definitely after a favour of some sort – he's never this nice. But I will deal with that later – of course I want to go backstage!

"Sure!"

I feel Blake shuffle around awkwardly next to me and I glance at him, Enrico acknowledging him too now.

"I'm gonna miss the last train…" the last time we had missed the last train, Blake had been furious. We had had to wait for the night bus, and once it had come it had taken a good hour and a half for him to get home. He had had work early the next morning and had not been pleased to be on a diet of cheap energy drinks.

"Early shift?"

He nods, solemnly.

Ok Alex, let's do the right thing.

"Alright, let's go," I say, about to wave at Enrico and make our way out when Blake forces a laugh.

"You're staying, lemonhead."

I frown. "What? But-"

He pulls me to the side by the arm, where Enrico is less likely to hear what we're saying.

"You're staying! Go backstage, go meet Pablo whatever, you've loved that guy for years. The gig was awesome, he's awesome, go meet him!"

He's telling me to go, I mean it would be crazy to say no….

"Are you sure?! Are y'gonna be okay?"

"The question is are *you* going to be ok with Mr Douche over there?"

I stifle a laugh. "*Him* I can handle," I tell Blake.

"And getting home?"

"Taxi."

"Just text me when you get home."

I nod and pull him into a hug.

"Have fun!"

I watch Blake disappear into the moving crowd, leaving me alone in the Forum with Buckteeth. I glance over at him as he fake-smiles at some passing Italians, and I find myself wondering what the hell I'm getting myself into.

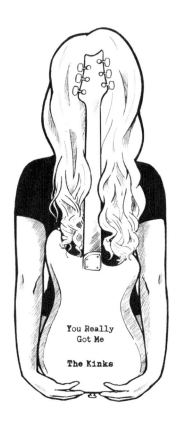

2

I have always imagined that everyone goes through this hell they call education so that they can live out the happiest day of their lives (graduation), get hired somewhere, and from there, their lives would slowly go downhill. A 9-5 job would slowly kill their soul.

But not me. I hadn't gone to my graduation out of sheer disinterest in participating in the happiest day of my life, and from there, nothing had gone the way I had planned.

Maybe that's why things are going wrong - I didn't go to my graduation.

My refusal to go had been a reflection of my desire to steer away from that stereotypical societal idea of getting a boring and uninspiring job, getting married, and having kids. In any which order.

But I'm beginning to think that life (or society) is punishing me for my fuck-the-system attitude, and instead of being ambitious, creative and driven, with absolutely no leads in the music business ten months after graduation, I am beginning to feel like a rather large loser. Like I am simply a huge fan of music and nothing more. A glorified groupie of some sort, and that doesn't make me feel too great about myself.

"Come on," says Enrico, and even from a metre distance he looks vaguely like a horse.

I follow him against the remainders of the moving crowd to the stage door, watching the back of Enrico's buzz cut head as he nods at some people we pass. A scrawny man in his early thirties wearing a fluorescent jacket stands in front of the door, arms folded.

I expect Enrico to get out a special backstage pass or something, but he simply nods at the scrawny man, who nods back and steps aside to let us through.

I smile at the security guard and scurry after Buck Teeth down the purple walled corridor.

I hate to sound like a groupie but this is pretty darn exciting. Stay cool though Alex, you've met loads of famous musicians and singers back at Slurp Radio, not to mention the internships...remember when you met Marilyn Manson and offered him a coffee? That was a good night...

The corridor is dark and cold, and we take a left down another empty corridor with only one door. Enrico opens it, winking at me, and we enter a spacious, lilac room. There's a mud coloured sofa, a coffee table with open packets of crisps and cans of coke laid on them; bass guitars, acoustic guitars, electric guitars all leaning against the wall.

There are two men in the room; one on his Mac on the sofa, and the other standing, gulping down a two litre bottle of water. They both nod at us.

"Great show, Kyle!" Enrico says to the man with the water bottle, over enthusiastically. I have already worked out who they are – the man drinking to replace his sweat is the bassist of the band, I recognise him from the ten seconds he had stepped forward to start a song. The younger guy on the sofa has to be a part of the tech team; he hadn't been onstage and he fits all the criteria – young, reserved, and on a laptop looking like he's trying to figure something out.

The bassist releases the bottle from his lips, wipes his mouth with his arm and blurts out 'thanks!' dribbling a little onto his dark purple Boston University t-shirt.

American.

I study the man carefully – he's in his mid-thirties, with green eyes and short brown hair, a few freckles on his neck and slightly pale skin.

Yeah, my Italian radar is not ticking here.

"The rest of the guys still recovering?"

"Paolo's doing a few press interviews, and the others are just getting changed."

Yep, that's definitely an American accent.

I notice a door on the far left hand side, and I assume the rest of the band is behind there. Looking around the room again, I notice a guitar lying on a chair and I'm sure I'm seeing things.

No, wait. That is...

"The Gibson ES-335!" I shriek, rushing over to the chair across the room. The other two look at me, taken aback, but my eyes are firmly fixed on the shiny red legendary guitar. Once in front of the chair, I lean in, my hands slowly reaching out to touch it…

"You like?" says a voice suddenly, making me jump back a little. I look to find the young guitarist standing at the Other Door, and he lets it shut behind him. He smiles and my heart begins racing as I remember his impressive solo. He slowly approaches, his eyes full of warmth and intrigue.

He's even better looking up close.

I study his face carefully as he approaches – olive skin, a perfectly shaped nose, big, brown charismatic eyes and a bit of stubble across his cheeks to his jaw, just enough hair for it to be sexy – really sexy. What is most attractive is his smile though - sincere and almost childlike, it connects with his eyes, as if his eyes are smiling, too.

He's now wearing a tight, grey t-shirt that shows off his toned chest and a black blazer with thin grey lines on it.

"Yes!" I manage to say. "I *love* this make, I'm so glad they brought it back, the ES-335 still takes my breath away."

He seems impressed as he stares.

"It *is* a pretty cool make," his voice is deep and sexy. For some reason a man's voice has always played a big role in my attraction to them, I can't explain it. It doesn't mean they have to sound like Barry White, but a perfect example of the sort of 'masculine' voice I like is Ric's – not too deep, but definitely not high-pitched. A man can be the best looking man on the Earth, but if he has even a relatively high-pitched voice, he has no chance with me.

The young guitarist slowly puts his fingers over the head of the guitar, affectionately.

"Do you play?" he looks up at me, waiting for my reply. His accent is a little difficult to read – it's almost American, but not quite.

I fling my hand in the air, as if shooing a wasp. "Hardly. I'm not very good," I tell him. "You were awesome tonight, by the way, awesome solo." *Stop saying the word awesome!*

"Thanks, what's your name?"

"Alexis."

"Ric," we shake hands, and as we do so it sends shivers down my spine. He's looking at me as if he is trying to see right through to my soul.

"Awesome job, Ric!" bellows Enrico, walking over to us. "Thought I'd bring her backstage with me – an old friend, worked in radio, sweet girl."

I want to roll my eyes but resist, and Ric doesn't even look at him, keeping his eyes on me. I, however, turn back to the guitar and keep my eyes fixed on the gorgeous Gibson ES-335.

"Oh yeah? What radio station?" he asks me.

"Oh, Slurp Radio – university radio, nothing amazing."

"You wanna play?"

I quickly look up at him, startled by the question. "No, no, no, no."

Did you say enough no's there, Alex?

He frowns, intrigued. "Why not?"

"'Cause I'd break it! Seriously, and I can't even play that well."

"Ooh, Alexis, come on!" Enrico turns to Ric. "She's played on my cherry SG'61 many times; she's not bad at all. Have you seen the custom new Cobra Burst?"

"Uh, yeah, it's alright. Prefer this one, to be honest," Ric seems to block out Enrico's bullshit the same way I do and this only makes me warm to him even more.

*Attractive **and** sharp – what a catch.*

"What?! It's so cool!"

Ric picks up the Gibson. "Here, come on, have a go, you won't break anything. Just be careful."

I swear with any other person on the planet I would *insist* that he keeps me away from his guitars, but he seems so sure that I won't break it, and he's giving me a pretty commanding look. He grabs the strap and slowly helps me put it over my head. I gently clutch the head of the guitar, my palms sweaty.

I look down at the beautiful guitar I'm holding, and he steps back.

Wow.

He smiles at the sight of the Gibson in my arms and I blush.

Be careful, Ric – I may just run away with this now.

"How old is he?"

"*She* is about a year now," he tells me.

"Wow, she looks brand new."

"*No* don't say that, I don't like my guitars looking brand new. They should look experienced and…full of memories."

"Just like your women," retorts Kyle, as he gets out a packet of cigarettes from his jacket, and I remember that there are other people in the room. For a while there it had felt like the Ric & Alex show.

"Shut up, twit face."

"Twit face?" I blurt out.

"Yeah, I heard someone say it earlier on today when we were in Soho and instantly loved it."

I smile. There's something pretty amusing about hearing an Italian say the words 'twit face'. I am sure at this point that Ric is indeed Italian, and this is from several clues: A), his olive skin really screams *Italian* B), the way he pronounces 'experience', like the Italian 'esperienza', and C), his I.D. pass dangling from his neck reads RICCARDO D'ANGELO. He is most definitely Italian. His accent is rather impressive, though – apart from correctly pronouncing most letters, it has a twinge of American to it, so people are more likely to assume he's American before they realise he's Italian.

"I'm gonna go smoke a cig, be right back," announces Kyle, as he disappears through the Other Door.

"So, you gonna play something?" asks Ric, as he searches the sofa for something.

"What are you…?"

"Pluck," he finds a black pluck on the table next to a plate of doughnuts that I only just notice and he passes it to me. It's only then that I realise that the guitar is already plugged in to a nearby socket. I relax a little as Ric goes over to the rest of the guitars, beginning to pack them. I'm relieved, as I can't play well under pressure.

I start fiddling with the pedal awkwardly, as I try to think of a good song but my mind goes blank. I glance at Enrico, who is texting someone now – probably Bianca, and I look at the tech guy who still looks like he is trying to figure something out on his laptop.

I adjust the chords and play with the pedal for a good couple of minutes. I then take a deep breath in, and begin playing the main guitar riff to 'Californication', by the Red

Hot Chili Peppers. I play with passion and delicate accuracy, with my eyes focused on the strings as I play. I don't dare look at Ric, but I see from the corner of my eye that he has looked up and is grinning.

"Bit mainstream but a classic."

I gasp, as I continue playing. "So what if it's mainstream? It's a beautiful guitar riff. Frusciante had it made with this song, even if they got too mainstream towards the second decade!"

Ah, music. The only thing on the planet that is able to make me switch from normal human being to passionate psycho in a nanosecond.

Ric looks a little surprised by my outburst and cocks up an eyebrow. "They were *always* mainstream."

"Oooh you think you have a better tune, do you? Go ahead and try!"

Of course he's got a better tune than you dumbass, he's a professional guitarist.

"Yes!"

I stop playing and pull the guitar over my head, as he comes back over to me. I hand it back to him.

"I can think of something much better I'm *sure*-"

"Buona sera, ragazzi!" roars another voice and Mauro Fontana now stands at the Other Door, letting it click behind him. I do not bat an eyelash.

There's something about Mauro that I distinctly don't like, but I can't work out what.

Maybe it's his nose, I think as I look at him. *He has that long, ugly nose that evil characters have in cartoons.*

He's wearing a flannel shirt now and a pair of old jeans; post-gig clothes.

"Mauro!" Enrico and Mauro throw their arms around each other, grunting and shouting "oh!" and "hey!"s to accompany their man hug. Mauro then turns to us and comes over, Ric putting the Gibson back down on the chair.

Ric doesn't seem quite so relaxed now and I could have sworn the atmosphere tensed as soon as Mauro walked in.

"Hi," I say to him, and we shake hands, giving each other the traditional Italian peck on each cheek. It's really awkward between us and I'm shouting 'POSER!' to myself in my head, repeatedly.

"Ciao! Nice to meet you, I'm Mauro."

POSER!

POSER!

POSER!

"Nice to meet you, I'm Alexis. You were great out there tonight, Mauro." I'm lying through my teeth, but what am I supposed to say? *'You looked nice out there whilst Paolo played the most important parts himself'?*

"Thank you Alexis, I'm glad you enjoyed the show." Mauro has looked at his reflection in the mirror three times since he's walked in, and he seems like one of those egocentric Fake Rockers – you know, one of those people that claim they *love* Led Zeppelin but really go home and listen to Taylor Swift.

"I think I may have swallowed a fly," says Kyle, reappearing. Ric laughs as he goes back to packing.

"You gotta shut that mouth sometimes, that's why, Kyle."

I stifle a laugh, but quickly realising Kyle is a stranger to me, I immediately turn serious again before either of them can notice.

"Ha-*ha*, you know, you should have become a comedian instead? You would have got more solos that way."

So I'm not the only one that noticed the fact that Ric only landed one solo?

Before Ric can reply we hear a voice I most definitely recognize.

"No, vabbè, lo prendo domani, ok ciao," Paolo Petrinelli stops in his tracks about halfway across the room, phone pressed to his ear. He hangs up and looks at Enrico, and then at me, wondering who the hell are the strangers in the green room.

"Paolo, you remember Enrico, he was also at Florence last year," Mauro says to Paolo in Italian, who seems to relax a little now.

"Ah si," they shake hands.

"Lovely to see you again, Paolo," Enrico says to him.

"You too Enrico," his eyes then turn to me, and I approach, my whole body trembling. Foo Fighters' 'I'll Stick Around' starts playing in my head, as I nervously walk over to him.

I've taken all and I've endured
One day it all will fade
I'm sure...

"Ciao Paolo, è davvero un piacere conoscerti, sei stato fantastico stasera," I say to him.

From the corner of my eye I can see Ric gawking at me.

Oh, did I not mention that I speak Italian?

Paolo gives me a warm smile, shaking my hand, and we exchange pecks on the cheeks.

Paolo Petrinelli smells of oranges.

"Grazie mille, come ti chiami?"

"Alexis."

"Grazie mille, Alexis."

"Ric here was showing Alexis the great Gibson ES," Kyle explains to Paolo, checking the inside of his mouth in the reflection of the mirror that hangs in the corner.

"Oh really? You like guitars? We really do need more female guitar players in the world."

My heart melts.

"She's actually quite good," Ric tells him, and I give him a gratifying smile.

"Well, keep playing then. Maybe one day I'll see you onstage," he winks at me and I blush, though I know the likeliness of that ever happening is pretty minimal. "I'd better be going – the family are all ready to go outside." He turns to the others, "don't forget any of the gear," he tells them in Italian, "and behave tonight, okay? I don't want to see on the newspaper tomorrow morning, 'Paolo's Boys Take London By Storm' for anything other than music, okay?" he turns to Mauro, "make sure they're not doing anything stupid."

Mauro? You're leaving Mauro in charge? As if he'd do anything in an emergency. He looks like he's the most likely to run in a bad situation.

Mauro nods and Paolo turns back to me. "It was a pleasure to meet you Alexis, I hope to see you at a gig again soon. Take care."

"Il piacere è tutto mio, Paolo! Grazie," I watch him walk out of the room, nodding at Enrico on the way, and my heart rate begins to slow down as he disappears.

I just met Paolo Petrinelli. And I didn't accidentally cough on him or sneeze on him or swear at him.

Five points to Alex.

I notice Ric still looking at me.

"You're Italian?" he asks. "Why didn't you tell me? Here I am talking to you in shitty broken English, thinking *oh what a nice London girl, let me just try to speak some decent English with her and*-"

"I *am* a London girl – my parents are Italian, they taught me it as a kid. I was born here."

"Smart people. Wait, why are we still speaking in English?"

I shrug. "It's easier, isn't it?"

"I guess. Gives me a chance to improve my English."

I watch him as he goes back to packing, his muscles flexing.

He is so damn attractive.

"Me, too!" Enrico wails, excitedly. "You know Ric, me and a few friends have formed a band here in London, and we're gonna record the album just outside of London, it's gonna be like Foo Fighters meets Led Zeppelin…" as Enrico rambles on about his crappy band I realise the favour he is after is probably going to be something to do with this.

Forget about that right now, Alex.

I glance at Ric and his chiselled jaw as he pretends to be listening to Enrico.

"So what are we doing then?" Kyle suddenly asks, snapping me out of my stare.

We? That obviously doesn't include me. I should go, leave them to it, don't hang around where you're not wanted, Alex…

Ric half-shrugs at him. "Pub?"

"Alright."

I should really go before they kick me out…

Ric turns to me. "You wanna come? Get a beer? There's a good pub next door."

My heart begins racing again. "Sounds great."

He smiles, and murmurs 'okay' as he puts the Gibson ES away.

And just like that, I've gone from girl in the crowd, to girl going to the pub with the Paolo Petrinelli band.

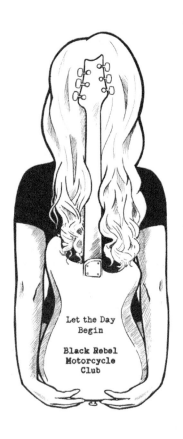

3

I was eighteen the first time I went out drinking with a band. It was when I was interning for a big radio station in London, and I was shadowing on the evening drive time show. Yellow Bandit was their name, and they were an alternative rock band with a splash of heavy metal. They were fairly well known and I had a copy of their debut album I listened to on loop. I had no idea they were set to play in the studio one summer's evening until I saw them in front of me.

At eighteen, I dressed a little 'dangerously', so to speak – miniskirts, makeup overload, and, let's not forget that innocent smile. I remember how all their chins dropped when I walked into the studio as they were setting up.

They got talking to me and turned out to be really nice guys, so much so that after the show they invited me out for a drink and we ended up going on a pub crawl. It was a spectacular evening, and I completely forgot that they were famous musicians. That stuff doesn't get to me; I only care about whether musicians are good or not, and if they're nice to speak to. Honest to God, that's all that really matters. All that other stuff is just bullshit. If it's fame and fortune that allures you to the music business, I won't be able to relate to you.

Anyhow, here I am several years later, going for drinks with a famous band again. Except, hopefully this time I've grown up a bit. Or I at least definitely wear less 'dangerous' clothes, and no longer strut across radio studios secretly smiling at having all of their jaws drop to the floor as soon as their eyes see my perfectly sized ass.

Oh yeah – I definitely have the best ass in the world, and it's been this way since I was twelve years old.

I offer to help Ric pack but he only shakes his head, so I take a look at the posters around the room whilst the rest of them put everything away.

There are so many posters in the green room – and they're promoting new bands, old bands, solo artists, guitar makes, festivals. I even find one in the corner promoting the legalisation of marijuana! I grin and shake my head, and just as I do I hear Enrico yell 'Alexis, come on!' and I follow him out of the room, the others not far behind us. I ask Enrico about the other members of the band (the keyboardist and drummer), but he tells me that they're busy and that they will join us later.

The tech guy on the sofa comes with us, but now he has his eyes fixed on his iPhone, still looking like he's trying to fix something. The guys put their gear in a taxi that's running out back of the venue, and some scruffy guy in his twenties escorts the gear to the hotel. The pub is not next door but down the road, and so we make our way down the lively high street that is Highgate Road.

This is my favourite time of day, and when I love London the most. A summers' day in London in May is one of the best things you can experience in this city. It's bright and lively and wonderful.

Highgate Road is just an ordinary road, but on evenings like this, it comes alive and I connect with it so well. Like two old friends reunited after years of separation; we remember our good times, and everything we have ever shared together.

We pass a couple of busking break dancers and a crowd cheering them on, happy tourists taking in the beauty of this city. We pass a group of teenagers talking about crack rather loudly, and a couple holding hands as if without each other they would disappear into oblivion.

All of this, is exactly why I love my city.

Enrico and I are leading the way, though not exactly in conversation – he's texting Bianca again. We're followed by Ric and Kyle, who are talking about some film, and finally Mauro and the tech guy, though Mauro is on the phone to someone. The air is cool and I look up at the full moon, grateful that I decided to take my jacket. Even in May, weather in London can be treacherously temperamental.

What is it about the full moon that always brings a certain magic to the night, I wonder.

Since Enrico and I are a few metres ahead of the rest of them, we enter the pub and head straight to the bar to order. Just as I'm about to attempt small talk, Enrico's phone rings.
"Ciao, amore!"

Bianca.

I sigh, and turn my attention to the alcohol behind the bar, just as the others walk in. Mauro, the tech guy and Kyle all go and sit down at a table in the corner, having told Ric what they wanted. He comes over to us, narrowing his eyes at Enrico, signalling for to him to go and join the others. Enrico gives him the thumbs up, revealing his buck teeth to the world once more, and walks away.

"Oh no wait, you didn't tell me what you wanted…" Ric calls after him but it's too late – he's no longer within earshot, especially over Bryan Adams playing in the background.

"A beer and he'll be happy," I tell him, smiling.

Ric turns to me as if he has only just noticed me standing there, and he gives me a hesitant look. "Are you two…?"

"No, no, **God** no!" I blurt out.

We've never even slept together!

Ric raises his eyebrows at my reaction.

"He's a friend…" *Too kind.* "A guy I know."

"Needs a favour?"

"Pretty much."

He shakes his head a little and turns his attention to the bar. There's a couple in front of us being served.

"What are you drinking?"

"Beer. You?"

"Amaretto."

"Cool," he says, not really sure what else to say.

"You ever tried it?" I decide to ask, to fill the time.

"Nope," he pauses, "I like my beer."

I laugh and he stares, puzzled.

"What?"

"Nothing…just the way you were like, '*I like my beer*'," I clench my fists in mid-air and deepen my voice. "*I am a caveman, I like my beer! Mmm…beer! Mmm women…mmm beer!*"

He grins, hardly believing what he's hearing. "Are you calling me a caveman?!"

"No, don't be silly! Just *like* a caveman."

We stare at each other and burst out laughing at the same time. He shakes his head and we relax, Oasis' 'Live

Forever' playing in the background. The couple in front of us look as if they are about to finish paying.

"Well I think I'm gonna try this Amaretto…"

"Really?" I say, excited.

"I think I have to don't I, or I'll be a caveman in your eyes all night."

That is a seriously gorgeous smile.

Once we head over to the table the atmosphere has changed. Enrico, Mauro and the tech guy are all engaged in banter, talking loudly in broken English and grinning at each other.

Ric asks where Kyle is, as we put down the drinks on the table. Enrico is sitting all alone on one side of the table, opposite the tech guy and Mauro. I sit down next to him, and make him move up a little so that Ric can squeeze in. He remains standing though, as he waits for a reply from Mauro, who tells him he's outside.

"Smoking?"

Mauro nods and Ric slides down next to me. Squashed up next to each other our arms are touching. Well, his blazer is touching my crimson jacket, but there is still something sexy about it. Our legs are also touching, my skinny black jeans to his casual blue jeans.

Ric explains to me that Kyle's wife is heavily pregnant, and that Kyle has said multiple times already that if she goes into labour whilst they're in London he's going to kill Ric, since he's the one that persuaded him to come.

"That's why I got him a lemonade – alcohol's too dangerous at a time like this," Ric tells me.

"Parla in Italiano!" Mauro suddenly yells at us, holding up his hands dramatically in the air.

What a walking stereotype.

"She wants to talk in English! So do I! And hey, what about Stan?"

"Poor Stan!" bellows Enrico, and Mauro puts the tech guy in a playful headlock as he blushes heavily, his iPhone still in his hand.

Kyle reappears and drops down in the small space next to Mauro opposite us. Ric narrows his eyes at him, a song from Boyzone playing in the background.

"Did you ring Caroline?"

He nods.

"All good?"

Again a nod.

As we dive straight into conversation, it's as if I have known the pair of them a hell of a lot longer than half an hour. Kyle is married, lives in Bologna, and both him and his wife are from Arizona. He's been playing since he was thirteen years old, and wouldn't give up bass for guitar even if you paid him (I tried to, then tried to make it look like I was joking).

I study Kyle's face as he speaks, scanning his eyes for some sort of malevolence, or arrogance, or drug addiction, but all I am able to see is a humble bassist, and I'm okay with that. Musicians tend to typically contain a dark side to them; more than narcissism, they are almost sadistic. It's this pain or darkness that tends to bring out their creativity. But I've always found that bassists are more likely to be the humble, peaceful member of the band.

They ask about me – what I do, what I've been doing, and all I tell them is that I graduated last year in physics, and that I want to work in the music business. They look at me as if I am from another planet.

"*Hold on,* you have to be the *only* person in the world who would do a degree in physics, and then want to work in the music business?!" Kyle tells me, and I suppose he's right.

I explain to them how I have a healthy interest in physics and thus proceeded with a degree in the subject, in order to dig deeper. It was interesting and it was hard and I loved it, but I have an unhealthy interest in music, and it's something that I simply cannot avoid or ignore. It goes much further and much deeper than any other love or passion in my life.

It has been this way since I was old enough to crawl, and I doubt it will ever change. My mum even says that when she would put on old Italian music as a baby, I would instantly stop crying. I'm talking the highest of the highest quality of Italian music – like Lucio Battisti and Franco Battiato.

Now those are what we call *legends.*

When Ric and Kyle ask me my age, they're shocked to find out I'm twenty-two. It's hard not to roll my eyes as they tell me they thought I was about eighteen. Not really what I want to hear when I'm trying to break into an industry that looks down at 'little girls', but I get it a lot. I look younger than my twenty-two years.

"How old are *you* guys?" I ask them.

A little surprised I've turned the question back on them, they shuffle around in their seats a little, Ric's jeans rubbing against mine.

"Well, *he's* thirty-five," Ric says and Kyle mutters 'thanks, man', "and I'm thirty-three in June."

It takes an impeccable amount of effort to stop my jaw from dropping.

*Ric is **thirty-three years old?!***
*He really, really, **really** doesn't look it!*
We're ten years apart.
Well, wave goodbye to that possibility Alex, it'll never happen.
As if you had a chance, anyway.

"You're gonna be thirty-three?!"

"Yeah, why?"

"I thought you were like…twenty-eight."

He grins like an excited school child and shakes his eyebrows at Kyle. "You hear that? I look twenty-eight!"

"Yeah, must be all that drinking and smoking you do – keeps you young."

Ric finally takes a sip from his glass and nearly spits it out, managing to swallow as he cringes up his face.

"Argh! What the…? That's so sweet! That tasted like cake!"

Kyle and I burst into laughter at his reaction, and he stands up. "Argh. No, Alexis! No. I'm going to go get myself a *beer*!"

"You can't!" I shriek, and they both glare at me. Ric stands in front of the table, baffled by my reaction.

"You can't, you have to try something else."

"I *have* tried other drinks, you know. I just happen to like my beer!" Ric tells me.

"Liar! I bet you haven't tried…Pimms!"

He stares blankly, as Kyle gets out his vibrating phone. "She's got you there man, that's a totally British drink," Kyle says to him, picking up. "Hello?"

"What's Pimms? Is it like Amaretto? I might as well drink a packet of sugar then. Argh," he cringes his face up again and I giggle.

Staring at Ric I realise that I've forgotten he's Petrinelli's rhythm guitarist, that just an hour ago he had been up on that stage with him, performing that amazing solo. It seems like two different people to me. The guy in front of me now is just a man that plays guitar and likes his beer. I don't know him, but I like him. You ever meet someone and just instantly like them? It's rare for me, but it's happening right now. There's nothing I don't like about Ric.

"Maybe I've tried it before when I've been in London, it sounds familiar."

"You come here a lot?"

"Yeah, yeah, used to, when I had a Britpop band, Red Bricks. I was the only Italian in the band, I sang and played guitar - we wrote Britpop songs and performed here a lot for gigs at small venues, all a few years back now. Was cool," he tells me. I try to imagine Ric at a younger age, in *my* city, singing Britpop songs passionately into a mic in a dirty, intimate pub, and it makes my heart melt.

"Awesome! Man, I would have loved to hear some of that."

"I can send you some tracks if you like," Ric tells me.

"Awesome!"

There you go again, repeating the word 'awesome' as if you only know five words in the English vocabulary.

Come on, Alex – use other words!

Fantastic.

Brilliant.

Amazing.

No, don't say amazing. That's a Dumb Blonde go-to word.

Kyle suddenly slams his phone on the table and shoots out of his seat quicker than I've ever seen in my entire life.

"She's in labour! She's in labour, man! Caroline's in labour!"

Oh shit.

"She's **what**?!" shouts Ric.

I gawp at them as they freak out, eyes big and scared, like two kids that have just been told all the chocolate in the world has been destroyed.

"She's in labour!"

"But…you just rang her! She was fine!"

"And then her water broke, man!" Kyle sits back down, "oh God, her water broke. Her water broke, and I'm in England."

Ric takes a nervous deep breath in, and puts a hand on the back of Kyle's neck, as if he has returned to strong, adult Ric.

"Come on, let's go. Airport."

Our entire table has gone quiet, and all eyes are on Kyle as Robbie Williams' 'Millennium' plays in the background.

"I'm gonna have a baby. A daughter. A daughter!" Kyle seems a completely different person from the one that had just been teasing Ric about his bad habits. He may be thirty-three but I swear to God, right now he looks about five years old.

"Yeah, I know. Come on," Ric picks up Kyle's phone and wallet, and tugs at the sleeve of his jumper. "Come on."

"I'll call Adam," Mauro announces, getting out his phone.

"Yeah, tell him we'll need him next Friday."

"Oh God, I gotta play next Friday!" squeals Kyle.

It's hard not to laugh at Kyle's sudden change in character, and I can't seem to get myself to look away.

"No, don't worry about that. Adam will step in. Come on, we gotta get you to the airport."

"What if there's no flights? What if I'm stuck in London?! *Oh God!* I'm going to hail a cab!" he runs out of the pub without taking his things from Ric, who begins to pick up his own stuff with his already full hands – jacket, phone, wallet.

"You gonna find a flight at this time?" Mauro asks him cynically in Italian.

"Yeah, saw one earlier. Leaves in less than two hours. Had a feeling this might happen. Gonna call now and book. Let's hope there's a seat left." I watch as Ric continues to fail to pick up his own stuff from the table. "Argh!"

I get up and grab them for him.

"Thanks."

I follow him out of the pub, where Kyle has just managed to hail a black cab.

"You coming?" he asks Ric, with puppy dog eyes.

"Of course I'm coming," he hands Kyle his stuff and then turns to me. Ric looks curiously at me, as he takes his things and presses his phone to his ear.

Well that evening ended quicker than anticipated. Oh well, at least you got to go backstage, meet Paolo, meet Ric, and hey, he said he'll send you his old songs so maybe he'll ask for your e-mail address now.

Say goodbye before he gets through to someone at the airport-

"Good luck!" I say to him, "it was really good to meet you... good luck next Friday, too!"

Ric continues to stare, squinting his eyes at me. "You wanna come with us?"

Which e-mail address should I give him actually because-

Wait, what?
Did he just ask if I want to go with them?
He's joking, right?

My eyes widen and I stare at the gorgeous face looking back at me, waiting for a response. He is definitely not joking.

I need to call the store that I bought this top from tomorrow and personally thank them, clearly this thing hypnotises people or something.

"What?" I manage to say, trying not to sound shocked.

"Well, what are you going to do in there with those three?"

"I was actually going to go home..."

He glances at his watch, "it's early. You're twenty-two, live a little! Come on, come with us, help me accompany this bundle of nerves to the airport, and then we can come back here and you can drink some sweet drink made for teenagers that will put you in a sugar coma for a month."

I smile, but in all honesty, I don't know what to say.

I've only just met them, isn't this a bit weird?

I study his attractive face, taking in his big brown eyes as they stare back at me, waiting for my answer. I do want to go. I'm curious, about where the night could go from here, and I'm not tired. That feeling of not wanting to do anything

39

from earlier on, from the past ten months, has vanished. Just like that. And suddenly, I have all the energy in the world.

"Come on, live a little."

"Ric, come on!" shouts Kyle from inside the taxi. Just then, Ric turns away from me as someone at the airport picks up.

"Yes, hello, good evening, I'd like to book a one-way ticket to Milano Malpensa please, first available please." Pause. "That's wonderful, exactly what my friend was after. Hold on, I'm going to pass you to him so that he can give you his details," he leans into the taxi and I briefly glance at his perfectly shaped butt through his jeans.

Well, well, what do we have here?

Could this be the male equivalent best butt in the world?

I quickly look away as he slides out of the taxi and turns to me, smiling.

"So, you in?"

I don't care that I have to get up early to take the damn cat to the vet, I don't care that I barely know them at all (though I probably should).

I want to go.

"Okay."

Ric's smile grows bigger and he steps to the side.

"Alright,London-Girl-With-Ambition-To-Work-in-the-Music-Industry, get in."

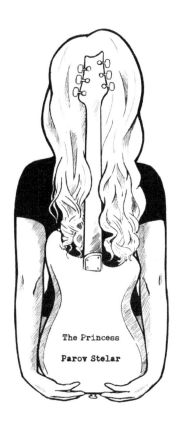

4

When I was eighteen, I got lucky. Strolling through London one fine Sunday afternoon, I bumped into a famous radio DJ. We got talking and I asked him if I could intern on his breakfast show.

"Of course – I'll sort it out for you," was his response. It turned out that 'sorting it out' was simply telling reception I could enter on Monday morning. That's all it took to intern at a famous radio station. I thought of all the applications I had sent, emails chasing anyone and everyone at these places, and though I was happy I had found a way in, I was also a little bit sad for those sending application after application, not knowing that anything in media takes *who* you know, above all else.

I was only supposed to intern there a couple of weeks; I stayed six months. I made coffee, sorted the post, wrote short articles for the website, and was the general support for everyone in the office. I got to welcome celebrity guests into the studio, I got to small talk with them, and I got to watch magic as it happened on critically acclaimed radio shows across the country.

What I think was most valuable about this experience however is that I had to really push and develop my skills for working in a fast-paced environment. You just never knew what was going to happen next. From running to a costume shop at 9AM on Halloween morning to *beg* them to find me a witch outfit, to entertaining a world famous wrestler for a good twenty minutes as we remained stuck in the office building lift. I had to think on my feet, and I had to be good at it.

I really did well at that place, and they loved me. But I wanted my degree before entering the work world. It's the way I grew up, it's the way I was raised. I wanted to be college educated, and I am proud of my degree. But by the time I graduated, everyone I knew at that radio station had moved on. And it was as if I had never even entered that building.

The journey to the airport with Ric and Kyle is anything but boring, and if there's supposed to be any awkwardness between us deriving from the fact that I have only just met them, it's expelled completely by Kyle.

He spends most of the journey drumming his fingers on the window, agitated as hell, as Ric tells him that labour usually lasts a hell of a lot longer than an hour and a half flight. Kyle then proceeds to sing Aerosmith classics such as 'I Don't Wanna Miss A Thing' and 'Crazy', sticking his head out the window and singing to the motorway. He stops only once it starts pouring down and Ric has to physically pull him back in.

"What if he had drunk alcohol?!" I say, trying to refrain from laughing.

"*Exactly*," is Ric's reply, shaking his head and scrolling up the window.

When we arrive at the airport an hour later, Kyle's ticket has been booked, he's checked in and all he needs to do now is go through security. It's still pouring outside, and I grab the only newspaper in the cab to put over my head, as the other two pull their jackets over their heads.

"Come on!"

Why am I here? This is seriously weird. I woke up this morning with one intention: to go to the Paolo Petrinelli gig. How did I end up here?

We look around for departures.

"There it is!" I squeal, and Ric sighs in relief as we scurry across Stansted.

Airports always remind of that excitement you have right before a holiday, and it depresses me to find myself standing there with no holiday prospects for the summer as of yet, and it's nearly June.

Going abroad, leaving London for a week or two, is something really important to me. Travelling, visiting places where you can actually see the sun for more than a day at a time, is important to me. I love London, it's my home, but like any other city in the world, it has its downsides too.

My last holiday was last August – Italy, to visit my relatives by myself in my parents' hometown.

It's been nearly a year, how depressing.

You better get a job quick Alex and then you can afford as many holidays as you want.

I know Ric and Kyle are better off with a private man hug, and so once we arrive at customs I tell them that I'm going to go have a look in the book store. Ric nods, but Kyle only stares at me.

"Alright, Alexia."

"*Alexis*," Ric corrects him.

"Right – Alexis. It was nice to meet you."

"You too Kyle," I walk away having shaken his hand only to turn back and add, "oh yeah and uh, congratulations."

He smiles and I find the bookstore I usually pop into when I get to the airport early. I wonder how Ric and Kyle have said goodbye. If Ric patted him on the back and said, 'you're a father now'. Or if they have hugged it out.

Ric looks the type to have probably patted him on the back. I'm not sure why but I find it easy to envision. Either way, they seem to be really good friends. It must be nice to tour Europe with a bandmate you're also good friends with.

I'm flicking through a book on the music business when I hear Ric's voice behind me. It's music to my ears, so much so that I can't help but smile as soon as I hear it.

"Any good?" is what he says.

I turn around to find his eyes on me. "Uh, seems…interesting."

"I'm not sure how much these books really help, you know Alexis. It's better to go out there and work in music. I prefer fiction books on the music industry."

"But this *is* a fiction book on the music industry," I say, playfully, "it's about a girl in the music industry and the problems she faces."

"Like?" he asks, scanning the other books on the shelf.

"Like people thinking *girls can't play guitar*. And *girls can't get jobs in the music industry without sleeping with someone important,*" I roll my eyes, but in truth the conversation has become much too personal too soon, "anyway, did Kyle set off okay?"

"Yeah, yeah. He'll be fine," he says, "oooh look at that," he picks up a copy of The Unbearable Lightness of Being, "one of my favourites."

I frown. "You read?"

He chortles, "of course I read. What kind of a question is that?"

"No, it's just…" *It's just that men who read turn me on **so badly.*** "Erm, nothing."

"Okay. Shall we go get a taxi back? It's depressing being here and not actually going anywhere."

"Exactly what I was thinking."

Arriving back at the entrance of Stansted Airport it's still pouring down. I sigh and put the newspaper over my head again, as we go over to the taxi area. Ric digs his hand into his inside jacket pocket just as we call one over, and he freezes.

"Oh God," he searches his other pockets and gulps, "shit! I can't find my wallet!"

What?

The taxi driver forces a laugh and scrolls up the window.

"No, wait! Shit!" he hisses. We scurry back under shelter and he searches his pockets again.

"You must have left it in the cab," I tell him softly, wondering how much cash I have. "I think I can cover us…" I tell him, getting out my purse.

"*No*, it's not that, Alexis! It had my passport! VIP passes, personal documents, ID cards…apart from not being able to leave the country tomorrow, if someone *Italian* gets a hold of that I'm fucked!"

Oh crap.

"Paolo is going to kill me! And Mauro is going to say, "*I told you not to hire such a young guy, he's too **immature**!* Argh!" Ric is panicking like a little kid, cringing up his forehead in anguish, as if his mother has just told him he has no choice but to go to school. There's something very odd about the rest of the band seeing him as so young when to me he's ten years my senior.

"Calm down," I say firmly, surprised by my own tone, "look, we're going to find it, okay? The taxi driver probably picked it up. I'll call the company."

The night manager for the taxi company we had used is able to deduct which driver we had had, and says he will ring him up for us.

It's a good ten minutes later that he calls us back.

"He did find the wallet and passport of a Riccardo D'Angelo," the driver tells us on speakerphone.

"Yes!" Ric's eyes lit up.

He explains that the driver would drop the items at the main office. Luckily for us, their main office is ten minutes away from the airport. Unluckily for us, the driver is on his way into central London with another passenger.

"He will be here in approximately two hours when his shift ends," the manager tells us. Our faces drop, and Ric groans in annoyance, as I thank the night manager before hanging up.

"Well…that's great," says Ric, "if you wanna go home I can pay for it via my phone, I'll cover the jour-"

"No way, I'm staying here."

He smiles gratefully at me.

I don't want to go home, anyway.

"Two hours. Two hours that we will be reminded that we are *not* going on holiday."

"Of course, *you* are technically on holiday right now so you don't really count."

"This is work, it's different," he tells me.

"Ha! Yeah, playing guitar, the awesome ES Gibson to be exact," (here Ric smiles sweetly), "yeah that's work alright."

"How about learning songs so perfect you could play them in your sleep because if you fuck up once, just once, you're out."

"And apparently Mauro would be *right*."

He seems slightly embarrassed, as he remembers what he had blurted out earlier. But he keeps quiet.

Change the subject quickly. "Airport bar?"

"You read my mind."

Arriving at a cute little bar inside the airport, the place is empty apart from a young, skinny man in a suit sitting in the far corner, reading a newspaper. Some cheap jazz plays softly in the background and Ric turns to me, signalling for me to choose a table.

Oh I hate this responsibility. Why do I have to choose? I can never decide.

I glance around and walk over to a two-seater table in the middle of the bar.

"Okay, what are you drinking?" Ric asks, leaning over the table at me as I sit down.

"Um, a beer, I guess."

He frowns at me.

"What?"

"Do you know *what* beer?"

I shrug. "Any, I don't care."

"Okay, if I'm getting something new so are you," he tells me with a playful smile.

I may just jump you right here right now if you continue smiling at me like that, dearest Ric.

"Gosh, really?"

"Gosh, really."

I laugh a little, but he keeps his eyes fixed on me. "Okay fine, Jack Daniels."

He cringes his forehead at me in surprise. "You've *never* had Jack Daniels?"

"I keep meaning to but-"

"Okay, hold on," he scurries over to the bar murmuring 'never had Jack Daniels' under his breath and an old, beer bellied man behind the bar serves him. I rest my head on my hand and watch them chat, curiously.

How the hell did I get here?

I've never been the spontaneous type, even when friends call me up asking if I want to get drinks 'later' I make up some excuse, because I don't like surprises or spontaneity of any type. I like knowing when I'm going out and with whom. It's as if I need mental preparation for everything. But nothing could have mentally prepared me for this night and yet, I'm doing fine. I'm not freaking out, and I'm not nervous anymore. Ric is a normal guy and the events of tonight so far are making me feel more alive than I have done in months.

I am liking this adventure, and I am liking the unknown.

Ric returns with two full glasses and places them in front of me, as he sits down opposite me. I glance at his fruit drink.

"Pimms?"

He nods, "don't think I've ever tried it."

We drink and we talk about the usual stuff people talk about when they first meet – our families, our childhoods, our smothering parents. I tell him about my average bring up in suburban London with my older brother, Leo, and he tells me about his average upbringing in suburban Siena, Tuscany. Ric seems like a pretty relaxed guy, as far as Italians go.

Most Italians I know are anxious people, always yelling and agitated about everything, but Ric is a little more relaxed. It doesn't mean he's one of those laid back 'dudes' that lets life pass them by. By all means, Ric is definitely not a dreamer. It's obvious to me that Ric has focus, and he's worked his way into the industry. He has his beliefs and his ideas, and he isn't afraid to share them, and I like that.

What I also like is that when he makes a point, he has facts and statistics and explanations to back up his points, and it's something I find rare and intriguing in a person. I know so many bullshitters. So many people that just read a couple of newspapers and think they know everything.

Ric, I quickly come to learn, reads about twenty different sources before he even dares to open his mouth about a subject. And anyway, I much prefer a person with opinions and ideas, even if a little ridiculous, than a person with no opinions and no ideas.

He moves his hands a lot when he speaks, like a typical Italian, but I do that too. He has this light in his eyes when the subject turns to Dale Carnegie or Led Zeppelin – they sort of dance. I learn early on that Riccardo D'Angelo is passionate about three things: music, politics and brilliant thinkers, such as Carnegie and Dalio – I have no idea who they are, but apparently to Ric they have brilliant minds.

When one of these three subjects are mentioned, Ric almost looks like a child; excited and passionate, his face lighting up like a drunk Christmas tree.

And then the subject changes to the state of the Italian economy, his jawline tenses, his eyes turn darker and well, who can blame him? But despite the dark cloud, Ric has all these ideas on how to fix Italy's problems, dancing around the ideas of various Italian political parties before I realise he's completely in his own league. Some of his ideas I totally disagree with, like his belief in the Italian judicial system, and I tell him.

After all, I realise I am not afraid to tell him what I think, to tell him his ideas are ridiculous. He seems surprised by my sincerity, but is more than happy to get into an argument over our clash of ideals. I'm not too much of an expert when it comes to Italian politics, but I skim over various sources at least once a week; I know enough to argue back with him using facts.

I'm sure my eyes turn into heart shapes when the topic turns to guitars. We both love the same Gibsons and the same Fenders, and he owns a few of my favourite guitars. Ric began playing guitar at twelve, after 'nearly shooting himself with a farmers' gun' after six years-worth of piano lessons.

"I hated it," he tells me, "it was such a boring piece of shit."

Ric has this way of telling stories with such charisma that I just never want him to shut up. I don't know if it's the alcohol or just the right atmosphere, but we share a lot of stories.

I tell him about how I used to sneak out of the window at night to go smoke weed in a van with my high school buddies, and the time I got lost at Hampstead Park and asked Hugh Grant for directions to 'my house'. I tell him about my older brother, Leo, how he lives in San Francisco, and how I sometimes wished we lived closer, but know full well I love him more because of it.

He tells me about a school trip to the zoo when he was eight where the only animal he had been afraid of were the owls, and the one time on tour his luggage had flung open in a moving taxi in Napoli, his clothes flying out, never to be seen again. And the time he got emotionally blackmailed by his friends as a kid to perform a dance routine to Human League's 'Don't You Want Me Baby' in front of his school assembly.

The thing that stands out the most about Ric is his honesty – he isn't afraid to tell you what he thinks, and I didn't know just how much I admire this quality until now. If he likes a crap band, he isn't afraid to tell you. If he thinks a band that is seen as legendary by most is phoney or overrated he isn't afraid to say it, and every time he does it, I'm that little bit more attracted to him.

It's three Jack Daniels later that I become a lot braver – alcohol has a way of doing that. Ric gave up on his Pimms about halfway through the evening and ordered a Jack

Daniels, catching up with me in quantity fairly quickly. We are now near the end of our third drinks.

The bar has since become a lot hotter and I have taken off my crimson jacket; both our faces red from the alcohol and all the laughing. We're chuckling at the littlest of things, the skinny young man in the suit looking at us occasionally, wondering what the hell could be so funny.

"Didn't you ever just do it for fun?" Ric asks, taking a sip from his glass.

"Yeah, there was one summer I smoked quite a bit, out of pure boredom of suburban London life, but then I quit once school started up again," there's silence between us and all you can hear is the cheap jazz music still playing, every song worse than the last.

"I started when I was sixteen, never looked back," he gets out his packet of cigarettes and caresses the front gently.

"You okay there? Want me to leave you two alone?" I say, trying to contain my laughter.

"Maybe later, when I've got my passes back. Me, my passport and the cigarettes – threesome seems likely."

I instantly burst into laughter and slap my hand on the table for dramatic effect. Ric smiles, laughing a little as he watches me. I notice that when he looks at me he focuses so hard it feels as if he is making mental notes on every detail of my face.

"It wasn't *that* funny," he tells me.

"I know!" I say, in-between laughs, "I so wanna marry Jack!"

He leans in, sexily. "Oh Alexis, I'm sorry," he lowers his voice, looking at me with a serious expression,

"Jack's dead, and has been for a *long* time."

The partially drunk version of Ric makes more facial expressions and talks in a slightly higher pitched tone. But then again, what the hell do I know? I only met him a couple of hours ago, for all I know this is his sober tone.

"Noooo!" I wail, making the bartender turn and look at us, "noo! That's not fair! All the good guys are always...dead!"

It's Ric's turn to laugh, and he cringes up his nose as he does so.

"They're always *what?* They're always dead?!" he continues drunkenly laughing, a little confused. To be fair, I have no idea what I'm saying. I don't secretly have dead ex-boyfriends buried underground. You know how it gets when you drink too much alcohol – especially as I had been a Jack Daniels virgin.

"Yeah! Along with my career," I remark. Suddenly things aren't so funny, and we both tense. The self-pity is beginning to ooze out of me with no way of stopping it.

"Alexis! You're twenty-two!"

"Twenty-three very soon. And in that time I've done so much, I should have a job by now! When I was sixteen I wrote for the college magazine, I then worked in radio, had my own show, interned for a music TV show, helped the selfish twits (musicians), interviewed the selfish twits (musicians) and set up gigs for the selfish twits! I should have a job by now!"

"If you hate musicians so much, why do you wanna work in music?"

It's a question far too common sense for someone drunk, and I wonder if Ric is actually as intoxicated as me.

He can probably hold his liquor better than you, Alex.

"I don't *hate* them, I just recognise their egocentricity, and I resent them sometimes because I know my career will always revolve around them and their needs."

Look at you using big words when you're drunk. I usually can't even pronounce ego-uh-ego-uh egocentricity when I'm sober.

"And ~~why~~ shouldn't it? They, or, *we,* are the ones that make the music, so everything in music *should* be based around getting that absolutely right," he tells me, "but the 'selfish brat' thing, the 'I'm too cool to talk to you' attitude is understandably annoying and unnecessary. I've never been able to do that. At school I *was* that kid."

"What, the self-obsessed one?"

"No, the one that the cool kids never talked to."

I try to imagine Ric as an uncool kid at school and it's impossible. I find it hard to imagine anyone ignoring that smile.

"I know what it feels like and it isn't very nice."

"I had blonde hair in school," I blurt out. *Damn you Jack, you are powerful.*

Ric cackles. "You what?"

"I dyed my hair blonde when I was fourteen, was supposed to be subtle dark blonde highlights but I somehow ended up doing half my head and it was bleach blonde. My mum loved it but when I went to school the next day I got mega teased. And I got mega teased for the rest of the year."

"You didn't dye it back?"

"My mum liked it."

"Oh, right," he stares, "that's pretty rare."

"Yeah, well, my point is, I know what it feels like too," I tell him, and there's a moment of silence between us.

"What was their worst nickname?"

I gawp. "I tell you that story and *that's* what you wanna know?!"

"Yes!"

"That is absurd!"

"Come on! You know wanna-"

"That was supposed to be a serious story!"

"Spill!"

I squint at him, debating telling him or not.

"I'll go get us some more Jack as soon as you tell me. You know you want some more Jack…"

I sigh. "You're a tool," I lick my lips, "light bulb."

An instant uproar of laughter from across the table. I want to playfully be angry at him, but I'm too pulled in by his laughter. It's loud and it's innocent and it gives me goose bumps.

"Stop it!" I slap him lightly on the arm and he gets up, still in fits of laughter.

"Oh that's beautiful!" he says as he walks back over to the bar. I look around and meet eyes with the skinny man in the suit. He gives me a glum smile and turns back to his newspaper.

What's his deal? Maybe he comes here every night. Maybe he lost his job, and then caught his girlfriend screwing his boss, followed by the death of his parrot.

Alex, you are way too dark for your own good.

"Our fourth Jack is free! According to the bartender, Constanzo, from Athens!" Ric puts down both glasses on the table and I wave at a smiling, old Greek man behind the bar.

"That's nice of him."

"So what are you going to do next?" Ric asks, sitting back down, and looking rather serious. Much more serious than when he had left the table.

"How do you mean?"

"Well, you say you've done all this great stuff to start your career, but you're not working right now, right?"

"No, not since I finished uni last year," I sigh, "it's *really* difficult."

"What stuff are you looking to get into?"

"Radio, record labels, presenting. I *really* wanna present and I *really* wanna work for a record label," I say, passionately. I haven't said this with such passion since the day I graduated.

"Well, are you applying?"

"Yes! And I either get no reply or the lovely rejection email. *We regret to inform you that you are shit and we don't want you.*"

"Have you had anyone look at your CV?"

"Actually no, I don't think I have."

"You might want to do that. CVs are a tricky thing. I know because my brother's was the same. He wasn't getting call backs because his CV was written badly. All the right criteria but not written well enough to catch someone's eye."

"What does your brother do?" I ask him, wondering if he looks anything like Ric.

"Advertising up in Volterra."

"Nice."

He gulps down the remains of his Jack Daniels and leans in a little.

"If you want to go somewhere in life Alexis, you better grab every opportunity you can. 'Cause I can promise you now that it will never jump out and grab you."

Just as I try to think of something to reply to that, his phone buzzes and he gets it out.

"Message from Kyle; he's landed."

My eyes widen and his shocked expression mirrors mine.

"Already?!" we both say in synch.

He looks back down at his phone. "Wait, oh shit, Alexis!" he laughs a little, "you'll never guess what time it is!"

"What time?" I search my jacket for my phone.

"4:03AM!"

"You're kidding me?!" my own phone reads 4:05AM and I gasp. "Geez, I thought it was 2:30 max."

"Me too! Come on, let's go. The driver must have dropped off my things by now."

Ric pays Constanzo using his phone and we make our way out of the airport. My legs are like jelly and I'm finding it hard to walk straight, but I try to pretend I'm a person that can handle her alcohol.

At least I can still see straight.

Outside the sky is now a light crème colour and it's stopped raining.

"I don't know about you but I *cannot* walk to this place, let's get a taxi," Ric announces, walking over to the same spot we had stood at only several hours ago.

"We're gonna take a taxi to the taxi place!" we both laugh drunkenly at my inane joke. I follow Ric, still trying to maintain my balance, and as I do so I suddenly have an epiphany. The alcohol probably slowed down my reaction rate, as I'm only just starting to process Ric's words.

Grab every opportunity you can.

It will never grab you.

I stare at the back of his head, as he leads the way over to a free taxi.

He *is an opportunity.*

I could interview Paolo Petrinelli.

I could post it on the Internet.

I could interview the biggest singer in Italy!

"Ric…"

He turns around. "Yep?"

"Could you get me an interview with Paolo?"

He smiles. "Sure," he says, with a look as if to say, *I thought you'd never ask.*

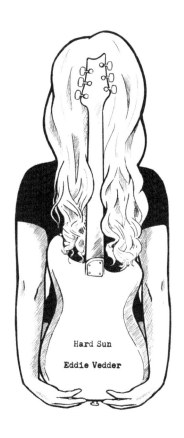

5

I have always been a rock music lover. Even after my detour into pop as a teenager, I managed to find my way back to it. I discovered Nirvana at eleven years old; I remember listening to Smells Like Teen Spirit and getting goose bumps. I wasn't sure why, but I knew there was a certain magic to it, to all of Nirvana's songs. Kurt Cobain's voice held a supremacy that was both unique and unexplainable.

I remember scribbling down the lyrics to 'Lithium' and just staring at them, trying to understand them. Even at twenty-two, I still don't fully comprehend the meaning to some of their songs. I remember listening to Pearl Jam's 'Black' and skipping track on Leo's CD player. I know now that I just wasn't ready for it, not at eleven. I would go back to it at twenty, just after my first break up. That's when 'Black' makes sense. That's when you lose yourself in the pain and darkness that Eddie Vedder's voice can transport you to – when your heart has been broken for the very first time.

I became truly enticed with the Seattle Sound at age eighteen, when rock started to really reel me back in. From thirteen to fifteen I was listening to pop, don't ask me why. I was temporarily engrossed by the let's-be-like-everyone-around-me route. Pop, however, is just not music that I can feel a deep connection to. For everybody it's different, and for me, listening to the Top 40 doesn't evoke in me even half the powerful feelings that say, a Pink Floyd song can.

Nobody in my class at school liked grunge or any type of rock at all. Nobody. But when I started to venture out, go out looking for good rock music, that's when the fun started. And funnily enough, that's when I started to break away from the social cliques at school. Not that I had ever really belonged to any of them to begin with.

I soon discovered that I much preferred listening to Kurt Cobain's voice than going shopping for nail polish and talking to boys. To this day, listening to bands from the Seattle Sound takes me to that place, that place that makes me feel like it's okay to be alone. Because I am not alone – I have

Kurt Cobain, and Layne Staley, and Black Francis. I can breathe, and I can be myself, because they understand me.

I pull my headphones out of my ears, put down the luggage in front of the single bed in my hotel room, and step out onto the terrace. Pixies' 'Debaser' can still be heard blaring from my headphones, as I look out at Italy's fashion capital. The morning sun shines on my face, and the view of Milano is atrocious. It's of a few dirty streets – nothing tells you it's Milano.

It might as well be Neasden.

I look out at the palazzi across the street from the hotel, the only clue that I'm in Italy. The Italian architecture makes me smile like it always does – those white walls, narrow rectangular windows with brown blinds and those window doors you just never seem to find in England.

As a little girl, Italy was the best place on Earth. During the British winters I would pedal away on our home exercise bike, pretending it could fly and that I was making my way to Biella. I had been in love with my parents' small suburban hometown in Piemonte ever since I could remember. There was something about the fresh air, mountains and warm smiles that always made me feel so good. It was the place where I had had my first kiss, my first motorbike ride, and I had even spent a summer dating the town rebel, Antonio.

But as a kid, before all of that, it had been the place where I was the happiest for no particular reason at all, other than being in Italy. There could be absolutely nothing going on and I was happy just breathing in the fresh air, admiring everything Italian – the houses, the cobbled streets, the people – it all seemed so magical to me.

I breathe in the polluted air of Milano as I lean over the balcony.

I've got to make some money and fast. Then I can afford better hotels for jobs like this. Even if this is my first one, and who knows how it's going to go. Maybe I'll ask Paolo Petrinelli the wrong questions, maybe it'll be so awful his representatives won't let it go on the Internet...

I inwardly sigh and step back into the small hotel room, the lilac walls making me feel as if I'm stepping into a nursery. I zip open my luggage, pulling out my microphone and camera.

When I was a kid I used to pretend I was an anchor woman on the news, reporting on the 'local crime'. My dad would be filming us on a family holiday somewhere and I'd pop my head in front of the camera, pretending my hand was a mic. "Hello, my name is Alexis Brunetti, I'm reporting live from…"

People would tell my parents what an 'active and charismatic child you have', and from school plays to my own radio show on Slurp Radio, people said I would go places.

You're going places.
You're going places.
You're going places.

They had said it so often that I had started to believe it, and when you start to believe something that hasn't happened yet, it's the easiest way to stop it from becoming reality.

Why work for it, when it's going to happen anyway? You begin to relax, you begin to get lazy, and that split second you take your eye off the ball, it's gone.

I can safely say that this is not how I imagined my life would be like at twenty-two. It's funny, I've always imagined my desire to work in the music business as an oval light guiding the way in a dark tunnel, showing me the way, but never revealing its actual identity to me. Not yet.

Do I want to be a presenter?
Work in artist management?
A record label?

Whichever one of these it is, I know one day that oval light has to reveal itself. It just has to. The thought that this interview could change everything, the *hope* that it could help in any way, is what is driving me now.

After ten long months I have something driving me. I know it will only be for a few days, until I go back to London, back to my parents' house, back to the chicken shop on Enfield Street, but I've chosen to let it soak in, to let the drive take over. And forget about the life that awaits me back in London. That person is someone else, another Alexis Brunetti, another girl with cherry red hair.

I put down the equipment on the bed and pick up my notebook. Inside are the questions I plan to ask Paolo, and I scan through them for the thirteenth time today.

I look down at what I'm wearing – exactly what I had picked out just four days earlier, when Ric had sent me an email confirming Paolo's consent to the interview, followed by a contract from his representatives. You know, stuff I can't ask, etc. Four days to pick out your debut as a 'journalist' of some sort is just not enough time.

What am I, anyway? A journalist? A presenter?

I press my purple jeans mini skirt with my fingers, as I stand in front of the bathroom mirror. The Rolling Stones t-shirt goes well with the occasion, the semi-transparent black tights and flat knee-high black boots match the skirt perfectly. My freshly re-dyed cherry red hair shines brightly in the sunlight. I look back at the reflection of my face – a curious, nervous look in my eyes.

You're going to do fine.

I take a deep breath in. All I need now is a retouch of my make-up. Stupid aeroplanes.

Just as I search for my make-up bag, my phone sounds a text message.

Mamma:
Have you reached safely? Ready for the interview? You'll be fine. X

I smile to myself. I'm glad my parents are finally on board with the whole idea. The morning after the night at Stansted Airport, I had announced to my parents that I was going to go to Milano to interview Paolo Petrinelli.

For free.

'Why don't you get a nice admin job, Alexis?' my dad had said. 'This music stuff will never pay well.'

Why is it that as a child your parents tell you you can be whatever you want to be, when in their eyes it's simply not true? At sixteen the illusion dies and your parents decide to tell you 'what you have a shot in'. At least, that was how it went with me. Occupations appropriate for Alexis Brunetti: teacher, office assistant, museum guide. Seeing them written down like that I am even more offended. Was that all I was capable of in their eyes? I love my parents and they have always been good to me, but I just don't quite understand how a parent wouldn't want their child to pursue their dreams rather than make a decent living in a job they hate. Maybe it's an age thing – maybe when I'm their age I will see the world how they see it. But right now music is all I want, and without it, I simply do not have purpose.

It's half an hour later that I arrive outside Luna Hotel. I look up nervously at the big sign, as my taxi purrs and takes off. My phone sounds again.

Blake:
You better knock 'em dead! X

I grin and suddenly hear voices. At the entrance of Luna Hotel the doorman is hailing a taxi for a very posh Italian woman in her late thirties. She's wearing tight, white trousers with expensive-looking black heels, a tight white top with her black bra underneath showing, and pearls around her neck. She walks proudly towards the taxi as she speaks loudly on the phone in Italian, her head titled upwards as if to say, *I am better than everyone else*.

I do not belong here. I really do not belong here.

Just as I watch the stuck up woman get into the taxi, I notice Ric stroll out of the revolving doors of the hotel with a duffel bag over his shoulder. He spots me and smiles, putting up his hand and giving me a motionless wave. Wearing silver sunglasses, semi-tight grey jeans, a tight, plain white t-shirt that highlights his abs, and the black leather jacket he had been wearing the night at Stansted Airport, he looks the part of a rockstar.

Oh boy. I forgot how attractive he is.

It feels like the night at Stansted Airport had happened a month ago, when in reality it has been exactly a week. After Ric had got his wallet back that night, we had shared a taxi back and he had dropped me off at home. The following afternoon, he had called me to tell me Paolo had agreed to do the interview. He called me whilst they were at airport, waiting to fly back.

His voice had sounded even sexier on the phone, pausing every now and again I would have paid good money to have known what he was thinking. He had then proceeded to add me to his private social media page (to my delight), and then emailed me to confirm the interview. He text me before my flight that morning, telling me to meet him at Luna Hotel at 3pm sharp. As I learnt the night at Stansted Airport, Ric lives in the outskirts of Milano. But Paolo, who lives in Bologna, is staying at the Luna Hotel.

I meet him halfway up the pathway to the hotel and we smile at one another.

"Hey," he says, and we give each other the two traditional pecks on the cheeks, his breath smelling of tobacco.

Argh. The only negative to you, Ric.

"Ciao!"

"How was your flight?"

We walk back down the pathway together, where the doorman has already hailed us a taxi. I watch Ric put his duffel bag in the boot.

"It was good…" I continue, as we get into the taxi, "is Paolo still in the hotel?"

"No, no…he's having lunch with his family. Just came by to pick up some stuff. The rest of the band and the crew are staying here, too."

"Oh."

"San Siro per favore," he tells the driver.

Hearing the name gives me shivers and I smile to myself, hardly believing where we are heading.

San Siro stadium is the biggest stadium in Italy; it hosts football games and some of the biggest concerts in Europe. In all the times I have visited Milano over the years, I have not yet had a chance to visit the stadium, and tonight I not only get to enter for free *and* go backstage, but I also have the privilege to be the first to interview Paolo Petrinelli in thirteen years.

That's right – Paolo Petrinelli hasn't allowed anyone to interview him in thirteen years. Ever since his wife had a miscarriage and a journalist pushed it too far by asking about it a few days after the tragic incident. He is notoriously known

61

for his reaction in what must have been a very painful period for him.

"*How do I feel?* I'll show you how I feel!" he famously is heard saying to the journalist.

Footage of Paolo's fleeting moment of anger and his attempt to punch the journalist circulated the media across Italy and 'I'll show you how I feel!' became the catch phrase most used by Italians that year.

Since then, Paolo has not allowed *anyone* to interview him. He held a press conference where he announced to Italy that he and his family will not be doing any more interviews. Journalists tried for years and years but to no avail. They still try now of course, but he continues to refuse.

Except for me. I am the lucky one that gets this honour, in thirteen years, and all because Ric had asked him. I know – I'm asking myself the exact same question; how the hell did I get this lucky?

But I'm not going to waste it.

"So how many D'Angelo solos are planned for glorious San Siro tonight?" I ask Ric.

"One."

"*One?* Again?" I blurt out, and I lower my voice in case the taxi driver is a secret spy for Mauro Fontana. "Look, I don't mean this in a poisonous, I'm-a-bitch way, but Mauro is not that amazing a guitarist. I mean, most of the things he's supposed to do Paolo does. And his solos – not that clean. You on the other hand…" I tilt my head to one side and he smiles, "granted I've only heard one, it was one pretty damn awesome solo."

Ric gives me an appreciative smile, and I realise we have already relaxed around one another again. It's crazy how you meet people sometimes and feel comfortable with them straight away. As if they have always been with you; you just hadn't crossed paths yet.

We talk about London and the gig as we make our way to the stadium. Ric at one point scrolls down the window to have a cigarette and the wind does insane things to my hair. My hair is naturally curly but I hardly ever let it loose – as soon as I wash it, it's straightened right away. I don't like my hair curly; it's messy and unpredictable. Plus, I get tired of people asking me why I don't brush it.

You can't brush curly hair!

Having said that, I turn into an eighties icon every time it rains.

Or it's windy.

Or it's humid.

I suppose England is probably not the right country for you when you have curly hair.

"Siamo arrivati, signore D'Angelo," the taxi driver suddenly announces to us.

"Already?"

As we get out of the car, my eyes slowly trail the huge building all the way to the top, hurting the back of my neck. San Siro stadium is across the road from us, and it looks just as huge as it does in pictures. I am in complete awe, and the information I have previously read up on the infamous building years ago regurgitates itself in my mind.

This stadium was built in 1926. The first event ever held at the stadium was a football match between A.C. Milan and Inter. A.C. Milan lost 3-6...

Ric gets out his duffel bag from the boot, as the taxi driver hurriedly gets out of the car.

"It's okay, I got it," Ric tells him, putting it down as he gets out his wallet. I snap out of my daydream where I own San Siro and hold monthly barbecues, and walk over to Ric. We lightly argue over who is paying for the taxi, and in the end, Ric wins.

I look up at San Siro in awe, as we cross the road and walk up the pathway to the entrance. The place is practically empty, but I notice a man standing and smoking not far from the entrance, looking right at us. He's in his mid-forties, with a beer belly and big arms with tattoos half hiding under his black t-shirt. He has a silver hoop earring in his right ear and he looks terrifying.

Who the hell is this guy? He looks like a hooligan.

I want to warn Ric of the weird thug looking at us when the stranger speaks.

"You're fucking late!" growls the scary-looking man in Italian to Ric with a huge grin, dumping the cigarette on the floor and squashing it with the heel of his dirty trainer.

Do these two know each other?!

63

"Listen, Willy's already in there getting drunk, you might wanna stop him."

Ric shakes his head and we come to a halt in front of the stranger, Ric gently putting his duffel bag on the floor and it confirms that they are friends of some sort. I would care more to question their chalk-and-cheese dynamic if only we hadn't stopped less than a hundred metres from the double doors of San Siro. I look over at the entrance, longingly.

So close and yet so far.

"He needs to be put on a leash," Ric gets out his phone and reads something, as the stranger and I stand in silence.

I am dying to know who this man is in relation to Ric. Family? Good friends? Colleagues?

"Is Franco here?"

"You know he never gets here before five," the thug replies.

Ric sighs, looks at me and then at the tattooed man. "This is Alexis, she's from London, here to interview Paolo."

The stranger frowns, and puts out his hand. "Oh!"

"Alexis, this is Vinnie. He's a bastard. He also lives near me."

I stifle a laugh and take his meaty hand. "Piacere."

"Piacere," he stares, "is this your first time in Italy?"

"Can't you feel her accent is legit, idiot? She comes to Italy every year, her parents are Italian, her parents taught her Italian before English." He picks up his duffel bag once more and we head into the building. It warms my heart that Ric remembers my basic info – we haven't seen each other in a week, and when you're the guitarist of the most famous man in Italy, that's a lifetime.

"*Ooooh,* well how am I supposed to know?" Vinnie continues, "so, is it your first time at San Siro?" he looks at Ric, "can I ask her that or you gonna snap at me again?"

"Uh, yeah," I reply, as Ric ignores him.

I'm not sure what to think of Vinnie. He seems to be a good friend of Ric's – I can tell that much, but the idea of them spending barbecues and pub nights together seems difficult to imagine; they're so different. Ric has no tattoos, is polite and doesn't appear to swear much. Vinnie on the other hand, looks like someone that regularly appears on the local papers for rioting and vandalism. They also look at least ten years apart. Worst of all, Vinnie seems like one of those people that claim they're 'honest' but are really just plain rude – you know what type of people I'm talking about. There's a big difference between the two and I wish someone would explain this to them.

"Oooh, well then you're gonna have a fucking brilliant day! You know Sting arrives later on-"

"What?!" I shriek, as we pass a billboard with a huge poster of Paolo Petrinelli singing passionately into the mic.

"You're a fan?" Vinnie seems surprised and I feel sexism is behind this one.

"Yes."

"How much of a big fan? Can you name his first solo album-"

"The Dream of the Blue Turtles. Amazing album, also a fantastic phrase for a tattoo, if I ever feel like getting words."

Vinnie stares. "Thinking of getting a tattoo some day?"

I peel my top down at the shoulder to reveal my 'FF' tattoo as we walk.

"Holy shit. Foo Fighters." Vinnie forces a laugh, clearly impressed. "Now I understand why Paolo has allowed you to interview him."

Ric blows out smoke and gives his friend a quick smile, as we make our way through the revolving doors.

We're here. Finally.

I look around the reception area – there's already a queue forming when the doors are not set to open for another six hours.

Some of the women roar in excitement at Ric and he smiles at them, though there's slight discomfort in his eyes. I can tell he's relieved to make it to the staff entrance before anyone can reach us. The receptionist presses a button and the door labelled 'INGRESSO VIETATO' buzzes open.

"Favourite three tracks?" Vinnie asks me.

"Best of You, Arlandria, and the awfully underrated 'The One'."

We walk down an empty corridor filled with posters. Bob Dylan, Bruce Springsteen, The Doors – they have all performed here at some point.

Vinnie's eyes light up. "Oh, that's the one that was made for that film with Jack Black…what's it called again, uh…"

"Orange Country," I tell him, without a blink of an eye.

"Yes! Yeah, I remember really liking that track," Vinnie smiles and shakes his head, his eyes on Ric. "this is so the girl for you, Ricco."

"Just don't bring up the Red Hot Chilis or she'll throw a fit like she did with me the other night," Ric tells Vinnie, giving me a smile.

"*The other night*'?" Vinnie repeats, with bewildered eyes. "What happened *the other night?* Not breaking poor Valentina's heart now, are we Ricco?"

A punch to the stomach.

So there's a girlfriend. Of course there's a girlfriend – he's the guitarist of the most famous singer in Italy. Do not even concern yourself with his love life, Alexis.

We arrive at a plain black door with a security guard standing outside. He has a big build and his olive skin muscles pop out from his t-shirt like massive rocks. He's wearing a security pass round his neck with a moody picture and his name: MASSIMO CONSTANZO.

I would not want to mess with you, Massimo.

"Carte d'identita'?" they both get out their backstage passes and Ric hands me something – my very own laminated backstage VIP pass.

PAOLO PETRINELLI TOUR NAZIONALE
VIP PASS
SAN SIRO

There is a picture of Paolo Petrinelli playing acoustic guitar and singing into the mic. I smile.

"You got me a pass," I say softly, as I stare down at it, rubbing my thumb affectionately over it.

"Yep. Well put it on then, or guys like this will stop you everywhere in this place."

"Okay, avanti," Massimo moves to the side as I put the VIP pass round my neck, and we walk through to the backstage area. The place is buzzing with people and filled with all sorts of different noises; people talking loudly in

Italian, hammers, a vacuum, and cheesy Italian pop music playing. There are lots of people around; moving, carrying things – most of them roadies and tech guys. We walk further on and I realise we are walking onto the stage, just as three or four guys rush over to Ric.

"Where have you been?!"

"Riccardo, you're here!"

Whilst Ric and Vinnie stop to talk to them, I continue walking, as if in a trance. As if the front of the stage is calling my name, luring me in. I'm in awe, taking in my surroundings, drowning out all the noises around me. As I look around, studying every detail of the stadium, I am hit with a thousand emotions.

Call me crazy, but it's as if I'm suddenly surrounded by something bigger than me, bigger than Paolo Petrinelli, bigger than anything else on the planet. This is a place where music is shared, where it collides with emotion for the ultimate effect. This stadium brings people together, aspires epiphanies, dreams, goals. It creates memories that last a lifetime. It changes peoples' lives. It may sound dramatic, but when has the power of music ever been dull or normal? Music has always been dramatic, music has always been able to change our mood; darken us or brighten us, scare us or motivate us, inspire us or drown us, and that's why we love it.

"So, you're back?" says a voice that sounds vaguely familiar. I turn around to find Mauro Fontana standing there, smiling at me with those sly eyes. I try not to frown, but in all honesty, I'm surprised he even remembers me; he had barely spoken to me back in London.

"Yeah, yeah. Can't get rid of me that easily."

He holds two bottles of beer in his hand and he has this look on his face – a sort of curious expression that makes me uncomfortable.

"Well you are *very* lucky to be at this gig, you know that? Not many people get this opportunity, especially young women at the start of their careers."

When he says 'women' he looks me up and down, and I swear that for a second, a split second, I see an element of perversion in his eyes.

"Yeah, I know. I'm grateful to Paolo," there's silence between us and I can hear Ric and Vinnie chatting loudly to some of the crew about Bobby Brown.

"Here," he hands me one of the beer bottles, "for you. I'm going to go set up. See you later and, enjoy the show. Maybe one of my solos will inspire you."

I very much doubt it.

"Thanks," I watch him walk away, wondering what the hell just happened. I take in the strong Italian sun hitting the back of my head and take a gulp from my ice cold beer. I decide I don't want to think too much about Mauro's motives, after all, it could have been for a range of reasons. Perhaps he wants to launch a solo career in London, or perhaps he's one of those manwhore musicians that can never keep it in his trousers. Whatever it is, I won't think about it now.

I sit down at the edge of the stage, my legs dangling down, and I stay there a good while. I take in the sun beaming down on my face, and enjoy my ice cold beer, my eyes never leaving the beautiful stadium in front of me. I cannot believe where I am, and I cannot understand how I got here.

All I did was accept Enrico's invitation to go backstage at The Forum.

Is this how it works for everyone? Know the right person, ask at the right time, and the world is your oyster?

And, if that is indeed the way, does that make hard work alone worthless?

The thought saddens me and I shake it off, for this is absolutely not the time to be sad. This is the time to be excited, to be brave, to be ready.

And I *am* ready.

This is going to be the start for me, I know it. I *feel* it. Something is happening, something is different, since the moment I asked Ric if I could interview Paolo. I am suddenly on a rollercoaster, and I don't want to ever get off. The exhilaration, the excitement, the motivation; it's bringing me to life.

I am fucking ready for this.

I'm eventually asked to move from the stage by some roadies dressed in black; a young, cute Italian in his midtwenties politely asking me to get up.

"We really don't want to electrocute you, not until after the gig," he tells me, smiling with big, dark eyes.

Don't even think about it, Alex. You're here to work.

Though, a fling could be a nice bonus, it has been a while…

No! Focus.

I walk around backstage for a while, investigating the inner workings of the stadium and reading over my questions a few more times. Ric in the meantime sets up with the rest of them, whilst simultaneously gossiping with Vinnie and a few guys that look a lot like Vinnie.

Are these his friends? Doesn't he have friends his own age, and who don't look like hooligans?

Eventually everyone makes their way to the green room, and by 'everyone' I mean the band (minus Paolo) and their loved ones. It appears Ric's loved ones are Vinnie and the Vinnie lookalikes, but I wonder rather nervously if Valentina will turn up later. I wonder what she looks like, how she dresses, what her favourite Pixies album is. Does she even like the Pixies?

The green room at San Siro is five times bigger than the one back at The Forum, with a mini bar and kitchen added to the mix, it's also five times cooler.

There's great energy in the room; the drummer is playing his drumsticks on the table, as Ric plays Guns n' Roses – 'Sweet Child O' Mine' on his Gibson Les Paul. People are clapping and moving their heads to the song.

Ric at one point plays some John Mayer just for me, with me clapping and *woo*ing.

John Mayer is one of my favourite guitarists and I had mentioned this to Ric the night at Stansted airport. We were three or four Jack Daniels in, discussing guitarists and I name dropped John Mayer. When he starts playing 'Slow Dancing in a Burning Room', I give him a smile as if to say: *thanks for listening to me that night.*

He returns the exact same smile.

Then Mauro walks in and ruins the good vibes. And to be honest, I hadn't even noticed he wasn't with us. His presence isn't actually missed.

"Can't you cut that shit?" he snaps in Italian to Ric. The singing dies down and Ric stops playing, sighing.

"We're warming up, Mauro. It helps us relax, ease the tension," Ric tells him.

"Yeah well, we're on in less than an hour so it might be time to stop 'relaxing' and start tensing up."

I don't like the way Mauro speaks to Ric, the way he looks at him as if he's better than him. It doesn't seem fair to me that Mauro gets so many of the solos when Ric is clearly more capable, and it's hard to believe that he is the main guitarist of one of the biggest singers in Italy.

Maybe Mauro had been really good years ago and had then had a car accident or something and now he can't play as well, but they can't fire him. Or he's secretly the prince of a country we've never heard of and his wishes *have* to be granted, no matter what.

There *has* to be a logical explanation as to why Mauro Fontana is the main guitarist. I want to find out what it is, I *need* to find out what it is, because it sure as shit isn't talent.

The evening flies by, chatting and getting ready for the gig. Soon enough the concert is to begin, and everyone is making their way to their seats. After wishing Ric and the others good luck, I follow Vinnie and the lookalikes to the booths. They're high up and have a great view, but this is not the view of the concert that I so very desire.

"Do you think I'll be allowed in the standing area?" I ask Vinnie, as the others take their seats. I look at my empty chair, and my soul saddens at the thought of wasting such an incredible night observing it from this view.

"Of course you can, you can go anywhere in this stadium with *that*," he nods at the pass dangling round my neck. And so I tell Vinnie I will see them all after the show, and make my way to the standing area of San Siro stadium. It takes a hell of a lot of pushing to get to the front, but I stop at about fourth or fifth row. Everything here is huge, and I feel about the size of an ant. But this stadium is something else – it really makes you feel like you are a part of something truly special, before the concert has even begun.

I take some selfies and send them to Blake. In return, he sends me some pictures of the grey skies near Charing Cross and they make me shudder.

I love that I am in Italy right now. I love that I am at San Siro, about to do what I am about to do. And most of all,

I'm glad I asked Ric for this opportunity. That I had the balls to ask. Because it was such a batshit crazy idea, if you think about it. And I had envisioned thirty different ways Ric could have responded, with twenty-nine different mimicking laughs.

After swapping pictures with Blake, I put my phone away and look around me at the thousands of people surrounding me. They look like tiny ants, and I hear Vinnie's Fun Facts on the stadium earlier.

San Siro stadium holds a capacity of 80,018...

That's a hell of a lot of ants.

The crowd goes crazy with screams and woos when the band eventually come onstage at a late 9:30pm, and I am the most excited I have been a long time. I join in with the screams, except this time my screams are directed mostly at Ric. I keep my eyes on him throughout, watching him nod his head as he plays, my eyes sometimes trailing to his butt when he walks across the stage. Girls near me scream his name, others screaming Paolo's or Mauro's.

I'd be lying if I said that I wasn't waiting impatiently for Ric's solo, continuously smiling at him. There is an eagerness in me to see him play, as if to confirm that the solo I heard a week ago was actually real.

It's two hours later that it's finally his song, and I've enjoyed the entire set. It's just that when I recognise the track straight away and start *woo*ing like a crazy person, it's a different level of excitement than the rest of the gig. I've been waiting (impatiently) for this moment. The moment when I get goose bumps, when I lose myself in Ric's playing, when his solo speaks volumes.

The limelight shines onto him and I *woo* at the top of my lungs. It's the same solo, but it's so damn good that it sends shivers down my spine as powerfully as it did at the Forum. As if it is the first time I am hearing it. The first time it is reaching my soul, the first time I am connecting to his playing, and it feels so damn magical. I jump up and down, taking it all in, knowing that Ric possesses the talent to go far. That he *will* go far. He has to.

Once his solo is over, he grins at me, putting his arms in the air and I do the same. It's crazy but I think I'm proud, proud of the talent of someone I hardly know. It's bizarre, I know, but I welcome the feeling. There's never anything wrong with a bit of pride for someone talented. Raw talent needs to be supported, shouted about, praised. Always.

Out of all the thousands of faces in the crowd, his eyes are locked with mine, recovering from his amazing solo like a couple recovering from amazing sex, and we continue to look at one another as the screams keep going. Somehow I feel connected to him through his playing.

That was the last song of the night. And as the band walk offstage, nerves hit my stomach, my legs turn to jelly, and I realise that it's time.

It's time to interview Paolo Petrinelli.

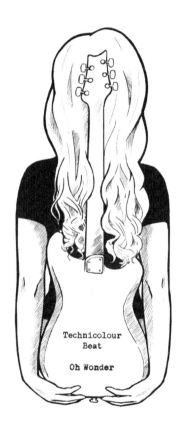

6

The first time I ever interviewed a musician I was seventeen years old. I was passing through Covent Garden on a busy Saturday afternoon when I heard a beautiful male voice performing in front of the London Transport museum. As soon as I saw his face I knew I was going to interview him for the college magazine; his blue eyes, impressive guitar skills and soothing voice were something I very quickly realized was going to be worth writing about.

And so I introduced myself to him after his set, and asked him if I could interview him. He was honoured, and so I began reading out questions I had written down on a napkin from a restaurant nearby. The college magazine liked the article so much that they prompted me to invite the singer in to perform a concert. I created posters for it and designed the tickets, selling them in the college canteen at lunchtimes. It didn't seem to be working as well as I had envisioned, and so one lunch time, tired of not selling many tickets, I stood up on the table and started selling the shit out of the musician.

"Listen up everyone, a very cute, Italian busker is coming to OUR college! Can you believe it?!"

I had no idea if it would work, and if it didn't, I would be the laughing stock of the entire college. But I was okay with that, with taking that risk, if it meant there was a chance I could get what I wanted.

Luckily for me it worked, and within thirty minutes, the concert was sold out. Nobody had organised a concert at our college in over twenty years, and I had to sit in meetings with our head master, deputy head master, and head of year, just to fight for it to happen.

Pitching it.
Selling it.
Giving it my all.

And in order for it to go ahead, I had to sell out the venue, which I had already done.

In order for the musician to show up, I had to fight for the busker to actually get *paid* for performing at our college, which was on the other side of London. When I told the busker how much he'd be getting paid, I still remember the way he had scoffed, and said, "that's enough to cover my travel to your college, and a sandwich," and he couldn't have been more right.

I think that was the moment I realised how little musicians get paid when they're not Prince, and that's when they actually get paid at all. It's not an easy industry to make money from, as we all know. You're either making millions or barely anything at all.

The gig was a success, and the singer and I became friends following the event. In fact, we're still friends now; he's toured the world and his music only gets better every passing day. It's crazy how our friendship was born of one simple interview. All in that one decision to get up, go over to him, and introduce myself.

I look around the empty green room of San Siro at all the posters – Bryan Adams, another Jim Morrison one, and then, one of Paolo Petrinelli. I walk over to it, my eyes fixed on his face. He's showing that warm smile of his, but the photo seems quite old – he has no wrinkles. I wonder what it must have been like, to go from being a 'normal' guy living in Bologna to Italy's biggest singer.

How does that transition even happen? One day you're a struggling, hungry artist, and the next you have more money than you know what to do with. You go from a nobody, to people fainting when they see you. To knowing that your fans are going to treasure any interaction they have with you for the rest of their lives. Whereas to you, you will have forgotten them by tomorrow.

How incredibly odd it must be to be a celebrity.

The floor suddenly creaks and I immediately turn around to find Paolo Petrinelli walking slowly towards me. He has the exact same smile on his face that he has in the poster, and in practically every photograph I have ever seen of him. It's the smile he reserves for strangers.

"June 1995. That was a great night," he says to me in almost perfect English. It still seems bizarre to me to find myself standing in the same room as the Great Paolo

Petrinelli. There are Italians that would do virtually *anything* to be in my position right now. I think after seeing a certain amount of posters, billboards, and music videos of a musician you deem them Untouchable and Inhuman. They are something *higher*, and of course, this is the general motive behind the PR team of a singer like Paolo – who would buy his music if he was just a regular Joe?

But Paolo *is* just a regular person – *everyone* at the end of the day is just a regular person. We all get the flu, get our hearts broken, cry at the end of Titanic and say 'aaaw' when we see puppies. Fame is an illusion. But it's an illusion that manages to fool of us, and as he approaches me, I begin to tremble.

"I saw the footage of that night on the Internet, it looks amazing," I tell him, "you were incredible tonight too, Paolo, really. I'm always blown away."

His smile seems to appreciate the compliment and not see it as ass-kissing, which I'm very grateful for.

"Thank you, Alexis. Shall we start the interview before the boys get here and start causing chaos?"

"Of course," I reply, as my heart starts pounding out of my chest. I grab the camera out of my bag and set it up on the coffee table, lightly pulling the mic wire over to the sofa in front of us, where Paolo has already taken his place. He looks curious as to what I have in store for him, and a little on edge, but he tries his best to hide it with that smile of his, that smile that reads: *everything's going to be okay, Paolo's here.*

"What I thought is, since we said a 'brief' interview, I just planned five questions. They're sort of *big* questions, but five nonetheless, so it'll be over in no time."

"Okay, Alexis."

Every time he says my name my heart quadruples in beats per minute.

"Okay, so I'll introduce you, and then I'll dive straight into question number one."

"Sounds perfect."

"Are you ready?" I ask.

"Yes."

After hitting 'REC' on the camera, I walk back over to the sofa, where I take my place next to Paolo and smile. I turn to the camera with the mic in my hand.

"Buona sera! I'm Alexis Brunetti and I am backstage at San Siro stadium in Milano with one of Italy's finest singer-songwriter guitarists Paolo Petrinelli, after a fantastic performance tonight," I pause and look at Paolo, who knows exactly what to do.

"Buona sera, Alexis!"

"Buona sera, Paolo! How are you feeling after this incredible event tonight?"

"Oh I feel amazing, Alexis. There is nothing like it."

"Well it's wonderful to be here today, to have the honour to interview you here backstage at San Siro."

"The honour is all mine, Alexis."

I beam. "Paolo, you've been in the industry nearly twenty years now, you've released thirteen albums, sold over three million copies of your singles worldwide, which song do you think has been the most important to you?"

He takes a deep breath in and stares into mid-air, as he thinks about his reply. I, in turn, keep my eyes fixed on him, smiling.

"Uh, I would have to say…the first single we ever released, Se Non Ti Ho. I know, it sounds crazy! But, you know, as a musician, it's really hard to get started, you know? Everyone asks, *so what do you do?* And you say: well, I'm a musician, and they say, oh let's hear some stuff! But…it's tough.

You get scared, because you don't *know* that anyone will like it, you just know that *you* like it, and so to go ahead and spend all the money you earned working at the local shop in a small town in Italy, plus half your rent, on something that is so likely to fail, that's a big step, it's such a huge leap of faith on yourself."

Paolo Petrinelli is a natural interviewee, probably helped by his twenty years' experience in the business, but it definitely lends a hand in easing my nerves. In the past whilst working in radio, I have occasionally interviewed artists that either had nothing to say, *ummed* and *erred* too much, or were just plain blunt in their replies. There's nothing more awkward than an interviewee that has nothing to say.

"Well I think many, *many* people are glad that you did take that step."

He smiles. "Thank you very much, Alexis."

"So out of the thirteen albums you made, which was the most enjoyable to work on and why?"

"Uuh, that's a tough one because I loved working on all of them."

"They weren't too stressful?"

"No, no, I mean, yeah it's always stressful, of course, but because we're working on music, and music that I love, the stress is a small price to pay."

Smooth.

"I guess if I had to choose one, it'd have to be La Vita Di Lei, because I made that album the year I got married and my wife was pregnant with our first child, Matte, and it was an amazing time, so I was very happy."

I notice Mauro appear at the door, and he tiptoes into the room, followed by the rest of the band, Ric last.

I suddenly feel the pressure a hell of a lot more.

"That sounds amazing Paolo, but now I have to ask you a peculiar question."

Paolo tenses slightly but tries his best to hide it. "Go on."

"If you weren't a musician, what do you think you would have been?"

As he *umm*s, I notice Ric leaning against the radiator, his toned arms folded, and he winks at me. I notice some significant others of the band are now in the room too, along with Vinnie and some of the Vinnie lookalikes.

Good God, this is getting nerve-racking. Why not just invite the fans in, too? All 80,018 of them.

"I think I would have become a pilot."

"A pilot?"

"Yes! I had an unhealthy interest in planes as a child, and I kind of still do. Got a couple of models in my house even today. My wife swears she's going to get rid of them whilst I'm sleeping one night."

I laugh. "Might get one of your children to 'accidentally' break them."

"Yes, actually, I had a really ugly plastic fish that I bought many, many years ago in Brighton and my wife hated it from the first time she saw it, but naturally, I wouldn't get rid of it. So when our second child, Maddalena, was five, my wife broke it and said it had been our daughter!"

I laugh again and so do some people in the room.

"Seriously?!"

"Yeah! And then of course, my wife, being of a pure heart, she couldn't keep the truth to herself for long, and so she told me…" Paolo explains, and I see him relax a little.

"Poor fish! Did he have a name?"

"No, but he was a good friend of mine."

"On that note, a little side question…"

"Sure…"

"Do you ever give your guitars names?"

It's a question I have always asked guitarists, because I name all my guitars. Back at age seventeen, I couldn't afford brand guitars, so when I bought my beautiful acoustic guitar off Denmark Street, I named him Joe (after the Jimi Hendrix song 'Hey Joe'). I loved the name and the guitar so much that it became a tradition with each guitar I bought.

"My guitars? No…"

I study him, trying to work out if he knows what I'm going to ask next.

"Would you like to today?"

He frowns. "Name one of my guitars? Yeah, okay….uh…"

I quickly catch Ric's glance and he's beaming at me.

"…How about my acoustic Fender…ok, uh, well, all my guitars are definitely girls…uh, how about…Jasmin?" he tells me.

"Jasmin? That sounds cool."

"Yes! I heard it whilst on tour in America and instantly loved the name."

"Great! Jasmin it is." I look at the camera. "You heard it here first, Paolo's acoustic fender here is called Jasmin!" I turn back to Paolo. "Right, my next question is a little on the odd side," I can feel all eyes in the room on me as I pause, Paolo watching me curiously. "I recently learnt that you like to moonlight as a rapper in your spare time."

He instantly grins, looking away as he shakes his head. When he looks back at me he is a bucket of nerves.

Will he go for it?

"It's a very little, *tiny* side hobby I have."

Paolo is probably the last person in the entire world that you would guess could rap. And no fan has ever actually heard him do it before, it's something he only shares with his family. I made sure of this before adding it to the interview.

"I was wondering if, perhaps, tonight…you would like to freestyle for us?"

Some people in the room turn to each other with surprised looks, and Mauro breaks into a soft cackle.

He's either going to like the question and try, or refuse and kill me afterwards.

It's a risk I take…

"Noooo, really? Me? But I'm so terrible…"

"It's completely up to you, I know everyone here would love to hear something…" I say to him, and he watches me, pensively.

"What would you want me to freestyle about?"

YES!

VICTORY!

WE HAVE A VICTORY ON OUR HANDS!

"How about…this moment right here."

He continues to smile at me, and I study him carefully – he seems genuinely interested in the challenge, so I keep going.

"Do I have to move my hands about?" he jokes, and I laugh.

"Not at all! Unless it helps…"

He rubs his hands together, concentrating hard. "Okay, alright. I got this."

YES!

"You got this!" I tell him, smiling. There is complete and utter silence in the green room, as Paolo thinks of a verse.

It's the slowest few seconds of my entire life. It feels as if an hour goes by in what is only a moment, a moment where Paolo tries to think of a verse to rap for me. Is this really happening? Is my idea actually working? Is he really going for this?

He suddenly looks at me.

"Sitting here backstage with a very cool girl,
Her vibrant, red hair makes her stand out in the world.
With my band as an audience,
And a crowd that shone bright tonight,
I am very happy to be here,

San Siro… you were a delight!"

There is immediate applause from around the room, and I join them, heat rushing to my face.

I just got Paolo Petrinelli to rap.
I just got Paolo Petrinelli to rap.
I JUST GOT PAOLO PETRINELLI TO RAP!

The lines had just rolled off his tongue, and everyone in the audience looks completely gobsmacked as they clap.

"Wow, that was incredible, Paolo!" I tell him, and he beams at me, red in the cheeks. He looks completely chuffed with himself, and not as if he's going to kill me afterwards.

"That was harder than I thought it was going to be!"

"Really? You made it look so easy!"

He breathes out heavily, fanning his face with his hand.

"Is it just me or it's hot in here now?!"

I laugh.

"Making me rap! You see, this is what happens when you allow yourself to be interviewed by a Brit!" he jokes, as he eyes the audience.

"You enjoyed it though, didn't you?"

"You know, I did."

"You're thinking about including it in your next show, aren't you? A rap intro at your next gig!" I tell him, playfully.

"Oh, yes! Definitely, Alexis!" he says, sarcastically.

"With some back-up singers maybe, get Eminem to join you onstage, too..."

"Oh my God, this woman! Would you like to become my new PR manager, Alexis?!"

I just got Paolo Petrinelli to rap.

People around the room laugh. "I would like that very much Paolo, where do I sign?!"

"She's got my next tour campaign set up already, ladies and gentlemen!"

"Yes, I do!" we both laugh, bright-eyed and enjoying the moment.

This is going well. This is going really well.
Keep going, Alex.

"Well that was a wonderful verse, thank you Paolo. My last question for you, you could say is the *ultimate* question…"

"I'm listening."

"What advice would you give someone just starting out in music?"

He narrows his eyes at me.

"A singer or…?"

"Anyone that's just starting out, that loves music."

Me.

Me.

Me.

Me.

Me.

"Well, this industry is pretty tough. *So* many people want to be a part of the phenomenon, want to be a part of music, it's such an incredible thing to be a part of, and well, you *will* get rejected. All I can say is that if you really want something, like anything else in life really, you have to keep going until you get it. The ones that give up, they are the *only* ones that don't make it."

I smile. In a way, I had expected this to be his advice. It's the advice I give myself everyday. But, coming from Paolo seems to soothe me. "Thank you very much Paolo, it has been a pleasure to talk to you tonight. And to meet Jasmin."

"Thank you, Alexis, it's been a pleasure to be here. You are lovely."

I blush. "Thank you, Paolo!" I turn back to the camera, knowing I am red in the face. "This is Alexis Brunetti reporting live from San Siro on the night of Italy's biggest concert of this year, have a fabulous evening."

There is uproar from the audience. Paolo and I shake hands, smiling at one another, before I get up and press 'STOP' on the recorder. I am still red in the face from Paolo calling me lovely and the applause only encourages more blood to rush to my cheeks. I smile in gratitude however, as the audience begins to disperse around the room and I realise my palms are sweaty. Paolo walks over.

Whatever you do, don't shake hands with him again.

"That was wonderful!" I tell him, "thank you so much."

"That was a great interview, Alexis. You are a natural. I will no doubt watch it once it's ready," we walk out of the green room together and stand in the corridor where it's much quieter. I am still trembling, reeling from what was such a wonderfully exciting seven minutes. "I think it's going to be great, you will send a copy to my manager, Tommaso, yes?"

"Yep, and I will send it to him *before* I post it on the Internet, so if there's anything you would like me to edit I'll be sure to do that," I say to him, secretly hoping that no further editing would be needed and I can post this video out to the world as soon as humanly possible.

"Okay, thank you, I hope you had a good time tonight," Paolo says to me.

"I most certainly did, thank you *very* much for everything."

"My pleasure."

We give each other pecks on the cheeks.

He smells like oranges again.

"I'm sure I will see you again very soon."

I watch him walk down the corridor to his dressing room, turning around and giving me a motionless wave, I do the same.

"Paolo! Wait!" his family wails after him.

I stand outside the green room for a moment. I put a hand to my temple – I am still boiling hot.

I just interviewed Paolo Petrinelli.
I just got Paolo Petrinelli to rap.
To fucking rap.
That was a good idea, Alex.
You achieved something tonight.
Well done.

After taking a moment to be proud of my achievement, I walk back into the green room as if walking on a cloud. I go straight over to Ric, who has his back to me. He's talking to Vinnie, and I tap him on the shoulder. When he turns around, I notice he is holding two bottles of beer, and his eyes light up at the sight of me.

"You were awesome!" Ric looks just as excited as me.

"Yeah you *were* awesome!" Vinnie chimes in. "Good questions, too."

"You just got Paolo Petrinelli to rap! To *rap!* This is gonna go viral in only a matter of hours! You realise this, right? No one has *ever* asked Paolo to rap!"

I grin; it gives me such a warm feeling to see Ric excited for me.

"Well done. Good thinking."

A well done from Ric means the world to me and a wave of emotion hits my stomach. He holds out one of the beer bottles and I gently take it from him, thanking him under my breath.

"Ready to celebrate?"

"Hell yes!" we clink bottles, exchanging smiles.

The band, excluding Paolo and his family, all stay and relax in the green room, along with Vinnie, his lookalikes and Kyle's temporary replacement, Adam. I get an official introduction to the drummer, Roberto, and keyboardist, Martino. Roberto is the manwhore of the band, with lots of tattoos and big, crazy hair; he is constantly surrounded by random, slutty women. The keyboardist, on the other hand, is quiet and timid; he doesn't speak much to me at all or to anyone else for that matter.

The rest of us talk about the greatest and worst rockstars to have ever lived, drugs, Italian politics, popstars, British indie bands and Dave Grohl as we drink beer, smoke and enjoy the Friday night atmosphere. Okay, I never usually smoke. I hate the stuff and stay away from it, but there's something about tonight – the magic, the excitement, that makes tonight some sort of weird exception.

I don't know what it is, whether it be following the success of the interview or simply being at San Siro, but I keep sharing cigarettes with Ric as if I'm an addict.

At about 2am, the drummer leaves with three women (three!) and the atmosphere seems to mellow down, after all, he had been the loudest one in the room.

I'm sitting on top of the white marble kitchen top, my legs dangling down, my feet kicking the cardboard boxes beneath it, and my third cup of beer in hand. Ric is sitting next to me sharing the kitchen top and his knees bent, but he's holding his fifth cup of beer, and a lit cigarette. Adam, Mauro and Martino are all sitting on the sofa opposite us, Mauro leaning forward, always alert, whilst Adam slouches back, not a care in the world, smoking a joint and blowing out smoke rings.

Martino is texting his wife and not paying attention to anybody else, whilst Vinnie and three of his lookalikes sit in the corner on wooden chairs, most probably discussing Italian football. Attractive women have come and gone, but none of them seem to hang around too long after Roberto left.

"But he *did* change music," Adam says, blowing out another smoke ring. Somehow from the genius of Freddie Mercury, we have switched to the genius of Michael Jackson.

"For sure," Mauro tells us, "but I just don't like him. I acknowledge his waves of change, his talent, I appreciate it, but I just don't like him."

"Well I think he was a musical dancing genius, whatever he was in his own life," I declare to the room. Ric smiles at me and I gently take the cigarette from his fingers, taking a swig. We don't take our eyes off each other as I inhale, and it's outrageously sexy.

Ah yes, perhaps there is another reason I am smoking tonight; the way Ric passes me his cigarettes. It's like a strange sort of chemistry is passing between us.

Call me crazy, but it seems to me like something has shifted between us tonight. Ric is looking at me in a different way; he is looking at me in a way that my ex-lovers have all once looked at me: with that sort of lost look, like they want to dive into my soul to have a look around, to learn something, to discover something, anything. I am new, I am exciting, I am like nobody else that you have ever known, and you want to see me naked.

Little do they know that later, much later, that look will no longer exist, because they've discovered me, they're learnt me, they've seen me naked, and the flame has died.

Every flame burns out.

"He was pretty cool," Ric says, his eyes still fixed on me. I attempt to blow out a smoke ring but only a puff of smoke rushes out of my mouth, and I cough excessively.

"What are you trying to do?!" Ric asks, drunkenly laughing.

"I'm trying to blow out a smoke ring like Cool Kid over there," I nod at Adam, who is now in conversation with Mauro about The Jackson Five.

"Have you never done one before?"

"Do I look like a frequent smoker?"

"Well you don't look like a music journalist either but…"

I give him a stern look.

"Joking! Okay, look, put your lips together, and make a circle."

I take another swig and try again, following Ric's vague instructions but only another pathetic puff of smoke steams out of my mouth. I cough again and he stifles a laugh, as I hold out the cigarette to him.

"Forget it."

"What? No! Try again!"

"No!"

"If you go for a job interview at some big music magazine and they reject you, you just gonna give up? Or you get an interview with Bono and you fuck it up, are you just gonna give up?"

I raise an eyebrow at him. "How would you fuck up an interview with Bono?"

"I don't know, you could ask him to take off his sunglasses or something."

I laugh and as Ric continues to refuse to take back his cigarette, I put it back to my lips.

"Brava. Now, imagine a circle in your head, what you want it to look like, and do that shape with your mouth. Then, breathe out a small portion of smoke."

Pessimistically I follow his more specific instructions, and suddenly I see smoke the shape of an outlining oval descend from my lips. My eyes widen in disbelief.

We grin at one another and I hand him back his cigarette, taking a gulp from my bottle of beer.

That's right Alex, give into the rockstar lifestyle tonight – beer, cigarettes – all that's missing now is some cocaine.

It's a pity you're anti-drugs.

Oh and that you suffer from heart palpitations.

Yes, I suffer from heart palpitations. It's not like there's anything wrong with me or my heart or anything – it's just that I have a naturally fast heartbeat. This means that I have to be careful when I drink a lot of alcohol, it means I can't try any sort of drugs, it means I have to keep an eye on my heartbeat when I exercise. Most of the time I don't even remember I suffer from them, I mean I'm anti-drugs and I hardly ever drink more than one glass of alcohol (excluding this past week). I guess the only real time I remember them is when I haven't exercised in a while, but I make a habit to run five times a week. If you don't stay in shape, you're more prone to have them. Thinking back now, I cannot even remember the last time I had one.

They can be a little bit scary, at least they were the first few times I had them – the very first one was when I was eighteen and on my gap year. I was hardly moving from the sofa for the first three months, applying for internships from my laptop and watching daytime television. It came on when I stood up too quickly. I was *really* out of shape.

I didn't know what they were and hadn't ever even heard of them, so it was a little scary to suddenly have my heart race and beat out of my chest as if it is going to explode. You feel dizzy and you have to sit down but it still doesn't go away. It eventually died down itself, and I pretended as if it had never happened.

After my second one, I decided to do some research. I went to a doctor and they did tests on me. My heart was fine, it's just that I didn't do any exercise. To help an 'episode' recover quicker I was told to drink cold water, lie down, and take deep breaths in. I found forums online of people who suffered from them, most of them were neurotic or had other physical issues.

I began to exercise, and I chose running. Since then, if I avoid caffeine like the plague, I don't tend to suffer from them, but I am still careful.

Ric and I continue drunkenly laughing and messing around, whilst the rest of the room starts to clear out. One by one, people start to leave. First it's Mauro, and once Mauro leaves, the others start following.

It's been a good night, a really good night, and I don't want it to end. I actually quite like Vinnie too now – I don't know how I went from being repelled by him and his whole hooligan look to actually liking him, but it happened pretty fast. One minute I'm rolling my eyes at him, and the next we're laughing over each other's impressions of Diana Ross. I obviously beat him – I am the queen at impressions.

He may give off the impression of being a thug, but underneath he is a big ol' lovable teddy bear. He kept repeating throughout the evening how great I had been and how he couldn't wait to see the interview on the Internet.

I guess the fact that Ric and Vinnie are really close influences me too. You can tell, simply by watching them converse with one another, that there is a real and pure friendship there. They tease each other non-stop and call each other bad names, but underneath it all, there is very clearly a strong bond between them.

And it makes me miss Bailey and Blake a little. I wish they were here, that they could have seen me tonight in action. Full of energy and positivity. After nearly a year of darkness. They will be so proud of me when I show them the interview.

Once everyone has left, the green room is unbearably silent. It's just Ric and I left backstage at San Siro, and I cannot think of one thing to say, not *one!*

We're still sitting next to one another, and we've been talking all night non-stop, but as soon as we are left alone, I cannot think of one interesting thing to say. All that comes to mind is the weather and I don't want to drag our conversation down to that level after a wonderful evening of intellectual discussion. After all, we may not see each other ever again after tonight and I want him to remember me for my knowledge on how Muse first got together, not whether it's due to rain tomorrow or not.

Ric digs his hand into his inside jacket pocket, fishing out his packet of cigarettes. It's suddenly so silent that every movement either of us makes feels much more notable than usual. A deep breath in, a scratch of a nose. It's so tense that I am trying to breathe as quietly as possible.

Vinnie and his lookalikes were the last to leave, and he had given Ric a cheeky grin as he left us. Is it weird for us to still be here? Does he think something is going to happen between us?

I lightly kick the boxes underneath the kitchen top as I swing my legs, not sure what to say, but feeling obliged to say something. "How many do you smoke a day?!"

"Enough," he pauses, as he lights one up coolly, "fifteen to twenty."

"Geez."

"Ooh, watch this!" he blows out the most perfect smoke ring I have ever seen and smile.

"Show off!"

His smile turns into a grin and I giggle uncontrollably. We are met again by silence. How odd this is, to be here right now.

How did I even get into this situation?

Suddenly a man bursts into the green room panting, grinning at the sight of Ric, and I am grateful for the disruption.

"Riccardo! Franco is at it again!" shrieks the scruffy man in his mid-twenties with crazy, curly hair in Italian.

"That mad bastard!" Ric looks at me as the scruffy guy continues to exhale loudly, "come on, you gotta see this guy!"

The stranger leads us back out onto San Siro stage; the place is now empty apart from a couple of tech guys still taking a few things away. I look out at the stadium as we approach the front of the stage – all that remains now are empty bottles of beer, and an old man in the middle of the standing area of the stadium, dancing by himself. The view is incredible, highlighting the humungous size of the venue, even in the dark, and the night lights circling the venue flicker in the distance, illuminating the stadium.

I am hardly paying attention to the old man drunkenly dancing, but Ric and the scruffy guy laugh.

"Riccardo! We meet again!" the old man suddenly shouts, and I peer out at him. He's wearing an old brown suit, top hat, and a faded, grey beard.

"Buona sera, Franco!" Ric bellows with a grin.

"Tell him his imaginary wife looks great out there," the scruffy guy whispers, and I glance at the stranger beside us. He is looking at Ric with such wonder in his eyes, as if Ric himself is Paolo Petrinelli. And I realise suddenly that there must be a lot of younger guys that look up to Ric.

*You say **younger** musicians Alex, but Ric's thirty-three. Is that old?*
When I was twelve, he was twenty-two.
Wow.

Ric moves in a little closer to me. "This man is a massive Paolo Petrinelli fan, he's always here whenever we play at San Siro, or anywhere in Milano, and then he stays

89

here afterwards until security throw him out. And he does strange things. Once he started singing 'Oops I Did It Again' and he sounded surprisingly like Britney."

I stifle a laugh and we notice two security guards approach him from behind. We can't hear what is being said at such a distance, but he's clearly being asked to leave. At his refusal, the guards begin to physically pull him out of there. The old man looks at us as they drag him out, still smiling.

"See you next time, Franco!" Ric yells, waving.

The scruffy guy sighs and claps his hands together, as if he is satisfied. "Well, I'm off. The night wasn't complete without seeing Franco. Goodnight!"

"Goodnight, Cesare." Ric says to him, looking out at the stadium, as the scruffy guy walks off stage. We are once again left alone, except this time we're standing on the stage of San Siro stadium, looking out a view that has me completely and utterly mesmerised.

There is silence between us, as we take in the stillness of the night. The wind blows softly, and we hear a couple of cans roll around in the standing area. I take a deep breath in, fully aware that neither of us has said anything for a good sixty seconds or so. Yet there's a relief I feel in knowing neither of us in this moment has an actual problem with that. We don't feel the need to fill the silence with something irrelevant. We are both taking in the view, the moment, the magic.

Because, and I don't know why, but as I look out at the incredible view, there's something about this evening that makes me almost believe that actual magic exists.

It is beautifully pure, this moment, and this night. The sky could be straight out of a painting, as could the lights that illuminate this enchanting stadium. I am happy, I feel alive, and I am *proud* of myself.

I smile, as I breathe in the cool Milanese air, and bask in the perfection of this moment.

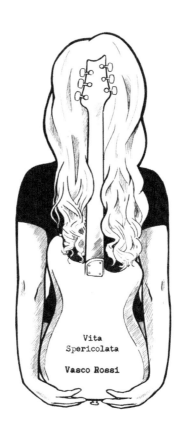

7

Hey, I have an idea!" Ric declares, and I watch him run backstage. "Come on!" he calls after me.

I follow, bewildered, and he leads me back to the green room. My stomach rumbles however, and I make my way over to the fridge in my tipsy state. "I'm hungry!"

When I open the fridge I gasp to find it filled with goodies. "Holy shit." Amongst the ridiculous dessert plates is chocolate cake, sponge cake, custard pie, strawberry sundaes, and jelly. But there's one plate in particular that has caught my attention, the one thing that has always been there for me, always comforted me no matter what, the absolute love of my life – tiramisu.

"Alexis, come here," Ric tells me, and I watch him kneel at one side of the sofa. "Come on, you take the other side."

I freeze, as I slam the fridge shut. "Are you kidding?"

"Just take it, come on."

I slowly walk over and put my hands on my waist. "Aren't we gonna get in trouble for this?"

Ric smiles back at me. "Yes, I suspect the Green Room Police will be here at any moment," he tells me sarcastically, "relax. It's fine."

I shrug and we carry the heavy sofa out onto the stage of San Siro, placing it exactly where we had been standing – right at the front. One tech guy passes us on the way, but he doesn't blink an eye. Once we let go, I walk back over to the edge of the stage; slowly, carefully, as if if I were to make a wrong move, I may wake up from this dream.

I know I was just here two minutes ago, but I'm taking in the view as if it's the first time my eyes are seeing it. I mean, it's so incredibly beautiful that it's hard not to. Your eyes almost feel as if they cannot take it.

"It must be so amazing to play here," I tell him.

"Damn right. There's no words for it," he tells me, and I hear him sit down on the sofa. "What about you?"

I turn to face him, walking back over. "What *about* me?"

"To play on this stage," he tells me as I sit down. "You're pretty good, I mean, if you practised every day, a few hours, you could be pretty awesome. Didn't you ever wanna be a musician?"

I'm a little taken back and flattered by Ric's words, but am finding the question odd. In all honesty, I've never thought about it. Nobody has ever asked me if I want to be a musician. When I was eight, I told my dad I wanted to be a singer like The Spice Girls, and he said 'absolutely not, they all ruin their lives by becoming singers, you're *not* becoming a singer' and that was that.

Do I want to be in the limelight? Write songs? Be self-righteous? I don't see myself as a musician nor a singer, simply a spectator of it all, and hopefully, one day, a part of the industry itself.

"Um, no, don't think it's for me. I like to play guitar, mostly so I understand the power of playing, to relate more to musicians, to the music, and it can be like therapy to play, but I don't think I could ever make that my career."

He hands me his cigarette and I take a swig. We sit in silence for a few minutes.

This is so damn poetic. Sitting where we are, seeing what we're seeing, all whilst sharing a cigarette.

Once we eventually break the silence, we spend the next hour discussing why Ric became a musician, and he explains to me that if his music reaches just one soul, inspires just one person, then that's enough for him. He loves creating, but most of all, he loves inspiring.

When I tell him that that sounds great but also super cheesy, he brings Bruce Springsteen's name into the conversation as an example of someone cheesy but effective. When I mutter under my breath that Springsteen is not *that* cheesy, he gets up and stretches out his arms as if he's about to start star jumping. But instead of star jumping, he begins singing the chorus to 'Born in the USA' to prove a point – Springsteen is the King of cheesy, I'm completely wrong, and Ric is not ashamed of his cheesy goals.

"After all, if you get cheese just right, it's really a very effective weapon to have," he tells me.

I finally get up the courage to ask him why Mauro gets all the solos, and I find out that it's because Paolo knew him

93

in college and they're all buddy-buddy. "That's all going to change now," he tells me. Ric has been playing in the band five years, starting at twenty-eight, and he doesn't want to go solo until he's built up a good enough career in the band.

I tell him that that's fair enough but that he shouldn't wait too long – I see him as a solo artist, and I can't wait to see him make it a reality. He smiles at this, and it's a smile I have yet to see – almost childlike, as if thirteen-year-old Ric flashes in his eyes, taking in my compliment.

The most shocking revelation however is that Ric used to be a drug addict. He shows me a video on his phone from four years ago – someone filming him backstage at, once again, San Siro, and whilst he's being interviewed he's twitchy and agitated, with black bags under his eyes and a sort of dark, strange expression on his face that doesn't exist now.

He looks much younger than his twenty-nine years, and I find it hard to comprehend that it's the same person sitting next to me now. I would never have pegged him as a druggie, someone who gave into that lifestyle, and allowed drugs to be his escapism. But that's not what Ric used them for – he tells me that he took cocaine to stay awake during tours and recording sessions, apparently it became all too much to bare and everyone around him was using. He said that when everyone else around you is taking drugs as casually as vitamins, you start to think that that point of view and world is reality, when it's not. He seems embarrassed of the fact that he is a former drug addict, and of the person he used to be.

When I ask him how he stopped, he simply replies 'I just did'. But I feel as if there's more to the story than that. I mean, if you've been taking cocaine for two solids years, even a person with the strongest self-discipline is going to have trouble 'just stopping'. Once I say this to him it is revealed that his then-girlfriend of one year gave him an ultimatum – stop using or I'll leave you. He cleaned himself up, or at least he tried, but it wasn't until she left him that he sunk to his lowest, and decided to go to rehab.

"You went to rehab?" I repeat back to him uncontrollably, and the sentence comes out with more judgement in the tone than I intended. He becomes uncomfortable, says 'yes, it was a long time ago' and changes the subject.

I explain to Ric my dislike of drugs, how my friends in radio would always use and I'd always decline – I even tell him about my heart palpitations.

Only three people in the world know about those – my parents, and a former lover, who unfortunately had the pleasure of witnessing me have one during sex. Just as I was coming, actually. Never had I felt less like a woman in my entire life.

And no, I didn't manage to orgasm in the end. It was a terrible evening all round.

It's an hour later that we are sitting in silence again as we look out at the amazing view. How much I love these silences, delight in them. I think Ric is the first person I have ever truly enjoyed them with. Then again, I've never sat on a sofa on San Siro stage after hours with an attractive, interesting and charismatic Italian guitarist before.

"I'm gonna go get another beer, you want one?" he asks me, getting up.

"Yeah, okay."

He disappears backstage and I look back at the view.

What the hell are we doing? We're sitting on a world-famous stage, talking about our lives as if we're on a date. This is weird.

I get up and look out at the stadium, imagining what it would be like to perform in front of so many people.

I look out and imagine all the chairs filled with people, cheering and screaming, laughing and crying as they sing along to *your* songs, and shout *your* name.

I suddenly put out my right hand, pretending it's a microphone, and clear my throat. "Buona sera, Milano! Thanks for being here tonight, I would just like to say how vonderful it is to be here," I pause, realising my accent is unintentionally turning German, I decide to go with it. "Oh, but *vat* an honour, to be called up from Berlin, just to be here, wiv you vonderful people, to play tracks from my double platinum album, The Vonderful Times of a German Lady. Now-"

"What are you doing?!"

I turn around to find Ric standing there, two bottles of beer in one hand and a slice of tiramisu on a paper plate in the other.

"I got you some tiramisu," he walks over and hands me the plate and spoon with a smile.

I glare at the plate. From all the desserts in the fridge, how the hell did he know that I would want tiramisu? That tiramisu is my *soul mate*, my love, my other half? That I have dreams about him when we are apart, that I have dreams about him even when I have him for breakfast? (And yes I have had tiramisu for breakfast before – trust me, I am the biggest pig you will ever meet, and tiramisu is the most delicious breakfast you will ever have).

I shake the shock off, and remind myself that it was simply a lucky guess.

He puts my beer bottle next to the sofa and we sit down.

"Oh, thank you!"

"This is the best tiramisu you'll ever taste."

"If that's true, why does it get left behind?" I ask him.

"Paolo gets a lot of tiramisu, Alexis." He pauses, as we look at one another. I have a sudden urge to kiss him, to wrap my body around his and attack him, hard. The feeling is *huge*, hits every inch of my body, and I'm wondering whether this desire has been here all night and I just haven't noticed. "So what were you doing just now?" he asks, breaking our stare, and I'm grateful.

"Well, if you must know, I'm Anna…Danke. Do you not know me? I just went platinum with my latest single," I tease, as Ric takes a swig from his beer. "Called… Don't Forget to Schlafen."

Beer instantly floods out of Ric's mouth in laughter. It lands on his jeans and on the floor in front of us. I cackle, as he tries to wipe the dark patch on his thigh. He shakes his head at me, but as I try to come up with my next imaginary persona, Ric throws me off with an unexpected question.

"How come you don't have a boyfriend?"

I glance at him immediately, and he quickly adds, "it does seem like the appropriate question to ask in this situation."

"What situation is that? And how do you know I haven't got one?"

He shrugs at me, blowing out a smoke ring.

"I don't know, you don't seem…tied down. I mean, you seem sort of free, as a person, of all that."

I look out at the beautiful view, and take a deep breath in, as Ric waits for a reply, but I know that with my answer comes with risk. Risk of being seen as weird, or different. And yet somehow, I proceed anyway.

"I've done all that, and it bored me. Again and again, I hurt people. And hurting them hurt me, so I just decided…not to have relationships anymore." I look at him. "I think there are bigger things in this world to focus on than having someone by your side."

I search his eyes for a reaction. He suddenly throws his cigarette to the floor and squashes it with the heel of his shoe.

Shit. He thinks I'm weird. He now sees me like most people see me – odd, strange, an aspiring crazy cat lady...

"I'm weird, I know. Or some people think I talk absolute bullshit and I secretly cry in my bedroom at night wishing-"

He gets up and takes a few steps forward, until he's only a metre from the edge of the stage. "Come here."

Puzzled, I put down my untouched tiramisu, and walk over to him. We both once again look out at the view in awe, and he takes his place behind me.

So many dirty jokes, so little time.

"Look out at the stadium," he orders and I obey. "Think about your life and who you are. Think about your past, the lessons you learnt, and the person you became because of them. Think of the pain you suffered, the joy you had the pleasure of experiencing, and how these two things added to your growth." He pauses, as I take in his words and obey. "Okay, now, I want you to imagine you meet a guy, um, his name is…" he lowers his voice, "what male name do you like a lot?"

"Adriano."

I have always loved the name Adriano. For my tenth birthday, my parents took Leo and I to Rimini. After a wonderful few days at the beach, we then went up to Biella to visit our relatives. We went by train, and on our way, we got talking to a young, handsome man called Adriano that sat opposite us.

I still remember everything about him; he was in his early twenties with freckles on his neck and massive dimples when he would smile. He had emerald green eyes and a dark brown mop of hair that he would flick to the side when he would pause in conversation.

He was working as an engineer near Rimini and was going to meet his girlfriend in Milan for the weekend. I had had a huge crush on him and had been so very jealous of the girl he gets to call his girlfriend. And from the second I had heard the name Adriano, I had fallen in love with it.

"*Really?* Adriano?" Ric says, unconvinced.

"Yes!"

"Okay, okay. So…you meet Adriano…" again he whispers, and it sends shivers down my spine. "Do you like brown eyes and brown hair on a guy, or blue eyes and blonde hair?"

"Brown hair and brown eyes," I tell him, and there is an awkward pause between us as I realise that that fits Ric's description perfectly.

"Uh, okay, and he's sweet and he's loyal and he's mature, and he's crazy about you. It's not just about sex, he wants to be together *officially* and you say, what the hell, let's give it a go. So you text all the time, you go out Saturday nights, you spend Friday nights cuddled up on the sofa watching romantic films, his social media profile pics are always one of you two, and you see sex as making love-"

"*No!*" I open my eyes, and put out my hands, open-mouthed. "No, no, no, no, no, no, no, no, no, no, no, no, no, no, no, no, no, no, no, no, no!"

He grins, a little surprised, and puts a hand on my lower arm. I shiver at his touch.

"It's okay, it's all imaginary. I just wanted to see if deep down you really wanted it or not," he laughs, "man, you *really* don't want a relationship."

"First of all, no one's sweet and loyal and crazy about you unless they're creepy, needy, gay or a character from a Hollywood film. Texting the same person *all the time?* Going out with the same person *all the time*? You can't get chatted up by somebody else or even *look* at another hot guy, let alone have the possibility to sleep with them!? That eliminates spontaneity completely!" I tell him, passionately. I am sure my cheeks have gone bright red.

It's all true; I'm not the relationship type of girl. Monogamy to me is like when you catch a flight too early in the morning; you book it perfectly convinced that getting up that early will be worth it for wherever you're headed, but you're wrong. You're always wrong. Because when it comes to that morning and you have to force yourself to get up, you end up grumpy and moody, regretting the fact that you chose this flight. Because if it was up to you now, you would never have booked it, as no matter how great the destination was, you do not like early morning flights, and you probably never will.

It's true that I have 'been there done that' with relationships. Don't get me wrong, I don't for a second pretend I am not human – I have been attached before (once), and loved someone (once). But it wasn't enough for me. I am at my happiest when I am alone, and I cannot explain to you why I am this way, for I don't know myself.

In terms of hook ups, I do tend to get jealous rather easily (something about being dominant/possessive), but it doesn't for a second mean that I love them. After all, sex and dominance walk hand-in-hand.

Once I worked all this out, I stopped being a girlfriend. The term to me now seems completely and utterly separate to the person that I am. I am not girlfriend material, and I'm okay with that.

"So you like the spontaneity element of being single?"

"Yes! And I don't wanna spend all or most weekends with one guy! The chances of that working out at twenty-two are pretty damn slim, max he'll persuade me to marry him *somehow* (even though I don't believe in marriage) and ten years later or even five we'll be divorced because we will have realised that people don't stay together forever and we actually don't like each other very much once the sex gets boring.

I'll be single again but this time I'll be 50kg more and *triple* as cynical as now. I'd probably go on a sex spree to make up for lost time," (here Ric laughs) "and catch some STD. Super. And the cuddling on the sofa on a Friday night? What a waste."

To me the term 'forever' is as humorous and unlikely as me becoming prime minister of England. A relationship lasting 'forever' or even a *really* long time is unnatural and unrealistic; the bond between two people that truly love each other the same amount and live in contentment without wanting to kill one another, that's all a fantasy.

It's an idea made up by the human race to make life seem sweeter than it really is. After all, isn't that what Hollywood was built on? The sweet whispers of unrealistic dreams?

"So you like your Friday nights to be a bit more fun."

"Hell yes, Friday night is much better than Saturday night, there's a hell of a lot less pressure to do something fun, thus you have more of a chance of ending up actually *doing* something fun," I take a deep breath in, realising I have rambled on a little.

He must think I'm nuts.

To me life is nothing short of one person trying to make it on their own, in their own story, with their own voice. They may meet characters that they get attached to along the way, taking wrong turns when distracted by these characters, but always finding themselves back on the main road; *your* road, the only road that truly matters.

When people give up this road to get on a motorbike and take a shortcut with some random yet alluring other person, I find it baffling when they return later on alone, with no motorcycle, surprised that no, it didn't actually last forever, and this new found addiction they now have to latching onto someone, anyone, just so that they aren't alone, makes them weak, and makes them blind.

Somebody please tell me what the fuck is so wrong about being alone? I'm not talking about *forever*, forever is a whole different discussion, and I find nothing wrong with being alone forever either.

I'm talking about being alone at any given age for a given amount of time for any given reason, from not wanting another relationship, to wanting to rediscover yourself, to a tragic incident leaving you isolated. What is so wrong about a person getting up in the morning and doing things alone? Going to the cinema alone? Eating alone? These are things I try to do as often as possible; I enjoy the silence, the time to hear myself think. There is something so great about going into a café and eating lunch alone; not having to think up 'dinner conversation' or laughing at unfunny jokes, constantly smiling or the second you unintentionally drop the smile you hear, 'what's the matter? Hey?'

I *hate* explaining the expressions on my face twenty-four hours a day. Because I'm a woman I'm 'supposed' to always be smiling, always be happy, always be full of sunshine or otherwise it means I'm on my period?

Fuck. You.

"Wow, you are one no-nonsense, commitment-free, post graduate, you know that? But it'll change," Ric tells me.

I don't think so, and I tell Ric that, to which we argue for a good ten minutes about it. He believes that because he's a good ten years ahead of me, he knows a thing or two more about how our brains work.

I tell him to go suck a lemon.

"So basically, if I ever meet Adriano, I should take down his number?" I eventually say, admitting that perhaps Ric has a point. I mean, life is long. My perspective on so many things is going to continuously change and evolve over time. I may one day not even recognise the morals and values of twenty-three-year-old me.

"Yes, Alexis. That's exactly what I'm saying."

Duly noted.

Ric is right about the tiramisu – it *is* the best I have ever tasted. So much so that I keep going back for more every half an hour. Ric laughs every time I get up; I could be going to the bathroom or to get another beer, but he *knows* I'm heading straight back to the fridge for another slice.

"How much do you eat?!" he asks me at one point, with a big grin on his face.

"Now, now, Ric. That's not a question to ask a *lady*," I tell him playfully as I scurry off backstage. Once I return, and once we playfully fight over the best Pink Floyd album (I vote for Dark Side of the Moon, whereas Ric chooses The Division Bell), I delve into a completely different subject entirely.

"Isn't it annoying how people are always ready to tell others what music they like that is labelled as 'genius' or 'cool' but not so much when it's 'uncool'? I think everyone should just admit to their secret music mistresses that they're keeping in the closet, we've all got them."

He tilts his head slightly at me with curious eyes. "And what's yours?"

"Katy Perry," I say without hesitation.

He laughs.

I really do like that laugh.

"Are you serious? I kissed a girl and I liked it? Are you sure you're not trying to tell me something, Alexis?"

"No! I only really like Last Friday Night."

He frowns, still laughing. "Seriously? Alexis? I thought you were cool," Ric teases, and I force a laugh.

"Whatever gave you that impression," I retort.

"Bet you listen to the entire album. What's track eight? Nine? Do you dance to it in your room?"

"Stop!" I start hitting his arm playfully, and he grins, as he tries pathetically to defend himself against the abuse.

"…with your hand as the mic like I saw earlier."

"Shut up or I'll start singing it!"

"…and dress like her and pose in front of the mirror with that pout she does…"

I instantly get up. "Last Friday night!" I sing, his jaw dropping.

"What are you doing?"

"Yeah we danced on table tops," I circle the sofa with the cake in my hand, moving sexily and imitating Katy Perry as Ric's eyes remain fixed on me.

"Stop!" he says in a much stronger tone and a big smile.

"…And we took too many shots-"

"Alexis!" he instantly comes after me, and I squeal as he catches me by the waist from behind, covering my mouth with his hand playfully. "Much better!"

I giggle, begging him to let go of me. "Are you going to behave?"

I nod.

"Are you going to sit down and eat your tiramisu?"

I nod.

"Brava!" when he slowly lets me go and I turn around, we are both grinning at one another. Except, Ric is looking at my lips, and I am looking at his.

There is something strange about this moment between us, as if there is *even more* tension between us now, and it makes me want him so much more. There is chemistry here, I can feel it.

Tension.

Magic.

But something is holding me back from attacking the handsome, charismatic person in front of me.

I don't know what exactly is holding me back, making me fight against the chemistry pulsating between us, but it feels as if I am being cautious. He's helped me get to this magical night and I don't want to ruin that. Yet looking at him, and the way he is looking at me, I can see it. I can see he wants me, and I know he can see that I want him. His eyes are fixated on me, looking deep into my green eyes as if searching for a 'yes' from me.

A yes that it's okay to proceed.
To kiss me.
To fuck right here on this stage.

But Cautious Me is holding Sexual Me back so much that I dilute the moment instantly, break eye contact, and go back to the sofa, where I take a deep breath in, mentally apologise to my vagina, and take a gulp from my beer.

When he comes back over to me, I smile and pretend I am *not* envisioning us fucking in twelve different positions, or guessing the size of his dick by having a quick glance at his jeans, or wondering if he's any good at oral.

I'm a sick, sex-obsessed dog, if you haven't worked that out already. But, I can still control myself.

I am oddly comfy on that sofa, as if we have known each other a hell of a lot longer than a week. As if, we have been sitting on that sofa for twenty-three years. We look out at the view and continue to talk about music; whenever I'm with Ric it always feels as if we could talk about music forever. It just never ends.

We always have an album to dissect, and we break it down into melodies, guitar riffs, guitar solos, and lyrics. Sometimes the bass comes into conversation, and the voice, and we alight with excitement with whatever element of music we are breaking down.

We both understand how powerful music really is, and how much it influenced us growing up. I don't think I've ever met someone with whom I can connect with music over like I do with Ric. This bond right here between us, it's turning out to be pretty strong.

My favourite part to our conversations is when we disagree on an album or a band or a guitarist's technique – adrenaline rushes through us when we both bring our arguments to the table, trying to figure out who is right. Usually we agree with some of each other's points, but we have a hell of a lot more fun disagreeing and shaking our heads at one another as we argue our points.

We spend the rest of the evening like this, remaining on the subject of music; good music, *really* good music, bad music, *really* bad music, embarrassing music, funny music, and any other kind of music we can think of. Our mutual first love is running the show, and we love it.

We eventually hear footsteps coming our way, and I turn to see a security guard walking across the stage with a serious expression.

"Buona sera signori," he says, "San Siro is closing, I'm afraid."

I glance at Ric who gets up instantly, probably remembering that he hasn't packed his gear yet.

"Okay, I'll just go get my things," Ric says to him in Italian. The security guard nods and I follow him back to the green room.

As Ric packs I try to ignore the tight knot in my stomach that has formed the second I had seen the security guard. The evening is coming to an end, and soon all of this will just be a memory.

Suddenly I want to throw myself at him, kiss him, and have sex right here in the green room. But I know I can't. Not now. The moment has passed, and it's time to go home, in more ways than one.

"Y'want me to help?" I ask, as he lugs a massive guitar bag onto his back.

"It's fine."

I'm finding it hard to stand properly following the abnormal amount of alcohol consumption tonight, and so I decide not to insist in fear he will hand me something heavy and important and I'll break it before we even reach the exit.

Once outside the entrance of San Siro, the streets are quiet and we find ourselves looking up at the stadium in awe, just like we had done eleven hours earlier.

I love this place.

"Well, now you've been to San Siro."

"Indeed I have," our eyes remain on one another. "Grazie, Ric."

"You're welcome, Alexis. I'm glad you were here, I'm glad you got to be here."

Our eyes on one another seems to last forever, before Ric takes a deep breath in.

"Alright…"

"Buona notte, Ric."

"You gonna get a taxi?"

I nod.

This is it. Our goodbye. We will not see each other again. I fly out in a couple of days, and I'll never see him again. We may talk on social media or whatever, but how long will that last? One week, two?

This is it. The Ric and Alex conversations are coming to an end.

"Okay, you said your hotel is in south Milano, right? We're going in different directions."

We cross the road and walk a few metres to the taxi place. There are two parked on the side of the road, the drivers inside.

This is it. The last pecks on the cheeks, the last time smiling at one another and-

"There's a party on Sunday, come. I'll text you the details."

Oh.

I guess I will see him again.

Just one last night.

Yes, I could do with one last night of amazing conversation.

"Alright," I smile and walk past the first taxi, leaving it to Ric, and stop in front of the second. I take in the cool night air, knowing there will never be a night quite like it. I turn around and wave at Ric before getting in, and he winks at me.

Yes.

There will never be a night quite like this.

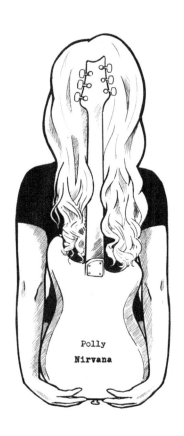

8

My third passion, after music but before the world of physics, is art. I love to draw. I have been drawing since I was six years old. And I draw anything – from dogs with cat-shaped pupils, to people with tails eating large bowls of tiramisu whilst dressed as firemen. Most of the time, my art doesn't make sense to anyone but me, and there's something about that that I truly love. Like a secret the rest of the world doesn't know or see.

My love to draw is directly connected to my love for music – I only get inspired when I listen to a good song. A song that is able to reach my soul, connect with me, and light up that part of me, the part that draws. The part that wants to express something, something that lives inside of me, deep, deep inside, waiting to surface, to show itself, when my entire body and soul is encompassed in a good song.

But it's been a year since I last drew. It seems the rules to how I get inspired are a bit more complicated than I had originally thought. I have of course heard good songs in this past year, but they don't seem to inspire me. I think it is something to do with Unemployment Oblivion – I am unable to draw when I am unhappy, uninspired by my life in general. A good song can make me feel alive, sure, but my life must do so also in order for me to create something.

Arriving outside Gino Marchetti's villa in suburban Milano at 10:45PM, I stand in front of the massive red gate in awe at the striking villa before me. The taxi disappears into the darkness, as it begins its descent down the steep hill to which Gino's villa sits upon.

My eyes remain fixed on the dream house, taking it all in. The walls are crème and on either end of the villa are two huge terraces on the second floor with black iron fences, and big, white pillars that remind me of Greek mythology.

With every window comes Italian blinds and brown shutters with thick, dark brown frames around each window. A big porch circles the house, with white, knee-high mini-pillared walls guarding the home. There is a small tree planted in a big, brown vase next to the front door, but you can tell, even from a distance, that a woman doesn't live here.

Gino Marchetti is one of the most famous guitarists in Italy. He has played for some of the best artists in Europe and I have adored him (from a distance) for a few years now. Tonight is his birthday, and Ric has invited me to his party before I'm due to set off back to London tomorrow.

I've spent the weekend walking on a cloud, recovering from a perfect Friday night, and not wanting to leave Italy. I have spent it drinking decaf cappuccinos as I sit outside cafes and read book after book with a smile on my face. Walking around Milano and discovering the best places to eat. Sitting in Parco Sempione with the sun beaming on my face as I listen to nature. It's been a really good weekend.

Laughter and splashing in the pool can be hard from what I can only assume is the back garden. There is nobody in sight however, and Nirvana's 'Lithium' can be heard playing.

"Well it looks *goooood* from here," Bailey says, putting her silky black hair behind her ear. I look at what my friend is wearing – a sexy yet elegant black cocktail dress that clings to her curvy figure and shows just a glimpse of her outstanding cleavage, alongside her favourite black ankle boots that we found last winter at Camden market. She has on black eyeliner and blusher to hide her pale complexion after a very British winter, and in the reflection of the lampposts, her perfect cheekbones stand out impeccably well.

I nervously press the button on the intercom, where above it in steel it reads 'RESIDENZA MARCHETTI GINO'.

I look down at my Led Zeppelin dress, my knee-high, high-heeled black boots, and my makeup consisting of dark purple eyeliner and dark red lipstick. I'm not a fan of blusher, it always reminds me of Snow White, and my skin tone is always olive no matter how bad the British winters get.

"Pronto?" says a deep, serious voice, shortly followed by 'stop it!' from a high-pitched female voice in the background, giggling in synch with another girl. You can hardly hear them though over 'Lithium' playing through the speaker.

"Hi, we're here for the party, Alexis Brunetti plus one!" I bellow in Italian, hoping he hears me over the music. The stranger hums along to 'Lithium' as I assume he scans the guest list, and you can hear girls gossiping next to him, talking about some guy's hair.

"Uh, cool! Come right in, Alexis plus one!" the deep voice tells us, "beautiful women are always welcome here."

The gate buzzes and slowly opens inwardly, as Bailey and I exchange smiles when I translate that last line to her. I notice a camera on top of the gate and wave seductively at it.

"You're not too bad yourself," I wink as Bailey giggles, and we make our way down the garden path to the front door.

"If we get there to find he's some ugly dude, I am going to laugh my butt off," Bailey tells me.

"No rockstar is gonna put some ugly dude at the door; what kind of impression would that give his guests?"

"Good point."

We follow the gravelled path, passing a huge lawn and sprinklers. Just as we arrive at the rather large brown door, it flings open and a good-looking topless man in his mid-twenties with abs as fine any I've ever seen, stands there with two girls in bikinis and hot pants, gawking at us as they stand behind him.

"Ma Giovanni, ti avevo detto di lasciare aperta 'sta porta!" *Giovanni, I told you to keep this door open!*

The hottie looks at us and smiles, and I don't know about Bailey but I'm temporarily distracted by his abs; he looks like he has just stepped out of a fashion magazine – the Rockstar Party Edition.

"Buona sera, ladies! Come in, come in!" he steps to the side and we walk in, the two slutty girls giggling as they look us up and down.

Probably wondering who Led Zeppelin are.

"I've never seen either of you at one of these parties before, how do you know Gino?"

"We don't – Riccardo D'Angelo invited me," I explain to him, using that semi-friendly and semi-cautious tone I reserve for strangers.

"Aaaah, okay! Cool! Ricky's cool! I'm Marco," he puts out his hand and I resist reaching for his chest as I shake it.

"Alexis."

He pulls me closer to him and gives me a peck on each cheek.

109

He smells of apricots.

He does the same with Bailey, who is not used to Italian customs and borderline-squirms as Marco pulls her close, wishes us a good evening and is onto the next guests; a group of girls in mini dresses that have suddenly appeared at the gate.

It's only then that I realise we are standing in the most beautiful lobby I have ever seen. The walls are white marble, as is the floor and the ceiling, and there are paintings of Italian philosophers my mum taught me about as a child, and a copy of Dante's Inferno.

The lobby feels more like a five-star hotel than a person's house, and I study the marble staircase as it curves to the right artistically. The last thing I notice, at the very same time as my friend, is the chandelier that hangs above our heads. We exchange smiles in awe.

We're a long way from Enfield.

We walk down the corridor where the music seems to be coming from, passing mantelpieces after mantelpieces with expensive-looking plates from Egypt, and Greek vases. You have to bear in mind that Gino is a little different from your average rockstar – he's is in his late forties and only shot to fame with his amazing guitar abilities at age thirty. That's the trouble with guitar – to be really good takes years and years of practice.

From interviews on the Internet I've seen over the years, I have this idea that Gino is quite an educated man, admiring his philosophers and probably his prose. I am sure that growing up with rock musicians (he went to a prestigious guitar academy in Milano) he got teased for being who he is and liking what he likes, but I admire him for it. Life is all about breaking boundaries. Why should he be a dim-witted, long haired druggie because society says so? (Well actually, he's been to rehab twice, and has long hair, in fact so long that it reaches his elbows, but at least he's crossed dim-witted off his list).

We enter a massive room painted an alluring crème colour, the place buzzing with people. I'm not a big fan of crowded rooms – crowded gigs are fine, because you get your favourite bands as a reward and that relaxes me, but random rooms filled with people puts me a little on edge. I feel trapped, suffocated, small. But I guess I can manage it for a few hours.

There are some people standing and chatting, an unofficial dance floor in the middle, a couple of crème sofas, sofa chairs, and bright bean bags. Guests vary in age from twenty to forty, but it seems most of the older people are sitting and chatting with cups in their hands, and the younger ones are moshing to Pantera's 'I'm Broken' out on the unofficial dance floor, spilling beer onto Gino's beautifully tiled floor.

"Hey there's another room," Bailey says to me, and I look to find she's right – at the far end of this ridiculously large space is an arched doorway with what appears to be gold-patterned framing around it.

"Know anyone here?"

I shake my head.

"Alright let's check out Room Number Two, geez this place is big!"

Passing stoners and a guy with a blue Mohican, we find the second room of this jaw dropping villa to be remotely similar to Room Number One, with the same mix of people, the same walls, and the same tiles on the floor, only perhaps there are a few differences in furniture that a girl like me would never notice even if you paid me, and a karaoke machine in the far right hand corner.

Bailey and I gulp at each other, reliving our friend Piper's surprise party the previous year and our rendition of Britney Spears' 'You Drive Me Crazy' after a few too many cocktails. Guitar I can handle, even a little drums, but singing drunkenly in front of strangers is out of the question for me in any situation. I learnt that the hard way.

We don't exchange words on the subject, we simply hurry back into Room Number One in fear that the karaoke machine will follow us, and as we do so, someone crashes into me.

"Sorry!"

I look up to find Vinnie standing in front of me holding a cup of beer, wearing a white vest that reveals a lizard tattoo right above his heart, his flabby arms and beer belly standing out like a sore thumb.

Why is he in a vest? Put some clothes on Vinnie, please!

"Hey, hey! Alexo! You came!"

Despite being taken off guard at the vision of Vinnie in a vest, I'm glad to see him – it's funny how in a crowd full of strangers a person you have only met once can feel like a friend you've known for years.

"Vinnie! Hey! Yeah, we couldn't miss this! And you in a vest."

"Yeah I'm waiting for the swimming pool to warm up a bit…"

"Oh yeah, the swimming pool! We haven't found that yet," I tell him.

"Right this way!"

We follow Vinnie through the crowd, passing a group of giggly twenty-something women in miniskirts, and a zealous couple making out. I introduce Vinnie to Bailey, explaining that Bailey is my close friend from London and that she's come out to see me since back in England it's a Bank holiday weekend and she's been bored out of her mind.

He tells us both that because it's our last night in Milano, we have to make the most of it. I know what he means by that and want to point out that Bailey isn't a fan of casual sex and will probably be in bed by midnight, but decide against it. Vinnie leads us to the back garden, where the view from the top of the huge staircase makes us both gasp. It's hard to know where to look first.

Following the trail of the split white staircase (Gino sure likes white), the left leads you down to the huge rectangular pool, lit up by underwater electronic bulbs, deck-beds circling it, and groups of people standing near them smoking or sitting on them. Next to it is, of course, a white pool house the size of a suburban house in London, with a pillared porch and a few more deck-beds. If you follow the trail of steps to the right, it leads to a patio guarded by a wooden square-fence that is engulfed in green vines.

The view from the top of the steps is incredible, other than the mountains in the distance that instantly remind me of Biella and make me homesick, there are fire-lit lamps circling the garden, and a rather romantic-looking apple orchard next door to the villa.

I take a deep breath in of fresh air as we follow Vinnie down the left steps, thinking of Blake heading out to O'Neill's in Soho as he does so every Sunday night. I imagine him walking down the polluted streets of Piccadilly, battling through the hustle and bustle of Sunday evening tourists. It's probably raining and some dazed girl has accidentally poked him in the head with her umbrella.

Oh London, how I don't miss you.

The air is warm and I half wish I had packed my bikini. Vinnie begins his verbal tour of the party, explaining that the back garden will get much more packed later on, and that by midnight someone will have thrown up in the pool, most likely with people inside.

"Eeew!" both Bailey and I shriek, cringing up our noses at each other as Vinnie leads us over to a few free deck-beds next to his friends.

I'm about to ask where Ric is when I hear a "hey!" that I recognise, and I turn around to find him walking over to us with an unlit cigarette between his lips and smiling eyes. He seems happy to see me.

"Oh, *of course* he has a cigarette in his mouth! Of course!" I tease, and he instantly picks me up from the back of my thighs, lugging me over his shoulder as he casually walks over to the pool.

I'm so taken back that I don't know what to do or say, and so I just squeal like a twelve-year-old girl.

"What did you say?! You'd like to go for a swim?!"

The feel of his hand on the back of my thigh is firm, and it sends shivers down every single part of my body.

"That you're a tobacco-addicted, pompous-"

"*What?!*" he bellows, bending down next to the pool as if he's going to throw me in. He grips my thigh tighter and I'm finding it hard to concentrate on the conversation.

"*Don't you dare, D'Angelo!*" I squeal, in-between giggles. He slowly puts me down, my heart sinks as his hand leaves me thigh, and we smile at one other.

"Jackass!" I wail, as I playfully punch his shoulder.

"Welcome to the party, Brunetti!" he tells me, as he lights up. "Pretty cool place to live, right?"

"Not quite up to my standards but near enough," I reply jokily, just as Bailey approaches us with a curious smile.

113

"I was kind of hoping you'd chuck her in!" she tells Ric.

"Me too!" he frowns. "Oh my *God*, did Alexis bring a friend?!" Ric says, putting out his hand to her. "I'm Ric."

"Bailey!"

"Better to wait a while to throw Alexis in – you know, build up to it," Ric tells her, winking at me. "So how do you two know each other?"

"We went to college together. She was bored on her bank holiday weekend, so I said come out and see me in Milano," I explain. The way Bailey is looking at Ric is making me uncomfortable, and I try instead to focus on the pool and the couple swimming in synch.

They're swimming as if the rest of the party doesn't exist.

"Well, where are your drinks?" Ric asks, staring at our empty hands, and I look at him.

"Oh! Bails, shall we go get some?" I ask her, and she nods. "Want anything, Ric?"

"Don't worry, I'll finish my cigarette and then join you guys."

I nod, glad to get Bailey away from Ric as we walk back up the stairs.

I know exactly what's coming next.

"He's *hot!*" she tells me, and I force a half-smile. "Have you tapped that yet?"

"Nope."

"Why not?!"

It's a good question, and I'm not sure what the answer is. I've been focusing so much on the interview that the possibility of sleeping with Ric has completely slipped my mind. Over the weekend I *have* been thinking a lot about San Siro and being up there on that stage after hours. If we hadn't been kicked out, would something have happened? *Could* something have happened?

We did share a moment where it looked possible we were going to kiss. There was a tension, a chemistry. Or did I imagine it?

If I didn't, why did I hold back? It was me who stepped away, who went to sit down on the sofa and pretend like it didn't exist, like I didn't tense up in that moment, looking each other in the eye with such intensity.

But like I said, maybe I imagined it.

"Boh. I just…I'm here to work. And anyway, he might not even fancy me back."

'Boh' is like the Italian equivalent of 'I dunno'. I say it all the time, so much so that even Bailey knows what it means.

"*Alex*, I saw the way he picked you up. Definite chemistry there, only a matter of time."

I choose not to reply and instead pull her over to the bar to get our drinks. Mine, is of course, Amaretto on the rocks, and Bailey opts for her usual Gin Martini. I don't think there's anyone in the world more of a Martini girl than Bailey.

Looking around at the party, I search the place for Gino but am unable to spot him in the crowd. I would love to meet him and have a little chat. From his interviews he seems real humble for someone of his stature. I would love to just shake his hand and tell him I think he's great. That would make for a really great evening.

I look out at the pool and see Ric chatting away to Vinnie. I imagine what it would be like to kiss him, to have sex with him, and I grow ever more curious about the possibility with every passing second.

I've already done the interview, there is nothing professional remaining between us – we get on, he's hot, and it's my last night in Milano. What a great parting gift it would make. After all, I'm probably never going to see him again after tonight.

The thought brings a certain unexpected sadness to me, and I take a huge gulp from my Amaretto, pulling Bailey back outside with me. Once we reach the pool, we notice a crowd has formed around some deck beds. As we curiously make our way through the crowd, I spot Ric and go over to him.

As I approach however, I realise the crowd all have their eyes on two particular individuals – Vinnie, sitting on one deck bed, and a beautiful young woman, sitting on the deck bed adjacent. They are facing one another, arm-wrestling on the table between them.

It's such an awkward pairing that it makes me frown, and I study the beautiful woman in detail. She is wearing a gorgeous, long red dress that highlights her big, round boobs, with long, silky straight black hair that hovers above them. Her lips are big and red, with a shade of lipstick that perfectly matches her dress. Everything about her is sensual, and I am instantly intimated by her.

Vinnie wins in an instant, and I am secretly happy. The crowd roars and applauds, but Bailey and I only look on in intrigue.

"Silly duck! I'll get you next time!" the woman tells Vinnie, as she rises. She appears to be coming our way, and so I move to the side to let her through, but she stops in front of us. And to my upmost surprise, she trails her fingers down Ric's forearm intimately, before linking her arm with his.

"Babe, I can't believe he beat me again!" she tells Ric, Bailey and I gawking.

"You will never be able to beat me, Valentina!" Vinnie tells her, as he joins us.

A punch to the stomach, much like the one back at San Siro when I first heard the mention of a Valentina. This is Ric's girlfriend. The one Vinnie mentioned when we first met.

Not breaking poor Valentina's heart now, are we Ricky?

I'm not sure why it's a punch to the stomach when I already knew she existed. I'm not sure why it's a punch to the stomach when I was already fully aware that he's the guitarist of the most successful singer in Italy and that he had to be sleeping with *someone.*

Yet heat is rushing to my face and I am instantly trembling.

"Alexis, Bailey, this is Valentina. Valentina, these two girls are from London visiting. Alexis interviewed Paolo yesterday."

Must. Find. Voice. Box.

"Nice to meet you," I manage to say, as I shake her hand. She looks me straight in the eye with her beautiful, big black pearl eyes.

"Oh, how lovely! Babe, since when did Paolo start doing interviews again?"

What's with all the babe-ing? Ric doesn't look like someone who should be babe'd.

Ric looks just as uncomfortable as me, if not more. And I realise he has not said a word yet.

I have a flashback of us sitting up on that stage at San Siro at three in the morning.

Someone with a girlfriend should definitely not be doing that.

"Uh, he made an exception," he tells her.

I'm feeling fifty things at once – sadness, that Ric has a girlfriend and I can't jump him tonight, or have him pound me like I had been fantasising about all weekend.

Anger, for someone I had thought was really nice turning out to disappoint me, yet again, and treating his girlfriend this way.

And claustrophobic, for I have to get out of here and away from this couple as fast as humanly possible.

"Do you want to go get another drink, Alexis?" Bailey asks me, and I'm grateful that she is here tonight, that she flew out, that we are friends. I am no longer irritated at her for the way she had been looking at Ric earlier, for the way that she had stripped him of his clothes with her eyes. None of that matters now that I am standing in front of this so-beautiful-she-could-be-a-supermodel girlfriend.

I feel ugly, very ugly. And small. And stupid, for thinking I was going to get him tonight. I was never going to get him, kiss him, ride him.

He is not mine to ride.

"Yes, let's go!" I reply.

"But you just got one?!" Vinnie points out, eyeing the ¾ glass of Amaretto in my hand.

"Ah, but I drink these babies like shots!" I blurt out.

"You drink Amaretto like a shot, Alexo?" Vinnie repeats, and all eyes are on me now. I can either go along with this bullshit, and get out of here, or I can go back on my stupid point and come up with another excuse to get out of here. Either way, I'm going to look fairly stupid.

"Yes! It's the latest thing back in London, haven't you ever tried it? Bailey and I discovered that as a shot Amaretto can taste *really* good. Especially in a regular sized glass."

How am I able to come up with such bullshit on the spot? And how is it that I am still, at twenty-two, shocked when I find myself in this sort of situation? Come on Alex, you should have seen this coming. You *knew* Valentina existed, you knew, for fuck's sake!

Before I know it I'm lugging down the entire glass of Amaretto. I can almost hear my teeth crying as they overdose on the sugar. Bailey cringes slightly, and I wipe my mouth. "Mmm, tastes so good! Gonna go get another, anyone want one?"

Everyone apart from Bailey shakes their head in bewilder, and we make our way back up the stairs. I let out a huge sigh as soon as my back is turned. Relief. Pure and utter relief. My self-esteem, my ego, it can relax now. Things are better now. And the more seconds that will pass, the more I will get back to cool, relaxed, confident Alex.

Just don't go back there.

"I'm sorry," Bailey tells me, bringing me back to reality. "That looked really awkward."

"It felt really awkward too," I reply. She takes my empty glass out of my hand and sets it down on an empty table. We make our way through the crowd with no actual idea of where we want to go.

"I guess you don't want another drink?" Bailey yells over Metallica's 'Enter Sandman', and I shake my head at her. "That looked so awful – definitely never doing an Amaretto shot!" she tells me. There are suddenly people pushing us back and forth, and I look around, realising we're in the middle of the unofficial dance floor. Losing myself in Metallica, I begin to laugh as I re-live myself gulping down the Amaretto.

"An Amaretto shot!" I tell her, in-between cackles. Bailey attempts to laugh with me, but she's suddenly disappearing in the crowd, unable to understand how to defend herself against the moshers currently surrounding us. She's never been in a mosh pit before.

Bailey is not what you'd call a rocker – she mostly listens to pop music, and for some reason, the Gypsy Kings. So watching her in a crowd of heavy metal moshers, I'm now laughing like crazy as she struggles to make her way back to me. I coolly pull her back to me and tell a couple of the rockers to back off.

"EXIT, LIGHT! ENTER, NIGHT!" I sing at the top of my lungs, as I hold onto Bailey to make sure she doesn't disappear again.

"Why is everyone pushing?!" she exclaims.

"It's called moshing my love, push back or they'll destroy you!" I tell her.

I lose myself in the music, the way Metallica always manages to transport me somewhere else. Have you ever heard such an incredible blend of instruments in your life? The first time I saw them live, I swear I nearly fainted from how fucking good the music was. I connected so Goddamn well to the guitars I really thought I wasn't going to survive the night.

"Phantom Lord was the first band Hetfield's played in," says a man in front of me to his friend - both of them in their late twenties and dressed grunge.

"Actually, James Hetfield played with Obsession first before Phantom Lord!" I shout over the music. They turn around to look at me, and as male rockers tend to do, they look me up and down, as if to say: *you're a **girl**, what the fuck do you know about metal?*

We complain and complain about how pop music rules the masses and rock music, *all types* of rock music, don't get the exposure they deserve. Whilst this may be true and something that often saddens me, I am much more affected and disappointed by the fact that women in rock music seem to hold no place. Or at least, not the place they deserve.

I've interned in so many different fields of the music business – radio, niche rock labels, huge brand distribution companies. They look at you like you're cute and they may even be nice to you, but as soon as you open your mouth to contribute to a conversation where rock music is the topic, you are not taken seriously. They look at you as if you are nothing, as if you know nothing, and as if your words mean nothing.

Even if you are an encyclopedia of rock music knowledge. Even if you have been to more rock gigs than most musicians in London. Even if you fucking play guitar, and are self fucking taught. It does not matter.

Take for example these two Italian grungers in front of me. They are looking at me as if I am an alien, as if I am a joke, as if I shouldn't ever have an opinion on rock music. Even if I can recite every track of every Metallica album ever made, and in order. Even if I can play three of their solos in my sleep. Even if, I know more trivia on the band than they do. None of it matters. Because I'm a girl, and my place in rock music is far, far away from the 'real' rockers.

"I guess you won't be going back down to the pool?" Bailey asks me, breaking me off from my stare with the two Italian grungers, who are still giving me perplexed looks. Smashing Pumpkins' 'Bullet with Butterfly Wings' starts blasting from the huge speakers, and I turn to her. "Not a chance in hell," I say.

She lasts another thirty seconds on the dance floor before begging for us to go and sit somewhere. Neither of us are in the mood to go and meet new people, especially as they are half likely to not speak English and Bailey will be left out. So we go and get another drink, sit on bean bags in the corner and talk about London, about Bailey's job, about boys. These are the general things we tend to talk about, and it's okay. I guess every person should have someone they can talk to about fluffy things.

Bailey is the type of person to go on about three dates a year. She's picky, and she's lonely because of it. She's looking for Mr Right and has yet to realise that he does not exist. We don't live in a fucking film. I want her to start casually dating, to have a one-night stand and see the positives to it, to understand how life can be good if you just focus on sex instead. But she doesn't want to and I don't try to persuade her to, I am simply hoping one day she will come to me and say, 'show me how to use dating apps'.

Take me for example – I aim to have sex once every six weeks. I go on an app, filter down to the top five hotties on there, and choose one. I've been doing it for years now and have become somewhat of an expert on how to look out for certain signs – if they look crazy, emotionally available, or shy in bed, I know to delete them. I try to look for the handsome, good abs, not too douchey but is incapable of developing feelings, type of guy.

They usually have three brain cells and you have to teach them what to do in bed, but at least they don't get attached. That, after being crazy or dangerous or having a small dick, is my main concern.

I look for guys who are uninterested in something more with me, whilst Bailey looks for someone who can love her. Funny, huh?

We have a good time even if the conversation is a little bit too fluffy for me, and I wonder what Ric is doing. I don't dare look up or go back downstairs to have a look, in fear of seeing him cuddled up with the most beautiful woman in Italy.

I don't know why my ego is taking this so personally but I honestly don't want to see any of it. I'm like that sometimes – I may not get emotionally attached to people, but like I said, I can get jealous and competitive when I see their interests have been swayed towards someone else. I *have* to be the best, I *have* to have your attention, or it hurts.

I know. I have a shitty personality.

I really just want to leave this party but that would mean the night is over. That would mean that we are closer to my flight back to London, and I'm not ready for that. As Bailey gets up to go find the bathroom, I make my way over to the drinks table for a refill. I push thoughts of the interview and Ric out of my head as they try to resurface, and I try to relax and enjoy my last night in Milano. Before reality is set to kick in, because boy, that's going to sting.

It's coming and soon – reality. To remind me that there is a whole different life waiting for me back home. There's something about when you travel to another country – you see your life far more abstractedly than when you're there, living it. And I can see that there is not one thing I can think of that excites me about my life in London, and that there is something fundamentally wrong with that.

I try to choose my next poison as I bop my head to the classic Verve song 'Bittersweet Symphony', scanning the different spirits on the table.

"The Vodka and melone is divine," says a voice in Italian, and I turn to find Gino Marchetti standing next to me. My eyes widen.

"Oh yeah? Always wanted to try it; doesn't exist in London," I reply, also in Italian.

He frowns with a smile, as I study him. He's wearing black jeans, and a black buttoned up shirt. His hair is shorter than when I've seen it in interviews, just reaching his shoulders and curling under his chin. His eyes are brown and big, so very friendly and at the same time cautious. He looks like someone you'd have a great Sunday afternoon with, playing guitar and talking about The Verve.

"Let me pour you a glass."

"Oh, that's very kind of you," I manage to say, as I continue to study him. There's something very gracious about him, and it makes it hard to remember that he's a world-class guitarist. He hands me the glass of vodka and melon with a smile. "Grazie!" I put out my free hand. "Alexis – piacere. You have a lovely house."

"Piacere – Gino. Grazie Alexis. So you're from London?" he asks me, as he pours himself a glass too. "Oh wait, are you the girl that interviewed Paolo at San Siro?"

Holy shit.
Gino Marchetti knows of you.
What the fuck?

"Erm, yeah. How did you know…?"

"Ric told me. He speaks very highly of you."

I look out the window at Ric in the garden, talking to Vinnie about something and laughing. My anger and sadness towards him melts in an instant. How foolish of me to be mad at him; I have no right to be angry at him for having a girlfriend. All he's done since we met is help me, and he never once made a pass at me.

"That's nice of him," I take a sip of my glass and my eyes light up. "Oh my God, this is amazing!"

Gino's smile grows wider, and he too takes a sip. "Aaah, heaven." We both look out at the party across the room, studying the craziness going on around us. We watch on in silence for what seems like forever, and I am happy, so very happy, just standing next to Gino Marchetti, sipping my vodka and melon.

"Interesting playlist. Very eclectic," I eventually say, as Depeche Mode's 'Personal Jesus' starts playing. Both of us bop our heads to it as we continue to study the crowd. "Though Johnny Cash's version isn't that bad either, just a totally different vibe to the song."

"Some covers are able to do that," Gino says. "Make a song completely their own."

"Running up That Hill."

"Hurt."

"Killing Me Softly."

"And the obvious one…" we both look at one another.

"Hallelujah," we say in synch, and we instantly laugh. I like Gino. His warmth completely elevates you. I wish more musicians could be as humble as him.

Someone calls Gino from across the room, it's a woman's voice, and Gino turns to me. "Gotta go," he gently takes my hand, and bows as he kisses my knuckles, softly. He keeps eye contact with me and I do what I always do when someone decides to kiss my hand – I instantly blush. "It was a pleasure to meet you, Alexis. You are a rock queen. Make sure you send me a link to the interview once it's ready."

"Yes, sure, of course. It was really great to meet you too, Gino."

"I'm sure this interview is going to bring you great success." And from that, he disappears into the crowd, and I am left beaming to myself.

I just met Gino Marchetti. Not only that, but I made an actual connection with Gino Marchetti. And it wasn't over his house, or his life, it was over music. The best possible thing we could have discussed. It couldn't have gone any better than that! I stand there, taking it in, trying to make sure I didn't just imagine it.

"Hey," says Ric, as he appears next to me. I turn to find he's a little more relaxed than when we had been outside.

"Hey."

He picks up a bottle of beer and opens it.

"I just met Gino Marchetti."

"I saw."

"He's pretty nice." There's silence between us and all you can hear is the rest of the party; people shouting over the music to be heard, and girls screaming for no reason. We both look around Room Number Two in curiosity, just as 'Last Friday Night' (Ben Wolsey's version) starts playing. It's out of tune and it's not professional and it's far from perfect, but I do like it. I occasionally listen to this version; it's definitely the best rock version out there.

It takes Ric and I a few seconds to remember our connection to the song, to suddenly have a vivid flashback of me singing it with my hand as a microphone onstage at San Siro only two days earlier. When we do I grin, and so does Ric, and we look at one another, now totally relaxed.

"Aha! It's your song," Ric says, pointing his finger to the ceiling. "Would you like me to create a quick stage for you, I mean I assume you need to sing this one out-"

"*Haha*, you're so funny. You should start a one-man comedy show, you know that?" We continue to stare at one other with smiles, as the song blasts. I really, really want to kiss him, to feel his lips on mine, to taste his beer on my tongue, for him to taste my vodka and melon on his, but I instead take a huge gulp from my glass. I know I can't do it, that the moment has now passed, that it probably had only ever been in my imagination.

"Not drinking Amaretto?" Ric asks me.

"Well look at that, he knows my drink! And he's not an Amaretto virgin."

"Yeah some crazy bitch made me try it once and jinxed me for the entire night."

I chuckle. "That was a good night, you can't call it a jinx!"

"As soon as I tried that drink Kyle's wife went into labour, I lost all my passes, we were stranded at the airport and barely made it to the taxi with our legs moving like zombies, especially yours! I thought I was going to have to carry you!"

"Yeah, I'm a lightweight."

"Light as a feather!" he pauses, "but yes, it was a good night."

As nostalgia for a night that had only happened a week ago takes over, I decide to change the subject. "Is everybody still out there?" By 'everybody' I mean Valentina and he knows it.

"Yeah, looking out for who is gonna be the first to throw up in the pool."

I cringe up my nose and chortle.

"So send me the link to the video when it's ready, yeah?"

And there it is. The sentence to officially confirm that my time in Italy is up. Tomorrow I will have to leave all of this for London. For my real life. The one where I am not happy. The one where I am not achieving anything at all.

"Yeah, of course." I say to him, trying my best not to sound sad.

After all, I wouldn't be here if it wasn't for you.

"It'll be good to see you in action and see how it turned out. It's gonna get a lot of hits."

My heart sinks as I can no longer keep reality out – I'm going back to London tomorrow. This dream world I have been living in for the past few days is coming to an end. It's nearly time to go back to grey skies, to living with my parents, to not seeing Ric, to not having Gino Marchetti serve me drinks.

The melancholy hits me hard, and I look around the room instead of at Ric, in fear it will only make me sadder – knowing that tomorrow I won't see him, that none of this is my life. It's a cruel teaser that feels good in the moment but is going to sting tomorrow.

Ric talks and I listen, but as I do so I spot Marco – the hot model who had greeted Bailey and I at the door, looking over at me. He smiles, and I return the smile. And I suddenly remember what the best temporary remedy for blocking out reality is.

As I try to decide whether I will take Marco back to mine or go to his, I realise I must accept that this not my life. That it probably never will be, not for a long time, anyway. That I have to go back home tomorrow and sort out my life. That I can't let things go back to how they were before, I can't.

And yet that's exactly where it's heading.

Back to Enfield.

To a life like before I had even heard the name Riccardo D'Angelo.

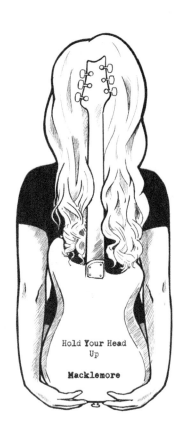

9

When I was eight, we had to sit around the class in a circle, and the teacher asked us the following question:

'If you could be any instrument in the world, what would you be?'

We went around the room, and I was one of the last to have to stand up and declare my answer, so I got to see what the rest of the class said as a response. It became abundantly clear pretty quickly that all the boys chose guitar, and all the girls chose flute.

I couldn't understand it – the gender divide. In my head none of that malarkey existed when it came to music. You loved what you loved because of what it was able to give you, of the ability that an instrument or song had in connecting to you in some shape or form, and that was that. Whether you were a boy or a girl was irrelevant; an instrument or a song could belong to anyone.

The more I listened to my fellow classmates give their answers, the more I felt the pressure. None of them were daring to name something else. I was eight but I knew exactly what I wanted to be, and I wasn't going to pretend otherwise.

It eventually was to my turn – I stood up with confidence and said:

"Guitar. Yahama. White."

Yahama was the only guitar brand I knew at age eight; I had seen it being played by the house band at a hotel restaurant whilst on holiday the previous summer with my family. I had loved not the look of it, but the *sound* of it. The man played incredible solos on it (at least, they were incredible to eight-year-old me), and I resonated with that guitar like no other instrument I had previously ever heard.

Everyone in the class gawked at me, as if I had declared I was going to live in Antarctica to try and clone polar bears. I pretended not to see their judgemental eyes trying to pierce through to my soul, and remained calm, confident, and sure of my decision.

I knew who I was, and I wasn't afraid to say it. And I knew then that I would never be afraid to admit what I liked, or what I stood for, no matter how strange it would seem to everyone else.

"Alexis!" a voice booms from across Studio 1. "Can you pass me that boom pole over there please?"

I squint at the bright lights of Penn Studios as I walk over to the desk carrying a shock mount and a light reflector. I spot the boom pole and pick it up, marching over to Harry, the executive producer.

"Alexis! Can I have that shock mount please?" orders Louis, and I scurry over to him. "Thanks," says the over-friendly, Portuguese assistant director.

"No problem."

Louis and I look out at Diesel & Diesel, the rap duo from Ireland currently shooting their music video. We have transformed Studio 1 of Penn Studios into a Funhouse, with dancing spiders and gunge baths. I don't really understand the concept of the music video, other than they're supposed to be fearless twins that love to bathe in green gunge.

"So Alexis, last day as our intern," Louis tells me, and I grin.

"I know, where has the time gone?!"

It's hard to believe I've been interning for Penn Studios for three months now; it's been great fun and educational, to say the least. I've learnt what it takes to build a set, and construct/direct a music video. Most of the acts that come in here are crap, but that's besides the point. London is always going to be London; so many musicians trying to make it, or trying to continue to make it; you don't really have much of a part to play in choosing where you end up.

Be grateful that you have an internship, that you're learning what you're learning, and worry about working with talented people later. When you're good at what you do.

Okay so I don't really want to work in video production, but it's something to have on your CV, to add to your list of expertise, to build a name for yourself. Musicians are a hell of a lot of trouble when it comes to music videos (*my hair doesn't look right – my face doesn't look right – my outfit doesn't look right*), and directors spend most of their time pulling out their own hair because of them.

But I'm glad I did it, that I was offered the role and that I accepted. Sure, it was tough in the beginning, especially when I didn't know what the names of any of the props or equipment were, but now thanks to this internship I do.

What next? I hear you ask.

I have no idea.

But I know I'm going to have to jump on something else and fast – the music business waits for no one.

"They just flew right by! I'm sorry that we won't be able to offer you a job, especially as you've done a terrific job for us. You really have."

I'm not sure whether to take it as a compliment or not – all I've done the past twelve weeks is chase after the members of the production team through every music shoot, through every artist that has walked through the door, from kooky female singer-songwriters who don't shave their legs, to groups of deluded men completely convinced that boy bands are going to make their way back into pop culture this year.

Have I done a good job? It depends, does making coffee for artists and handing people equipment equal an actual job and can you really be praised for it?

It's been fun though, I must admit. To wake up and take the tube to a well-respected studio in London, to be contributing to the music business, no matter how minimal the contribution. I have felt as if every day has been a step closer to obtaining my goal of working in this industry full time, with an income, and that can only be a good thing.

"Remember, anytime you want to come and see my music studio, you're more than welcome," Louis tells me for the fifteenth time today. "You have my number."

The director, Harry, gives me the thumbs up from across the studio and I smile at him, waving. It's time for me to go. I turn to Louis. "Huh? Sure, thanks Louis. Gotta go."

"Take care, Alexis."

I clean myself up, re-do my make-up, and say a mental goodbye to Penn Studios before heading out into the car park. It's been a great twelve weeks. I have no idea what I'm going to do next, but I'm allowing myself fifteen to twenty seconds to bask in my glory. I didn't fuck up majorly at this internship – I didn't accidentally set a musician on fire, or drop coffee on someone, or cry in the corner when I didn't understand the difference between one light reflector and another.

I did alright, and I should be proud.

My twenty seconds are up and I look around trying to spot Clay but he's nowhere in sight. I get out my phone to text but am distracted by notifications.

15 new comments to your video 'Alexis Brunetti interviews Paolo Petrinelli backstage at San Siro'.

Smiling, I open them up and scan through them. It's been three and a half months since I interviewed Paolo Petrinelli that fateful night in Milano. The video went instantly viral, just as Ric had predicted. By the end of the first week the video had reached 30,652 views.

Comments included 'she's hot!' and 'he's such a sweetheart', and of course your usual set of haters who are *always* moody virgin loners commenting from their mother's basement. Always.

Paolo's rap became a national sensation in Italy, and even my relatives in Biella told me that everyone was going around regurgitating the rap to each other. It's so damn strange to think that I had done that interview; I feel detached from the entire experience, like someone else flew to Milano, someone else planned those questions, and someone else executed the entire thing.

Three and a half months later and I'm up to 1,927,652 views. That's 1,927,652 people that have watched my questions being answered by Paolo Petrinelli. That's 1,927,652 people that have seen my purple skirt, my blushing cheeks, my smile and my red hair. That's 1,927,652 people that have watched something *I* have done.

It's a bizarre feeling – to have something you created become popular on the Internet. All my friends posted it on social media and messaged me praise. Even on a night out with some of them, I was toasted to for 'going out there and doing what I needed to do in order to follow my dreams'.

But, had I really done that much? To me the praise is a little overstated; all I did was fly out to Milano, ask a famous singer a few questions and film it. The rest of the trip had been spent drinking and blowing out smoke rings with handsome musicians – can I really be toasted to for that?

I haven't even begun the real work to climb my way up in the music business; praise for something so miniscule only leaves my subconscious raring to go, raring to do something worth being praised for.

And then maybe, just maybe, I will feel true fulfilment.

"Quick, we're late!" wails Clay, who comes bursting through the double doors of the back exit of Penn Studios. He pulls a fresh t-shirt over his head, and jogs down the concrete path to me. "Come on!" he pulls me gently down the street by the arm and we jog rather embarrassingly to Kings Cross tube station.

"Is it really necessary to run?!" I ask him, as I try to put my phone away.

"We're late Alexis, you can *never* be late when meeting Gavin Heath!"

Watching Clay, I realise he is a much more embarrassing runner than me. You can tell that he doesn't get much exercise. It's okay because he's skinny, despite the alarming amount of junk food he eats for breakfast, lunch and dinner, but he spends all his time either in the studio making music or working, so it's no surprise that his metabolism probably sucks. I wouldn't ever sleep with him, that's for sure.

Clay is a singer, bassist and drummer working on a solo project called Hands to the Wind. It's supposed to be a cross between Massive Attack and PJ Harvey, but at the moment it sounds rather weird and uncomfortable to listen to. There's too many instruments and too many sounds to take in. But it's only a demo, and I don't think even he knows exactly how the finished album will and should sound like.

He also works at Penn Studios as a (paid) assistant to learn how to shoot his own music videos. Clay's a pretty sharp guy, and one of those 'jack of all trades' type of people who believes doing everything yourself is possible in this day-and-age. I respect him a lot for this, but I really hope he gets somewhere better with his music, or all the hard work he puts into it will be for nothing.

We're running like idiots to catch the tube to Piccadilly because we're off to meet Gavin Heath, an artist manager who is a friend-of-a-friend of Clay's. He heard that Gavin, who works for Ruby Records – an indie record label who have just been bought out by an absolute giant of the music business, TGI Records, is looking for an intern. This intern would be looking after an Italian rock band who have just been signed. How perfect would that be for me?

I don't know their name or anything about them, but I'm interested. Like, I haven't slept since Clay told me about it three days ago type of interested. Especially now that I've finished at Penn Studios.

Sure, it would be another internship and I'd have to continue working late night shifts at the chicken shop like I've been doing the past three months, but it just might be worth it. And that 'might' is what is keeping me going. If music is what I want to do, if the music business is where I want to be, then I have to be willing to sacrifice.

When I got back from Milano and posted the video, I started job hunting like mad, and created a blog. Within a couple of weeks, I got this internship at Penn Studios – the interview and blog helped tons. I knew I had to start changing things in my life in order to move up. My life is, surprisingly, something that is in *my* hands. If I'm not getting anything it's because I'm not willing to put in the effort to get it.

Returning back to London after Milan was melancholic to say the least – to miss a life and a country that I had only experienced for three days was beyond bizarre, but it made me come back to London feeling different about myself.

Suddenly twenty-two felt exactly as it should, and I was ready to take the necessary steps in order to earn my place in the music industry.

I knew that not taking any action would make everything stay the same, and that the only one to blame for that would be me. I don't want to end up one of those old, lame people who moan about how their life *could* have been if only A and B had happened. *No*, it's up to *you* to make it happen. And I'll be damned if I'm just going to let my life pass me by.

We arrive at the pub and scan the place, though I'm not even sure what he looks like. I did research him on the Internet but all his photos were either blurry or really dark. From what I could make out he's in his early forties with really intimidating blue eyes.

Of course they're intimidating – this man has managed some of the most successful British bands to come out of the music business in the last ten years. What are to him just clients, are to me some of the best albums I've heard since the Arctic Monkeys released 'What People Say I Am, That's What I'm Not'. Now that's a high level of quality.

"Is he here yet?" I ask Clay, impatiently.

"Nope, doesn't look like it. Let's get a drink." We queue up and order our usuals – Clay's generic pint of beer, and my Amaretto on the rocks. Both of our phones buzz, and we get them out, giving in to our anti-social Millennial selves.

You have 33 new followers on your blog.

I created my blog as a place where I can post my opinion on new music, old music, and interviews that I do. I made the decision to continue interviewing musicians for one main reason – I live in London, a city buzzing with music. I don't need to fly to Milano to repeat a video going viral.

Once I realised this, I put together a media strategy of my own: once a month I interview a well-known musician, and once a month, my videos get at least 10,000 hits.

How do I manage to nab the interviews? I've got contacts from all my internships over the years, contacts that I've never used due to embarrassment. But now the embarrassment is gone, replaced with drive. And you'd be surprised just how many contacts are willing to help you out.

In return, I write pieces on those contacts, whoever they may be – roadies, musicians, writers. They get a shout out on my blog, and with 4,000 followers and growing, they're happy for the publicity.

I get a text from Blake – it's more pictures of Indonesia. I gasp at the sunny beaches and then groan in envy. Blake finished his degree a couple of months back and decided that instead of getting a job, he would instead hop on a plane and do a gap year in Indonesia, teaching English to children. He secretly saved up enough money to get started and didn't tell anyone about it until a week before his flight.

I was at first annoyed with him for having not told me and for having kept it to himself, but the truth is I'm a little envious of his ability to take risks like that. I always have to plan and be sure and assess everything a thousand times over and even then, in all honesty, I usually don't make that sort of risky decision.

Except for the night of the Paolo gig at the Forum. And look where that moment of spontaneity got me.

I really need to learn to take risks more often.

"There he is!" Clay suddenly bellows, nudging my shoulder. I look up and scan the pub, until I spot Gavin Heath in the crowd, walking over with his eyes on us.

The photos didn't lie – his blue eyes are *really* intimidating, in fact the closer he gets to us the more intimidating they look. He has this smile on his face, like a cunning fox who already knows the entire outcome of this afternoon before either of us. As if he has planned the whole thing out and we are just his puppets.

He's wearing a reasonably elegant black coat, and a suitcase in hand. He licks his lips as he approaches. I am suddenly trembling and I have no idea why – or maybe I do.

Come on Alexis, he's not that scary.

But he is. And the more I study him, the more I can't see myself working for him.

I did of course research him in detail before this meet – Gavin is forty-five years old, the former bassist of a semi-famous rockband in the nineties called Havana. They all did drugs and were alcoholics, ending up in rehab a few times, of course. They eventually split in 1999 and that's when Gavin got into artist management. Apparently he knows everyone and is the 'best networker in the business' according to various music websites and forums.

He's tough, and he still drinks, though he claims he is disciplined now, and he does not take drugs anymore, apparently. He's fired multiple bands and artists over the years, and has been fired by a couple of labels himself, though it doesn't say what for.

One artist claims 'he did not give a fuck about my career, just money' and another wrote 'he is a piece of shit'. Current clients write 'he's fabulous and so, so smart', and my favourite: "he's such a silver fox', even though, he doesn't appear to have any grey hair. But yes, he is not ugly to look at. Though I personally wouldn't ever sleep with someone his age if we were to meet in a non-professional environment – I mean, how the hell would he ever keep up with me? I really don't want to give someone a heart attack; I assume it would take the fun out of sex.

Gavin and his wife are recently separated, with two kids – one boy and one girl, both under the age of ten. He's quoted in one article saying that he will be excited to bring his son to the label one day 'soon' as he is already a heavy metal drummer. ("Self-taught as well! What a little musical genius I have.")

Most people on the Internet describe him as 'tough' and 'strict' but that there's a reason his clients are all multi award-winning artists. He knows how to get them there.

"Hi, Gavin! Nice to see you!" Clay shakes Gavin's hand, who in turn grins back at Clay.

"Alright, mate? Nice to see you." His accent is quite chav-like, which I didn't expect at all. Never have I ever seen someone look so elegant and speak so chav before. His eyes move over to me and I smile as I put out my hand.

One interview he did with one of the biggest music magazines in the UK quoted him as 'cold' and 'calculated', but the interviewer contemplated that that's the attitude needed to make him as successful as he is.

"Hi Gavin, nice to meet you – I'm Alexis."

"Hi Alexis," we sit down at a free table near us, Clay and I on one side and Gavin opposite. His eyes don't leave mine and I am tense.

So, this is how it works in music. You don't have to turn up to an interview wearing smart clothes and listening to pretentious next-big-thing music in reception as you wait nervously to be called. No, that's not how it works when you know the right people. When you know someone who can introduce you to someone, a pub meeting is all it takes.

Now let's see if I can win this.

"Nice hair!" he says, nodding at my high ponytail. "You look like Madonna in that music video, what's it called?" he thinks about it for a minute and my mind goes blank. I'm not really a huge Madonna encyclopedia. Great singer, love the way she reinvents herself again and again, I love her really inspiring feminist speech when she won Billboard's Woman of the Year, but I don't tend to wake up with a craving to listen to her songs or watch her music videos.

I try to work out whether Gavin's comparison is a compliment or not, tempted to even get out my phone and type 'Madonna' to see if the video he's talking about comes up. But I decide against it – better to keep my eyes focused on him. "Anyway, so! How are you?"

Just as he asks, I remember something very important as I look at the two glasses on the table. "Oh Gavin, we didn't get you a drink, what would you like?"

Shit. Shit. Shit.

How could I be so stupid? An artist manager who could change my entire life has been kind enough to come and meet with me, and I don't even offer him a drink?

What the fuck is wrong with me?

"Oh don't worry, I'm about to shoot off to a business dinner where there will be lots of alcohol."

About to shoot off? But he just got here.

There's definitely an aura of importance to the man sitting opposite me, and I imagine his diary to be ridiculously stacked, people at the office being scared of him, being afraid to approach him. I try to imagine myself in his position at his age, and I just can't see it.

Come on Alex, this is just the negativity in you. Someday you will be someone important in the music business too.

"So! Tell me Alexis, why do you want to work in artist management?"

Clay shuffles about anxiously next to me, waiting to see how I will respond. He is hoping Gavin is going to take him on as an artist at Ruby Records when Hands to the Wind is ready. So if I mess this up, it will reflect badly on him.

The pressure is on and at first, a buckload of shitty, generic answers pop to mind.

Because I love music.

Because I want to explore every field in the music business and I've never really done much on the artist management side.

Because I desperately want to make money in this business.

Every answer seems to be getting shitter, and so I take a quick sip from my glass to buy myself time. I try to clear my mind and think rationally. Both of their pair of eyes are on me when I gulp, and the answer is suddenly on the tip of my tongue. "Because I like digging to find gold."

Gavin looks at me curiously, his blue eyes only getting more intimidating by the second.

He just looks so authoritative. Like if you did one thing wrong he would roar at you in a way that there would be smoke coming out of his ears. People like him scare me the most; people who are not afraid to show you their anger. I wouldn't want to mess with him.

I feel Clay relax next to me and I think I've done okay. At least it wasn't generic.

"First time digging?"

"First time digging, but not the first time I've spotted gold."

I can *feel* Clay's smirk, even if I can't see it as I'm keeping my eyes firmly fixed on Gavin.

"Care to elaborate?"

I take a deep breath in, as if I've been expecting this question, and in a way, I have. I have for a long time.

"A few years ago, I went to see No Doubt in concert. I know, not the greatest band on Earth, but I love Gwen Stefani's style, so I went and I took a friend of mine from school. We were in first row, we were super early, and we waited *ages* for the support act to get onstage.

Once she did however, she was a beautiful, young, attractive woman. But apart from an aura of desirability that followed her around like a lost puppy, once she began singing, both her voice and the songs she sang, had you hooked.

Not because she was my taste in music, absolutely not, but because I could see her songs playing on radio stations all across the country, and across the US – how much fun interviews with her would be, to have her sing live on TV shows, to shoot music videos with that rack.

To have men all across the world with their hands in their trousers when her music videos came on, and 12 year-old girls dancing around to them, wishing they were her or that they could have her as a big sister. I could see it all, a year before it happened." I pause for effect, as I clearly have both of their full attention. "And that singer, was Katy Perry."

Gavin resists frowning, but I can see that there is a slight glint in his eyes. The tiniest, most precious element of interest – in me. I hadn't planned any of what I said at all, but as soon as he had asked the question, I had had a flashback of the No Doubt concert.

He licks his lips as he keeps his eyes on me. "I think I'll get a beer," but as he gets up Clay does too.

"Don't worry Gavin, have mine – haven't touched it yet, I'll go get another. Be right back," without waiting for Gavin's response, Clay has disappeared into the crowd. I catch him look back and give me the thumbs up. I turn back to Gavin, who has sat back down.

"Has Clay told you about this Italian band?"

"Just that they're an Italian rock band."

"Good. That's all you really need to know. I need you to look after them for two weeks, three max. Then from there we can see where else to put you. I've got many clients. Are you interested?"

YES. YES. YES.

"Very much so."

"Great," he takes a glug from his beer and half the pint disappears. "Their lead singer is the son of Irish tycoon, Brett Gardner, heard of him?"

I shake my head.

"Well, look into him. As of two months ago, he owns half of Ruby Records. And the first thing he did with the new role was sign his son's band. They were due to start recording their EP in the studio last week, but apparently they've not shown up.

I've had a word with them and they promise to start on Monday; I do not believe them. Your job is to make sure they fulfil their promise. Sound good?"

So, be their babysitter?

Shut up, Alex – this is Ruby Records!

I nod and he takes down another gulp of beer, this time finishing the pint and wiping his mouth with the sleeve of his elegant coat, of which he has yet to take off.

"Good, I'll be in touch regarding the details," he rises to leave and I frown, hungry for more information. "You'll leave for Milan on Sunday night. I'll come out in two weeks to see if it's of a quality to go ahead for mixing.

If it is, we'll come back to London together to leave them to finish. Their move to London will then be three-four weeks after that. There might also be other artists that you can get involved in following the trip," he smiles. "It's a mad house – my clients. Hope you're up for the challenge."

I remain frozen, having not heard much of what he said after *'you fly out to Milan on Sunday'*.

"Nice to meet you Alexis, I have your contact details from Clay."

"Wait-" I say, as he disappears into the crowd and I go after him.

This cannot be happening.
Flying out to Milano?
For work?
But I just got Milano out of my head, I mentally closed this chapter – it's done, .it's gone! I've been focusing on London and now, now I have to go back there?

Gavin turns around in the middle of the packed dance floor, confused. I have so much I want to say – I want to scream and ask him why, why Milano? Why can't you give me a client in London?

I love Milano too much. I love that lifestyle too much. I may not make it this time if I go there again and then have to come back here.

*Ah, but Alex – you're forgetting one important thing: you **are** changing your life here. You **are** making something of yourself. Come on – you're going to be interning for Ruby Records!*

You can do this.
Don't be stupid.
Don't fuck up this incredible opportunity for you to get your foot in the door.
This is the moment you have been waiting for.

Gavin looks at me, waiting for what I have to say, and I smile, relaxing.

"Did you say…Milan?"

He returns the smile. "Why yes – that's where they live. Until autumn anyway. Your flight to Italy will leave on Sunday."

And from that, he sets off through the crowd to the exit, and I remain immobile in the middle of the crowd, as The Killers' 'Somebody Told Me' begins to play.

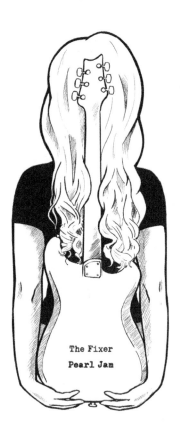

10

When I was eighteen, I fell for a Spanish bassist. He was sweet, shy, and terrible at communicating – we lasted just under a year before I realised I couldn't stand his evasiveness any longer. That was the closest I ever came to a real relationship.

About two months before the break up however, we were sitting on a packed tube going to Nottinghill when I decided to tell him something really personal about myself, something that I had never told anyone.

"I've started a blog."

He frowned at me, further hiding his eyebrows under his mop of black hair. "*Really?* What is it about?"

I shrugged. "Interviews with unknown musicians, music that inspires me, what's wrong with music today, etc. But I've stopped – nothing will ever come of it. No one will ever read it, anyway."

"*No way*, Alexis. You cannot give up. Imagine if you get just one reader, just *one* person who wakes up in the morning looking forward to reading your blog, wouldn't that be just such an incredible feeling?"

I may have forgotten the way that bassist smiled at me or held my hand or made me laugh, but I have never forgotten that sentence. The power of that one question. And I constantly ask myself that question in everything I do, since the day I got the Paolo Petrinelli interview.

Milano looks even brighter than the last time I saw her. I watch her in anticipation, as the plane lands. I think about how the last time I had been here it had just been the beginning of summer, and now here we are, near the end of it.

This is the time of year that Milano is at its hottest. This is the time of year that Milano is at its smoggiest.

And I've never been happier to be here.

I clamber down the plane stairs with my luggage, and take in the gorgeous sunlight on my face. It feels as if I never left. It feels as if she has been waiting for me.

I re-live leaving my house, my parents, my city, the grey skies and rain, and I smile.

Hello home, for the next two weeks.

Ruby Records have put me up in a studio flat in middle class Milano. It's a tiny place, with just the essentials, but I'm ecstatic. I'm in a place that is all mine, and I feel more mature, more serious about my role at Ruby Records than any other previous internship. And even if I am not getting paid, my accommodation and food is paid for!

My phone buzzes and it's my mum wishing me luck. I tell her that I love her and not to worry. I know my parents will never understand my love for the music business, they were brought up in a different time. But I'm glad they didn't try to handcuff me to the stairs when I announced I'd be going to Italy to babysit a band, for free. It's not right, I know. But if I want something this much, surely I need to work damn hard in order to obtain it.

I have a shower in what is my flat for the next two weeks, re-do my make up, and get out my phone.

Blake:
You ready?

Bailey:
Good luck tonight!

I smile, overwhelmingly grateful for my friends. I put on my blazer and call a cab using a taxi app, just as I step outside. The evening air is warm, and instantly amplifies my already happy mood.

I'm excited for the evening. For the adventure. For the change of air currently immersing my nostrils. It feels right, to be here. To be back. To be in Italy, and most of all, to be in Milano.

I have to prove myself, my worth, to Gavin. I want to work for Ruby Records – I'm *so close* to having a paying job in the music business. So damn close. I know I can do it, I just need to keep pushing myself.

The band I've been sent to 'babysit' are called the Devilled Eggs. Yes, I shit you not – that is their name. They are a teenage Italian rock band who misbehave, a lot. That, is actually everything I know about them.

I've researched them on the Internet a million times but always find nothing. Gavin mentioned on the phone that they've not created any social media pages yet, a decision made by Ruby Records to keep everything under wraps for now.

But I looked anyway, even researching the lead singer's father, Brett Gardner, to try and find anything on his son, but instead learnt a lot about Brett himself (forty-three years old, womaniser, his wife died five years ago, and sometimes he punches the paparazzi).

I did manage to find one thing on the band though – a gig they're playing tonight at a bar called Il Bireno. I found this information on a forum and am not sure how reliable a source it is, but I guess we'll soon find out.

I want to see them play live, and then introduce myself. I feel like this is a better way to meet them than just turning up to the studio on Monday and demanding they stay there till they finish. I mean, who am I to tell a bunch of musicians what to do?

I'd rather become friendly with them and take it from there. Musicians love me, or at least rock musicians do, anyway – DJs tend to look at me and my Foo Fighters tattoo as if I am an alien.

I'm excited and a little nervous to meet them – will we get along? Will we talk about music for hours on end? I also have to be extra cautious as the lead singer's father owns half of Ruby.

I'm surprised at just how big a venue Il Bireno is when I arrive. In London a venue for start-up musicians is about the size of a box room, but Il Bireno is more like a school assembly hall.

I hear some great rock music playing when I enter. The stage is pretty huge, and there are about two hundred people moshing and/or bopping their heads to the music in the crowd, with a bar at the back.

I stand on the outskirts of the crowd, lightly bopping my head to the music, taking in the music. It's crazy but interning at Penn Studios I didn't have time to go to *one* gig. I was always too tired to go anywhere in-between my internship and my job at the chicken shop. That's when you know I'm serious about something – when I sacrifice my gig time for it.

Gigs relax me, they send me to another place, another universe. There's nothing I love more than standing in front of a band playing good live music and taking it all in. The instruments, the vocals, the vibes good live music is able to give you. It feeds you, it brightens you, it gives you energy.

Back when I was artistic, my best drawings would come out right after a gig. Right after I had stood in the middle of a crowd, closed my eyes and smiled, as I took in every note.

The band playing onstage right now are pretty decent – I wouldn't go out and buy their music or anything, but they're okay, manageable – they don't make me want to cut off my ears or anything. And that's okay, because there's nothing worse than being at a gig where the band playing suck. What an absolute waste of my eardrums' time.

I feel someone appear next to me. "Great song," he says.

"Alright band," I reply nonchalantly, without looking at him.

"Crap bassist." I turn to look at Ric, just as he turns to look at me, and we grin at one another in the darkness of Il Bireno. We instantly hug like old friends, and not two people that have only met three times previously. "Welcome back to Milano!" he shouts over the music.

"Grazie! How are you?!"

Ric and I stayed in touch when I returned from Italy three and a half months ago, starting off by mostly commenting on each other's social media posts. He posts a lot about Italian politics and I like to counter one of his points just to rattle him – I find it so much fun.

In return, he comments on my music posts, trying to be controversial in his opinions. He really irritated me one day when I posted a song by The Cure and he decided to comment stating he didn't like The Cure 'that much'. I mean, that's absolute bullshit – no one in the world can live their lives without absolutely loving The Cure. It's impossible, it's outrageous, it's an alternative reality I want no part of.

I hadn't been sure if we would remain in contact – I envisioned us talking up until the release of the Paolo interview, and perhaps for a week following the buzz, if it were to receive any.

To my delight however, that's not how it went – we continued to talk, to chat, as if we were living in the same country, the same city – hell, sometimes it felt as if we lived on the same street. We didn't speak everyday but every other day and honestly it does feel like we never seem to not know what the other is doing.

"I'm good, I'm good. You? Ready for two weeks in Milano?"

I study Ric as I take in every inch of his face after three and a half months of not seeing it. Though we talk all the time, I hadn't thought we would ever see each other again.

Or at least, not for another couple of years – when I would perhaps visit Milano on holiday or he would visit London. My mind had mentally prepared me for not seeing him and his face up close for a very long time, if ever, and yet here we are, reunited once more.

It's strange how life goes sometimes.

His face is more tanned than the last time I saw him, and his arms slightly more toned. His smile, beaming back at me, manages to light up the whole venue. I had forgotten how attractive it is.

He has Valentina, remember this Alex.

When we speak online, we only talk about music and work, nothing personal. Nothing about Valentina, or love or sex or dating. He knows about my internship, that it ended, and how I've ended up in Milano. He knows why we're at Il Bireno.

I, in turn, know that he's just finished the Paolo European tour, and now all that's left are national cities, starting with Milano. So he's going to be around for the next couple of weeks too, before heading down to Mantova.

The gigs in Milano will be at big venues, sure, but nothing like San Siro. San Siro is the queen of venues around here, and I beam every time that I remember I've been there.

We get drinks and Ric fills me in on all the gossip about the European tour; they visited and played in: Barcelona, Lisbon, Paris, and... well, after that I stop listening. His smile and those eyes are drawing me in to the point that it's hard to concentrate.

Has he always been this attractive?

It probably doesn't help that I haven't had sex in two months. Yes, that's right – Alexis Brunetti, the girl with the sex drive worse than a man, has not had sex in eight weeks. I guess it's what happens when you're busy working, busy trying to make things happen – something has to pay the price, and in this case it's my libido. It's fine though, I'll just find some hot Italian whilst I'm out here. Dating apps are my saviour.

I learn that Vinnie shaved his hair for charity and looks even more like a hooligan now, especially when he wears his hoop earing. Kyle is back at work following paternity leave, but keeps messing up on chords as if he hasn't played in a year, and Ric is a little worried.

"And Valentina?" I manage to ask, once my second Amaretto allows me to get the words out of my mouth.

Ric looks a little surprised by the question, and gives me a look as if the name doesn't ring a bell to him.

"We broke up months ago."

And there it is.

In one line, your entire idea of a person changes. Alters. Re-makes itself.

My eyes widen, and he takes in my reaction with a certain smile in his eyes.

"We weren't even together at Gino's party. I called it off a few days before that, but she kept appearing at events she knew I'd be at, and I didn't want to set her off," he pauses, "she suffers from depression, triggered by a God-awful event many years ago. Didn't want to give her a reason to go off the rails."

I remember her beautiful face, her perfect body and that sensuality about her that had made me green with envy. I know everyone has an internal battle you have no idea about, but it still shocks the crap out of me every time I find proof of this truth. "And now?"

"Boh, she's shacked up with some drummer."

And just like that, 'Ric & Valentina' has a huge cross through it.

Just like that, the image of them together as a couple disappears, and it's replaced with just…

Ric.

Single Ric.

I stare at him, taking in the news, and I swear to God, for a split second, I see my desire reflected in his eyes.

Just as I try to read into it, there's a sudden mic screech and we both quickly look to see an emo band getting ready to perform onstage. The lead singer, a skinny emo boy who looks no older than fifteen, with a huge mop of black hair covering his entire left eye, takes to the mic.

"Hey there, buona sera! Thank you for being here tonight."

I look at Ric and raise a judgemental eyebrow at him.

Emo went out of fashion a very long time ago, my dear.

Ric smiles at me, as if he can read my thoughts.

"We are…the Devilled Eggs!"

My pupils grow bigger and I turn back to the stage in horror.

What the…?

No!

You have got to be joking?!

The band begin their first song and it's an influx of badly played instruments. I mean, it's really hurting my ears. As if in a trance, I am up in an instant, making my way through the crowd to the front – I need to get a better look. I need to see this. To see if this is the band that I've flown to another country to ensure they record their debut album.

I look up at the five boys onstage as I come to a halt in second row.

My eyes first dot to the lead singer, who is wearing a 30 Seconds to Mars sleeveless top and tight, black skinny jeans. The jeans only make his thin legs look even skinnier. He has on black eyeliner and keeps waving his hand near his face as he sings, as if it's an effective part of his performance, but in actual fact it's just making him look really weird, and borderline-possessed.

When he sings he widens his eyes so much that they look as if they are about to pop out of his head, and he stays put in his spot, as if held there by drying cement.

Singers are supposed to move around the stage!

He's singing out of key 80% of the time and the song is shit. I mean pure and utter shit. The guitar riffs are simple and repetitive, the bass can't be heard and the drums are too loud. Somehow I doubt very much this is due to Il Bireno's technical capabilities.

I look down at the singer's shoes – black Adidas trainers. This guy has combined three different styles – emo, alternative and sporty, in one. Already feeling my stomach tense with nerves, my eyes glaze over to the rhythm guitarist – again a mop of black emo hair covering his left eye, piercings popping out from practically everywhere, and he's dressed in all black.

Well at least he knows he's an emo.

The lead guitarist is dressed a little different from the others – tight grey jeans and a bright, white sleeveless Rolling Stones t-shirt. He has light, brown hair that he's stuck up with way too much gel and is the only one that moves around the stage the way he is supposed to. He is also the most handsome.

The drummer, a chubby man that seems the eldest out of them all (at least eighteen) also sports the black mop, black clothes and emo make-up, as does the bassist.

I glance at the bassist – he seems shy and awkward onstage, too scared to even look at the audience, probably unaware that his bass is too frekin' low to be heard!

I stare in disbelief at the band in front of me, and I only have one thought:

Do I really want to associate myself with such a bunch of cretins?

It really just continues to be one constant thought, one constant fear, that this band will fuck up any chances of me having a career in the music business. And I start to really panic, really become anxious about the band who stand before me.

The group of teenage boys playing onstage are worse than those shitty support bands I used to groan about at gigs, who used to make my heart ache, who used to make my ovaries fight to burst out of me and run in the opposite direction. This is far worse, and far more tortuous. And I realise I have no idea what the hell I'm getting myself into.

A hand suddenly appears on my shoulder and I know it's Ric. "Let's go get another drink," he yells over the awful nonsense playing.

I nod, and follow him out of the crowd to the bar, glad to get away from them. "Come on, relax. They're kids," Ric tells me, as we wait in the queue. "My first band was awful – Pink Slippers. I was fourteen, we thought we were punk but we were just twats."

I laugh nervously and put up my hands. "Hey, Ruby signed them not me. I'm just here to do a job, and that is to make sure they get to the studio."

"Well, at least now we know why Ruby signed them."

We both look at one another. "*Money*," we both say in synch.

"Welcome to the music business," Ric adds.

We get our drinks and catch up some more as the Devilled Eggs finish their set. I'm no longer paying attention to the band, in fear of throwing my drink at them, of booing them offstage, of crying in the corner on behalf of my ears.

I instead engross myself in conversation with Ric, who talks to me about great books he's read recently, of Vinnie's pub in north Milano that he promises to take me to, about the new Arctic Monkeys album (yes it is awesome, and yes they do get better with every album).

I light up in delight when he tells me he's thinking of 'maybe' starting his own solo career soon. I tell him to go for it with a huge grin on my face – the thought of Ric living up to his potential makes me beam with happiness. I can see it – the solo music videos, the solo songs, the solo tours. Ric can do it, I know he can. I just don't think he believes it himself yet.

It's so good to see Ric again, and to be reminded of how easy it is to talk to him about absolutely anything, from albums we love or hate, to the state of the Italian economy. We make jokes, we tease each other, but we also understand one another, and it's crazy but in the four times we have seen each other, I have had deeper conversations with him than I've ever had with Bailey or Blake.

And, I've missed him.

Once the Devilled Eggs finish their set, we wait near the stage door for them to come out as we chat. I want to meet them, I want to introduce myself, and I want to get to know them. I wonder what they'll say, how they'll react to me, if they'll have a drink with me. I could introduce them to Ric and they can get excited to meet 'Riccardo D'Angelo'. We could hang out and have an awesome time! That will definitely earn me some brownie points.

It's a good half an hour later that the door suddenly bursts open, and out pops the lead singer, followed by the rest of them. I instinctively go after Brett Gardner's son; the singer.

"Hey," I say, curiously awaiting his reaction. He slowly turns around, and smiles at the sight of me. But it's not a normal smile, it's one brimming with cockiness.

"Hey there gorgeous," he tells me, eyeing me up and down. "Where would you like it?"

Before I can say anything, he pulls out a marker from his jacket. "Boob?" he leans forward with his hand, pen aiming for my chest, but I push it away in one swift move.

"I'm not after an autograph," I tell him, trying to dial down the outrage in my tone. "I work for Ruby Records – Gavin sent me."

His eyes widen, and he stares at me, the other boys, who haven't heard our conversation so far, stop next to us now, wondering what's going on.

I stand alone, with all five members of the Devilled Eggs opposite me. Ric is off chatting to someone else, the way I knew he would. This is for me to handle – I can introduce them later.

"You're from, wait, what? Gavin sent you to Italy, why?"

"Just to help out, if you need any help in the studio, etcetera."

"What, are you an engineer?" Damiano asks me sarcastically, and the others laugh.

So he's a smart alec, is he?

"No, I'm on the artist management side and I've been sent out to make sure recording goes smoothly."

"Pity – I really had you down as an engineer."

For some reason, I am trembling. I am trembling pretty bad. Damiano looks like a total douchebag, with his cocky eyes and bastard smile. I hate him. I hate him already and it's only been forty-five seconds.

"So you've been flown out to babysit us," he slaps the arm of the guy next to him, the lead guitarist. "Elliot! Ruby Records sent us a babysitter."

"Hey, look, I'm just here to make sure-"

"Tell me something, what exactly is your job title?"

I gulp, trying to form the most confident tone possible for what I'm about to say, but it takes forever. His eyes remain fixed on mine as some shitty (yet better than the Devilled Eggs) band play onstage in the background. "Intern, I'm interning for Ruby Records."

The boys roar with laughter, and though Damiano's eyebrows are not visible under his thick mop of emo hair, I can tell he's frowning as if this is an April Fool's joke. "Tell Gavin we're good, thanks."

I want to call him back here, *demand* he speak to me, that he listen to me, but I can't. I lose control of my voice box, unable to call after them as I watch all five of them disappear into the crowd. I have never in my life felt so embarrassed. So weak. So much like a coward.

Did that just happen?
Did that really just happen?

I hear feminists around the world booing and hissing at me, and I try to drown them all out with the loud, getting-worse-by-the-second rock music playing. Somehow it doesn't work.

In only a few seconds, a fifteen-year-old untalented singer with an identity crisis has completely humiliated me. I know I should go after him, shout at him, at all of them, prove that I am older and wiser and they should listen to me.

But I just don't know how.

In a complete daze, I walk back over to Ric who is chatting to a forty-something year old man.

"How did it go?!" he asks me, and they both turn to me. "Alexis, this is Aldo. He owns Il Bireno – we've been good friends for many years. So anytime you want your Devilled Eggs to perform here again, he can sort it out super late notice."

"Great," I manage to reply, grabbing Ric's beer bottle from him and gulping it down. They both stare, and Aldo mutters something to Ric before disappearing backstage.

"What happened?" he shouts over the music, as he stares at me.

"I need beer," I tell him, "lots and lots of beer."

"They're closing in five," he tells me.

"So early?!"

"It's Monday night. This isn't London."

Suddenly, I miss my city. I miss my parents, and my house, and my bed, and my friends, and the weather, and the tube, and everything that makes my city mine. It's all so far away from here, from me, from everything that I call home. My safety blanket of a city is nowhere in sight. I feel stuck in Italy.

And it's not even been a day.

"I know somewhere we can drink," Ric suddenly says to me, and I see it again – that desire in his eyes that reflects mine. And this time, it remains.

Ric's flat is on the fifth floor and the lift is out of order. We huff and puff as we climb the stairs two at a time, beer bottles in our hands. "I thought you don't drink beer?" he asks me.

"Only when there's nothing else to drink and I need it."

"Are you going to tell me what happened with the band?"

"They're assholes. Hey, please tell me you have other alcohol at your place?"

"I'm sure I do. I'll check when we get in."

There's tension between us as we climb those stairs, knowing that inside his flat there is possibility for more. To cross that line. To explore each other's bodies and –

Argh. I'm so fucking horny I can't even think about it, or I'll mount him before we even reach his flat. That would actually be quite fun – riding him on the stairs of his flat building.

Speaking of flat buildings...

I laugh to myself, the way only really horny people who don't drink beer often do, hoping Ric hasn't heard my snigger.

My crazy sexual desires aside, the question remains:

Will either of us actually make a move?

My body is jiggling with both nerves and excitement, and we don't seem able to look at each other. Even when he drove us here, he had kept his eyes on the road, and I had kept mine looking out the window, as if searching for solace from the houses of Milano racing past us.

Ric's flat is white marble and spacious. You enter the living room to be surrounded by everything music-related, from the posters of David Bowie hanging on the walls, to the pile of music documentary DVDs on the table. The thing that stands out the most to me however, is the red Fender Telecaster Shawbucker leaning against the wall.

"You leave your baby out like that?!" I squeal, running over like an excited kid in a sweet shop. "Someone ought to call NSPCA!"

He cocks up an eyebrow at me with a smile. "It's only been there a few hours. I dropped it there after rehearsals, had a shower, and came straight to you. You can play if you like."

I'm suddenly shy and turn away. "Oh, no, it's cool. Maybe later."

Ric cocks up an eyebrow at me in confusion, dismisses it, and heads to what I assume is the kitchen. As I hear the fridge opening and closing, I scan more of the living room. There's post-it notes everywhere with neglected reminders, old gig tickets, train tickets, plane tickets, guitar plucks, The Who albums…

Wait, what?

I immediately find 'Who Are You', and put on 'Trick of the Light'. I blast it, but even at maximum volume I can hear Ric singing along from the kitchen, and I smile. It really helps that he has awesome taste in music.

My libido is slowly building and building and I tell it to shush. I must be an adult. I must stay on guard. Who knows if he wants it too, who knows if he's half as horny as I am. Who knows if anything will happen at all.

"Alexis! Come in here a sec!"

Intrigued, I leave The Who blasting and walk into the kitchen to find Ric holding a plate of tiramisu in his hand, grinning at me. "I stole it from the show yesterday! Thought you might like it."

"Oh *no*! But what will the rats outside the venue eat?" I tease, and he narrows his eyes at me playfully. "Thank you, I feel so honoured! I have my own cake thief stealing tiramisu for me."

"Want a piece?"

"Of course I do – here, let me get it." I cut the tiramisu into square slices, as Ric tends to the drinks. We are not even touching, just standing next to one another, but the tension can be felt a mile away. I want his body. I want to attack him, to have his tongue all over my body. But I can't, and I don't know why I can't, but I can't.

He takes a swig from his fresh bottle of beer, and pours coke into what I assume is my glass. He then pulls out the vodka, and looks at me.

"Tell me how much."

I let him pour quite a bit before I say 'stop'. Maybe a stronger alcohol will help ease me. Either that or I'll start touching myself in front of him.

My libido is dying!

I imagine his hands all over me and I gulp, not daring to look at him in case I lose all control of myself.

"Ice please," he tells me and I casually walk over to the freezer, pulling out the bag of ice. I walk as if my entire body isn't completely and utterly ready to pounce at him, to show him how wild I can really be.

As I grab the bag of ice, I suddenly have an idea. I freeze.

"Alexis…" he looks over at me, and notices the smug look on my face. I hide the bag of ice behind my back, and he smiles. "Ice please, Alexis."

I remain mute, speaking only with my eyes.

"Alexis," he says, this time calmer. He walks over to me, slowly, and stands in front of me.

"You know this song is about a hooker falling in love with John Entwhistle?" I tell him.

"Thunderfingers. I know."

Don't. Say. Fingers. To. Me.

"Rest in Peace," I pause. "If you want the ice," I lick my lips, cunningly and pausing for effect. "You're going to have to come and get it."

Ric gulps, but his eyes only become more confident, as I confirm what I want. What I've wanted since the moment we met. He can know now, he *must* know, for I am ready, I am hungry for this, and have been getting hungrier every single day since that first moment I saw him.

He steps forward, cautiously, and I grip the bag of ice as it remains behind my back. I hold it up high behind me, with an expression that screams one thing.

COME
AND
GET IT.

He slowly approaches with a cunning smile, and I am unsure of what is going to happen next. Is he going to tease me, jump me, reject me?

But I keep my cool, and remain confidently in place, keeping the ice away from him. He has to *earn* the ice.

He continues to approach me cautiously, and as I lean my back on the kitchen table, still keeping the ice firmly behind me and at the highest I can reach, he abruptly pulls me close to him by the waist; tightly, possessively, authoritatively. He grabs the ice bag off me, and kisses me instantly.

Finally.
FINALLY.

The bag of ice drops to the floor with a *thud* as we explore each other's bodies with lustful hands. His kisses are just as aggressive as mine, and I'm impressed. I give as much as I receive, pouncing at him and wrapping my legs around his chest.

He catches my legs and holds onto them as he continues to kiss me zealously. We crash into the washing machine, the kitchen table, the cupboards. Plates fall, ice gets crushed, all with The Who's 'Trick of the Light' playing.

Meanwhile, I can taste the ice cold beer on his tongue and I just want him to take me to the bedroom.

Now.
Now.
NOW.

He holds me upright, stripping me of my clothes as I strip him of his, and I realise we are not going to make it out of the kitchen.

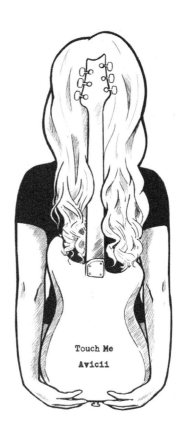

11

I can't remember a time that I ever was not completely and utterly sex obsessed. A time where I wasn't thinking about sex, or dreaming about sex, or fantasising about sex. It's always on my mind, always has been. You think men are sexual perverts? They have nothing on me.

Everyone I meet, I imagine what they're like as lovers. Whether they are attractive is irrelevant, it's the curiosity to imagine exactly what they do when they are in bed with someone. I imagine their groans, their thrusts, their orgasms. It's the way I am, it's the way I've always been.

I remember being eleven and creating sexual fantasies in my head with actors I fancied on my favourite TV shows.

But my high sex drive is something I have always kept to myself; you have to be in bed with me for me to reveal that side of me.

Why? Because being a woman with a high sex drive in our society only gives you a bad name. You'd think in this day-and-age that it would be different, that something will have changed, but if you look really closely, there is a hell of a lot that has remained the same.

Tell me that when I said that I had sexual fantasies at age eleven, that you didn't automatically assume I lost my virginity at fourteen? That I'm careless, easy – hell, I may even not use condoms I'm *that* careless. Isn't that what you subconsciously created in your mind? That idea of me?

People look at you differently when they learn you are a woman with a high sex drive, that sex is a high priority for you. And that kind of impression lasts; once they see you that way, you can never undo it.

So I choose to keep it to myself, to only share it with whom I please. And sure, sometimes it's the beautiful bodied Fuckboy-scumbags with two brain cells that get to share my body and my bed, but remember that Fuckboys are excellent secret keepers. Also, if you instruct them well enough, they can become great in bed.

They might even, dare I say it, make you actually orgasm.

Oh, and I lost my virginity on the night of my eighteenth birthday with a guy who loved me very much (the sweet bassist). I am very selective with who I choose to go to bed with, and I have never had unprotected sex.

But there's no point explaining any of that to the rest of society; if you're a woman and you love sex, you're a whore, and there's nothing else to it.

I collapse on the bed next to Ric in the darkness of his bedroom. Both of us exasperating, I am finally able to take in the contents of his room. We have had sex three times so far; twice in his kitchen, and once on his bed.

On the wall is a poster of Pink Floyd's last album, The Final Cut. It's my favourite Pink Floyd album and I smile, before scanning the rest of the room – an acoustic Fender in the corner, his desk scattered with albums, post-it notes, and DVDs.

I catch a glimpse of Shutter Island on top of the DVD pile, and a polaroid of Ric and Vinnie in the corner of his mirror in what appears to be a pub. They are holding pints of beer in their hands and have huge, drunken smiles on their faces.

I glance at the watch – 5:55am. *We've been having sex for five hours straight.*

I look over at the handsome man lying next to me, naked. I can't believe we have now crossed all lines. We are no longer friends, we are two people that just had sex, multiple times. That just made each other orgasm, multiple times. And yet, it feels as if we had never been just friends to begin with.

Ric leans over to the nightstand on his side, pulls a cigarette out of the pack, and I watch him as he searches for a lighter.

I have to say, he's much better in bed than I had expected. I had expected him to be good, sure, but I hadn't imagined him to be as aggressive and energetic and skilled as he is. He's practically just as sex crazy as me, which is good. Which is very good.

I coolly take his lighter off the nightstand on my side and tap him on the shoulder. When he turns around to see what I'm holding in my hands, he relaxes and takes it gently from me.

"Grazie."

I wait for it to become awkward between us, or tense, as we realise we weren't supposed to have sex, or that we are now simply two people lying in a bed naked together. But it doesn't happen. There is *no* awkwardness between us. I feel no regret, and neither does he it seems. It feels completely normal.

"Well that was a long time coming," he suddenly says, as he lights up. I can just about make out his face in the darkness of his bedroom, and he blows out a smoke ring.

I turn to lie on my side facing him, and watch his arms flex as he smokes. "I've wanted to do that for a long time," he says, as he tickles my nose with his free hand. He then turns his head back to looking straight at the Pink Floyd poster, pensively.

I open my mouth to say lots of things; how it's been the same for me, always. Since the second we met. That I've wanted to mount him since day one. That I've been wondering what he would be like in bed and none of it could have prepared me for *that*. To tell him he's definitely in the top three of my best lays. That I just want to attack him repeatedly. That he smells really good, all the time.

But I don't. And I don't because I've learnt that when seeing someone casually, the less you say the better. Because I've learnt that when it's only about sex and nothing else, there is only one thing to say, one very important thing to make clear. And the sooner you say it, the better.

"Let's keep this casual, yeah?"

He turns his head to me, but I can't read him. His eyes are neutral, and he's neither smiling nor frowning.

Again another smoke ring blows out of his mouth, and I wait for a response.

"Agreed," he tells me, using a neutral tone. And I sigh in relief, for losing my friendship with Ric, at least whilst I'm out here, would probably ruin me.

The next morning is the first day the band are due to turn up in the studio, and though I detest them, I have to make sure they actually do make an appearance. I didn't get much sleep as I got back to the flat at 6AM, following four rounds of sex with Ric.

159

He told me I could stay the night if I wanted, which was kind, but I need to always sleep in my own bed – I can't sleep with other people. Call me weird but I find sharing a bed with another person far more intimate than sex, and it's something I detest. I just never get to sleep – I lie awake, staring at the ceiling, counting down the hours until it's light enough for me to go home. I decided a long time ago that it's definitely worth getting that taxi home to sleep in my own bed.

When my phone alarm wakes me at 7:45am, I groan in frustration, have a shower, and leave. I grab a decaf coffee on the way (the downside of suffering from heart palpitations means I can't have normal coffee), and hop onto the train, nervously remembering the events of the previous night with the band.

I had tried to block it out by sleeping with Ric, by drinking a little too much, by having a really great time. But the thing is, and I know this well, but no matter how much you avoid something in the magic of night, dawn will always eventually rear its ugly head.

I have a flashback of the way the lead singer had laughed at me when I had said I'm an intern. The way they had all laughed at me, and looked at me like I was a joke.

Forget them, Alex. You can do this. Be tough. Make them scared. Make them fear you. You are older than them. You are smarter than them. And they will not make you feel inferior.

It comes to no surprise when I arrive at the studio to find it empty, except for the producer, Giuliano. I introduce myself to him, and we small talk for a while – he's in his late forties, obsessed with music and the entire industry.

He loves sixties classic rock, and Led Zeppelin are his favourite band. We discuss albums for a good hour or so and he's a pleasure to talk to, I do so love talking about good music.

I am however also nervously glancing at the watch. Once our conversation eventually dies down, I sit myself down and get out my copy of The Unbearable Lightness of Being.

Time passes very slowly, until it is eventually noon, and I give up. I surrender.

I get out my phone, and I call Gavin.

"Hello?"

"Hi Gavin, it's Alexis. How are you?"

"Good thanks Alexis, what's up?"

"Erm, I just wanted to touch base about something and update you – the boys are not at the studio. I tried to approach them last night at a gig-"

"No shit, Sherlock! Are you seriously calling me to tell me that? The point of sending you out there is to *get* them into the studio! I didn't fly you out there to point out the problem we have, Alexis-"

"I understand, but-"

"No Alexis, if I was dealing with this problem myself, I would be there. Instead I hired *you* to deal with it. So deal with it. And if you can't, no problem – come back to London and I'll find someone else who will. But I only have the time and patience for *one* intern, so stop being a baby and find a solution."

From that, he hangs up and it takes a lot of willpower to take that phone call in my stride. Giuliano is eyeing me in the corner and I gulp, forcing a smile. I am sure that Gavin was heard through the phone – he was yelling pretty damn loudly.

I remain cool and collected on the outside, but on the inside however, I am having some sort of panic attack. I feel stupid for calling Gavin up like a lost child that has lost her mother in a supermarket.

He's right, stop being a baby.

His rough and rather aggressive tone has shaken me a bit, and it takes another ten minutes before I find the courage to get up and leave the studio. I take deep breaths in, listen to some music (Oh Wonder are so wonderfully relaxing), and close my eyes to let it all pass. Once I'm ready though, I am *really* ready.

I march down the streets of Milano like a woman on a mission. I *really* look like I have a plan, but in reality, I have no idea where I'm going. I've walked straight passed the subway station so I'm clearly sticking with walking.

I walk and walk and walk and walk.

Solution?

Nada.

So I continue to walk and walk and walk and walk.

It's a powerwalk and I soon start sweating, and breathing heavily, and damn it, I need to stop for some water.

I do so and then I'm on my way again – walking, and walking, and walking, and walking. Until finally, I stop, in the middle of a busy street, a woman swears at me in Italian as she crashes into me, and I have an idea.

I get out my phone, and start researching Damiano on the internet. What am I looking for? His address. And where do I end up just forty-five minutes later? In front of his huge villa, just on the outskirts of Milano.

The goal of being here? To get him in the studio. And how am I going to go about doing that?

I have no clue.

I can hear 'What's My Age Again?' by Blink 182 blasting from inside, and I find it rather ironic. I also hear laughing, and general merriment, realising that they're having a party. I think of Giuliano back at the studio, waiting to record with them, and it feels as though steam is going to come out of my ears.

When Damiano opens the door, he's only in a white vest and boxers, and he reacts as if sunlight is the enemy. He peers at me, shielding himself from the sun with his hand. "You're a little late to the party."

Again he mistakes me for a fucking groupie. What the hell is wrong with this guy?

He does not recognise me, his humiliation of me last night so miniscule to the rest of his fake rock star life that it only adds to my frustration.

"You're supposed to be at the studio."

He cocks up an eyebrow in confusion. "What?"

Jesus, is he high too?

"I work for Ruby Records, and you're due in the studio today."

Slowly but surely, a sly smile appears on his face as he continues to squint at me. He's looking at me the way kids do when they figure out a knock knock joke. "Intern Girl?" Before I can reply, he bellows. "Hey boys, Intern Girl is here!"

I detest the newly appointed nickname, but try to focus on the fact that the other boys are also at Damiano's and that it saves me having to track them all down too. They appear at the door next to Damiano, looking just as dishevelled and hung over as Damiano, all of them in t-shirts and boxers.

"Sorry to have wasted your time Intern Girl, but we're not going into the studio today. We are at a creative impasse. We'll go when we're ready."

A creative impasse?! How deluded are you boys?! You'd need to have talent first to reach a creative impasse! The cheek of him, of them – you are not The Beatles!

You are far, far, FAR from being The Beatles!

"This is not a request Damiano," I tell him using my strict voice, which is new to me too.

"You can't make us go."

"Oh actually, I can," I reply, with sass.

"And how exactly do you see yourself doing that?" Damiano smarms at me, and I feel like whacking him in the face with my handbag like old ladies supposedly do to thieves. I decide to pull the Gavin card.

"I'll call Gavin and he won't be happy about this-"

"Do you know who my father is? Do you think he'll care for-"

"Listen kid, do you think I care who your father is?" I blurt out.

It throws him for a second, as if he's never heard these words come out of anyone's mouth before. I realise that Damiano is that stereotypical, spoilt rotten rich kid with daddy's credit cards at his disposal.

He doesn't give a fuck about anyone but himself. And he holds onto his band and their music for dear life because it's the only thing he cannot control – his pathetic lack of talent. Money cannot buy that, and so he desperately wants it in his possession.

"Did you just call me a kid? How much older than me are you, two years? Three? You can't be more than twenty?"

"I'm twenty-three actually, how old are you – twelve?"

Some of the boys laugh and Damiano narrows his eyes at me in fury. "I'll be sixteen in November."

"Good for you, maybe then you'll be able to fit into some big boy pants. Until then, you need to get to the studio."

"Baby!" a woman suddenly yells from inside, as we hear a plate break. "Baby, where are you?!"

"Sounds like a great party," I retort.

"It is," he attempts to close the door in my face, but I block it with my hand; the amount of force I had to put into the slap of the door stings my palm but I try my best not to let it show.

I am tough, I am dominant, and you *will* listen to me.

"I'll call the police if I have to."

"Go on, call them. And please, explain to my father why Ruby's intern got his only son arrested for drugs."

He's right. He's right and I can't do a thing to change it. I back away, and he slams the door in my face. I scowl, realising he has won.

The fifteen-year-old spoilt rotten, twat of a singer has won. He beat me. With all my years' experience, and the fact that I must surely be three times more mature than that pitiful boy, he beat me. He's right, I can't call the police – Gavin would never like it.

I can hear his voice yelling at me – *I asked you to do one simple fucking thing, and you go and call the police on them? On Brett Gardner's son? Are you joking?*

I scowl again as I realise I'll have to go back to the flat and re-think my strategy. That this could be the end for me. I cannot fail. I have been sent out here for this *one* task, if I cannot deliver Gavin is going to send someone else to do it. I'll be out of an internship with an incredible record label, will live with my parents forever, and work in that damn chicken shop for the rest of my life.

They will put my picture up on the wall for 'employee who has been with us the longest' and Blake and Bailey's grandchildren will come in and see me and refer to me as the person who didn't make anything of herself because she wanted to work in the music business.

"Everyone knows it's *super* hard to make it in the music business – practically impossible," they will say to each other.

"I *know*, how could she have been that naïve?"

Imagining myself returning to London a failure because of a fifteen-year-old jackass angers me to no end and makes me feel like an absolute coward. Yet there's nothing I can do, nothing I can say in this moment to turn things around – I need more time, to reflect on what just happened, to come up with a plan. I can beat them! I just need time.

But halfway down the garden path, I stop. I imagine Giuliano in the studio, twiddling his thumbs, and I realise this is a battle I need to win, not whenever, but right now. Now or never, for losing is simply unacceptable. It is not in me, I will not allow it to become me.

I feel a surge deep inside of me, as if I am going into battle mode. I am emanating strength and confidence and the sheer determination to not be beaten by this teenage emo twat.

And it takes me all of ten seconds to realise what I must do. What has been on the table as my solution since this whole thing began last night. Since the moment that wretched singer sniggered at me.

I get out my phone, and I call the person that is going to fix this.

"Hmm?"

"Still sleeping? Man, I must have tired you out," I tell Ric playfully, as I stand in Damiano's front garden with the sun shining onto my face.

Did I really miss London yesterday?

"Excuse me, you'll find that it's *me* who tired *you* out."

I roll my eyes but I'm smiling. "Listen, I'm having some trouble with the band."

"What kind of trouble?" he asks, and I can hear that he is now pulling himself up in bed. I imagine him naked in his bedroom exactly as I left him and it makes me want to run over and-

Focus, Alex. "They're having a party at the lead singer's house, rather than recording. I can't call the police, because of his father. There's probably tons of drugs in the house and he'll get arrested. I do, however, have another idea."

"Uh-oh, and it's something that involves me," Ric states, matter-of-factly.

"Yes," I purse my lips, nervously. "It most *definitely* involves you."

It's a good hour later that Ric arrives – even with minimal hours sleep and very little time to get ready, he looks good. He looks *really* good; the rough look suits him.

We 'hey' each other and I knock on Damiano's door. We stand side-by-side very awkwardly, and I can feel that Ric is uncomfortable.

165

He's a well-known guitarist, and well-known guitarists certainly don't go around knocking on doors of shitty, unheard of 'musicians' like Damiano.

I am however so unbelievably glad that he has agreed to help.

"Here we go," he tells me, as we hear footsteps and the door opens, Damiano cocking up an eyebrow at Ric.

"Riccardo D'Angelo?"

"Hi Damiano," I answer before Ric can, and his eyes dot back and forth between Ric and I, confused. "I would like to reach a compromise with you. If you come to the studio with me, and every single day that you need to until the EP has been completed, then Riccardo D'Angelo will accompany you guys on days that he is free, helping with your guitar, drums and vocals."

Damiano's eyes widen and I feel all giddy inside.

"…not only that, but once the EP has been completed, the Devilled Eggs will support Paolo Petrinelli at Verona at the end of summer."

"What's going on?" says another voice, and the bassist appears next to Damiano.

"Oh my *God!* It's Riccardo D'Angelo! *Guys*, Riccardo D'Angelo is at the door!"

The other three suddenly appear at the door, their eyes popping out of their sockets. I feel Ric tense a little bit more beside me and I want to put a hand on his arm, relax him, telling him non-verbally that I'll protect him from these cretins.

But I can't. The last thing I want is this silly band working out I'm sleeping with Ric, or, should I say, *Riccardo D'Angelo.*

"Hi guys," he says, rather formally.

"Intern Girl says we'll support Paolo Petrinelli at *Verona* if we finish this EP."

Stop fucking calling me that. "In the next two weeks," I add. "That's the deal you struck with Gavin, and that's the timeframe we would like you to finish."

I study Damiano, clearly the leader of the band. He's pensive, deep in thought, not willing to look weak in front of others, but at the same time, he will not give up this once in a lifetime opportunity to open for Paolo Petrinelli. I see it in his eyes – his internal struggle.

He coolly crosses his arms. "How do we know this isn't bullshit?"

I pull out a napkin I stole from a ristorante down the road whilst I waited for Ric. My ally eyes the napkin and then doubles back to have a second look, not quite believing what he's seeing.

"This is a contract," I tell the band, and Ric's eyes grow wider as I show them it. In a blue biro pen I have written the following:

> I, Riccardo D'Angelo, promise to get the band to perform at Verona for Paolo Petrinelli on September 29th.
> Signed:

Ric is taken aback, as I failed to mention this in my plan. But in my defence, I only came up with the contract part whilst waiting for him to arrive. This is essentially his fault for taking so long in the shower!

"It's not signed," Damiano points out and I want to give him a patronising round of applause, but I'm in character. I'm pretending to be someone that can actually stand him.

"I'm signing now," Ric announces, and he reluctantly takes the napkin from me. I hand him the biro and he gives me a stern look before using my back to sign. Once done, I grin, and say, "here you go, all done."

Damiano stares at the napkin a good ten seconds, and I hate that he has all the power. I want to shove his head through a bush or scrunch up the contract and shove it down his throat, but I know I can't. I have to be nice, and I have to be civil.

Fuck the rich, spoilt sons of the western world. Go out and learn to hunt for yourself, motherfuckers. And stop acting so damn entitled.

"Fine," he eventually says.

"Great," I reply, instantly. "That means get to the studio now. Not tomorrow, not this afternoon, but now."

The other boys nod, but Damiano remains cool. "Fine."

"I'll wait here," I tell them, and as soon as the door closes, I sigh in relief. I feel Ric's eyes on me but pretend not to. I cover my face with my palms, recovering from battle.

"A contract? Seriously?" he says. We turn to one another as we make our way down the gravel path to Ric's car. I feel the sun on my face, and I can hear birds chirping.

I won.

"I had to, I didn't know what else to do – he's a self-righteous bastard but he's not dumb."

"Well, you predicted it all rather well," Ric tells me.

"I mean, who wouldn't want help from *Riccardo D'Angelo*?" I tell him, throwing my arms in the air as if shouting his name to the stars.

"Or the chance to open for Paolo."

I study him as we walk. "Are you going to be alright swinging that?"

"Oh yeah. One of the tour managers owes me big, so yes, it should be fine."

I nod, and we stop in front of his car.

"You gonna be alright with them?"

"Uh, well, I was sort of hoping you could come and help with the first session?"

"Alexis!"

"I'm *sorry*!"

"I have practice in three hours. I was kind of hoping to get some sleep before then. You know, I had sort of a very eventful night with a very attractive, but very hungry young lady."

We smile flirtatiously at one another, and I feel as if I'm going to jump him there and then. "You always that hungry?"

"Yep."

"Me too."

"Then we're going to get on just fine," I tell him, and I'm tempted to pull him into the nearby bushes for a quickie.

He sighs, and looks out at the empty road. "Fine. I'll come for an hour, help them set up. Then they're all yours."

I give him a gratifying smile and am about to start some dirty talk about how I'll reward him later when we hear the front door fling open. All five boys come rushing out as if the world is coming to an end and we laugh under our breaths.

"Well I guess they're ready."

Damiano's designated driver takes the boys to the studio, whilst Ric and I make our own way there in his car. Once we arrive, Ric helps them set up, and the boys ask him lots of questions about Paolo, the tour and the new album.

They don't ask him any questions on their own music, except when they play him their demo. Ric eyes me midway with a 'help me' look as he nods along to it and pretends to find it okay, but I can tell he hates all of their tracks as much as I do.

We eventually make it to the end of the EP, and by now even Giuliano looks suicidal. The boys have been ignoring me since we left Damiano's, but I'm not taking it personally. It does not bother me in the slightest, as long as they stick to finishing their terrible, terrible EP on time. Then I can fly back to London a hero and move onto a more interesting client.

I've been following Ruby Records on social media and there's quite a few artists that have been signed recently, ones I'd really like to assist on their album releases.

I just need to get this EP completed, and then the world is my oyster. At least in the world of Ruby Records.

"I much prefer you over Mauro Fontana – that guy sucks," the only real emo in the band says, and I stifle a laugh quietly to myself.

"That's why Mauro never had a solo career."

"Actually, Mauro had a very impressive solo career before he joined Paolo's band, but he then developed a drug addiction and had to go to rehab, so when he came out everyone had forgotten him. Some years later, he got the gig as Paolo's guitarist that gave him a name again," I blurt out.

There is silence in the studio, and nobody but Ric looks at me. I am completely and utterly ignored.

Shit, remember not to speak, Alex. They will only ignore you, and you are fine with this, remember?

Ric shakes his head at me with a smile and gets up. "Right, I have to get to rehearsals now. It's been fun, see you either Wednesday or Thursday, okay?"

The boys immediately get up, all speaking at once, both groaning and asking why he must leave, and simultaneously excited for his return later in the week. They're all talking fast and elated, like kids in school to a really cool, rebellious teacher everyone loves and wants to be close to.

When he leaves, the boys begin recording track one, talking amongst themselves and paying no attention to me whatsoever. It's as if I do not exist.

And so I pop out, buy Paulo Coelho's Adultery and some ear plugs. Once I return, I sit in the corner of the sofa, and I get on with my day.

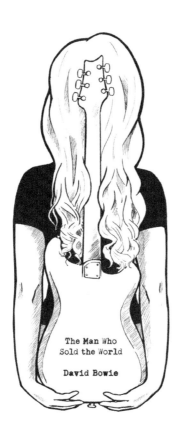

12

My fear of being boxed in started at an early age. I was ten when my phobia of ending up in a dead-end office job kicked in. The idea of doing the same thing every day for the rest of my life scared the shit out of me. Repetition gave me nightmares, as did low life ambition.

"You'll find something you like," my mum would say, but really she was wondering how the hell a ten-year old could already be worrying about such things.

If I'm honest, I never wanted to be 'like everyone else'. The things that 'everyone else' wanted to do, like get a decent office job after graduation, get married, have kids, are things that have never been on my list.

I was not that little girl that dreamt about her wedding, and when women share their childhood memories with me that involve pretending to put on veils and walk down the aisle, I cannot relate to them whatsoever.

I don't believe in marriage and I never have – I think if two people want to stay together they can do it without a piece of paper or a big party. If you want a big party that revolves around you write a book, write an album, create something, and then throw yourself a launch party. And you won't even have to share the glory with someone else.

Maybe one day I'll sketch something really good and do that for myself. The idea of celebrating an accomplishment by throwing a party for myself excites me much more than the idea of throwing a party to celebrate me committing myself to *one* person for the rest of my life.

Even M. Scott Peck says it – love is simply chemicals that trick us into marriage, to get us down the aisle, because honestly if we thought about it logically, who the fuck would do that to themselves?

I stand at the very edge of the stage, looking out at the sun going down in the distance. The sky is orange, that kind of beautiful dark orange that appears right before night fall. The air is still warm though; teasing you. It is still day. It is still summer. Not for much longer, but it's still all here, at your disposal.

I take a deep breath in, closing my eyes as I do so. Roadies can be heard moving about onstage, Ric too. He's talking to one of them about his pedals. When Ric speaks about his guitars or his gear he uses his most serious tone; the one that reads, *listen carefully to everything I have to say.* It isn't a request; it's an order.

I put out my hand as the wind blows. I want to feel it against my palm, as if there is a magic in the air tonight you do not need to see but feel.

This is it. This is the calm before the storm. I am standing on the edge of the stage of Arena Civica; a venue I have watched on Italian TV on numerous occasions as a kid, hosting some of the biggest concerts in Italy. And here I am now, backstage, having the privilege of being a part of this moment, of truly living it.

Sure, it isn't San Siro, but then again, San Siro is the *queen* of Italian venues. Arena Civica, however, is still big and beautiful nonetheless.

The stadium is empty but soon it will be filled with happy Italians, for whom some this concert is something they have been looking forward to for months. Fans are outside queueing in the heat and smog of Milano's streets; they are giddy with joy even though they are dehydrated and in desperate need of the toilet.

They're probably hungry too and their legs have already started to ache, but none of this matters because soon they will get to see Paolo Petrinelli play live, to warm their hearts, to set their souls on fire on a beautiful summers' evening in Italy.

People will go to great lengths to hear their favourite music live, to hear it in their ears on the way to work, to take it in before they go to sleep. They will go to great lengths to buy that new album, to purchase those gig tickets, to keep good music with them.

I love music so much, and every day more, but sometimes I do think it is a pity that the rest of the world does not stop often enough to think about the incredibly beautiful power of music.

I stand on the edge of that stage with a plate of tiramisu in hand and Bowie songs playing in my head, one after the other, perfection after perfection, as if the quality of music Bowie produced is in line with the quality of this night.

With my eyes still closed, I take in all the sounds around me: Ric, the roadies, the wind blowing gently, footsteps across the stage. I smile as I do so, thinking that there is nothing more perfect to listen to than this moment right here. It's a particular type of beauty, that time before a gig.

Exciting. Nerve-wracking. Brimming with possibility.

"Alexis! Come here!" I hear Ric yell, and I instantly open my eyes.

With a smile still planted on my face, I skip over to Ric as he gets out a black Classic Series '72 Tele Custom. The roadie he was talking to walks away, and Ric grins at me like a kid in a sweet shop.

I gush over the guitar, just as Ric expects. Guitars are able to excite me and overwhelm me so much more than anything else in this world – including sex and tiramisu. That's saying something.

I notice Paolo walk onstage as I stand there adoring the Tele, and he comes straight over to us with that wise smile of his. My body still manages to tense and my back straighten whenever Paolo comes within a hundred metre radius.

He pats Ric on the back. "You ready?"

"Definitely."

Paolo nods at me, and walks away. He's used to me now; I've seen him twice already this week. When I'm not sitting in a recording studio with a shitty band who ignore me all day, I'm with Ric at whatever venue in the city he's playing at that night.

They have four dates in Milano this week, and this is their penultimate one. It's fun to come backstage, to hang out, to see Paolo and the band perform. But I have started to ask myself how they manage to play the same songs every damn night and not want to throw themselves off a building. It must get tiring.

"Ready for what?" I ask Ric, intrigued.

"Well...I got more solos," he tells me nonchalantly, and I gawp. "*Six* more, to be exact."

YES, YES, YES!

"And for that, I get *this* beauty," he nods at the '72 Tele Custom in his hands and I beam.

"Six?! *Six?!*" I bounce up and down in excitement. "Oh that's brilliant! Tonight?"

He nods, proudly.

"That's so great, Ric. How did you get them?"

"I, uh, I asked."

I frown, as I have a flashback of us in bed the other night, in-between our fourth and fifth round of sex. We had gotten onto the subject of Ric's *one* solo situation, and I learned that he was still performing the same one I had seen him perform the first time I met him.

It made me instantly fill with outrage; Ric deserves more solos, more play time, more exposure. I don't want his excellence as a guitarist to go to waste.

"Why don't you just ask for more?" I had said, and Ric had forced a laugh, pushing my hair away from my eyes as we lay facing one another in the darkness of his bedroom.

"Because you can't just ask Paolo Petrinelli for more solos."

"Why not?" had been my response.

My heart warms at the thought that he had listened to me, and I watch him as he gets up. "So…you wanna test her out for me?"

"What kind of a question is that, D'Angelo?"

"A stupid one, Brunetti."

I move in closer and he swings the guitar off him and over me. The tension builds as our lips remain just inches apart. "You're gonna rock those solos," I say, softly.

He looks at my lips with that spark in his eyes, and steps back as I take hold of the beauty in my hands.

"*Porca troia,* she is so damn divine in my hands," I say rather loudly, just as Kyle appears next to us with his bass around his neck.

He's been back from paternity leave a month now and I've already bumped into him a couple of times. Our conversations are mostly small talk, but there's a fondness for one another that burns subtly in the background.

"Oh wow, look at her! She looks like she just won the lottery."

175

"She has good taste in guitars," Ric tells him, winking at me.

Kyle disappears and as Ric fiddles with the pedal at my feet, the only question on my mind is, what the hell do I play?

I have a painful want to play something by Pearl Jam, so I go through the options in my head.

Jeremy?
Black?
Scorch?
Or…Alive?

Hmm, Alive. I know it well enough to not fuck up on Paolo Petrinelli's stage.

"I'm gonna play Alive. Yes, yes, yes!" I tell Ric and he smiles without even looking up at me.

"Well this is a rare sight," says a voice. I turn to find a very attractive man in his mid-twenties standing in the middle of the stage, his eyes on me.

He has wavy dark brown hair that reaches his ears, black eyes and sexy stubble on his jaw similar to that of Ric's. He's dressed in tight, black jeans, a black buttoned up shirt, a black blazer and a black top hat.

He is sexy; very sexy.

He smiles slightly at me as he approaches us, his eyes still fixed on me. "Nice to see a girl so into guitars."

American.

"There's lots of us out there," I tell him with a smile I reserve only for attractive strangers. *Who is he?*

Ric looks at him but doesn't say anything, still fiddling with the pedal.

"Well *I* haven't met them! Not this attractive, anyway."

Don't Blush.

He puts out his hand. "Parker May."

That name sounds familiar.

"Alexis," his hand is soft, like he wears too much hand lotion, and the moment we touch it sends butterflies to my stomach.

The way he is looking at me forces me to gulp; his eyes are focused solely on me, and they read intrigue. They are big and black and powerful.

He looks like one of those strangers that if you were to meet on a group night out, he'd stick out like a sore thumb, even if everyone else in the group were GQ models. There's something about him that makes him so damn addictive to look at. As if there is simply never going to be enough time to take in everything standing before you.

"Aren't you supposed to be setting up, Parker?" Ric says bluntly, and the attractive stranger glances at him as if he's only just noticed him.

"Ric! How are you? When are we going to play some guitar together, man?"

His silver rings, his silver dragon pendant, the sexy, smooth chest that pops out of his black shirt – the more I spot on the attractive stranger before us, the more it makes me want to mount him right here on this stage.

"You're a guitarist?" I blurt out, still trying to take in his attractive self. I had of course worked out at this point that he is a musician (who dresses like that if they're not?), but I had assumed he was a singer, or at the most, a singer and a guitarist. A man with this much charisma and confidence shouldn't be anything but centre stage, surely?

"Yeah, lead guitarist of Luminous."

Paolo's second support act for tonight.

Luminous are a relatively famous Italian pop-rock band from Ravenna, trending mostly amongst late teenagers. I like a few of their tracks but they aren't super inspirational.

"So many Italian bands with American members," I say, as if to myself.

"You got something against Americans?"

I chortle. "No, I-"

"I'm messing with you."

"He does that a lot," Ric adds, clearly not a big fan of the musician standing next to us.

"And Ric here acts like an old man a lot," he winks at Ric, who only continues giving him a blank look.

"Parker!" someone calls from across the stage.

"Uh, I gotta go, see you later. We should jam some time," he winks at me and I watch him walk across the stage with swagger.

That man is yummy.

I look down at the guitar in my hands and play a few chords, hoping to distract myself.

"That guy is an idiot," Ric mutters, as if to himself.

177

Before I can reply, my phone starts playing the Smiths 'This Charming Man'. I get it out, see 'GAVIN' flashing on the screen and immediately pick up.

"Hi, Gavin!"

"Alexis, how's it going? Are they ready?"

"They're in the studio recording! Every single day!" I don't know why I say it with such an enthusiastic tone, as if I am waiting for Gavin to give me a gold star or something.

This is the way I seem to speak to him though – as if I am a child in primary school and he is the big, scary headmaster.

"I know. I asked if they've finished?"

I take the phone away from my ear, cover it with my hand, and breathe out heavily. It's always so stressful to talk to Gavin.

Ric peers up at me curiously, and I put the phone back to my ear.

"Not yet, should be just under a week to go. Two weeks in total, just as you said."

"Right. Keep me posted," he pauses. "Everything else okay?"

"Yes, everything else is fine."

Another pause. "Fine. I'll be out in a week to see you and hear the EP. We'll fly back together."

When I hear 'fly back together' I am temporarily sad for a moment, and I realise I like my life in Milano. I don't really like having a non-existent relationship with a shitty band or hanging out in a recording studio wearing ear plugs (a bit like going to a sweet shop and not buying any sweets), but I like going backstage to Italy's biggest venues and having rough sex every night with a handsome guitarist.

I guess it's not really why I'm here, or helping my career, but it sure is helping my soul (and certain parts of my body).

He hangs up before I can say 'bye' as usual, and I sigh as I put my phone away.

"Artist managers suck," I mutter under my breath, and Ric stands up.

"It's their job, Alexis. You can't expect him to sit around babysitting you. He chose you for a reason and he has excellent judgement – don't prove him wrong."

I gulp, and am half inclined to ask him how I can do that, but I don't want to seem clueless or needy.

"They have not said a word to me, not one. Not since standing outside Damiano's house with you," I shake my head.

I thought it wasn't bothering me, but it is. Even if they are the shittiest band in the world, I still want to communicate with them, to at least acknowledge each other, say hi in the morning, say bye when they leave. But nothing. And I'm starting to realise that it bothers me more than I have let myself believe.

"They're seeing you as the enemy, Alexis. Damiano most likely has tension with his father, at least that's what I read about in the papers. Mind you, newspapers are not the most reliable source in the world. But maybe there's a little truth to it?"

"But then why would his dad sign them to Ruby?"

Ric shrugs. "To maintain a good rep? It's all about good reputation with tycoons like that," he tells me, as he moves some gear. "I'd try to talk to them. Slowly but surely, they will come around. You need to get them to trust you."

I stifle a laugh. "They will never look at me like an actual role model, they call me Intern Girl for goodness sake."

"Well you won't with an attitude like that. Remember that nicknames and ideas of people don't come from a person's imagination – it's in your output. You don't believe in yourself, and so they don't believe in you either."

I cock up an eyebrow at Ric. Who knew he was so insightful?

"Have you heard of NLP?"

I shake my head at him.

"Neuro Linguistic Programming. Our mind is the most powerful thing we possess, Alexis. Look into it. Tons of books out there on it."

I stare at Ric in curiosity, realising that the man in front of me is not just your stereotypical guitarist.

"Okay," I manage to reply. He nods at me with a smile, before carrying gear over to the other side of the stage with some of the roadies.

Meanwhile, I decide to play the main riff to 'Alive'. It soothes me and relaxes me instantly, making Gavin's phone call and the thought of a shitty emo band ignoring me just fade away.

I love how playing can do that, can lift you up and take you away to an entirely different place. I am at one when I am playing.

The others continue setting up and I watch on, as I play one of my favourite Pearl Jam songs of all time. I think about the power of Mike McCready's playing, and Eddie Vedder's gorgeous voice. They are definitely the best band out of the Seattle Sound scene.

Damn it, I wish I had been a teenager when all of that was going on. To go to a concert and see Kurt Cobain play and sing. To see Eddie Vedder in his element.

Playing 'Alive' is paradise and by the end of the song I am back to my normal self. And as soon as I'm done and I'm kicked offstage by the tech team, I get out my phone, and I type in 'NLP'.

Call me crazy or weird or whatever you want to call me, but I love recording studios. I could actually live in them, seven days a week. I mean, think about it – it's this super comfy place where music is created, where music collides with art, to become one, to unite, to become *something*.

Everyone in a recording studio is there to create music. And the signature black leather sofa, the soft pillows, the mini fridge, the impeccable instruments that surround you – who the fuck *wouldn't* want to live in a recording studio?!

I can honestly say I've never visited a *bad* recording studio, I've been lucky that way. There are some better than others, more extravagant than others, sure, but they've *all* been frekin' cool.

You enter and there is a certain magic that greets you at the door, puts a smile on your face. And sure, they can be really stuffy (I have yet to work out why – is it done by purpose or is it just that there are lots of people in an enclosed place at once?), but they're still my favourite place in the world.

It's 11am on Monday morning and I've been at Gateway Studios for a couple of hours now. I got up early, had a shower, and headed in.

Giuliano gets here about 7am, he's a cool guy – he kindly offered to let me in whenever I wanted to relax or be inspired. You see, the sound system in a recording studio is always out of this world, or at least, better than whatever your crappy headphones produce (unfortunately I made a vow to myself to never, *ever* again buy expensive headphones, as I break and/or lose all of them).

And so Giuliano lets me borrow a pair of his headphones (technically not breaking the vow if they don't leave the studio), and I get on with some sketching.

Yes, after a very long time, I've started sketching again. Random stuff, like a couple flying over some dark mountains as they strip their clothes but keep their shoes on. And a man with hearts for feet, and as he walks, pieces from them break off and leave a trail behind him, mice then eating them. All my sketches are dark; you'll never find me drawing sunshine and rainbows.

It's good to be back at sketching, even if I don't really know what I'm drawing until it's on the page. It never used to be that way; I used to have a vision of everything beforehand, planned out and ready to go. But now I'm sketching in the moment, and even *I'm* sometimes surprised at the outcome.

The boys are due in the studio any second, but I'm so in the zone that I don't notice them walk in. I'm drawing a triangular chandelier, with symbols of sixties rock bands all around the edges. Led Zeppelin, Cream, The Who, etc. All the classics.

Suddenly I feel the wires of my headphone get tugged, and the music switches from Ian Curtis singing in my ears to Ian Curtis singing to the entire studio. I turn around to find Damiano standing there, the others behind him unpacking.

"Jesus, I've been calling your name for ten minutes!" he tells me as the last two minutes of Joy Division's New Dawn Fades blasts from the speakers. "Gavin wants to talk to you." Damiano hands me his phone and I frown, until I remember that I left mine at Ric's bedside table the previous night.

"Hello?" I say, as I press Damiano's phone to my ear and lower the volume on Joy Division.

"Alexis! What happened to your phone?"

"I left it at home, sorry! Stupid me, I'll go pick it up now. What's up?"

"*Always* have your phone with you please. I wanted to tell you that Brett is flying out with me next Tuesday. Just a heads up. So make sure they're done in the studio by then."

"Okay."

"See you in a few days." And from that, he hangs up. I hand Damiano back his phone, and pack up my stuff, deciding I'd better get a taxi back to Ric's in case Gavin decides to call again.

"Who is this?" says a voice, and when I turn around I realise it's the lead guitarist who asked the question, and it's directed at me. I think.

His name is Elliot, I know this because he's the most popular member of the band – there is always someone saying his name.

When I look at him, I realise it is the first time we have ever made eye contact.

Elliot is by far the most handsome one in the band, not just physically – he has a charisma to him that adds to his good looks. I of course wouldn't ever hook up with him, I don't really see myself as a cradle snatcher, but I do acknowledge his good looks.

"Punk, right?" he adds, in case I didn't hear him.

"Joy Division," I tell him.

"Never listened to them. He has a nice voice," Elliot tells me, and I freeze.

I must have misheard – the possibility that a rock musician has never listened to Joy Division is just impossible for me to comprehend.

"Wait, *what?* You've never listened to Joy Division? And it's Ian Curtis – the singer." I hate to be that person that acts shocked when someone hasn't heard of something or someone that I know very well, but I honestly have no other reaction to this news. Elliot is the lead guitarist in a rockband. How can he not know Joy Division?

"It's kind of Sex pistols type of vibes?"

"Well, they formed after attending a Sex Pistols gig in the late seventies. And though they started heavily punk, they then created their own sound, a sound so incredible and unique that it would influence and inspire many bands after them," I tell him.

Meanwhile, Damiano, the bassist Matteo and the drummer Lino chat in Italian in the corner, ignoring us. I know I don't like any of them, or respect them as musicians, but it feels nice to converse. I guess after not doing it all day every day, you'll take any conversation you can get.

Plus, I love talking about music to virtually *anyone*.

"Maybe I'll check them out," Elliot says.

But that's not a good enough answer for me. I grab my iPod, scanning through my Joy Division playlist. I click 'She's Lost Control' and the drum kicks in. I watch Elliot in curiosity, as he bops his head to it.

"Nice bass," the bassist says, joining us.

What's his name again?

"Matteo, you should take tips from him!" says the emo of the band, slapping his black playfully.

Bassist – Matteo. Got it. And what about the emo/rhythm guitarist?

"Shut up, G."

Ah yes that's right, they call him G, whatever the hell his real name is – I bet it's Giovanni or Giorgo or something.

All three of them bop their heads to Joy Division, but my eyes are fixed on Elliot, as we smile at one another. The drummer, Lino, joins them, and I can hear G, Matteo and Lino chatting amongst themselves about the song whilst Elliot and I remain fixated on one another.

Don't ask me why, because I don't know. But it's as if we both like this song the same amount.

Damiano moans about the band slacking off and tells them to get ready to record, but the boys don't move. They tell him to chill out, to take it easy, that they still have time to set up. Everyone moans back at Damiano except Elliot, whose eyes do not leave mine.

He's really liking Joy Division.

I skip ahead to Heart & Soul, to which Matteo ears pop up like a cat that hears the sound of a tin can opening. "Holy shit that is an insane bass riff!" he exclaims, whacking Elliot's arm. "We should make more bass-centric songs!"

"Really? I thought guitar is your strongest voice," I blurt out, and suddenly all eyes are on me. They look at me as if I have just announced I am flying to the moon, except for Elliot, whose smile only grows wider, and dare I say, he looks like a little intrigued.

"I was thinking of changing sound; not really liking the Strat," he tells me.

"Why on Earth would you do that? Your guitar is a beauty." I skip forward to 'Isolation' and Matteo is losing his mind as he bops his head to the song. It's the most curious thing – to see guys who call themselves rock musicians listen to one of Joy Division's most potent and amazingly inspiring songs for the very first time.

"Peter Hook. Check him out – bassists worship him," I tell Matteo.

"Are we setting up or what?!" Damiano barks over the music.

Funny how Damiano has never shown any work ethic up until now.

"What do you mean when you say you think guitar is our strongest voice?" asks Elliot.

"I mean that is a beautiful instrument you are willing to give up on, and there is a voice coming from that Strat that can tell the story of your band."

The recording studio is silent, and all that can be heard is Ian Curtis' voice. Even Giuliano is looking at me now, his chair squeaking awkwardly as he turns around to peer at me. I feel weird and uncomfortable all at once, and I'm not sure where to look or what to do.

Yes boys, I know a thing or two about guitars.

Yes, I am a girl. You can check if you want.

Joking. That would be slightly inappropriate.

I remember Ric's words the other day, *'they don't believe in you because you don't believe in yourself'*.

According to NLP, there are various exercises to practise in order to tweak the idea you have of yourself. This, in turn, builds confidence, and creates better and more positive output around other people.

I've been practising some of these exercises every morning and evening since.

Elliot and I are still staring at one another, and I put out my hand. "May I?" I ask, gesturing at the Fender Strat he holds in his hands.

Elliot doesn't look at the others for permission or their opinion, he simply hands me his guitar, without any hesitation. And his eyes remain firmly fixed on me. I pause Joy Division and put down my iPod.

"What is she doing? Hey? We are supposed to be recording, for fuck's sake!" Damiano groans, but his complaining goes ignored by all of us as I fiddle with the pedal at my feet. Elliot smiles at me as he watches me set up, I'm not looking at him but I feel it.

I must say, if you were to ask me to choose one out of the band I dislike the least, it would be Elliot. He seems like the only one in the group that thinks for himself. Bear in mind, I have only come to this decision by witnessing him choose pasta over pizza at dinner time, watching Mad Men on his breaks, and dismissing himself from the conversation when the subject turns to crappy TV shows or pop culture.

Maybe, just maybe, someone in this band has a mind of their own. He can't play for shit, sure, but he might just have good judgement. And I can't ever put down good judgement.

I know straight away what I'm going to play; it's a song I know well. It's also something I think would be a good sound for the band. You know, if they learned to actually play well. And sing well. And perform well.

Once ready, I begin playing the main riff to Smashing Pumpkins' 'Cherub Rock'.

I love everything about this song. I love Billy Corgan's soothing and slightly spooky voice, to James Lha's guitar playing. Above all though, I love the guitar riff in this song.

I fell in love with it from the very first moment I heard it, aged seventeen. It was one of my favourite to learn to play, and one of the ones I have since remembered how to play. I would love to learn to play the solo someday too.

I play the riff a few times, bopping my head to it, and from the corner of my eye, I see Elliot bopping his head to it too.

I hear Billy Corgan's voice start the verse and take in the wonders of this song. I don't dare look up as I play, in fear that Damiano's withering stare will put me off and lead me to mess up.

I play the riff a few times, with no mistakes, and once I stop, I look up at the boys. Four of them are smiling at me, and as expected, one of them – good old Damiano, looks like he couldn't care less.

"Cool riff! What is that?" Matteo asks.

Again?!
Seriously, guys?
Again?!
What the fuck kind of rockband are you?!
"Smashing Pumpkins – Cherub Rock."

They look at me blankly.

"1979? Disarm? Ava Adore?"

Still blank faces.

"Dear Lord, what music have you been listening to?" Realising how rude I sound, I gulp and swing Elliot's guitar over my head, handing it over to him as I walk over to my iPod. "Okay guys, let me know if any of you recognise this song."

Stone Temple Pilots 'Plush' begins playing and I close my eyes, partly to take in the legendary music playing, and partly in hope that when I would open them again the boys in front of me would no longer be looking at me blankly.

It does not happen.

And so I continue through my music encyclopedia, making them listen to songs they are supposed to know as rock musicians and do not: Joan and the Jetts, underrated Rolling Stones songs, Black Flags, Dead Kennedys, The Strokes, Queens of the Stone Age, The Smiths.

Every sub rock genre, across every decade. I am determined to pass on my knowledge, in pure refusal to allow a rockband to walk around calling themselves a rockband without knowing these artists.

I tell them about the musicians, their history, and what made or makes them great. The boys, apart from Damiano, listen on in intrigue, taking in every word I say.

Damiano however, stubborn as ever, listens, but remains standing at the back with his arms crossed, as if to say: *I am listening, sure, but I will never obey.*

Well fuck you, Damiano. It's okay that you're not listening, you know why? Because I'm going to teach your band about real rock music whether you like it or not, if it's the last thing I do.

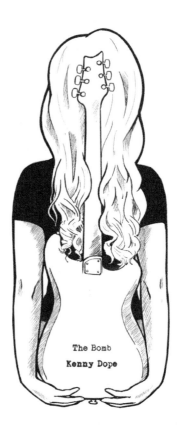

13

Okay, so I'm not just a rock chick. I know I have a Foos tattoo and I talk a lot about Pearl Jam and Van Halen and Pink Floyd, but I love other genres too. It *is* possible to love more than one genre of music, you know. Just like someone can be a corporate lawyer and a guitar player at the same time, someone can be both a rock chick and a classical music enthusiast.

And I think it's time I come clean about my other passions when it comes to music. Or, at least one of them.

I love nineties dance music. Yes, that's right. I'm talking about Sonique, I'm talking about Daft Punk, I'm talking about Faithless. I have to be in a particular mood when I listen to nineties dance music, usually when I have too much energy, or it's Saturday night and I have no plans.

I'll blast it as loud as I possibly can through my headphones and then jump around, as if I'm at a nineties rave.

Fun fact: I actually went to a nineties rave once; it was fun, and probably the only rave I've ever been to where I didn't stop dancing the entire night.

So that's exactly what I'm doing in Ric's living room as he gets ready in the bathroom. We just had two rounds of sex, the second being shower sex, and then Ric had remained in the bathroom to prepare for his last gig in Milano, and I had proceeded to blast Phats & Small's 'Turn Around' (the radio edit) and dance around his living room in my bathrobe. Or more, *his* bathrobe.

I'm also using a celery stick as a mic – there's always fresh fruit and veg in the fridge at Ric's, he's one healthy eating freak. I guess it's his way of making up for all the cigarettes he smokes and beer he drinks.

His bedroom always smells of sundried tomatoes (and I say this as a positive thing), and he simply cannot shower without his Bluetooth speakers playing something by Rino Gaetano or Pink Floyd or Springsteen.

When he's in a *really* special mood, he'll play Black Flags. And of course, I hop back into the shower to attack him when he does that. I do quite admire a man who knows his punk rock.

I think at heart, Ric is even older than his thirty-three years, that's why he's such good friends with Vinnie and his lookalikes, who are all a decade older than him. I find it cute, but sometimes, our age difference feels slightly bigger than it actually is, if that were even possible.

We went to Vinnie's work last night; he owns an English pub, even though Vinnie has never been to London and never set foot in an authentic English pub. This tickles me, or maybe it's the two Irish coffees I had that got to me.

Ric rubbed my back and cackled at the reminder that I am indeed a lightweight. We hung out with Vinnie, who told me stories about Ric that entertain me to no end – such as Ric once went on a dating app date with what he thought was a woman, only to find out when he met her *she* was actually a *he*.

Another interesting story Vinnie shared with me was that Ric once went out with a fan of his who had thrown her bra at him onstage at a Paolo gig.

To Vinnie, 'she had the craziest crazy eyes I ever seen – but of course, Ricky here was young and naïve, just starting out with the band – he couldn't see it'.

When I asked what happened with that woman and when exactly Ric figured out she wasn't who he thought she was, Vinnie explained that it was only when she broke off his car mirror for responding to a comment on social media to his female friend, Elena, that Ric saw her for who she really was.

The 'crazy eyes woman', as Vinnie called her, was convinced he was cheating on her because of that interaction.

"From *one* comment?" I asked, turning to Ric. "What the hell did you say?"

"I wrote, 'great song'," Ric replied, and we burst into laughter, all three of us. Vinnie narrowed his eyes at me, and I knew what he was going to say next.

"*She* doesn't have crazy eyes – you're safe, Ric!"

I got a little uncomfortable at the comment, as if Ric and I are dating, as if Vinnie is saying he approves of me or something, but I'm used to this happening when I'm banging someone. Sometimes people simply cannot differentiate between the two, so I waste no time trying to defend it or explain it. I simply clinked my glass with his, and asked for more stories.

Vinnie is great company, and funny as hell. It's hard to think of a time when I didn't like him, back when we first met. He's sincere, and sure, his jokes are sometimes a little vulgar and I can see how some people might be offended by some of the stuff he says, but, in all honesty, he's one of my favourite type of people. He's sincere, and of a pure heart, so much so that he has to mask it with tasteless jokes. What could get better than that?

I don't sleep at Ric's, ever; I always make my way home after a night of sex with him, but it always feels as though I do sleep there, that I have slept there since I arrived in Milano. It's the strangest feeling.

You know when you see girls dancing in movies and they look sexy and cool and just plain awesome? Yeah, that's not me right now. I'm dancing in the most uncool way possible – bopping my head, jiggling my butt as I jump on his sofa, every now and again taking a bite from the celery stick.

I'm singing along, loudly, my eyes closed for most of the song, so it takes me a while to notice Ric standing and leaning on his bedroom door, his arms folded, watching me with a smile on his face.

It's a smile different from every other smile he has ever shared with me, but I can't quite work out why.

"Hey!" I sing. "What's wrong with *youuuu,* you're looking kind of down to me!"

He watches me with that smile, and it's a pity he's dressed to leave and that we do have to rush out to get to the venue. We were already pushing it a bit by having that second round in the shower, it's just – if you were in a shower with Riccardo D'Angelo, you'd probably be distracted too.

I purposely make my dance moves even geekier than normal, and he stifles a laugh. I signal for him to come over with my finger and he slowly does so, as if to tease me, as if to build on the tension. It works, as we continue to fix each other with our sex-hungry eyes.

By the time he's close enough, he pulls me to him by the waist and we kiss aggressively. We fall backwards, and I stop him suddenly.

"Wait, you're going to be late to the venue-"

"We better make this quick then," he replies, as he pulls off my bathrobe.

Tonight is Paolo's last of the Milano summer dates. Next will be Mantova, which is two hours away, and then Verona. After that, they will continue around Italy through autumn, but by then I will be back in London.

I'm excited for tonight's gig - the last of four dates in what is deemed the music capital of Italy. I've noticed with last tour dates in a city, the band tend to do something special or mix it up a bit.

I'm *praying* that they do, as I know their set inside out now, word-for-word, chord-for-chord. But Ric is smashing his six solos, each one better than the last and I lose my voice *woo*ing at them all now.

Once we arrive at the venue, people are panicked that Ric is late and I feel a little guilty. As if he can read my mind, he puts a hand on the back of my neck and winks, before heading out onstage with some of the roadies.

I do some sketching in the green room as they set up, and when the band comes in, I take some pictures of them with the very beautiful camera that head of marketing, Luciano, leaves around.

I've become somewhat of an unintentional intern for the Paolo Petrinelli social media team, taking pictures and videos of the band as backstage content for their page. The fans love it, and I love photography, so it's a win-win for everyone.

I've always loved portrait photography – I love to take pictures of people, to capture their soul or their mood or that glint in their eyes. When I was a teen, I even bought a semi-professional camera to practise, but quickly learnt that not many people like to pose for photographs.

They shy away, become uncomfortable and ultimately ask the question, *'why me, Alexis? Shoot someone else.'* I at one point thought I was going to be a photographer, and I listed all the potential obstacles that could stand in my way. Never did I think that the real obstacle to stop me in my tracks would be convincing other people to be my model.

Time flies by, as it always does on gig nights, and the band are onstage in what feels like a nanosecond. I quickly make my way out into the crowd, having been distracted by some shots I had taken of Roberto, the drummer, with some trashy groupies (they kept telling him the ways they were going to suck his dick later tonight – I mean, keep that stuff to yourselves, ladies).

I was busy editing the shots and sending them onto Luciano, who said he loved them and will post tomorrow. As a result, I'm a little late and scowl under my breath as I realise the band have already all made an entrance. The intro is always my favourite part – when each member strolls onstage individually, leaving Paolo as last.

I *love* watching Ric jog onstage and pick up his guitar – he does it so nonchalantly, so sexily, so confidently. His half-jog, half-walk always gets such a great applause, and I'm a little pissed I missed it.

They're straight into their opening song, a rock-poppy song I can dance around to, and so I bop my head to it as I make my way to the front.

People tonight are wilder and antsier than usual, and I guess it's because the band is twenty-five minutes late onstage due to technical issues. Or because it's their last Milano date. It takes me a while to get to the front, the crowd going wild – moshing, jumping around, screaming their lungs out to the lyrics.

I stop at about fourth or fifth row from the front as Paolo Petrinelli begins the second song. I look up at the stage for the first time and smile at the sight of Ric.

The second song on the set list has one of Ric's solos and I gleam, waiting for his moment. It's another upbeat rock-poppy song and the crowd goes ballistic, jumping around and shoving each other. There are elbows in my face from all directions and I have to fight them off.

It feels like the area around me is such a small, enclosed space when in reality it's huge – there are just too many people being pushed together. I get shoved from left to right, throwing me completely off balance.

What the fuck is wrong with this crowd?!

It gets worse. Beer is thrown around and some lands in my hair. This continues to happen, again and again, no matter how much I try to duck out of the way. In only a couple of minutes, my hair is pretty much soaked through with beer.

I feel someone grab my ass and I turn around instantly, ready to slap someone silly, when I am suddenly pushed again. People shout and swear at each other dramatically in Italian and I find myself getting lost in the crowd.

The craziest thing of all though is that through all this chaos, people are still managing to sing passionately to the song. It's as if they are possessed, and no matter what is going on, they must continue singing along.

I've been to crazy gigs before, where moshers are out of control, where beer is flying everywhere and people are shouting, but never to this extent. Never with the ass-grabbing *and* the elbows in my face *and* the hair completely soaked through.

Wait, it's nearly Ric's solo, I can't miss this!

I push everyone around me with force as I try to avoid being pushed and pulled like a ragdoll. Ric starts his solo and I scream, *woo*ing ecstatically, though hardly audible over the crowds' insane cheering and screaming. It seems everyone else loves Ric's solo as much as I do, one girl even shouting 'ti amo, Riccardo!'

I roll my eyes as a pang of jealousy hits me.

*Excuse me, **I'm** the one sleeping with him right now.*

At the end of the solo Ric looks out at the crowd, finding my eyes and smiling. I grin, waving at him like a twelve-year-old at a Justin Timberlake concert. He waves back and I feel like the coolest person in the crowd.

The next song begins, another upbeat one and again the crowd goes mad.

What's wrong with these people?!

I decide there's only one thing I can do to avoid injure, and that is to join them. And so I mosh with the crowd, still being pushed around but not as much as the ones that choose to stay still.

Ah, solution found!

But just as I think I have it all figured out, my heart starts racing, and I am reminded of how I am different from the other people around me; something I try so hard to forget.

Oh shit, no.
No, no, no.
No heart palpitation, please no.
I can't have one here.

I am in the middle of hundreds of people in the standing area of Riviera Stadium – if I am about to have a heart palpitation there is no way I would be able to get out of here. When I have an episode, I need to drink cold water, lie down, take deep breaths in and relax. There is no way I am going to be able to do any of these things in this crazy crowd, and the thought only makes me panic even more.

No, no, no, Alex.
No!
This is not happening!

I turn around to try and attempt to get out of the crowd but find it impossible, the people behind me only pushing me further to the front, making me now third row from the stage.

I try and struggle to make my way through as Paolo and the band continue to play the upbeat rock song, but I keep getting pushed from left to right, forward and backwards, elbows whacking me in the face, in the stomach, and all with the occasional grope from God knows who.

The floor is already littered with beer bottles and cups, which make it difficult to balance on the ground. There's glass too, and you have to be careful to not step on any.

I look up at the faces around me; most of them seem to be having a good time, unaware of the havoc they are causing around them. Are they high? Drunk? I don't understand how they can remain oblivious to the elbows and arms they are hitting people in the face with.

My breathing is starting to become heavier as the heart palpitation kicks in.

Oh fuck, there it is.
You're having a heart palpitation in a massive crowd of hooligans.

I try to make my way through the crowd again but to little avail; people are pushing me, shoving me, elbowing me – no one is going to let me through.

I can hardly breathe, it's boiling hot and I feel extremely claustrophobic. Everyone is in my face, loud voices in my ears, elbows poking me everywhere. I am weak, exasperated, and panicked.

I try to use my voice box to communicate the problem, the fact that I need to get out of here, but nobody can hear me over the chaos, and even if they could, hardly anyone knows what the fuck a heart palpitation is.

I realise something in Paolo's song has changed, something is missing, and just as I do, I spot a white t-shirt appear at the barriers. I look to find Ric has taken off his guitar, jumped offstage and is at the barriers, trying to tell the security guards something over the music. He looks panicked.

Paolo and the rest of the band continue playing, but all eyes are on him, wondering what the hell he is doing.

I am still being pushed from left to right, but I put my arm in the air as if to call him, losing sight of him as I get pushed sideways.

"Alex! Come here!" I hear him shout over the music and the crowd.

He's here for me.
He jumped offstage to help me.
Get to him!

"Ric!"

"Alex, come here!" he puts one foot on the step of the barriers, leaning into the crowd with his arm out to reach me, but third from the front means he is too far to do so and even as he tries, lots of people are touching him and pulling his hand and arm for their own pleasure.

"I can't, I'm too far!" I manage to shout back, unsure he can hear me over the chaos.

"Let that girl through!" he demands to the crowd in Italian with some authority, but the crowd just continue touching his arm, his face, anything they can get their hands on.

"Push your way through, Alex!"

I manage to re-gain my balance and push my way passed two twenty-something guys who glare at me, trying to understand what is going on and why Riccardo D'Angelo is at the barriers instead of onstage. My heart continues to pound through my chest, my breathing heavier than it's ever been.

I need to sit down, I need to lie down, I need cold water.

Get me out of here, oh my God.

We miss each other by about fifteen centimetres and I am frustrated, scared and overwhelmed all at once.

Come on Alex, just reach his hand.

I push myself forward with all my might, and Ric steps onto the second step of the barrier in order to reach me. Half his body is now in the crowd and people are touching him everywhere. He ignores them, and I reach, reach, reach for his hand.

I am just about able to reach Ric's hand and I grab it. He holds on tight, the strongest anyone has ever held my hand, and Goddamnit, I hate to admit it but there is an element of safety and comfort that infiltrates my soul as soon as he grips my hand.

I feel a hundred pounds lighter, and I am able to regain some of my strength. He heaves me towards him, but it feels as if he is a million miles away.

"Bring her to me!" Ric orders some guys in the crowd, and this time they listen. They push me forward, and once I am close enough to Ric, he pulls me up from under my armpits and puts me over his shoulder.

"It's okay!" he tells me loudly in my ear, as he steps down from the barriers, all the security guards watching us in disbelief. I feel like a cat being rescued by the RSPCA. The only thing missing is a fucking blanket and an 'aaaaw' from the crowd.

Ric carries me backstage quickly, breathing heavily as he does so, and he sets me down gently on the floor of the corridor, as if he's too panicked, too worried, too concerned to make it all the way to the green room. He kneels in front of me as he exhales.

"Are you okay?!" he says, in-between breaths.

Security guards and men with clipboards follow. "Is she okay?"

"Riccardo-"

"Back off, I'll be back onstage in *one* minute, just give me a second," he turns to me, his eyes widening. "Oh, wait! I know!"

He runs down the corridor into the green room, and I wonder where he's going as I try to catch my breath. My heart palpitations are out of control, and the three men in front of me just stare in bewilder. No one offers to help me, they simply stare.

Pretty sure this is the most embarrassing moment of my life.

Ric runs back down the corridor to me. "Here!" he kneels again in front of me as he hands me a cold bottle of water.

He remembered. He remembered me telling him I suffer from heart palpitations, he remembered me telling him what I do if I have an episode.

I take a gulp and nothing happens. I take a few gulps and finally, my heart rate begins to slow. The beats are still strong though and I continue to breathe heavily.

"Riccardo-"

"One minute!"

"Go," I tell him in-between gulps of water. I only just realise my forehead is sweaty and I am boiling hot. I take off my cardigan as Ric continues to stare at me with concern. "Go, Ric. I'm fine. I'll be fine."

Ric and I keep our eyes on another, until he eventually gets up. "Keep drinking water and go lie down on the sofa," he tells me. "I'll see you after the show."

I watch him walk back onstage with the security guards, roadies and managers accompanying him, as if making sure he actually makes it there.

"Well, well," says a voice I vaguely recognise, just as I get up. I look up to see Parker May walking towards me. He gives me a charming smile as per usual and I can't help but smile back.

He's always dressed in tight black clothes it seems, and he looks as attractive as he did the first time I met him back on the stage of Arena Civica. "You just *had* to be a part of the show, didn't you?"

"I'm an attention whore, what can I say?"

He cocks up an eyebrow at me, playfully.

"Well that certainly got everyone's attention. Are you okay? Do you need a doctor? We have one around here somewhere-"

"No, no, I'm fine, don't worry."

"Let me help you," he gently puts a hand on my forearm, and helps me walk over to the green room just opposite us.

I crash onto the sofa, and he fetches me a cold towel. "Thanks."

"You should exercise more."

I give him a curious look.

"My little sister suffers from heart palpitations; exercise helps. Running, boxing, intense work outs."

"I usually run. I guess since I've been in Italy I haven't been taking it as seriously."

"Always take the health of your body seriously," he tells me. He's about to go on when he hesitates, tilts his head slightly and looks at me curiously. "Oh shit. You're that girl!"

I give him a baffled look.

"You interviewed Paolo Petrinelli at San Siro and got him to rap."

I always seem to forget that that happened, that sometimes, out of nowhere, people recognise my face. It's happened five times already since I've been in Milano. "Wow, that was a *good* interview," he tells me. "Getting him to rap was a fantastic idea – that shit went viral."

I give him a smile of gratitude to the high praise. "Thanks."

"Parker!" says a female voice and two slutty groupies appear in the green room. They look at me with the towel on my forehead and then at Parker. "Are you coming?" one of them is holding a bottle of champagne in their hand, the other a couple of plastic cups.

"Yep," he looks back at me, "see you later, attention whore. Look after yourself."

I nod. "Have fun, and thanks."

He gives me Charming Parker smile, and I am suddenly alone in the green room.

Embarrassed.

Weak.

Foolish.

Feeling as if, I should have known better.

I hate having episodes even when no one is around; imagine just how embarrassed I was to have one in front of thousands of people. I'm sure it was caught on camera – me needing to be saved by a man.

Me needing Ric to save me.

I want to continue feeling disgusted with myself but I'm exhausted; I fall asleep pretty quickly and only awake when the show is over and people begin to come into the green room.

Everyone in the band comes in except Ric. Everyone asks if I'm okay, and what had happened. I don't like that everyone now knows I suffers from heart palpitations and try hard to constantly change the subject as fast as I can.

I wonder how much trouble Ric is going to get in for leaving the stage for me, and I am filled with guilt. I wish I had stayed at the side of the stage or sat with the rest of the friends and family of the band.

I picture the label bosses giving him a stern talking to, tour managers asking him what the hell he was thinking.

You can't just stop a show to go and help a girl in the crowd, I don't care who she is! People pay good money to see Paolo Petrinelli and his band, and that's what they expect!

Ric is the last to come in. I am alone in the green room when he does so; everyone has gone home. I'm starting to drift off again when I hear footsteps.

He strolls in, duffel bag on his shoulder, and only one thing on his mind.

I get up instantly, throwing my arms around his neck. He welcomes them, dropping his duffel bag to the floor and wrapping his arms tightly around my waist.

"Are you okay? How you feeling?"

I don't say anything, I just keep hugging him. Somehow I need to hug him, to feel him close to me.

I don't care if a guy 'saved' me, I needed saving dammit. And I want to say thank you but the words can't seem to come out of my mouth.

"Hey...." he pulls away from the hug to study me, resting his hands on my waist. "You okay?"

"I'm fine Ric, how did it go? What did they say? Are you in trouble?"

"No, they just had a stern word with me, asked why I had come to help you, etcetera. But those fucking security guards were doing fuck all! Their job is to stop things like that happening, but they weren't doing shit!

Anyway Paolo sees it as a good thing, it'll probably be mentioned in the newspapers tomorrow and will make the band look good, so it's fine. In a way I did them a favour. You should have heart palpitations more often."

My eyes widen.

"I'm joking," he puts a hand on my cheek, "feeling better? God Alex, you scared the shit out of me."

"I'm fine, I slept a bit. But it's so embarrassing," I tell him, as I sit down on the sofa and he joins me with a confused look.

"What, why?"

"Because everyone knows I have heart palpitations now, everyone *saw* me have one!"

"Oh *no*, how will Alexis Brunetti survive now that everyone knows she has a weakness? That she isn't all strong and thick skinned? That maybe, just maybe, underneath that toughness there's a bit of human in her?" he tells me playfully, but I wonder if there is an element of seriousness to his words.

"Shut up," I blush and he kisses me on the cheek.

"Nothing wrong with people knowing you need taking care of sometimes," he gets up, "let's get out of here."

"Ric…" I look at him, remembering what I had felt when I had grabbed his hand in the crowd. He had saved me and I want to thank him, to tell him how much I appreciate it, but I can't.

The words can't seem to come out of my mouth. It's as if if I say thank you, I will seem weak.

He continues to stare at me curiously, wondering what I want to say. I suddenly pull him to me and hug him tightly once more. He hugs me back just as tightly, kissing my hair.

I may not have been able to *say* thank you but somehow, I think it reached him anyhow.

When Giuliano walks into the studio to see me eating apple pie straight from the tinfoil, I should probably be embarrassed, but I'm not.

"Buongiorno!" I chirp, and he returns a good morning in a much less enthusiastic tone. I'm eating apple pie with my left hand, and drawing with my right.

This time I'm sketching a bird singing happily, and he's pooping out a much smaller bird at the same time. Giuliano leans over me and glances at the sketch with a raised eyebrow.

"Very weird," he tells me, as he walks over to the coffee machine out in the corridor. I know his daily routine like the back of my hand – first he switches on all the equipment, then he gets a coffee, then he listens to some Led Zeppelin, and then it's down to work.

The door flings open and G strolls in. The band have been coming into the studio early for quite a few days now.

"Morning G," I say to him.

He nods at me, keeping the grin, as he carries guitars into the studio. It's funny how he's the only real emo in the band, but he's also the most smiley.

Since that afternoon of rock education a couple of days ago, the band have been acknowledging me. Just hi and bye, little things, but it makes such a difference to my day.

I think they appreciated the legends I introduced them to, and call me crazy, but I've seen them be brighter, happier individuals since. It makes me glad. They may be shit musicians, but they're alright to talk to.

It's G's guitar parts today – Lino's drum parts are finally done, and it feels as if it has dragged on for several years. I didn't remember how strenuous it is to record an EP.

Lino broke down, cried, procrastinated, ate, got drunk, got high and even spent an hour laughing on the leather sofa at absolutely nothing, before he finished all the drum parts.

I am a huge, huge hater of procrastination. I say get shit done, to get more shit done. The greatest musicians, leaders, and successful people in this world did not spend an hour of their day laughing into a pillow. That's all I'm saying.

Elliot comes bursting through, holding some gear in his hands, followed by Matteo, which I am now used to. It seems Matteo is always a metre or two behind Elliot, wherever he goes. I suppose that is the stereotypical insecure and shy bassist role, but he does often remind me of a timid chipmunk.

"Buongiorno, Alexis!" Elliot wails, and my smile only grows bigger. He hovers over my shoulder as I draw.

"You're good – that's an interesting sketch," he tells me, as he takes a bite out of his pizza slice. Elliot has a similar habit to me in that he never stops eating. Pre, post and during recording. If I were a musician, I'd probably have a slice of pizza in my mouth whilst playing too. As Bailey always tells me, *I hope I meet someone who looks at me the way you look at carbs.*

I love food, and I have never been ashamed of it.

"Thanks, Elliot." He goes over to his gear and starts to unpack. I finish my drawing and get up, walking over to him as the others disappear into the studio. Before I can say anything, Elliot plays a riff and I frown.

"The Fight Song," I say. *He likes Marilyn Manson?*

Elliot gives me a smile. "Yeah, you know it?"

"Do I know Marilyn Manson? That's like asking me if I know Hendrix. The question is, do *you* know Marilyn Manson?"

"I do. I may not have listened to any joy Division, but I know my Manson," he tells me. "He's the reason I became a guitarist."

My respect for Elliot is rising and fast. But I can't work out his taste in music and it begins to irritate me. You can tell a lot about a person if you know what their taste in music is. I study Elliot as he tunes his guitar, and I suddenly get an idea.

I grab my iPod and go back over to him. "Tell me when you like a song," I order, and he replies 'okay' in intrigue.

First is Limp Bizkit's 'Take A Look Around' and he shakes his head.

Second is Metallica's 'Whiskey in the Jar' and again he shakes his head.

Third is System of a Down's 'B.Y.O.B' and the head just keeps shaking.

Fourth is Royal Blood's 'Figure it Out', and Elliot slowly stops shaking his head as he listens. I wait in fascination for a reaction as the music builds and builds. I stare at him as he listens intently, and I find him a rather curious character. He has friendly eyes, but you can somehow tell that he grew up rough, that music is what triumphed over what I can feel was not the simplest and innocent of childhoods.

Perhaps it's his tattoos or the way he holds himself, but I just know he's been in a few scuffles in his life so far, and yet, he has the softest teddy bear eyes.

We reach the chorus and the real guitars kick in. Elliot is now grinning as he begins to bop his head to the music.

And we have a winner.

"Royal Blood," I tell him, before he can ask. I skip ahead to 'Little Monster'.

"Hey, I was listening to that!" he says, but before I can reply he is lapping up the guitar riffs of 'Little Monster'.

Okay, so he's a Royal Blood type of person. He appreciates good guitar riffs, with a dash of heavy rock.

Excellent taste.

"They're a Scottish duo – fantastic musicians!" I shout over the music.

"I love the guitar riff!"

I skip track again to 'Hole'.

"Alexis, can you stop changing song?!" Elliot tells me, about to moan at me some more before his eyes widen at the beat drop. "*Holy shit,* what is this song?!"

As the music hits and I can no longer hold back, I bop my head and play air guitar, my red hair flying everywhere. Elliot beams and goes nuts too. We hop onto the sofa as we air guitar in synch and laugh as we do so. I can feel Elliot's love for good music and it's connecting us in the most potent way.

This is what music should be about – the capability to give you the most beautiful and potent energy out there.

The doors burst open suddenly and out come the band from the studio.

"Ready?" G asks him, and Elliot nods, turning to me.

"Come on, we have to show you something."

Oh shit, did they break another instrument?

Before I know it, Elliot grabs my sleeve and pulls me into the recording booth, where all the boys have set up as if they are about to play something.

"Guys, only one of you can be in here playing at a time," I explain, and I notice that an element of anxiety is present in all of their eyes, except Damiano's.

He looks his usual stubborn and moody self as he adjusts his mic. And yet, as I look a little closer, I manage to spot a tiny glimmer of hope in his eyes.

Has that always been there or is that new?
It's definitely new.

"What's going on?"

"So we wrote something," Elliot explains to me, "and we'd like to see what you think."

"Something new? A new song?"

He nods with a proud smile.

"But we're halfway through recording the songs Gavin agreed? We wouldn't be able to fit in any other tracks-"

"Just hear us out," Elliot tells me, and before I can reply Lino has started playing. Damiano nods his head to the beat, and Matteo jumps in on bass.

But it's only when Elliot begins the main guitar riff that my eyes widen in curiosity. It is a simple riff, and yet it is alluring; good chord structure, and he's playing in tune. It's catchy, and rocky, and…it works.

It frekin' works.

G follows in on rhythm, and finally, Damiano's voice. His voice is out of tune, but it doesn't phase me. It can be worked on, fixed by going to singing lessons; I know if he is trained properly he will be able to really soothe you with his voice.

It's the guitar riff that has my full attention, and rhythm too. They sound exceptionally, well, decent, and I find myself listening to every element to the song, as if my heart is singing along too, connecting to the band, and their music, for the very first time.

The song is growing on me more and more with every passing second, it's not quite done or complete – it is after all a demo, but there's something about it that is truly, truly magical.

And you know what it is? It's original. They took inspiration from great music of all decades, and they created something new.

It is in this moment that I see the boys in front of me as musicians for the very first time. It brings me instant excitement, as I see their potential in front of me.

Behind their shitty dress sense, Damiano's awful singing voice, and crappy stage structure, the fundamental underlying truth, as I suddenly am able to see, is that they have the potential to actually become good musicians.

Artists.

Creatives.

I listen on with an overwhelming smile on my face, nodding my head to the song. They all keep their eyes on me as they play with smiles on their faces, except Damiano. He is looking at me as if he is looking straight through me, unphased by whether I like the song or not.

It's the way he has always looked at me and it doesn't bother me.

It feels as if everything has suddenly slowed down as I watch them play. They are playing in joy, in the sheer pleasure of creating music, of creating something to be proud of. Up until then, I'm not quite sure they were proud of what they were creating.

As an artist, if you're not proud of your own music, why are you releasing it? Above and beyond what the audience will think, an artist should love and be obsessed with what they have created.

And it's only now, as I watch them play a semi-decent song, that I see that in the boys. And it makes me giddy inside; privileged to be the person able to witness this very important moment for them. And grateful that they chose me for it.

We have only known each other a week and a half, and we have only been properly conversing for three days, but I feel like I've known them a lifetime.

Everyone except Damiano, of course.

Once the song ends, they look at me for my reaction. I slow clap with a grin on my face, not sure how to even begin to express my surprise, excitement and pride at what they have just played me.

"*Guys!* Oh my God. I love it. What *is* this sound?! Could it be the real sound of the Devilled Eggs? The one they've been hiding from the world up until now?!"

They beam back at me.

"Ric helped us," Elliot tells me, "and your playlist the other day helped tons."

"Wow, that's amazing! I'm so excited for the next EP-"

"We want it for *this* EP," Matteo declares, and I am not sure what to say as I take in this information.

All I see is smoke coming out of Gavin's ears as I suggest the idea to him.

"THEY WANT TO DO WHAT?" he would say. "WHO THE FUCK DO THEY THINK THEY ARE, WRITING NEW SONGS AFTER WE SPENT A TON OF MONEY TO RECORD THE ORIGINAL ONES? ARE THEY FUCKING KIDDING ME?"

"Um, guys, Ruby wants an EP of the songs Gavin already agreed-"

"There's always time to change tracks," Elliot continues, "we could write a whole bunch of new songs, we just need somewhere to practise."

"My father won't lend us any more money," Damiano chimes in, and even he looks hopeful about a new EP.

"Could you ask Gavin for us?" Elliot says, and I gulp.

"We really want to get this right," Lino adds.

"Yeah."

Without thinking twice, I find myself nodding. And the words that then follow shock me more than they shock the boys.

"No worries, I'll ask Gavin. And I'll find you a rehearsal space too."

Are you insane, Alex?
How the fuck are you going to do that?
And with what money?
Are you out of your mind?

I drown out my inner voice with the sound of the guitar riff Elliot has just played me, and I'm suddenly okay.

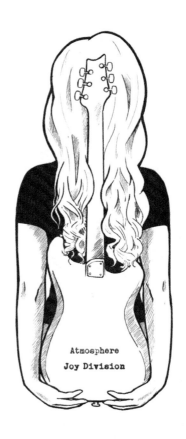

14

When I first heard about the recession I was eighteen, and I swear to God, I thought it was some sort of perfume. Kids brought up in the late eighties or early nineties grew up under the impression that once they would graduate, it was a *guarantee* that there would be jobs waiting for them.

They grew up watching uncles and aunts get into the line of work they wanted; they were taught in school that they could literally be whoever they chose to be. And I truly did believe that after university, there would be companies lining up to employ me.

I mean, I'm talented, so everything else had to fall into place, right?

Wrong.

I struggled that first six months after graduation. I struggled with getting to grips with the fact that the world didn't exist the way it had been described to me throughout my childhood and my teens.

Nobody warns you of the issues out there in the 'real world', nobody even teaches you how to do your taxes. You have to learn to do everything yourself, and if you want to earn something in this world, you better fight like crazy to get it. Because, and I wish they would teach this in schools, but the greatest lesson I have learnt in life so far is that the world doesn't owe you a Goddamn thing.

It takes me seven hours to find a decent rehearsal space for the Devilled Eggs. It's in southern Milano and it's a loft on the top floor of an art building. The lift opens into the room itself, and you're faced with a garage-sized space with typical lofty vibes. I pay for a week's rent with my own money, and I call Elliot to let him and the others know.

I don't know what has possessed me to take control of this band's career when up until three days ago we all hated each other's guts.

The truth is I suppose that I never really hated them – I could never hate anyone. But a band that is willing to learn about other bands, and then incorporate that into their music in order to become better, to evolve. I mean, how could I not support that?

They're kids, and yet it seems they have a hell of a lot more ambition than they first led on. And this only makes me want to help them, to encourage them to take themselves further, to ultimately see them create good music.

They didn't *have* to write new songs, they didn't *have* to beg me to find a way to make it their EP, but they did. And this in turn, turned me into a super determined crazy bitch.

I take pictures of the loft and send them to Ric. He usually replies in-between rehearsals, telling me how his day is going.

My phone buzzes as I'm plugging in my iPod to the speakers. I put on Viigo's 'Beautiful' and check my messages.

Ric:
Nice place!
Should be interesting
Meanwhile, here Kyle is messing up on some chords
I feel as if becoming a father has him really struggling to be a musician at the same time
Will try to give him a pep talk at our next break
See you tonight x

I smile, and just as I'm about to reply, the lift bells and out step the band. They look around in intrigue.

"Wow!"

"You like?" I ask.

"Oh, hell yeah!"

"Yesss!"

"Awesome!"

Even Damiano comments, saying a very quiet 'nice' under his breath.

"This place isn't first class or anything, but it's a place where you can create music that is truly your sound as a band. This is where the magic for you guys is gonna happen, I can feel it. And this place is yours for the rest of the week. Let's see where we get by Thursday, okay?"

They nod at me, and I plop myself down on the sofa, exhausted. I close my eyes for a moment as the band start to set up, excited.

"What's that?" I hear a voice say, and I open my eyes to see the shy bassist standing near me, pointing at something. I turn and spot the book I'm reading peeping out of my bag.

"Oh, Kill My Friends – a fiction novel on the music business. Pretty good."

"…but?"

A little surprised that Matteo has spotted my hesitation, I shake it off. "Uh, I guess it'd be good to read a book on the music business from the female perspective. You know, it's a little different to the male perspective. The challenges differ."

Matteo nods in agreement, though I'm not sure he entirely understands what I mean.

"*WAIT! WHAT, THE FUCK?* Alexis, is this you?!" Elliot bellows, rushing over to me with an open newspaper. I look on in intrigue until Elliot shows me the double page spread and my eyes widen.

It's a picture of Ric carrying me over the barriers at last night's gig. I cover my mouth with both my hands and mutter 'oh shit' under my breath. I pull the cover of the newspaper to discover it is a national paper.

I curse in Italian under my breath, wondering if my mum has seen this.

"What the hell happened?!" Elliot asks, all five of them gathering around to check out the article.

"Nothing, I just got lost in the crowd."

"But how does that even happen?!"

"Yeah, what's the deal with you two anyway?" G asks, as if the entire band has been dying to ask me this since the day we showed up on Damiano's doorstep.

"We're friends. We met in London," I tell them, deciding to leave out the part where we're also fuck buddies.

211

"So what happened out there?" Lino asks, and the rest of them, apart from Damiano, chime in with 'yeah!' and take their places on the sofa surrounding me.

I have their full attention, and it feels as if I am their nursery teacher and they are the toddlers gathering around me to hear a story. It's funny to think that just a few days ago all five of them were ignoring me.

And so I tell them the sequence of events that took place last night – how I always love to watch a gig as part of the crowd, as if I am part of something much bigger than me. How I could tell straight away that it was a wilder bunch of people in the standing area than it usually is. How the moshing was out of control, and I got groped a few times. How the elbows to the face were dangerous and the broken glass on the floor even more so.

They seem shocked and outraged that women can get so mistreated at gigs, all the groping and physical pain something they have never heard about.

I ask them if they've ever done anything like that and they shake their heads, Damiano included. "The only groping I do is on a bed," G adds, to which Elliot snorts and calls him a square.

"Why is he a square? Are you saying what men do at gigs is okay?" I ask.

"No, of course not. I'm just saying there's better places to grope the girl you're dating – like public bathrooms, on the train, on a plane-"

"Okay, okay, okay-"

"Rooftops, sofas, rollercoasters..."

Yes, Elliot is definitely the lothario of the band, and it makes sense. He is the most handsome one, and he brings the most charisma when they perform. He is also the most confident.

I tell them all how Ric dropped everything, ran offstage and came to help me out of there. I leave out the part where I suffer from a heart palpitation, as I don't think that's necessary for them to know. I'm trying to portray myself as mature and reliable – they do not need to know my weaknesses.

Matteo, who is becoming less and less shy by the minute, shares a story of when he saw a woman getting hit on at a restaurant by a 'sleezeball' and the manager, who was apparently very well built, stepped in and got the supposed 'sleezeball' to back off.

The woman ended up leaving her number to the manager, but once she left, this 'sleezeball' and manager high-fived one another. Apparently it had been a scam all along, and Matteo can't believe it.

He's so shocked as he tells the story, as if he can't believe scams actually exist, as if he lives in a world where birds dress you in the morning and the tooth fairy leaves you money. It makes me smile as I watch him tell the story with stunned eyes.

I realise that the Devilled Eggs are just a bunch of innocent boys playing music together. They are not manipulative, or severely unkind to anyone. Except Damiano, but that's okay.

There has to be a black sheep in every band.

I enjoy spending time with them, and I want to help them with their new set of tracks as much as I can before I am due to fly back to London. That only gives me a few more days, but I'm confident a lot can be accomplished in that time.

Plus, they'll be moving to London before we know it. Maybe Gavin will let me work with them again, continue with them, since I helped the band in the beginning. It makes sense.

I stay until late, we order pizza, they perform the new track a couple more times and I fall more and more in love with it every time I hear it.

I can't help but grin every time I hear it, and I do so as I bop my head to it, gulping down pizza slice after pizza slice (Elliot at one point even saying, "*Girl*, you eat a *lot.*"

Well, they were bound to find out sooner or later I suppose.

The boys get up and set up, whilst I lie back on the sofa. I have a good feeling about this, about them, about where they could head from here. And when I agreed to help them it didn't feel like an option. I'm in Milano to help them with their music; I know this now.

Elliot's playing snaps me out of my thoughts and I turn around to find him approaching me as he plays a Blink 182 riff. I groan in playful frustration and hide my head under the pillow. He knows I am not a fan of Blink.

Elliot pulls the guitar as close to my ear as his guitar strap permits and I squirm.

"No, go away!" I squeal, as he laughs.

"I thought you loved Blink?!"

"Fuck you, Elliot!" I hear him cackle some more as he steps back and I get out my phone to order some pizza.

"You ready?" G asks Elliot, who nods. I watch them as all five of them step out to take a hit. I'm not sure what they take but I can guess it's probably more than a joint or two.

They step out at least twice in a recording session, and it's always all five of them, as if they can only take them when they are together.

I hate drugs, but I've decided I can't say anything – being anti-drugs in the music business instantly makes you either too *old* for this industry, or too young.

It's probably the thing I hate most about working in music – drugs are seen as the complete norm. If you're not on them, you're not 'normal'.

But I just have to grin and bear it – if I go around starting in on my anti-drugs rant, I am the only one who will lose.

Once they return, I play them some indie music – Metric, Augustines, Band of Skulls, and then some Kings of Leon, the more unknown songs – such as 'California Waiting' which is one of my favourite songs. They seem to like it too.

It's past midnight when I decide it's time to go. Ric will be home by now anyway, and I need a good three rounds to sleep well.

I turn on my heel to leave, looking back at them. "I'll be back tomorrow. Good luck."

"Alexis!" Elliot calls after me, as I press the button for the lift. He comes over and stands next to me, as the others begin to set up. "This," he points up to the ceiling, referring to the rehearsal space, "is very cool, thank you."

"No problem. Just get out a legendary EP of songs please. Thanks."

He gives me a charismatic smile. "We will. Hey, have you asked Gavin yet?"

I gulp, and a shiver travels down my spine. "Not yet. Gonna do it now, I'll call him now."

He nods, and my lift arrives. "See you tomorrow, Alexis."

"See you." A wave of nerves hit me as I step into the lift and the doors close. I know what I have to do, but I'm afraid to do it.

Surely if it makes the band better, then that's in the interest of Ruby Records? How could Gavin be mad at me?

I step out on the ground floor, and call Gavin. It rings, and rings, and I'm grateful when it goes to voicemail.

This is Gavin, please leave a message and I'll get back to you as soon as I can.

"Hi Gavin, it's Alexis. Just wanted to run something past you – as you know, the Devilled Eggs' music sucks. However, they have come to me with a new song, and it's really great. And the boys would really like to record a new set of songs instead of the ones previously approved by Ruby.

They're currently working on these new songs and they should be ready by end of week. The boys would really like to know if, um, if I sent over these songs, if you would be open to listening to them and re-recording?

I think it would really be worth it. Please call me back when you can," I hang up, just as I make my way through the double doors of the building and am faced with the busy main streets of southern Milano.

I feel nauseous as I head to the metro station, but I walk as if I am absolutely fine.

When I awake, it takes me a few seconds to realise where I am. I'm in Ric's bed, in Ric's flat, and, can you believe it – I had fallen asleep. My eyes widen in shock, as I sit up and grab my phone to check the time. It's 6:51AM.

I recall the evening's events – dinner with Ric, followed by three rounds of sex, and an episode of Breaking Bad, which I convinced him to start watching and now, surprise surprise, he's addicted.

What kind of a weirdo has never watched Breaking Bad, anyway?

215

I had then unexpectedly fallen asleep. Not in his arms, which makes it less bad, but, I mean, I still fell asleep *in his bed. With him in it.*

I haven't done that in, well, years. It feels weird, as if I shouldn't be doing it, for I do not belong in this bed, not to sleep. And yet, as I continue glancing at the time, I don't feel like getting up and calling a taxi back to my flat, which is all the way on the other side of town.

It's a practical decision to make, I decide. And so I stay. After all, we both have an early start heading to the stadium together for the final Paolo gig. So it makes more sense to stay. Much more sense.

I slump back into horizontal position, and close my eyes. As expected however, I can no longer sleep. I'm a strange human, in the sense that I cannot sleep in a bed with other people, whoever they may be. I feel uncomfortable and start to tense. I've been this way my entire life, and I doubt I'll ever change.

Okay, just remain awake, it's only another three hours until you both have to get up anyway.

But I get bored, and consider getting up to read a book or something. Yet at the same time, I'm determined to fall back to sleep. I *hate* that I can't do what most other humans do so easily. I've always wondered how other people manage it; how they can relax and become defenceless in another person's bed.

I can't do it. I've never been able to do it, I'll never be able to do it. Even for convenience. My mind, body and soul simply do not relax, they do not trust anyone, they do not allow me to sleep with someone else in the bed.

I toss and turn anxiously, trying to find a position that is comfortable for me, but I'm failing miserably. It feels as if I am not capable of falling asleep in any scenario, that I have never been capable of sleeping, and that I'm going to remain awake and an insomniac for the rest of my life.

Sleeping is suddenly the hardest thing in the world for me, and I feel intense frustration at this failure.

I am weak. I am weird. I am incapable of asking my body to do something, and of my body complying. I am incapable of being normal.

I feel Ric move next to me and a pang of nerves hit my stomach. Up until now, he has been completely still, and I had assumed he was a heavy sleeper.

I'm lying on my side facing him, and I see his eyes suddenly open. We look at one another in the darkness of his room in silence for what seems like an eternity. His eyes are so full of warmth, almost as if they could hypnotise me simply from how kind they are.

He slowly reaches out his hand, and caresses my cheek. "Relax," he whispers, and his touch soothes my soul, calming it instantly. I am not sure what is happening, but it feels so good. I don't say anything, I simply close my eyes to take in his touch.

"I'm trying," I eventually say, giving in to the fact that Ric can always seem to read me. Even when I don't want him to.

Uncomfortable and suddenly defensive with what I've just admitted to, I turn to lie on my back and stare up at the ceiling.

I don't want him to look at me, to connect with my vulnerability. I feel as if this was a bad idea, that I should have got up and left when I first woke up. That this is all wrong and useless and I'm only going to be seen for who I really am – a complete and utter weirdo. Because that is what I am, I mean, what kind of freak can't sleep in a bed with another person?

Ric slowly moves in closer to me, and rests his head on my chest. I haven't had someone rest their head on my chest in a very long time, and it feels weird.

I welcome it however, and I don't know why I do. My mind is saying different things to my actions – I put my arm around him, and run my fingers through his soft hair. It feels nice, and comfortable, and, almost even calming.

"Relax Alex," he tells me, and before I can reply, I fall asleep. Instantly.

I wake up at Ric's and it takes me a couple of seconds to remember where I am. I re-live my struggle to fall asleep, Ric's hand on my cheek, and my eyes instantly widen.

He cuddled me.
I cuddled him.

I gulp, and glance over at his sleeping face. He looks even more handsome when he sleeps.

My phone buzzes on the nightstand, and it's Elliot. He's sent me a picture of the other four playing at their rehearsal space. I smile, and text back.

Alex:
I better hear some legendary rock tracks tomorrow!

I turn and lie on my back, putting the phone back on the nightstand and studying the ceiling as I think about the boys. Gavin has yet to reply or call me back, and I'm getting nervous.

Should I call him again? Leave another voicemail?

I shake my head, deciding that one voicemail is more than enough.

I feel Ric move next to me and he groans. "Morning," he says to me.

"Morning," I reply, awkwardly. All of this feels so weird – falling asleep at his, cuddling, waking up to each other. It's way too coupley for my taste.

And yet you stayed anyway, Alex.

He moves over to me and starts kissing my shoulder, my neck, my left cheek. And I'm torn. A part of me very much wants to have sex, and very much wants to have sex with Ric.

The other part of me however, feels uncomfortable for the first time ever with him, and that part of me, the bigger part, needs to get out of this bed.

"Mmm, I'm gonna have a shower," I tell him, slipping out and leaving him in his bed alone. His arms are out, hugging the empty space where I had just been lying.

"Seriously? Never seen you reject sex," he tells me, matter-of-factly. I can see he is a little hurt and I try to perk up.

"Well you may just be satisfying me then," I wink at him and he brightens, as I slip into the bathroom.

Once I close the door, I sigh in relief. I am not sure what is happening, but I am relieved to be on the other side of the door.

It feels weird and uncomfortable, but I know it will pass if we just don't touch each other for a while.

Argh, touchy-feely coupley stuff.

Vomit.

Boundaries need to stay boundaries if a fuck buddy system is to remain intact.

Once we reach the stadium Ric is a little nervous – he has *nine* solos tonight, and some important label people are going to be in the audience. It's so intriguing to see him nervous for once, and I try to calm him with kind words as we walk through the backstage door.

I tell him a joke about girls fainting at his solos, just as he is suddenly approached by five different people in the tech team.

I leave him with them and spend sound check video calling with Blake, catching up on news whilst I wolf down Paolo's triple chocolate cake. There's always such delicious food backstage at Paolo's gigs and everyone else seems oblivious to it.

"I thought you liked being part of the crowd?" asks Kyle's wife, Caroline, as she nurses baby Mina in her arms. Caroline is the all-out American housewife – blonde, blue eyes, and she wears the trousers in their marriage. It takes two minutes of seeing them together to figure it out.

"Kyle didn't tell you? There was trouble last time, a few moshing maniacs. They went a little crazy," I explain, and she looks at me, appalled.

"Oh *no*, are you okay?"

"Yeah, yeah, just prefer watching from backstage tonight. Plus I know all the songs and solos off by heart myself now," I say, with a playful roll of the eyes.

The truth is, even if I know every song and every show inside out now, I always love watching the Paolo gigs, simply to see Ric perform, to get the solos he so very much deserves.

I do however wish that I had the guts to join the crowd. They don't look so crazy tonight, and yet I am unable to move from the side of the stage. There is absolutely nothing stopping me, that is keeping me from joining the audience, to take in the gig the way it is supposed to.

And yet, I do not move.

It's a terrific show, and the crowd go wild with excitement at each and every one of Ric's solos, with Mauro only looking on with a semi-miserable face. I feel a little sorry for him, but the sympathy dies fairly quickly as I remember that Ric worked hard for this, and that Mauro has been the lead guitarist for the past ten years. Also, he's not even good.

I watch Ric brimming with pride, *woo*ing from the side of the stage, as he delivers each and every solo exceptionally well. He looks so happy, so excited, as if he has been waiting a lifetime for this moment. And it really warms my heart to witness.

The emotional element to it hits me pretty hard – thinking about who he is, the fact that he is a self-made guitarist who worked hard to get where he is. No rich parents, millionaire cousin, or best friend record producer. He did it all by himself, and this is a fucking rare sight in the music business.

I don't know about other industries, but I know that in music it's *who you know* that will get you places. Not for Ric, though. He pushed through all barriers, through the strong friendship between Paolo and Mauro, by being talented. And he succeeded. I am inspired by him, by his drive, by his talent, and I am so very happy for him.

I want to be like Ric, I keep thinking as I watch him. I want to remain humble, but keep developing my skills, and someday, maybe I'll be an artist manager. Not through knowing the right people, not through using my contacts or my status, but through talent. And remaining grounded. Always.

I think I've decided what I want to be. Hanging out with the Devilled Eggs has made me see how much I enjoy looking after a band, and I want to do it full time, earning money from it.

I see it – me as an artist manager. I think I'd be pretty good at it; keeping artists away from sharks, helping them develop their music, advising them on how to keep their reputation clean, negotiating their record deals.

Yes, I want to be an artist manager, and I'm in the right internship for it.

Just don't mess it up, Alex.

As soon as the show is over, I remain to the side of the stage, taking a deep breath in or two to recover. I can't let Ric see me like this – emotional over his solos, over how far he has come. But I can't help it – when he's up there performing, I feel as if I am up there with him.

I watch the roadies carry everything offstage, as Paolo and some of the others pass me, giving me a smile. Ric is nowhere in sight.

Where did he go?

Kyle comes offstage, distracted, and he suddenly looks at me, smiling, as I spot Ric on the other side of the stage, talking to a man in a suit.

"Journalist from Rolling Stone Italy," Kyle tells me, pointing a thumb at them.

I frown. "Really? Wow."

"Yeah, exciting, eh?" he winks and disappears down the corridor, and I glance back at Ric and the journalist. He is grinning and moving his hands about passionately, recovering from a brilliant show. I feel the pride rush back to me.

He so deserves this.

I walk down to the green room where it is now packed with people and loud banter. I'm not in the mood to be social though, and so I keep walking before someone can spot me.

I want to be alone, I want to take in this moment, I want to have a moment to be proud of Ric. But I need to get out of this stadium, just for a second. And so I make my way down the corridor, trying to remember where the exit is.

This is going to be the start of a new chapter for Ric; he's going to become even more recognised and established as a guitarist, and then he'll start his solo career and everything will take off.

He is doing it, he is doing what he has wanted to do for the better part of his life. He is pushing past the boundaries of 'Paolo's rhythm guitarist' into his own persona, slowly.

I pass lots and lots of rooms, and the further I walk, the less people I find. I eventually come to the end of the corridor where there is nobody around, and curiously, I peek into the last room. My eyes widen as I spot an acoustic Gibson through the door window.

Forgetting my original intention to find the exit, I open the door in intrigue, and find the room packed with Gibson guitars – acoustic, electric, even a few basses. In the middle is a rectangular desk much like the ones I had had in school; grey, empty and cold.

What catches my eye is not the table though, it's all the SG Gibsons – 64, 65, 66…the possibilities are endless!

What the hell are all these gorgeous guitars doing here?!

I walk around the room, debating whether to touch them or not. It's a strange and overwhelming feeling that comes over me when I am around beautiful guitars. It's as if they are all looking at me, smiling back at me, telling me they love me too. My love for guitars and their sound is sacred, and I am always happier when I am around them.

Guitars take me to another planet, another universe, where everything is so much sweeter.

"Beautiful, right?" says a voice. I turn to find Mauro standing there, leaning on the door with his arms folded and that fake smile planted on his face.

Quick, Alex! Put on your fake Mauro-smile so you can match.

"Yeah."

"How long have you been playing?"

It's weird to see Mauro engaging in conversation with me – I don't think he's once made conversation with me since that day on San Siro stage months ago. He usually ignores me.

"Uh, since I was eleven. Not very good, though," I manage to say. He slowly walks into the room with that Mauro walk of his; like a king entering his kingdom.

"Not true, I've seen you play!"

It's a little weird that he is being especially nice to me when Ric is out there getting interviewed by Rolling Stone Italy, and I feel a bit bad. Mauro is getting old now and he'll probably never become famous in his own name. I can understand his envy.

"They're all Paolo's, can you believe that?" he briefly touches a couple of the acoustics in the corner as he passes them. "They're taken all around tour with us, taken well care of; treated like kings."

I don't say anything, I am instead just watching him circle the room slowly, eyeing all the guitars, until he reaches me.

He stops in front of me with that same smile he always has, that look in his eyes as if he has missed something in his childhood, something good, something warm. "There's even that Gibson 1957 LP."

My eyes light up in semi-excitement. "Really?"

"Yeah, it's back here. We can play a little if you want," he goes to the end of the square room and opens another door, revealing a second room with, from my angle, more stunning guitars. But to tell the truth, I don't particularly want to play with Mauro.

For him it's like he is offering me the world; to me it's like playing some amazing guitars with an old, egotistical and overrated guitarist. I know plenty of Italians out there that at this moment would scream, *'go! it's Mauro Fontana!'* but honestly, when have I ever done something just because it's cool to other people?

Fuck that. I don't like this guy and I certainly do not respect him as a guitarist. I will never play with him unless paid an extortionate amount.

"Um, thanks, but I think I'm gonna go catch up with Ric."

He approaches me with that fake smile never leaving his face for a second. "It'll only be a few minutes, I'm sure he'll be fine. Come on…"

I take a step back, also holding onto a fake smile.

"Maybe another time."

"You've *got* to see this Gibson, Alexis!" he puts his hands on my wrists, still smiling, his grip loose and playful. I'm hit with a feeling that this is turning a little strange. "Come *oon…*"

Why are his hands on my wrists?
How did they get there?
"Nah, I'm gonna go…"
Does he not get the message?

I attempt to shake my arms free from his clutches but as soon as I try, he instantly tightens his grip. I look at him and his eyes are blazing as he continues smiling at me. I gulp, becoming instantly claustrophobic.

Don't panic, he's joking.
He's going to let go now.
He's going to let go now.
He's going to let go now.
"Mauro seriously, let go."
Why the fuck isn't he letting go?!

"Alexis, come on! Nobody will see us back there!" I gulp, and I am now not only seeing the fire in his eyes, but also the evil, the perverse, sexual predator in him – it's there, present his eyes, as real as anything I've ever seen in my life.

Shit.
What the fuck?!

"Let go, Mauro!" his smile turns into a grin, showing me his yellow teeth. "Let go!"

"Alexis, I just wanna play for *five* minutes…" he begins instantly dragging me across the room by the wrists and I shout at the top of my lungs. I shout for help, for him to let go, begging him to do so, but he won't listen, and nobody else can hear me.

As I continue to shout, I try to wriggle out of his grip but Mauro is too damn strong. I try to kick him but he has positioned himself in such a way that I can't reach him, not even his leg.

Why the fuck did you go in here, Alex?!

I'm panicking, my heart is racing, and I'm terrified. He is in control, he has me in his control, and we sure as hell are not going to the back room to play guitar.

"Mauro, let go!"

I see the monster in him, the sordid fuck that he is, and I continue to try to break loose but it's just no use. I have never felt so weak, so powerless, and so humiliated. I wonder if I will ever be able to escape, if I will ever be able to get out of this room.

There are people so damn close to us, just down the corridor, and yet it feels as if I am on another planet, for no one can hear me, and no one can help me. In my mind I beg to be out of here, to make it, to reach freedom, more than I have ever begged for anything in my entire life.

"Come on, Alexis, it'll be fun!"

"No! Help! *Help!*" I wriggle as I try to make him let go and he suddenly swings me round and pushes me up against the desk, his face and body moving closer to me.

I feel a hard lump on my leg and I scream in pure and utter disgust. I am furious and I feel sick to my stomach.

"Energetic girl, aren't you?" he smells of dog biscuits and cheap aftershave, and he studies my face with malevolent eyes.

I impulsively spit in his face, followed by a swift kick in the balls as he takes a few seconds to react. He cries out in pain as he unintentionally lets go of my wrists, I shove him away from me and I run out of the room.

Fuck!

What the fuck was that?!

What the FUCK was that?!

I am free, and I have never felt more grateful to be alive, to be free, to be away from evil.

I run, and I continue to run, as fast as I can. From his touch.

From his breath.

From his voice.

I run to get away from it all, as hot tears invade my eyes, and I try to understand what the *fuck* just happened.

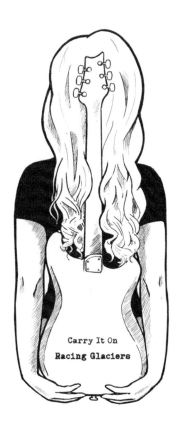

15

My legs are jelly as I run, in fact my whole body has now turned to jelly, and I have tears flooding my eyes, but I still manage to speed through the stadium.

I run down the corridor, arriving outside the green room, but even with poor sight and a trembling body, I don't manage to bump into anyone. Not until Kyle. By then I have wiped my tears away three times and luckily, my cheeks are dry.

"Woah!" he says, as I bump into him and grind to a halt in front of Kyle's bright, smiley face.

"Sorry!" I take off again before he can keep me around for small talk, and more tears rush to my eyes. I keep running, trying to remember where the hell the bathroom is in this maze of a stadium.

Just as I begin to run out of breath, I hear a bellow of 'Alex?!' and know it's Ric. I don't want to see him, I don't want to see anyone, not yet. I just want to go to the bathroom and try and take in what just happened.

What the *hell* just took place.

I begin running even faster, and he runs after me, realising that something is wrong. I spot the bathroom and am instantly relieved I can get away.

I quickly get inside and lock the door behind me. It's one bathroom but it's pretty small. I take a deep breath in, in-between tears, trying to calm myself down. After all, the last thing I need now is a heart palpitation added to the mix.

What the fuck just happened?
I sit down on the toilet seat.
What the fuck was that?
He's a pervert, a fucking pervert.
He was going to…?
Would he have…?

I relive his face and body pressed up against me, the lump on my leg, and I burst into tears. I haven't cried since I was seventeen years old, and it's a weird sensation. It's as if I am being sent straight back to Teenage Alex.

"Alex?!" Ric roars from the other side of the door.

I am still trembling like crazy and Ric's aggressive knocking shakes me so much that I nearly jump out of my skin.

It's Ric, it's not Mauro.
Calm down.
Ric's the good guy, remember?

But I don't want to talk to him, I don't want to tell him what just happened. It's embarrassing, it's humiliating, and it feels as if it is my fault.

It was *me* who went inside that room, it was *me* who didn't leave straight away, it was *me* who smiled at him.

I should have seen it sooner. I should have been able to spot that he's a sordid, twisted pervert.

But he did it all with a smile?
He was trying to confuse you, Alex.

"Alex! What happened?! Open up! Are you okay?" the aggressive knocking is only spooking me out even more and so I get up and open the door.

Ric looks at the sight of my tear-ridden face and gulps as he pushes his way into the bathroom, closing the door behind him with a concerned look. Both of us barely fit in such a small space but this doesn't concern Ric.

"What happened?" he asks in a much softer tone. I stand awkwardly next to him, too embarrassed to tell him.

I can't. It'll make it real.

"Alex?! You're scaring me!"

More tears roll down my cheek. He puts a hand on my upper arm but I instantly move away.

I don't want to be touched; I don't want anybody near me. Ric gulps, noticing the reaction.

He is about to say something when his eyes drop down to my arms. "What happened to your arms?!"

I look down to find that my wrists are red from where Mauro's repulsive hands had been, and it is only now that I realise how much they are aching.

"What the fuck happened to your arms, Alex?!" he says in a much louder tone.

Tell him.
Tell him!
Tell him everything!

"I found a room with Gibson guitars and then Mauro came in and he followed me in there, well I don't know if he followed me but he came in and-"

"*Mauro* did that?!" Ric booms. "*Mauro* did that?!" His eyes are like I have never seen them before; ablaze with anger and fury. He keeps repeating the same question as if even the possibility of it being true could make him explode.

"He tried to…I think he was going to…" my voice dies away with silent tears and Ric is out of there in a shot.

"Ric! Don't! Ric!" I don't know why I am shouting such clichés after him like girls do in films, 'no, don't do it!' when in all honesty whenever I watch those films I am secretly routing for the guy to punch the bad guy, hard.

I wish I could say it's different in real life, that I don't want Ric to humiliate him, but the guy has just fucking sexually assaulted me, can you really blame me?

I run after him, calling his name, recalling the hard look in his eyes before he had shot out of there, and I am now starting to worry, especially the way he doesn't even try to slow down.

I chase a raging Ric down the red corridor, passed lots of roadies and tour crew, skilfully managing to avoid bumping into anyone.

I, on the other hand, am not so successful, being slowed down by people refusing to move out the way for me. I can see Mauro in the distance, smiling and laughing with Roberto and some of the tour crew, and I gulp.

He's acting normal.
Like he didn't just try to drag me into a room.
As if I didn't just feel a lump on my leg.

Though I continue to chase Ric, I am now even angrier, and I turn vindictive. A part of me, the much bigger part, wants Ric to wreak havoc upon him, for Mauro to get a taste of his own medicine.

He stops running and powerwalks the rest of the way over to an oblivious Mauro, but I keep running to catch up, my eyes fixed on them.

Ric marches over and instantly swings a punch at him, Mauro bouncing back as blood floods from his nose. I gasp, grinding to a halt in front of them completely in shock. I cover my mouth with my hands as the people around us react,

229

Roberto quickly shouting 'Riccardo!' in disbelief, shocked eyes everywhere.

A crowd instantly form around us, accompanied by loud voices and gasps.

"You fucking bastard!" he yells at Mauro. Ric's eyes are ablaze with anger, like he doesn't have a care in the world. "You jealous fuck!"

When you see the good guy punch the bad guy it's nothing like it is in the films. For starters there's no slow motion; it takes only a second to punch someone, and then it's over.

Secondly, seeing Ric punch him came with 2% satisfaction and 98% numbness. What had punching him achieved? Other than making Ric look like a maniac? Because in all honesty, as soon as Ric's knuckles touches Mauro's face, he is instantly seen, in all eyes, as a hooligan.

"What are you doing?!" yells Roberto in Italian.

"Stop!" I wail, but it's of no use, Ric is onto his second punch, and just as he punches him in the lip two guys from the tour crew and three roadies step in front of him to stop him going any further.

There is shouting, screaming and panic in the corridor, and I can just about hear the 'that's enough!' in Italian from the people now holding Ric back. I realise as I look around in that moment just how much Ric looks like the monster; a psychopath having an episode.

I am filled with guilt for that split second that I had wanted to see what Ric would do, for that split second that it had felt good to see Mauro get punched and simultaneously have that smirk wiped off his face.

And I realise that there are going to be consequences, big consequences.

Everything good Ric has ever done is now out the window, replaced by an image of him as a thug. My guilt simmers and continues to do so as I watch the chaos unfold in the corridor.

I have a sudden voice in my head telling me to pull Ric out of there. There is too much anarchy. I pull him out of the crowd by the arm forcefully, and into a room as the crowd try to follow, but I quickly close the door behind us with some force. I lock it.

I exhale loudly, still in shock, as silence fills the room we are in. All that can be heard is shouting and yelling from the corridor, demanding to let us in, calling Ric's name. But I keep the door shut on the chaos that awaits us. It has been postponed. Delayed. Put on pause.

On the other side of that door.

"What the hell was that?!" I shriek, my voice becoming strong again, like before I had seen Mauro enter the guitar room.

"What?" he says calmly, as he nurses his red knuckles.

"That! Why did you punch him?! You're gonna get fired now! Oh shit! Oh *shit*! How could you be so stupid?!" I only realise in that moment the ripple effect of his actions.

Paolo is definitely not going to just let him keep playing in the band – this will hit the media, Ric will be seen as some sort of hooligan; his career as Paolo Petrinelli's guitarist is most likely over.

After all the work he had put into getting here. One wrong move, and it can all be taken away.

"He put his hands on you Alex, what the fuck did you think I was going to do?! Pretend like it didn't happen?! Continue playing with him after he tries to rape you?! Are you joking, Alex?!" he shouts back. I have never seen or heard Ric shout before, and it makes me grow an extra layer of skin.

"We don't know that he was going to…" my voice dies away, as I fail to get the words out. The extra layer of skin melts and I feel weak and fragile.

I try my best to snap out of it, gather some strength and raise my voice again. "You're gonna get in trouble for something *he* did! I can look after myself! And I did! I got out of there!"

"He was going to rape you, Alex!"

The word 'rape' sends shivers down my spine and I'm okay if I never hear the word ever again. "Oh my God you shouldn't have done that," I put my hands on my cheeks as I take in what has just happened; two incidents that are leaving me trembling. "I am able to take care of myself, Ric. I don't understand why you did that, oh my *God*. This is your career!" I yell.

"You think I don't know that?! You think I don't care?!"

"Then why did you do it?!"

He does not respond.

"Why did you do it?! Can you tell me why you did it?!"

But when I look into Ric's eyes, I suddenly see something I hoped I'd never see. Something I was so sure that I would never have to see in him.

I take a deep, and extremely anxious breath in, and he gulps, realising that I have seen it.

And it is irreversible.

"Oh shit," I manage to say, and there is silence in the room again.

"Don't be so surprised, Alex." Ric replies, softly.

"*Excuse me?* I told you, I told you from the start! From the fucking start!" this is the loudest I have ever yelled at anyone, and I never would have guessed it would be at Ric.

I am angry, I am very angry. And disappointed. This is not going the way I had planned, this is not going the way I had thought it was going.

I am suddenly regretting ever having decided to stay the night, and am feeling very stupid for breaking one of my own rules. Staying the night usually means something, at least to the other person it tends to.

Ric doesn't say anything. I look at him, and I start to see him in a new light. One that is no longer appealing to me, or attractive, or desirable. Our time is over, I see it immediately. The person in front of me now is seeking something in me that simply does not exist.

Who knows if it was always there, or if it developed in this past week and a half, but I cannot continue, I cannot deal with this, I cannot pretend to be someone I am not. I will only hurt him, for I do not feel the same.

I do not and cannot love him, only hurt him.

I study every inch of his face as sadness consumes me, whilst he looks anywhere but in my direction. He does it as if if he were to look me straight in the eye, I would only see more things that would disappoint me.

The silence between us now is excruciating, my soul drowning in pain and the shock of the three major events that have just taken place, one after the other.

I take in his face one last time, before I slowly turn my back, unlock the door, take a deep breath in, and throw myself back into the chaos ensuing on the other side of the door.

Life has a way of letting you know that an ending is coming, it gives you signs.

And as I walk out of that room, I feel it, and I know that I will never be back here again.

I blame films and books – always portraying the woman as the one that gets emotionally attached, but it's not always the case. I've had many the hook up in my twenty-three years, but every time that it's ended, every single time, it's been because the guy got attached.

I think it's something to do with not having me, or not having that attention they get from other women, which makes them think they want me or want to date me. I don't know, all I know is that I've never gotten attached to anybody in a hook up, and I'm a girl.

Just saying.

I feel bad more over having lost Ric as a friend than a fuck buddy, but that's the way these things go. I've had enough hook ups in my life so far to know that you can't be friends with them, and you can't continue fucking when the other person is attached. It doesn't work that way, and pretending it does only digs yourself a hole. No pun intended.

I'm glad for the time we did share, not just the sex but the conversations too, and the way we understood each other and could talk about music for hours on end.

I have a flashback of us lying opposite each other, naked, on his sofa, blasting Led Zeppelin and talking about our favourite Led Zepp albums. It was 3am and the neighbours were banging on the wall for us to turn down the 'racket'.

"Led Zepp is not racket!" we both fired back, instant bursting into laughter at how our minds had had the exact same reaction. We were a little tipsy.

I'll miss all of that, I will. But I simply cannot continue to see him, knowing what I know now. Seeing what I saw in his eyes.

I'm flattered, I am, and my ego did go up a notch or two, but at the core it upset me more than anything else. Because I knew I'd have to let him go. I will however always be extremely grateful for all of his help, and he will always remain with me.

The biggest thing on my mind however when I get back to the hotel is Mauro Fontana, and the incident comes back to me in waves.

I've never been assaulted before; it feels weird. It feels awful, to be frank. Even afterwards. Actually, just as much afterwards.

Though you know you are now safe, you don't feel as though you are. You have flashbacks and re-live the scene again and again in your mind, you remember what he smelled like, that damn lump, and how it felt against my leg.

I cry when I get home. Hard. And I continue to cry through the night. Taking breaks, sure, but then picking up again. I wouldn't say this to anyone and I've never used this word to describe myself before but, I feel extremely violated.

Scared.

Alone.

In shock.

This is the most upset I've ever been, and I'm also confused. Should I have called the police? Told them what he had done? But the thing is, when it's a big shot like Mauro Fontana, you're not going to win. And I'm not going to bother trying.

When I get home I don't eat, I just shower. I shower three times. And I don't sleep, all night.

Because I can't get Mauro's face out of my mind.

That smile.

His scent.

That lump.

I don't know what I'm going to feel next as I've never been through something like this before, and this scares me.

Just when I feel like I've calmed down, I burst into tears again. I hug my pillow. I wish I were in London, in my own bed, hugging my own pillow and not this damn *pink* pillow, which is cold and new and unknown to me. I would never buy a pink pillow case, and these are the words that repeat themselves to me as I cry.

How one person can think they can *own* another person's body, is absurd. It makes me fill with so much frustration that my chest starts to hurt. How anyone can have the audacity to think they can do what they want, when they want. That they can scar another person like that for their own pleasure.

I have flashbacks of his casual smile when I saw him hanging out with Roberto in the corridor just moments after sexually assaulting me. As if it was nothing. As if it *meant* nothing.

It was just some playful fun.

I'm not in the best mood when I arrive at the rehearsal space the next morning; with yesterday's turn of events and my sleep deprivation, there is not a whole lot to be excited about that rainy Thursday morning. It is, however, the day that the band promised me they'd have five new songs to present to me. So maybe I should be excited about that.

When I walk in, I am however grinded to a halt by what I see in front of me – it's Gavin. He's sitting on the old, musty second sofa G brought from his house, and he's looking at me with such a fixed glare that I stutter.

"Gavin…you're…here."

"I am, Alexis. I am. I got your lovely voicemail, and I thought I'd fly right over and see what the *fuck* the intern thinks she's doing. Have you lost your mind?"

I gulp. He does not like my idea. He does not like it at all. In fact, he looks as if he is just about ready to push me through the window a couple of metres behind me and see me land as twenty-five different body parts on the pavement.

"Listen, you need to hear their stuff-"

"I don't fucking care if they made the next Sweet Child O' Mine, you don't go making such judgements, you don't go telling bands to re-record when the label has spent a fortune to get them into the studio to begin with, you don't give any input on their music, their style, or their sound.

I flew you out here to fucking babysit them. You are an intern! I don't even fucking pay you! That's your worth right now, Alexis. You're not a manager. Not yet, and not for another fucking decade at least. I mean, what the fuck do you think you're doing?!"

"I'm so sorry Gavin, but I really didn't plan any of this, they just made some new tracks and it sounded *so* good, and what they were recording sounded *so* bad, so I thought-"

"You are not to have *any* thoughts! I am the only one who can think for this band. I get *paid* to think for this band. Understood?"

"Yes," I manage to say, but I am close to tears. Especially after everything that went on the day before. But I cannot and will not cry in a work environment – women are already seen as emotional. I can hold it in, I can keep going, I can win at my job and be successful. Even if the world is ending.

Before either of us can say anything more, the lift bells and the band walks in. I regain my strength, and even if I can tell Gavin has a lot more to say to me, we both know he will stop himself in the presence of the band.

"Hello boys," Gavin says, in a fake, cheery tone. The boys suddenly tense and look at him the way I look at mean bouncers at clubs. The band murmur 'hi' back and I watch them as they only become more uncomfortable. "How's recording going?"

"Um, about that Gavin-" Elliot starts.

"Alexis will be coming back to London with me tonight. And I'll be working directly with you guys from London, okay? Anytime you need anything, you call *me*, okay? Alexis will no longer be involved."

My heart sinks at the thought of returning to London, but perhaps logically this is the best thing for me. I mean, the band isn't going to be able to re-record, I've cut all ties with Ric, what's the point of hanging around?

I'll go back to London, and I'll start fresh. I'll make a good next move, a smart one. I won't piss anyone off or break any of the rules. I'll listen to the instructions and that'll be it.

I wonder, as Gavin gives the band a pep talk, if I'm fired. He didn't seem to specify, he just said that I won't be working or be involved with the Devilled Eggs, but does that mean I will still be a part of Ruby Records?

I feel foolish for having done all of this behind Gavin's back, like I'm some sort of pro, like I know what I'm doing, when in reality I am essentially a nobody at this point.

I should just be grateful for having had the opportunity to be a part of a great label. It'll go on my CV either way, I'll scream and shout about it to every other label and artist management out there, at every job interview I'll go to. I'll get a place back in the music business, I will.

As I watch Gavin talk to the boys, I'm well aware that he has most probably fired a ton of people in his life for a hell of a lot less.

Whether he decides to do the same to me or not, I wonder how exactly I'm going to make sure that I become one of the few to succeed. How exactly I'm going to ensure I become one of the selective few that bands and artists will *beg* to have as their manager.

Alexis Brunetti: Band Manager.

It has a certain ring to it, don't you think?

When Gavin leaves, he does not say a word to me. He simply hands me my flight ticket, which leaves at 7:30pm tonight, says goodbye to the band, and walks over to the lifts.

We wait in awkward silence for the lift to arrive, it bells, we hear Gavin walk in, and the doors close. Once we hear its descent, all five boys turn to me and start barking at me in panic, all at once.

"Why is he taking you back to London with him?!"

"Does that mean we're not re-recording?!"

"Why did he fly out here to piss us off?!"

"Does that mean our new music has gone to waste?!"

And they keep going, blurting out question after question, frantically. I squint at how loud and high-pitched they are getting, all competing to be heard over one another, all desperate to get answers.

I put my fingers in my mouth and whistle. Instant silence.

"Alright, I know Gavin's visit was unexpected. But not that much has changed. Yes, he has denied re-recording," the boys moan in synchronicity. "But we knew that was a huge possibility.

Ruby Records do things a certain way – it's very common at labels. And it doesn't mean it's the end of the world. You will get your chance, it just means it will require some patience. Keep your new music, *please* do not get rid of it out of spite or anger or anything like that. It's truly amazing work, and one day I believe it will be released."

"But you're going back to London," the bassist says, with surprising sadness.

"We were aware that my job was to be here only for two weeks. I'm simply going home a few days early."

"But we don't want to be managed by Gavin the Demon."

"That's what we call him."

"Guys, Gavin knows what he's doing," I tell them, "he's been in the industry for over twenty years, he has managed and continues to manage some really, really incredible bands. Stick with him, be kind."

The lift suddenly bells and out steps Gavin again. "Boys, Brett is downstairs. Wants to see hi, come on." The boys follow Gavin into the lift, all except Elliot.

I look at him as he unpacks his guitar. "Don't want to see Brett?"

"Ah, I've seen him enough."

"Hate him?"

"Pretty much."

I laugh; I knew there was a reason Elliot and I clicked straight away. I feel his eyes on me as I turn on my heel and go over to the sofa to pick up some of my stuff – books, drawing pads.

"So you're leaving us for London, eh?"

"Well it is my home, I was only supposed to be here two weeks all along, anyway." *Though it feels like a hell of a lot longer than that.*

"Right. You just fit in so well in this city, it's hard to remember you're actually from London." We smile at one another.

"You guys are going to be there too pretty soon. And you'll fit in there too, I know it." I go back to packing, and as I pick up my sketches, one in particular catches my eye, and I take it over to Elliot. "Here," I hand him one I did of Marilyn Manson playing guitar with a crow on his shoulder, and worms as hair.

Elliot really liked that one when he saw it. "Remember why you started playing," I tell him, and I see gratitude in his eyes as he takes it.

The lift bells again and out run the boys, minus Gavin or Mitch.

"Done so soon?" I say.

"Yeah Brett is *boring*."

There is a moment of silence before all four of them start barking at me again with their thousands of questions, as Elliot continues to unpack his guitar gear.

I don't have the energy to answer them all and to spend my last day in Milano assuring them that everything is going to be okay. That they will forget me after a week. Mostly because those facts upset me. I don't know how it happened, but I've come to like this band. They're actually not half bad.

I decide to get up, pull out a Queen record from my bag and walk over to the old record player Damiano bought in from home a few days ago. It found its home in this rehearsal place, and it makes me smile every time I look at it.

I do love vinyl.

I slip in the record, and like every time Radio Ga Ga begins playing, I take in the magic that is Freddie Mercury's voice. His presence. His charm. His everything.

I start swaying to the most enchanting music on this planet, and close my eyes as I do so. Once I open them, all five of them have stopped talking and are looking at me and my trance-like state.

I grab a marker and dance around the studio, their eyes fixed on me and my every move. I suddenly put the marker pen to my mouth as if it is a microphone.

"…I'd sit alone, and watch your light, my only friend, through teenage nights. And everything I had to know, I heard it on my radio."

I hop onto the sofa, as I continue to sing. It is impossible for me not to sing along when Freddie is singing. He is contagious, he is captivating, he is a legend.

And he is my last gift to the band.

I have always known Queen are one of a kind, ever since I was a kid and would hear their songs on the radio. But it wasn't until I was nineteen that I truly started listening to them, that I started taking in the genius music, the genius lyrics, the genius of Freddie Mercury.

It's not only that their music is out of this world, unique in every possible way, but it's the fact that Freddie has always been able to inspire me. He always knew he was meant to be Freddie Mercury, despite what everyone said, despite being picked on for his race, his sexuality, his teeth. He knew he was supposed to be onstage. And he got there.

Elliot is the first to join me, hopping on the sofa as he grabs a can of deodorant as his mic. We smile at one another as we lean in for the chorus.

"All we hear is…Radio Ga-Ga! Radio Goo-Goo! Radio Ga-Ga!"

Matteo and G are next, leaping onto the sofa so fiercely Matteo nearly falls right off. We laugh in-between singing as they join us, pretending to share the 'mic' with me.

Lino gets up and bops his head to the song, but is apprehensive to join us. And so I jump off the sofa and run up to him, using some of Freddie's onstage gestures, like punching the sky and swaying like him, as I circle Lino. He visibly relaxes as he smiles at me, and I pull him onto the sofa with us.

Damiano stands up but doesn't join us, as expected. He instead stands in front of us, his arms folded as he watches us with a smile.

He is the cool cat. He will never participate. But I have a feeling he too, has a hint of sadness at the fact that I shall be going back to London.

I watch him roll his eyes and get out his phone to scroll through social media.

Or maybe not.

I grab Lino's top hat off the arm of the sofa and put it on as we dance like looneys. For this is how I want my last afternoon with the Devilled Eggs to go.

I'm taking today to be happy, happy at having had the chance to meet the Devilled Eggs, to help them, and to genuinely grow to like them.

I do think they have the potential to be great, with the right management. Whether it will be with Gavin or someone else, I cannot tell. I just hope they stay in touch, as I would love to remain a part of their journey somehow.

As for me, it's time to head back to London, and face the consequences of my actions. I have no idea what is going to happen next for me, whether Gavin is going to fire me, or where my next adventure with the label will go.

I have no idea.

It was less than two weeks in Italy, but it feels as if it were a lifetime.

And I know what I want now, so no matter what happens with Gavin, this knowledge will be my greatest weapon, one I hadn't possessed up until now.

I'm ready.
I'm finally ready for you, London.

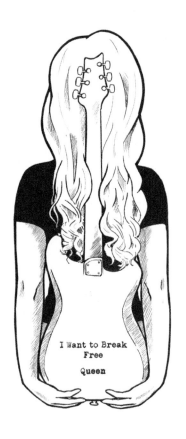

16

When I was fifteen I watched the film Vanilla Sky for the first time and I became instantly obsessed. The notion that our idea of something derives from a moulding of what we saw or experienced as a child, an angle, a moment, that defined our decisions later on, our view of the world, fascinates me.

It has always been something that I've believed in, from the first time Oliver, a boy in my class at school, said that love was for 'suckers' and I had then met his tattooed, beer bellied father at a parent's evening where he was hitting on our least attractive teacher, Mrs Barnes.

I have always known that our idea of something comes from another idea, another influence, another notion, but just because I know it doesn't mean it dissolves the element of damn right fear that comes attached to this truth.

Do you ever stop to think where your life could have taken you had you not seen Home Alone at seven, or had your mum not taken you to see Father Christmas, or if Backstreet Boys had never existed? Doesn't the possibility that our lives have taken a certain path because of the decisions of others scare the hell out of you?

If I hadn't grown up watching films where managers were 'cool' and the music business seemed fun and slick, would I still wake up every morning with the same passion to work in this industry?

If my parents hadn't been in an unhappy marriage the entire time Leo and I had been growing up, would we have seen relationships and marriage in a different way? Leo seems to have gotten over it.

And Alex?

Alex chose her career, the music business, as her one and only love.

Ambition is the only thing that drives me. I do not need or desire romantic relationships. I am a lone wolf, and I am happy this way.

I stare down at the five forks and five set of knives in front of me, in-between the ridiculously expensive white, shiny china plate and glass of champagne as Gabriella Reed tells Gavin and her PA, Ceska, about our afternoon at MTV.

Do we really need five forks, really? Why do rich people need five forks, anyway? Are they just too fussed to eat with one?

Now how does this work again? I've forgotten.

Damn it Alex, this is your third meal in a place like this this week and you still can't remember which fork to use first?

The one on the far left?

No, the one on the far right?

"Excuse me," Gabriella suddenly calls to a waitress passing by, "hi, we'd like to order." The waitress in her late thirties gives Gabriella a stern look.

Oh dear Lord, you'd be wise not to do that.

"I'll be right with you," and she is gone.

Oh-oh.

It doesn't matter where the waitress is going, whether it's to save a baby from a fire, a dying bird from the roof, or a pregnant lady from an Earthquake – it doesn't matter because when she returns she will not have a job.

"What the…? Did she just…? She didn't…?"

She's stuttering!

The waitress will never be able to work again.

"Excuse me," she calls to another waitress, this one in her late twenties with a sincere smile planted on her face stopping in front of our table.

"Hi, can I help you?"

"Yes, I was just rudely disrespected and brushed off by one of your colleagues, I don't know where she was going, but she's here to do her job, am I right? And she was not. *Does she know who I am?"*

I inwardly sigh, but am grateful it's a slow day with Gabriella. Usually it's her eighth or ninth time using that line this far into the day, but she's only reached number four.

"I mean, this is a six-star hotel, I am right now taking up half the rooms in this place with my crew, my boyfriend and his tour too, the least I expect is good customer service, is that too much to ask?"

The waitress tries to hide her hatred for Gabriella as hard as human possibly, and she is doing rather well.

That's not a sincere smile – that's a really good fake one!

"I'm sorry, Miss Reed, my apologies. She's new. Let me take your orders for you."

"I would like a vegetable soup," Gabriella tells her, pushing back her hair as if recovering from a long and bloody battle. She relaxes, using the menu as a fan as Gavin scans his.

"Hmm, I think I'm going to go for the oysters."

"You always go for the oysters," I blurt out and he smiles at me, handing the menu back to the waitress with his eyes fixed on me.

"Because oysters are the best."

I wave my hand at him as if he is talking nonsense.

"You would know if you ever tried any." He turns to Gabriella. "Did you know she's never tried oysters before?!" He looks back at me, "where have you been living all your life?!"

In an average, middleclass upbringing.

Gabriella seems uninterested in my food preferences and turns back to Ceska who has just ordered the salmon and is hiding behind her thick framed glasses, checking her email. The waitress turns to me.

"Uh, I'll have the salmon, too, thanks."

She nods and takes my menu, turning back to Gabriella.

"Anything else?"

"No, that's fine. Maybe have a word with your *colleague?* Teach her how to do her job?"

"Yes, I am so very sorry about that, Miss Reed. Who were you talking to?"

Gabriella looks around the restaurant and suddenly points across the room.

"The blonde," she says with assurance.

"Okay, I will speak to her. So sorry about that."

"It's fine, but she should learn to do her job," she says as the waitress nods and walks off in direction of the soon-to-be ex-waitress.

"Easy, Gabriella," Gavin says, picking up his phone from the table as another twenty emails buzz his phone into a temporary spasm.

245

"You have a nine o'clock appointment with Jez tomorrow," Ceska tells Gabriella, her eyes still glued to her phone, as Gavin's are to his.

Don't get out your phone, Alex. Don't. Don't!

Do not join them.

I've given myself a new challenge: to try and get through one dinner without checking my email.

Just one dinner, it can't be that hard?

But it is, and I have been dying to check it since the moment we had sat down twenty minutes ago.

You know those people you see in the music business in films and TV programmes that walk around with their eyes glued to their phones, with their fingers constantly typing, even when they walk, even when they talk, sometimes even when they're sleeping?

Yeah, that's me. That's the person that I have become in what seems overnight. But it's not like I chose this for me – I didn't just wake up one day and say hey, let's become one of those people that are obsessed with checking their email and don't have a moment to spare to listen to anybody or interact with real human beings.

No, I became one of those people because I had to. I had to or I would crumble. Somebody else would rush in and taken my job, one of the five hundred other candidates like me, just waiting for the opportunity to knock me out of the game and take my place.

And I couldn't let that happen.

It's been three months since I came back from Milano. Gavin, surprisingly, didn't fire me. Our flight back to London was in pure and utter silence, he even put on headphones and was listening to Daft Punk at maximum volume in order to not interact with me.

Once we landed, I was too scared to nudge him awake from what seemed a very deep sleep, and so I got one of the air hostesses to do it for me. She was scared shitless too, but she did it anyway and I thanked her in a whisper before scuttling off the airplane.

We parted at passport control, and he said, 'I'll see you Monday'.

On my first day, he called me into his office and said that he keeping me as his intern, and he assigned me new clients. He also told me however that this was my last chance, and if I even did *one little thing wrong*, he would 'fire me quicker than you can say 'abracadabra'.

I was so happy to still be a part of the label, even though he gave me a hell of a lot of shitty tasks for the next couple of months.

It's only the last few weeks or so that he has started really letting me step up and help out – from photocopying passports of artists and filling out their American visa forms, to fetching smoothies and soups for singers such as Gabriella Reed.

Now however, I'm onto assisting with tours, helping backstage, prepping artists for their radio interviews, and writing press releases.

As I've started doing more meaningful tasks, I've also started attending dinners and lunches and drinks at suave hotels where on a normal basis I wouldn't even be able to afford to buy a cocktail.

Life, as an independent twenty-three-year-old girl, is not easy. Doing it in London however, makes it just that little bit harder in terms of paying bills and the cost of living.

I have a breakdown at least once a day over how unfair my city is in its taxes, rent, food, and general living prices.

It's almost as if London wants you to fail at your dreams, and the rich are the audience, laughing at you and your pathetic attempt at succeeding in life.

I found a crappy little flat in Euston, sharing with three other people – two of them I'm pretty sure are batshit crazy in the head. I sometimes hear them talking to themselves, I kid you not. And I got a job as a cleaner in the evenings, to make rent. God only knows being an intern at Ruby Records does not pay. At all.

But this is what I want to do. It's the *only* thing I want to do, and I won't stop. Nor will I move back in with my parents and be judged, babied, and spied upon my every move.

This is my time to do what the hell I want, and though it's hard and tiring and yes my ego isn't doing that great lately, I am free, I am independent, and there is a joy in feeling those things that absolutely nothing on this planet can replace.

I wish I could say Gavin and I have become friends, but the truth is that whenever we are alone together, things are always tense.

But of course, when we are in company, especially of platinum album winners such as Gabriella Reed, he pretends he likes me and that we have a strong relationship.

I'm not complaining to be honest – the more clients like Gabriella see people like Gavin trust me, the more they trust me too.

But it's weird how much I know about Gavin's life now. I am just as much a PA to him as I am an intern to Ruby Records – he lost his PA, Emily, two months ago and hasn't had time to replace her yet. And so he uses me to do all his diary management, budgeting etc.

I don't mind, as it's character building for me, but it gets weird when I stop to think that I know crap so initimate about Gavin that I wish I could unlearn – such as Wednesday and Sunday nights are the times he has sex with his semi-famous actress, Delilah Barnes. Yeah, I really wish I could unlearn that one.

I learnt pretty quickly that the music business as an office environment is way more relaxed than most other businesses out there – you can stroll into the office at 12pm if you want and nobody says anything, at least not at Ruby.

The downside however is that, in the music business, you never switch off. You have to check your email *all the time*, because maybe someone important in New York needs something done straight away as they're at the office, and they need it done *now*.

If you choose to not check your email for an hour, because you're, say, out with your best friend at a bar in Covent Garden, be sure that once you do eventually check it you will find that a sports editor of a very big sports magazine in New York has sent you three very colourful emails demanding his documents and highlighting your incapability as an assistant manager.

Yes that did really happen, and Gavin had not been a happy bunny to lose that client to a rival record label.

One hour.

Just one hour on Friday night not checking my email.

And we lost a client.

Crazy, isn't it?

I look around the table at all three of them typing emails and sigh, getting out my phone and taking a deep breath in.

You have 78 new emails

What!? In twenty minutes?!
I check the time: 20:35pm.
The Americans are still at the office, that's why.
I quickly scan through some of them.

"Alexis, did you send the NDA to Taylor?" Gabriella asks me, and I put my phone away, knowing full well that she doesn't like it when you don't fully concentrate on her when she speaks to you.

"Yeah, this afternoon."

Gabriella Reed isn't actually as bad as she seems, she is pretty nice most of the time, to Gavin, Ceska and I anyway.

She is a three-time Grammy award winner with two platinum selling albums. She is an American beauty in her mid-twenties with a voice to die for, and signed to Ruby Records with Gavin as her manager.

Rumour at the office has it that the pair had once been lovers, but that once it ended he offered to be her manager. He does seem to act a little more personal with her than he does our other clients, but who knows with office rumours.

I'm hoping at one of our newly appointed social nights out with important clients he might declare to me his undying love for her once he's had a bit too much drink, but it hasn't happened yet.

I handle a lot of the Gabriella PR work now and am happy to do so when she isn't throwing a tantrum. I also work closely with two other Ruby Records clients: Dazza and moody alternative rock band, Mind Spin, who spend a lot of their time smoking weed and discussing their fascination with crappy adult cartoons.

"We can go see Fred tomorrow about his Visa," Gavin tells me and I look at him, playing with one of the forks.

"We can't, we have that meeting with Dazza tomorrow at eleven."

"Oh yeah, Dazza," Gavin smiles and I know what is coming next. He turns to Gabriella. "Gabs, did you know Dazza here has really taken a shine to Alexis?"

Gabriella gives us both a baffled look, playing with her hair, her phone still in her hand. She never places it down, even when she's eating – one hand for eating, one for her phone.

"Oh really?"

"Yeah, he offered to buy her a Lamborghini."

Okay so it's true – Dazza, a glam rock artist with a very sexy smile but about two brain cells to his name, wanted to buy me a Lamborghini. It doesn't mean anything though, he's just wacky and has so much money he doesn't know what to do with it. He is the son of British tycoon Philip Reading, who coincidentally is friends with the new owner of Ruby Records, Brett Gardner; Damiano's father.

Dazza recently signed to the label and Gavin put me in charge of his photo shoots for the next three weeks. Running around after Dazza is tiring to say the least; the man has more adrenaline in his body than water.

In only two weeks we have raced around central London on his Harley, done an unofficial duet at HMV and got drunk at Soho House with a famous film composer and one of the original members of the biggest video streaming website in the world.

All of this whilst I had continued to repeat, 'Dazza, we should really get back to work and get to the shoot,' to which he would reply, 'relax, Alexis! Got plenty of time for that!' in his Californian accent. Yes, Dazza actually grew up in Cali and moved across the pond only last year.

Despite having zero in common, we do tend to get along, and one day I dreamily expressed my love for Lamborghinis to him. Before I knew it, as sons of rich tycoons tend to do, he offered to buy me one.

'Come on, don't you wanna see the looks on everyone's faces?' he had said to me, winking.

I declined, because, well, I mean, it's inappropriate to say the least, but also, *I'll* be the one buying myself a Lamborghini, thanks.

"Really?" she looks at me, giving me her sincere smile.

Gabriella has two smiles: one for fans, and one for us. The smile reserved for fans is too wide and too bushy tailed to be real; Gabriella is never bushy tailed and bright eyed. The sincere smile Gavin, Ceska and I see, along with her famous drummer boyfriend Todd Baker, is smaller, with an element of exhaustion and boredom plastered on her face. "He must like you, Alexis."

"He definitely does, he doesn't do that for anyone else at Ruby. You should go out with him," Gavin tells me and I inwardly sigh, knowing where this is heading. "It's about time you went out on a date," he turns back to Gabriella, "she hasn't had a date since she started working for me." He looks back at me. "Pretty girl like you, twenty-three…make the most of it. You could get far with a guy like Dazza by your side. Crazy fucker, but all-round nice guy."

Unfortunately, no matter how much I deflect personal questions from Gavin, the man knows my life and weekly schedule better than anybody else in my life at the moment.

"I think Alexis will go on a date when she feels like going on a date, Gavin," Gabriella tells him, and I give her an appreciative smile.

"Yeah I know, I just think if Dazza seems so keen…"

"Oh you just want that to happen so that it'll be easier to get favours from Dazza's dad," Gabriella states, and I want to hug her. She is right, of course.

At the end of the day, to be good at his job Gavin has had to develop a talent for sniffing out a good opportunity. I sometimes worry that perhaps I, too, one day will have this 'talent'.

"Not true," he pauses as all three of us stare at him, "okay a little true, but my God if you did genuinely like him I would suggest you go out with him."

I slowly stand up.

"No thank you, Gavin," I tell him, as I scan through my e-mails. I suddenly look up. "Hey, do you think I can change my mind and order the oysters?"

Skipping down the stairs to the backstage area of the Royal Albert Hall, I get that buzz I always do when I go backstage at an event – the sight of roadies and Marshall speakers, any of the tour crew and VIP passes dangling from people's necks always gives me butterflies, the good kind.

I walk down the busy corridor until I find Gavin and Dazza talking, leaning on some gear. Dazza spots me approaching, wearing his usual tight black jeans and cool motorcycle jacket, as Gavin continues to talk to him, rubbing his neck as he always does when he's nervous.

"Alexis! There you are! You've been running around like a headless chicken all afternoon! It's starting in five."

Yes, it's typical of me to be running around and checking everything is running smoothly instead of soaking up the atmosphere, it being my first time backstage at the Royal Albert Hall and all. It's a prestigious venue that I've dreamed of going backstage to many times in my life.

Gavin looks at me and smiles. "Hello, you. Isn't it enough that I see you at the office every bloody day?" he jokes.

"*Every* day? Gavin you only come into the office about twice a week."

Dazza laughs. "Busted!"

Gavin rolls his eyes.

"So, everything okay? Did James find the drumstick?"

The entire afternoon has been chaotic, with gear going missing, musicians needing water, food, Wi-Fi or God knows what else. I swear I must have lost more weight running around after everyone than I could have done with a couple of hours at the gym.

This is Gabriella's last of three tour dates in London; she's off to Germany in the morning. I haven't said it out loud to anyone but, I'm very much looking forward to getting some peace and quiet whilst Gabriella is off on the rest of her tour.

I know she likes me and on a general level I like her too, but she is a *lot* of work and I could do with a break to focus on our other clients.

"Yes, he did."

"Alexis!" says Brian, one of the assistant tour producers; a sensible American with a penchant for Bob

Dylan. He pokes me playfully in the back with a sharpie as he powerwalks past us with a grin. "Jack Daniels is waiting for you in the green room."

"Thanks, Brian!" I've been dying for some sort of alcohol consumption all day and am wondering how the hell I had managed to make it this far into the afternoon without him. "I'm gonna go get some JD before the show, you guys want anything?"

"Nah, I'm good Alexis, we're gonna go find our seats, where are you sitting? With us?"

"Actually I think I'd like to watch it from the side of the stage…"

Gavin gives me a sly smile. "Ooh, the *cool* seat."

I nod at Dazza who wails 'see ya!' at me and I watch them walk off down the corridor before heading to the green room with a smile.

I love this venue, I love this atmosphere, and I love every moment of this day. I am backstage at the Royal Albert Hall because of where I work, because one of the artists I help manage is performing here tonight.

And it feels so damn good.

Quite a few of the crew are hanging out in the green room with glasses of beer, but the atmosphere is pretty low key when I enter. The green room at the Royal Albert Hall is pretty slick – there's a bar, stupidly strong air conditioning, and, oh, did I mention the alcohol?

Just as I head to the bar, I notice someone I know ordering. I smile.

His back is recognisable virtually anywhere; nobody else can pull off the tight black jeans and black blazer quite as well as him. Not to mention his messy yet sexy mop and the way he leans onto the bar with his tight, glorious butt sticking out.

He turns around, his eyes lighting up. "Well, hello there!"

Parker May arrived in London five days ago for the British leg of the Luminous tour. They have done two gigs at the Shepherd's Bush Empire where he put me on guest list, and we hung out afterwards, going to a bar near the venue with some of his crazy rock-obsessed American friends who had flown over for the gigs.

253

We became somewhat friends, or close acquaintances, following meeting in Milano when he added me on social media. One conversation about the influence of Led Zeppelin, led to the genius of Robert Smith, and suddenly we were friends.

But we speak mostly about music and the power of art, hipster kind of things. I'm content just watching his beautiful face move as he speaks, and it temporarily distracts me from my overly busy life. For a brief moment, I am simply just a twenty-three girl.

"I didn't take you for a Gabriella Reed fan," I tell him playfully, always uncontrollably smiling when I see his gorgeous face.

After the second Luminous gig he had asked if he could be put on guest list for the last Gabriella gig so that we could hang out once more before he was due to fly out to Paris with the band.

The bartender puts down two glasses in front of him and I cock up an eyebrow at him.

"What? I was coming to save you with a little bit of Jack," he tells me. He hands me one and we clink glasses, eyes locked.

"So when do you fly out?"

"Tomorrow morning," he groans.

"Oh, like Gabriella and basically everyone here," I say, nodding at the tour manager, Danny, who smiles as he passes us.

"Yep. Except I'm going on an actual half-decent tour and not some commercial, autotuned-"

"Sssh!" I hiss, "this is not the place to start one of your Parker May bitching fests!"

"You care *way* too much about who listens to our conversation, Alex."

We talk about music and Gabriella and Luminous and London, losing ourselves in entertaining conversation. I quite like Parker. He's a manwhore, sure, but he's got brains, and he's got charisma. He can talk for *hours* about Black Rebel Motorcycle Club and Portishead, he switches genre in a nanosecond, can learn to play impressive solos in just hours, and he's got that happy-go-lucky vibe and energy that you just get easily addicted to being around.

The only thing I don't like when I see Parker is that I can sometimes be reminded of Ric. Not because they are anything alike (other than they are both guitarists), but because of the way I met Parker.

I remember that day as if it happened yesterday. Ric had just got his new solos, and was setting up for me to play on that gorgeous Fender. I remember the way Ric hadn't liked Parker, and sometimes wonder why.

A week after I returned to London, I saw on Italian papers that Ric had been fired from the Paolo band. He was no longer Paolo Petrinelli's guitarist. As soon as I read it, I felt a part of my soul die. I had been aware that this was a likely result of Ric's actions, but when it's actually confirmed it's another story entirely.

I felt like total shit, I did. I shouldn't have left him in that stadium, I shouldn't have left Italy without even saying goodbye. But in my defence, I had been pretty shook up by the Mauro incident. Yet every time I say that to myself, I am aware with Mauro incident or not, I would have bailed on Ric either way. Because that's who I am, and that's who I will always be.

I did text him the second I saw the article. I said 'hey, just heard the news I'm so sorry, are you okay?'

He read it a good eight hours later and didn't respond. A couple of weeks later I tried again, this time with 'If you need help with finding another band I can put you in touch with some people I know'. Again, no response.

I felt incredibly silly – he had been Paolo Petrinelli's guitarist; he doesn't need help finding a new gig. And I don't even live in Italy! But it was clear he wanted nothing more to do with me, and I had to accept this.

Yet when I'm around Parker, I sometimes remember how truly awful a person I can be.

"Who's that?" Parker asks me, nodding his head to an overweight man, pacing up and down the green room, wiping sweat from his forehead every three to five seconds.

"Clive, the tour manager."

Parker cackles. "Only the manager of Gabriella Reed could look as if he suffers from constant anxiety."

We both laugh and clink our glasses a second time. We do that a lot.

255

Once the show is set to begin, I lead us down the corridor to the back of the stage, and we stand in an empty space next to some spare speakers and microphones. I walk a little on to the stage to look out at the crowd and gasp, Parker following.

"Wow," I say, as if to myself. The audience in front of me, above me, all over the massive venue, look like ants.

"Hey, hey, where do you think you're going?" says Mike, Gabriella Reed's lead guitarist. The man in his early thirties whose breath always stinks of red wine, stands behind us untangling some wires and giving me a sly grin.

Mike Patterson is a well known guitarist in Nashville, playing for mostly bluesy artists. He's on this tour because Gabriella's boyfriend, Todd, is good friends with some people in Nashville and called in a favour. Otherwise no serious blues artist would agree to go on tour with what is ultimately a pop star. Gabriella however wanted *'nothing but the best'*, and so Mike Patterson was called in.

He hates her guts.

"I thought I'd start off the show," I tell him, as we walk back over to the side of the stage and stop in front of him, folding my arms. "You ready?"

"Alexis, Alexis…I was born ready."

I grin and he pats my arm.

"See you later, sweetheart."

The venue suddenly goes dark and the screaming commences. Parker and I exchange smiles as one-by-one, Gabriella's band walks onstage, waving at the screaming crowd. Gabriella walks onstage from the other side, and it only fuells the screams and applause from the crowd.

"Hello, hello, London…wow, it's great to be here."

She is dressed in a sexy black cocktail dress, with hair extensions I bought online for her for £3000.

I'm so used to seeing her with no make-up and her hair in a bun that looking at her now I am reminded of just how beautiful she can really look with make-up.

"Let's start off the evening with one I think you should all know…"

Opening song and one of Gabriella's best-selling songs Everything You Wanted starts playing, and I move my head a little to the music, Parker gulping down his JD next to me.

This is so great. All three nights have been a success. Now I can focus more on Dazza, though Gabriella will still be emailing for stuff, but I can handle that, as long as I don't have to go through another stressful afternoon like today and the past two days for a while...oh who are you kidding, you know you love it. You love the adventure, you love the hectic side to it, and you like to be needed and so urgently.

Alex, we need you!
Alex, do you have the files?
Where have you been, Alex?!
This is your job, Alex. This is you in your element.
You're in the right place, you really are.

"Alex, is he okay?" I snap out of my thoughts and look out at the stage to find Mike struggling with his guitar strap. He looks at me for guidance.

"Oh shit, it's not his guitar."

Parker sniggers. "What do you mean it's not his guitar? Surely he would have noticed if the RC320 wasn't his?!"

"There's two, one was for the second set...." I tell him, starting to panic.

"Two sets?!"

"Yeah, she's doing two sets with two bands, one with the old stuff and one with the new…"

"God she really is a diva," he manages to say, shaking his head a little, but my eyes are fixed firmly on Mike. "Can't he just adjust the strap?!"

"Nope," and that's all I have to say to make Parker realise that even though Mike is a nice guy, he is a fucking diva of his own. He doesn't adjust his own guitar straps. He doesn't tune his own guitars. He just demands a ton of money to step onstage and play.

Someone was actually hired for the tour to comb his hair.

"Shit, I gotta go get it, it must be outside with his second set." I rush offstage and Parker follows. We run down the corridor to the instrument room, and enter to find the place stacked with guitars and bass.

"Holy shit, what the fuck kind of diva tour is this?" Parker says. "Luminous doesn't have half of this crap, and we're a *band*."

"Help me find the guitar Parker," I order, searching through every guitar case.

"Right, right, I'm sure it's here somewhere."

I find it, and we both pull it out from behind a few Fenders. Three roadies rush into the room.

"Oh thank God! Mike has the wrong guitar!" one of them tells me.

"No shit Sherlock," Parker says to them. He is never afraid to speak his mind and I love that about him.

I hand them the guitar and they disappear down the corridor with it.

Parker and I follow and watch curiously from the sidelines as the roadies walk onstage and swap the guitars for Mike, who looks like a lost child.

"Who knew the Ibanez RC320 could cause such a fuss?" Parker asks me in my ear, our eyes fixed on the stage. We bump knuckles, shrieking 'IBANEZ MOTHERFUCKERS!' a little too loudly in high-pitched voices, laughing as we always do. It's a little tradition we have whenever we see an Ibanez guitar.

Don't ask how or when we started this tradition, I don't fully remember how it came into conception. It was something to do with being backstage at a mini after party for Luminous, drinking a little too much, and laughing way too much.

Plus, Ibanez is a funny word to say.

"There you go, problem solved," Parker says to me, as the roadie walks offstage and shows us the thumbs up, Parker puts a hand on my shoulder. "Relax, the show's gonna run smoothly…for the most part."

And it does, thankfully. But that night, as stressful as it is, gives me a buzz. Not just any buzz, but that music business buzz I had been searching for and was certain existed from the first time I ever interned in music. It's a drug. And one I never want to give up.

Ever.

This is what I am supposed to do.

This is where I am supposed to be.

It's nighttime and I can't find the exit to the stadium. I walk and I walk until my legs hurt, whilst Paolo's band hang around in the background, laughing and joking amongst themselves.

They don't see me, but I sure see them. I try to call out to them and moan about my legs, but they can't hear me. I hear someone calling my name and turn to see Mauro walking towards me.

He has his usual vile smile that show his yellow teeth, and I want to get away from him as fast as humanly possible. I attempt to run, but my feet are now stuck to the floor. I call out to the band, Ric included, but nobody hears me.

They continue laughing at a joke Roberto is telling them, whilst Mauro approaches. He grabs my wrists, and I shout for him to let go, I beg for him to do so, but he does not listen.

He leans in, I feel a hard lump on my leg, and I scream. I scream so loud that only dogs can hear me.

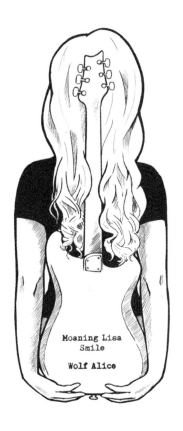

17

I cannot believe there was once a point where I was complaining about my inability to get into the music business, whilst spending the weekends in front of the TV, eating popcorn and checking social media.

I had no right to be complaining about the lack of leads. I had no right to be moaning about my living at home (where I at least had a roof over my head and lived rent-free).

To achieve anything takes persistence, hard work, and a little luck, sure, but once you start to focus and work damn hard to get where you want to be, it's incredible the things that can open for you. If you keep pushing, if you are always willing to go the extra mile, you may just start to see results. It's less about working hard, and it's more about working efficiently.

It took me a long time to learn this.

"Where the *fuck* is he?!" I roar into my phone, as Dazza's phone goes to voicemail for the fifteenth time in a row.

I switch to Bright and Perky Alex as soon as I hear the beep. "Hi Dazza, this is Alexis. Again. Your photo shoot was supposed to start *fifty* minutes ago. Where are you? This is the *final* shoot before your album release, let's try to get it out the way please? Call me back, thanks."

I hang up and shake my head, anxiously. Though I'm hard on Dazza in real life, I've learnt it's best not to be Bitchy, Bossy Me when technology is involved – any proof that I'm actually a moody, bossy bitch will never help you at a place like Ruby. Not if you're a woman.

"Where is he, Alexis?" asks the photographer, a prima donna, camp Argentinian guy with more 'tude in his face than any other person on the planet. He walks across the pavement of Tower Bridge carrying his camera around his neck, trying not to crash into people as he approaches.

"He'll be here soon, Cris."

"We can't close the pavement until he arrives," he reminds me for the eighteenth time today.

"I know Cris," I reply, as yet another person pushes into me as they pass.

I thought choosing Tower Bridge as Dazza's final photo shoot at 11am on a Wednesday morning was a genius idea when I had suggested it in the meeting, and so did everyone else in the room.

Now however, I have come to realise that I couldn't have been more naïve: Tower Bridge is *always* busy, no matter what time of day, and as a Londoner, I should really have remembered this.

I suddenly hear the roar of a motorbike engine and turn around, knowing it's Dazza before I can even spot him racing over to us. He stops two feet in front of me, and pedestrians scream as they run out of the way.

He takes off his helmet, waves his floppy, brown hair around as if he's starring in a shampoo advert, and smiles flirtatiously at me. I hold back my gasp as I spot his gorgeous and no doubt expensive black jeans and leather jacket completely covered in mud stains.

"Morning Alexis, great day for a cruise around town, don't you think?"

Cris looks over the bridge at the grey skies, and shakes his head, muttering something about singers under his breath. We watch him walk off, as if if he were to confront Dazza over his muddy clothes he would explode, and he instead orders some of the team to close off part of the pavement.

I turn back to Dazza. "Glad you could join us – where have you been and why are you all dirty?"

"I went to a mud track, oh it was so much fun!"

I've noticed a few things about the kids of rich, successful, and hard-working parents; other than the blatantly obvious fact that they are spoiled rotten. We all know that. But recently I've started to notice other things about them too.

For example, they tend to miss a few of the basic survival instincts that the rest of us possess (and quite early on). Let's take a look at Dazza – he doesn't know how to cook. And when I say that I mean that he doesn't even know how to boil an egg.

He's never put bread in the toaster, he's never boiled pasta, he's never grated cheese on top of anything. I guess this is normal for rich kids but I've never really thought about it before, as I don't tend to hang out with rich, spoilt rotten kids of successful parents. And I'm finding all these facts fascinating.

If we think about it, Dazza has never had to take out the rubbish, or go food shopping, or book a flight two months in advance and excitedly countdown the days until his holiday. Dazza can go on holiday whenever the hell he wants. Hell, he could hire a private jet if he wanted to (no, they don't own one, but they definitely could).

He's never had to fend for himself or worry about money, ever. I know some people get extremely envious over this, over the way they live, but I only possess a huge amount of sympathy for them. Sure, it would be nice to go on holiday whenever I wanted, order whatever I wanted, and have a gigantic door always open for me in so many different avenues. And yes, I plan to be well off someday. But, the difference is, I will have earned it.

It's funny, if you think about it. People who are only rich through their parents or their grandparents, through the success and hard work of other people, are able to live the way that they do because of other people. And it's scary because their parents think they're doing them a favour by giving them everything they want, but they're actually just doing the exact opposite.

If we think about it, some of the kids of hard-working, inspiring and successful parents are some of the weakest kids in society.

Isn't that ironic?

I take in his muddy clothes and cover my face with my palm. "*Dazza*!"

"I know, I know, I'm a bit dirty, but it's fine – nothing that can't be fixed with a good cleaner."

"We don't have a cleaner on sight that can get all that shit off of you!" I bellow at him. "You *knew* we had a shoot, Dazza!"

But he only smiles at me. "God, you're even more beautiful when you're angry, you know that?"

Before I can scream profanities at the spoiled brat in front of me, Cris is marching back over to us with ears very close to releasing smoke.

"Is this a joke? We've been waiting an hour for you, and now…now…"

This is a disaster. This is chaos. I can already hear Gavin shouting down the phone to me, telling me I'm useless, telling me he's going to hire someone else. His words in Milano ring in my ears and I have shivers down my spine.

One more thing and you're out, Alexis!

I cannot let that happen. I belong at Ruby.

"It's all part of the character," I blurt out, and they both turn to me.

"What? All I saw on the brief was that he needed to look dark and mysterious – dressed in black, handsome, and cunning," Cris tells me.

"Yes, but last minute we also added the whole 'dirty, rough' look. Women love a bit of rough."

"Don't I know it," Dazza adds, but we ignore him.

"So, this was done by purpose?"

I bullshit my way through and Cris seems to buy it, hesitating only for a few seconds before nodding and ordering Dazza to hop onto the bridge so that they could start shooting.

"Wait, what?" I say, but Cris ignores me. Dazza climbs the railings, and stands on the wall. This is the edge of Tower Bridge. And he doesn't look scared at all. He looks like he is, indeed, feeding off the adrenaline of the mud track.

He's a crazy fool, he really is. But I admire his guts. He may be spoilt rotten, but the man has guts like I've never seen before. Could this be what growing up rich does to you? You don't have any survival instincts, you cannot boil an egg, but you can stand on the edge of Tower Bridge as easy as you would your garden steps?

There is an element of envy that suddenly hits the pit of my stomach as I watch Dazza, an envy I've felt a number of times in my life – when my cousin was able to drive on icy roads, when Blake rock climbed barefoot, and whenever I watch someone deliver an incredible speech under pressure.

I am envious of people who are fearless. I wish I were that way. I wish I could encompass it.

I want to be fearless too.

I look up at Dazza and smile, as he gets into position without any direction, and the photoshoot begins.

Once I get back to the office, it's past 5:30pm. There's still a few people around, but it's quiet. Dazza did a great job on his last shoot despite his late arrival, and thankfully, no one ended up falling into the river Thames, which I'm noting as a huge plus.

I tried, for a second, to imagine calling Gavin to tell him something like that, but it terrorised me even at the thought.

Note to self: never again let a client climb the railings of a bridge for a photo shoot. It is definitely, definitely not worth it.

I pack up nervously and debate heading home, even though I know I have plans. Even though I know I paid *money* to go to something tonight. I remember Dazza's fearless self up on that bridge and I shake off my anxiety. I assure myself that I can do this, that I have nothing to be ashamed of, and I head out to get to the tube.

Once I arrive at Farringdon station, I follow the map on my phone to get to my destination. It only takes a few minutes, but it's raining, cold and windy; my umbrella breaks in a nanosecond, I throw it in the nearest bin and continue on my way in a huff.

As my coat, shoes, tights and hair get drenched, I find myself wondering why I have decided to do this. Why I have decided to endure this, against all obstacles. It is somewhat of a *pleasure*, not a necessity, so do I really need to?

When I eventually arrive at the venue I burst in through the double doors and into the foyer of the building. I shake my hair like a wet dog and grit my teeth in irritation. Sometimes, I really don't like living in London. I really, really don't.

"Hi! Welcome!" says a voice, and I turn to find a friendly-looking man in his early forties approaching me with his hand out, ready to shake mine. He has a ginger beard with eyebrows to match, and round, black glasses.

"Hi," I manage to say, looking down at his hand. "I'm soaked, I probably shouldn't."

He quickly puts his hand away. "Of course. It's lovely out there, isn't it?"

I remain mute, unappreciative of any type of humour in this moment.

"Well, we're about to begin," he looks around me. "Have you brought your…?"

Oh shit, oh shit, oh shit! I knew I forgot something! How bloody stupid are you, Alex?!

"Oh crap, I forgot it!" I blurt out, followed by a ton of Italian swear words to myself about how stupid I am.

"It's okay, it's okay, it's not a problem at all. I have a spare," he puts his arm around me, despite how soaked through my coat is, and he leads me into a room.

There are already plenty of students – about fifteen to twenty people, all practising electric guitar by themselves. I look at the man's warm smile, and then back at the rest of the people.

I instantly relax. I forget the journey I've had, I forget that I'm soaking wet, and I forget all my anxiety about coming here. I am suddenly no longer angry, or upset, or frustrated. For my day at the office is over, it is non-existent, once I enter this room. And I am definitely in the right place. The fear is still there, present as ever, but so is my excitement. They walk hand-in-hand, and I'm okay with that.

"Here," says the man, as he hands me his spare Fender Strat. "Please take a seat, and I will begin the class."

I hurriedly grab the cart of sandwiches and drinks and push it into the meeting room. I pull open the blinds, check the temperature of the room, and swap any chairs that are broken or ripped or dirty. I know the routine like the back of my hand now when a guest comes in for a meeting.

The only difference is, today I get to speak at the meeting. The next step for Dazza's campaign is finding the right radio plugger, and it was me who found this guy – Gary Watson. He's got a fabulous roster of clients under his belt, and he's been in the business a good thirty years.

Now, usually when you're old, people frown at you, worry that you don't know how to change with the times, but Gary is a chameleon. I've studied all his campaigns, the clients he made famous, and he knows better than anyone what is happening in the radio industry at any moment.

Some people say radio is dead, that there are much better avenues to focus on, but the thing about working at Ruby is that they can afford hefty budget for several multi channel campaigns.

Since I'm the one who found him and Gavin approved him with glee, he said that I could run the meeting. So though I am still the one setting up the meeting, coordinating everyone's schedules, bringing in the snacks, setting up the whiteboard and everything else that comes with a client meeting, today, I have a voice. And I can't wait to use it.

The glass meeting room door swings open and Gavin pops his head in. "Gary is here."

I nod, and hurry out to head to reception. I straighten my black pencil skirt and white shirt as I do so, and Dazza winks at me as I pass him in the adjacent room – Gavin's office.

I find Gary sitting at Ruby reception, watching the news on the comfy sofa as he unwraps a sweet from the bowl on the coffee table. I've seen pictures of him on the Internet, but he looks older in person. He's only fifty but I'd give him at least five years more.

I greet him and introduce myself, and he follows me to the meeting room as we small talk – how was the journey in, where do you live, isn't London awful in this constant rain?

Gavin steps in first, introduces himself, and they begin bonding over whatever was on the news this morning, as I go and fetch Dazza. He's still in Gavin's office, looking at something on his phone.

"Come on, Dazza! He's here."

But he doesn't take his eyes off his phone, as he chuckles. "Look, Alexis! A friend of mine in L.A. got super drunk last night, she's singing the national anthem in Chinese-"

"Dazza!" I hiss, as I scurry over to him, straightening my pencil skirt once again.

It creases so easily!

He looks me up and down as I approach, as if he has only just noticed the pencil skirt, even though we've been in meetings together all morning.

"My, my, Alexis. You do look lovely. Trying to look more like a woman than a girl these days?"

267

I tug at his leather jacket. "Up! Come on, no more messing around, he's in there waiting for you! You want a music career or not?!"

"Okay, okay, geez, keep your panties on. Wait, are you wearing any?" he pretends to try to kneel to take a peak and I slap his arm.

"Stop it! Come on."

He gets up with a grin and we walk over to the meeting room. When we burst in, I freeze. It is no longer just Gavin and Gary in the room. There is a young man, well – boy, with them. He can't be a day over twenty, dressed in a black polo jumper and black jeans with very slick shoes.

Confused as to who he is, it is Gavin who introduces Dazza to Gary, and they begin talking amongst themselves. Gavin, instead, looks at me and my clearly confused expression.

"Oh, Alexis – this is Martin, our new intern."

I frown. "Intern? For who?"

"Oh, he's going to be working across Peter, Sharon and my clients."

We shake hands amicably, but there is something about him I do not like. I assure myself that it is *not* that he is my competition. "Lovely to meet you, Alexis. I've heard so much about you."

And I've heard nothing about you.

Dazza turns to us, looking Martin up and down. "Well, you're no Alexis – which is disappointing, but okay." They shake hands, and I can't help wondering why this wasn't mentioned to me.

I attend all the weekly update meetings, I even write the damn weekly newsletters for all staff! There was no announcement about a new intern. I'm the only intern working for Gavin, never did I consider somebody else coming in to be my competition.

Does this mean something? Does Gavin not want me anymore? Has he not forgiven me over Milano? Did I do something wrong? Did a client complain about me?

"Oh, Alexis – I made Martin look through Dazza's portfolio and he had an idea for Gary. Do you mind if he starts the meeting?"

I open my mouth to speak, to respond, to push back, to scream in a variation of Italian swear words, but nothing comes out. My voice box is dead to me, refusing to help me right when I need it most.

I watch Gavin and Martin as they interact; they talk about football and I can't help wondering about their relationship. Where exactly did Martin come from?

Once we sit down and the meeting commences, I imagine Martin pulling out a USB and popping into the computer. On screen a presentation would appear, it's impressive, and it makes my envy only grow. I mean, that's what I had done – I put together some slides, and had learned the speaker notes off by heart.

But that's not what Martin does. His idea is to get Dazza on a very famous radio station, through, coincidentally, a friend of his who presents the breakfast show there. That's the big, amazing idea.

I admit, it's a great opportunity for Dazza and will no doubt be a great part to the campaign, but, it isn't exactly an idea, is it? He didn't look at Dazza's portfolio to get it, and he didn't exactly put thought and effort into this *amazing* concept. He knows a guy, and he's going to use this to get further in the music industry.

It's lazy. The ultimate shortcut to success.

And, completely normal.

I present my idea, which is to target certain radio stations who especially love the same sort of genre as Dazza's music, set up competitions, do intimate gigs with coverage streamed on radio stations.

It's well received, but all of it feels completely and utterly overshadowed by Martin's Great Idea. The saviour of the afternoon. And there's nothing I can do about it.

We spend the rest of the meeting discussing several different tactics, but every second that I am in that meeting my soul is dying just that little bit more.

I feel small, very small. Weak. And not confident at all. I don't even present that well, either – I envisioned it going a hell of a lot better than that and find myself disappointed with my performance, my reaction to competition entering the room, entering *my* territory, and my overall personality.

269

I hate all of it. Who the hell am I to be in the music business, if I cannot even succeed in a meeting with *one* radio plugger? One fucking radio plugger.

What happens when it's a huge meeting with label senior heads, when it's rival label heads, when it's potential clients, when it's anyone who is anyone in this industry? Am I going to remain a chicken the rest of my life?

Step up, Alex. You need to learn to step up.

Once the meeting is over, it is of course Martin who accompanies Gary to the lifts with Gavin, and me who is left to clean up. The only thing I can think is, I swear to God, if the other intern was female, they would be right in here with me.

Dazza is in the meeting room with me but he is silent. He is instead watching me clean up with a curious look in his eyes. I know I look miserable, but I don't care to show it around Dazza. Plus, I've been looking happy and full of joy for an hour and a half – I'm exhausted.

"He's a twat," Dazza eventually says. When I look at him, he shrugs. "He's a twat. I don't trust him."

I nod to acknowledge his words.

"But getting on Radio Star is awesome," he tells me, before walking out and leaving me alone in the meeting room.

"They're so fucking boring," Parker says, pointing his nose at someone as he gulps down his third tequila shot and slams the glass down on the table.

The someone he's pointing his nose at is the female folk singer onstage at the Balham at the moment. It's just her and her guitar, and I have to admit, I do agree with Parker. Her voice sounds like a thousand before her and a thousand of her to come. Can we please push folk out of the current trend and mix it up with something more interesting?

"Plus!" Parker barks, once he has ordered us another two shots when I have yet to touch my first, second and third. They sit in front of me, looking at me in unavoidable disappointment, as they await their eventual finish in my stomach.

Yet somehow, I'm not in a mood to drink.

"*Plus, plus, plus!* They're all blonde. Can we have a brunette please?"

It's Saturday night in London and I am scouting for an artist or band to take to Gavin. Nine days ago, he told me to bring him talent, and that 'maybe, just maybe, if they're good, they can be your client'.

So I've been scouting every single night since he said this to me, eight days ago. This is gold. This is my opportunity to show him and Ruby what I'm made of.

Imagine if I got to manage my own artist – brand them, help them with their music, structure their entire campaign. This is exactly what I've been waiting for.

And yes, everyday seems like a blur now, I don't even have time to wash my hair sometimes, I only get five hours sleep a night, I am most definitely overworked, and I don't remember what it is to have a weekend, but I'm happy.

Because I love what I do.

All the artists I've seen so far have been completely boring, however. So I'm starting to think it's me, that I always need to seek trouble, even when opportunity is handed to me.

What's wrong with me?

"What's wrong with you is that you are working everyday, all day, and you have given up your social life completely," Parker tells me, once I say all of this to him.

"That is not true-"

"When was the last time you saw your friends?"

I struggle to remember.

"And when was your last date?"

I squint my eyes at him. "Like I have time to date!"

"Jesus woman, you need to get laid, and you need to hang out with your friends. And if you can't do either of those things, talk to strangers!"

This is why I like Parker. He's the ultimate extrovert; the complete opposite of me. He always needs to be the centre of attention, he always needs to talk to people, converse with people, and share his stories with people. He gets energy from being this way.

Parker has always been an extrovert. Originally an actor before he decided to become a full time guitarist, he grew up poor on the wrong side of L.A. He earned some cash co-starring in a famous daytime show about a New York teenage boy being forced to move to a small town in the middle of nowhere. Parker played the boy's best friend.

He wasn't really interested in acting but it made him enough money so that he could quit and go into what he really wanted to be in – the music business.

From talking to the right people, saying the right thing, making himself present at the right events, Parker was able to find his gig as Luminous' lead guitarist. I wish I could be as constantly outgoing as he is, as charismatic, as interesting to talk to as he is. But his energy is infectious and I love being around it.

Before I can reply, Parker is on his feet and approaching a group of friends at the next table. I can't hear what's being said but I watch on in curiosity. Another pang of envy at someone being fearless. I have a flashback of Dazza hanging on the edge of Tower Bridge.

Fuck this.

I get up and walk over. There are three guys and two girls at the table, all in their mid-twenties with big, bright smiles. You can tell they're as young as me from how sweet their smiles are.

It turns out Parker has re-invented himself to this group of strangers; his name is now Todd, he's a fireman, and he lives in south west London. I decide to join him, and call myself Gwyneth. I'm twenty years old, I'm a stripper, and I moonlight as a cat walker.

Yes, that's a real thing.

Parker and I pretend to be engaged, and they tell us we make a beautiful couple. We thank them as we keep our arms around one another, playfully.

"Kiss!" Sherry, the drunkest of them demands, to which Parker leans in and I block his face with my palm.

"Awe, sweet pea, go brush your teeth before you do that." I know that he's up for kissing me, and though Parker is very attractive, and I am single, I like our friendship. I don't want to ruin that.

I know better now.

We spend a good few hours talking to the group, and I get a chance to test my new NLP knowledge on them: how to talk to strangers, how to read them (both their verbal and body language), and I get to talk confidently about myself. Sure, I'm pretending to be Gwyneth, but somehow, it gives me the confidence to be myself.

The more I read about NLP, the more I love it. The more exercises I do, the more confident I get. The more I understand people, the more I can communicate and connect with them. Now that I'm an avid learner, it's hard to think of a time when I didn't know about NLP.

And I never forget for a second that it was Ric who introduced me to the entire thing.

I miss him sometimes.

It's a couple of hours later that I am fairly tipsy. It's hard not to be when out with Parker; he practically shoves the shots down your throat.

We're all laughing and joking and being a typically annoying drunk group of twenty-somethings on a Saturday night, when the mic suddenly screeches. I haven't been paying attention to the stage for a while, but as I look up, I see a female rock group hitting the stage.

I suddenly remember that I'm there to work, to impress Gavin, to get a fucking *job* at Ruby. I regain my focus and concentrate on the stage as I watch the female rock group get ready to play.

They look pretty damn awesome and badass – dressed in black, dark purple lipstick, and Vans shoes with their dresses. There's an energy to them that doesn't allow me to look away. And they haven't even started playing yet.

I realise it's the singer in particular that has my attention, with her piercing green eyes and purple hair. She looks calm and collected as they set up, and I don't know why or how, but I decide that she's cool. She's so damn *fucking cool.*

"Er, Earth to Alex?" Parker says to me but I ignore. He follows my gaze and sits up in his seat. "Ooh. They look interesting. Thinking what I'm thinking?" he nudges me and I tear my eyes away to look at him.

"Orgy at yours following the gig?" I get up, as he shakes his eyebrows at me. "I, on the other hand, am thinking of something else entirely. I'll be back."

I walk over to the standing area to get a closer look at them, and just as I do they begin playing. Their music is not bad, the playing too, but it's the singer that has me hooked. She's mesmerising. She's enchanting. And I want to know her.

The first thing I notice is her powerful voice, it reminds me of a white Whitney Houston. And she knows how to carry it, this is very important.

Second is her beautiful face; it isn't conventionally beautiful, her lips are too thin, and her nose is crooked, but her eyes are a gorgeous green that stand out in the dimly lit venue. There is an aura to her, along with her confidence, that gives her immense power up on that stage, and this trumps conventional beauty, every single time.

All of this combined has me addicted to both looking and listening to her. I am instantly in love with her. I immediately imagine re-branding her to become a more neutrally powerful feminine, as opposed to the generic rock gig/dark mood feminist with the purple hair and mini skirts.

We can do better than that.

She is mesmerising in her performance, and a sensual delight to look at. She would make men come in their trousers and women want to be her.

I want to meet her so badly that it's taking a great deal of self discipline to not hop onstage during their set and just hug her, tell her I love her, tell her I'm taking her to Ruby whether she wants to or not.

Oh, how this woman would challenge the patriarchy.

Her eyes, her voice, her lyrics; they all scream feminist, and I have decided she is my Goddess.

The second the gig is over, I am immediately rushing out of the crowd and over to the backstage door. I imagine several different opening lines I could use, but none of them seem to work out, at least in my head.

I remember that the last time I waited outside the stage door for a band, it was my first encounter with the Devilled Eggs. I shudder as I remember Damiano thinking I was a groupie that wanted my tits signed.

I wait there patiently until they come out, and Parker soon joins with another shot of tequila for me. I'm starting to feel a little dizzy, but I shake it off. I'm excited to speak to them, to introduce myself, to get them to Ruby and show them off to Gavin.

They take an incredibly long time to come out and Parker leaves me to go back to the table. I don't care though, I'm waiting. I'll wait for however long it takes. I *have* to meet her.

Eventually, the door bursts open. The two other members are the first out, and they look angry. Infuriated, even. It is shortly followed by the singer, who looks just as livid.

"Fine! You can both fuck off! I *am* this band, anyway!" she yells after them, and she turns to me. She sees me gawking and blurts out, "What?"

"Uh, hi," I put out my hand, "I'm Alexis, I work at Ruby Records. Did you guys just break up?"

"Yes, we did. Sorry Alexis, looks like you're literally a minute too late." She makes her way through the crowd, she's not waiting for me and she doesn't care if I follow or not. She marches to the bar, full of power, and I try my best to tail her, though I keep getting elbows to the face as I do so.

She could have walked on the outskirts of the crowd to get to the bar, but then that wouldn't have been her style.

I know her already, and I love her.

"That's okay, I was more interested in you anyway!" I yell over the music – another female folk singer. She turns around to look at me and gives me a guarded smile.

"I thought you were brilliant out there. You had the audience captivated," I tell her, and I think she sees that I genuinely mean it. She's looking at me differently now, and I think I see a shred of respect for me in her smile.

She suddenly peels down the shoulder of my dress and peers at my Foo Fighters tattoo. "I like it. Amazing band."

"Thanks," I usher the bartender over. "What would you like to drink?"

Her smile grows slightly bigger and I know I have at least ten minutes of her time now. "Jack Daniels on the rocks."

"A woman that loves her whiskey – I am only more in love with you," I tell her and her smile now shows no element of apprehension towards me. We have eliminated our smiles reserved for strangers in less than a minute and I love it.

Her energy is so strong, so inspiring, so alluring. She comes across as a woman that would commute to work naked if you simply dared her. No money involved, no real reward other than to accept a challenge others would consider daunting or embarrassing.

With some people you can just tell straight away that they are fearless.

"So what happened with the band?" I ask her, as if we are friends that have come out to this venue together.

"They're kids. Twenty-one years old. I'm twenty-nine. My vision is different; my experience in this business is different. They wanted to go poppy, I didn't."

"You want to remain rock?"

"Absolutely. But, as I'm sure you know already, to get noticed by rock labels it takes a completely different approach to if you want a pop career. The girls wanted to wear pink mini skirts and sing about boys who broke their hearts."

"And you want to sing about…?"

"Growing up. Being a woman in this industry. The bullshit. The hypocrisy. There's much more to sing about than some fucking guy breaking your fucking heart. He's a fuck boy, we get it – just develop better taste in men, Jesus!"

She is one no-bullshit, tough woman in the music business, and I want to be her. And marry her. And have kids with her.

I laugh, and I wish so damn hard that I were a lesbian. I'd promise myself to this woman and be done with it.

"What's your name by the way?" I ask her, as our drinks arrive.

"Anastasia."

Ana and I become friends the quickest I ever become friends with anyone in my entire life. We discuss the best and most powerful female singers in the world (I vote Aretha Franklin, Ana votes Pussy Riot - the very camp bartender chimes in with 'Beyonce!' and we turn to him with our best bitch mode faces; he walks away with his tail between his legs).

We talk about our experiences in the music business, every single moment we have felt emancipated by a male, I share everything but Mauro. I am not yet ready to discuss that with anyone. It turns out she has a lot of stories similar to mine, and we share a mutual disgust towards each and every story we decide to share.

Ana tells me about her childhood - she grew up in south London, was adopted by her aunt, who had a 'mean' husband, and so she ran away at eighteen to attend music school.

She wrote songs for famous bands, then became a singer, graduated from music school, learned how to play bass, went on tour with a *very* famous singer as his bassist, and saw the world. She chose to leave the band, seven years later, to focus on becoming a singer in her own right. That was two years ago.

Since then, she's been in a couple of bands, recorded a couple of EPs, but self-funded, and they never really went anywhere.

The more she tells me about herself, the more I want to sign her. And if I had the power to, I would. She seems a little upset to have just broken up with her band of only three months, so I can only assume she had been emotionally attached to them.

"But I think it's good we broke up tonight," she tells me, an ounce of sadness to her tone.

"I think this is the best thing that could have happened," I tell her and she turns to me with bright eyes. "Now I get to bring you to Ruby with me and show you off as my finding of treasure. Treasure of finding? Finding of…? What? Argh, you know what I mean."

I've had too much to drink, but it's okay. Ana has had too much to drink, too.

She laughs loudly. "Alexis, I love how honest you are. This is very rare in the music industry."

"It might just be the tequila," I point out, and we both cackle loudly. It's fun to get drunk with a *female* in the music business.

"Well whatever it is, I'd be honoured to come into Ruby with you."

Yes!
Done.
Done.
Done!

"Fantastic!" I exclaim, and I hug her. She laughs, as she hugs me back just as tightly. She then gets up, telling me she'll be right back.

I nod ecstatically as she disappears into the crowd, and I get out my phone to text Parker, who left with two girls from the table an hour ago. Just as I unlock my phone though I notice a familiar name on my screen. My eyes widen, as I open a message from Elliot.

It's a video of the band, they're waving at me and I beam.

Oh, how I miss them.
Always.
Everyday.

Elliot points the camera at something behind them, and I realise it's Big Ben. I immediately squeal – I squeal so loud that most people in the venue turn to look at me.

I jump up and down in excitement as I read the message at the end of the video.

WE'VE OFFICIALLY MOVED TO LONDON, BITCH!
When can we see you?

It's time for bed, so I wash my face, and floss. I hate flossing and always groan in frustration as I stand in the mirror for what is to me such a boring task in daily life.

I stick the floss between two top teeth, and just as I hold onto the tooth, I jolt at the appearance of something behind me.

It's Mauro. He is smiling at me in the reflection of the mirror and I turn around to face him.

"Hello Alexis, shall we finish what we started?"

I try to run, but he holds me back by the wrists, as I shout for him to let go, begging pathetically for my body to be mine again.

I feel a hard lump on my leg and I scream, I scream as loud as I possibly can...

18

When I was a kid, I used to *wish* I could go back in time and make me born in the early eighties, so that I could be a teenager in the early nineties. Grunge always feels as if that should have been my time. I would have got to see and feel Eddie Vedder's energy in concert back then. What it must have felt like. What it must have done to your soul, your heart, your entire adolescence.

I am extremely envious of people who got to see Slash in Velvet Revolver, and Chris Cornell in Soundgarden. I love and appreciate so many of the rock decades out there, but it's those early nineties that I love the most. One day I will go to Seattle, and the city will touch my soul on a level I will never feel with any other city in the world.

I listen to Temple of the Dog's 'Say Hello 2 Heaven' as I sit on the tube. I pull out one of the two books I packed with me. I'm reading so much nowadays, from body language to self-help, I am continuing to learn and grow and evolve through other smart peoples' views on life.

Books are such an incredible way to gain knowledge, a way to feed the soul. And they are helping me, forming me, giving me a weapon I never really thought possible to get from books.

It's freezing cold when I step out of Queensway tube station, but I hardly notice. I'm too excited, too filled with adrenaline. I look for them at the exit, and then on the high street, but when I spot them, I have to do a double take before I realise it is indeed them. I gasp as I take in the fact that their emo looks are completely gone.

They are walking in my direction, on my side of the street, talking amongst themselves. I begin to walk towards them, realising that they somehow look older too.

They notice me suddenly, with big smiles, roaring in Italian, and I can no longer contain my excitement.

To see the Devilled Eggs in London is such an incredibly exciting feeling, and to have them in front of me now, after four months of having not seen them, is even more exciting. I didn't think I would be this excited to see them!

I race towards them, and my eyes narrow to Elliot. I leap into his arms in pure and utter happiness, his arms open and ready for me, he spins me around as I laugh.

"ALEX!" he bellows, and he slowly stops spinning me, gently putting me down. We gaze at one another in utter joy, though he looks as if he's a bit cooler and more collected about our reunion than me. "Hello, hello."

I am in shock over the boys' appearances – they are dressed in normal, colourful clothing, and I can see their foreheads!

They look nothing like when I last saw them, except Elliot who looks exactly the same. He had never given into the emo look and I had always been grateful for this. I look into his eyes, and I see the same warmth I had left in Milano four months ago.

So pumped with excitement and happiness to see them, I pull Elliot into my arms again and give him another hug. He hugs me tightly, and the boys watch on with smiles on their faces. Except Damiano, who looks both moody and bored, as always.

I guess some things just don't change.

"It's so good to see you all!" I tell them, as Elliot and I let go.

Since leaving Milano, I had kept in touch with the band. Mostly Elliot and Matteo, but even G and Lino would reach out sometimes. It started with comments on social media posts from Matteo, G and Lino that then led to private messages from Matteo mostly, and weekly updates.

They told me how it was going with the band, their move to London, their move from Gavin to another Ruby manager, Matt. I knew they were due to move to London soon, but I didn't know the exact date.

Elliot and I are the closest. He calls me when he creates a new guitar riff, new lyrics (yes, he's started writing his own songs), or when he needs my opinion on anything music-related.

Elliot, I've come to learn, is not an emotional person; he is very logical, and he takes criticism better than most. So after you give him feedback, he will not only listen, but he will go and improve on what he's doing wrong. And I find that a really incredible quality to have; it means he's going to go far in life. Someone open to growth usually does.

"What happened to the Emos I met last autumn?!" I say, as I turn to the others. "Oh my God, I can see your faces!" I playfully put my hand on Matteo's forehead. "Hello Forehead!"

He laughs, and pulls me into a hug. "We missed you," he tells me. I hug the rest of them, and Damiano is last. I hesitate, not sure whether to approach him with a hug or not, given we haven't directly spoken in four months.

"Hi Damiano," I say, and he nods at me with a semi-smile. I don't mind that he doesn't want to hug, I am actually impressed that he's here. I was half expecting him to not show up.

He can't not like me that much if he's here, right?

Anyway, I stopped caring what Damiano thinks of me a long time ago. He's the typical prima donna lead singer of the band and I've made my peace with that.

We make our way down the high street, as I lead them to the restaurant. As we walk, Matteo starts telling me about a bass he wants to buy, when Elliot puts his arm around me. I turn to look at him, and he messes up my hair, affectionately.

It's so good to see them.

"...so I don't know which one to buy," Matteo tells me, and we turn to him.

"Oh, Matteo, I'm sorry I don't know much about bass guitars I'm afraid."

He looks disappointed, so I quickly add, "but I know someone at Ruby – George, he's a bassist in his own time, pretty good too. I'll introduce you when you're in the office."

Elliot snorts. "*George?* What kind of a name is that for a bassist?"

"A mighty fine one I'd say," I tell him, "bassists are usually…" my voice dies away, as I realise Matteo's puppy dog eyes are on me. I clear my throat, deciding to change the end of my sentence. "...the most awesome, badass people in the band."

"Nice save," Elliot whispers to me and I cackle.

They all catch me up on stuff that they forgot to tell me via social media, and there's plenty to share. That's the thing with long distance, it can feel as if you are sharing everything that is happening in your lives, but you always forget at least half. So though I knew some stuff, there were some surprising new facts – such as Matt, their new manager, getting rid of their emo look, and re-naming the band Metal Cookie.

"*Metal Cookie*?!" I blurt out, even though I promised myself I wouldn't judge any of Matt's tactics with them. They are not my band, and I cannot act as if they are.

But Jesus, *Metal Cookie?*

Matteo and G nod with solemn looks on their faces, and I feel guilty for reacting less than positively to the news. "I mean, I guess it could work? You guys like cookies, right?" Silence. "Where did he get that name from, by the way?"

All five of them shrug at me, and I bite my lip in apprehension. I quickly change the subject before I blurt out stuff I shouldn't, and we walk happily through Queensway to the restaurant.

When we arrive outside Bel Canto, all five of them are looking puzzled.

"Can't we go to Shoreditch instead?' Lino asks.

"Yeah, I heard Shoreditch is full of cool bars and pubs!"

"It is. But Lino is the only one that can legally drink," I explain to them.

"So?" G retorts, cocking up an eyebrow at me.

"So G, this is not Milano. This is London, and I cannot let you drink. Come on, stop complaining, this place is awesome."

Yes, Bel Canto is one of my favourite restaurants in London. I tell the boys this as we are led to a table, but I fail to inform them that this place is a little different to the other restaurants in London. I fail to tell them that the staff are all opera singers, and that when they bring you their food, they break out into song.

It takes a while for us to choose what to eat and order, and as I wait for the food to arrive it feels as if time is standing still. I become slightly antsy, to the point that G asks me if I'm okay.

"Oh I'm fine," I tell him, waving my hand as if nonchalantly swatting away a fly.

But I'm actually getting excited for when the waiters and waitresses will arrive with the food.

I know it's only been four months since I last saw them, but my God, how much they've changed. I forgot how quickly you change when you're a teenager.

I remember going to Biella every summer throughout my teens, and each year the photos of me were completely different to those of the year before.

Every year the guy I would be into would change dramatically. One summer it would be the town rebel, the next it would be the town geek.

My fashion will have changed too, and my hair. As a teenager, I loved to change my hair at least twice a year. I've been blonde, brunette, purple - you name the colour and I've done it. I'd go through moods of wanting to grow my hair long, or wanting it really short. I just never felt like the same person I was the year before, and I guess that's what the Devilled Eggs must be experiencing too.

Matteo, for one, seems a little less shy and a bit more confident - and not just because he's become comfortable with me, but you can see it when he orders his food, he's grown more sure of himself, and it's nice to see.

Lino, who is usually more pensive and introvert, is interacting a lot more with the others, and G, who would usually take out his phone to check his reflection every ten seconds, has only pulled it out twice, and once was to text someone.

Damiano and Elliot are the only ones who seem to have remained the same. Though Damiano's emo look has disappeared, he seems the same bitch mode self I have known since the first time I met him. I guess for him to change would have me race to the window to spot pigs flying.

And dear old Elliot has remained the same, for which I am very glad. Though he's the second eldest in the band, it feels as if he's decades ahead of the others sometimes. He encompasses a maturity in him that is older than his seventeen years.

Or maybe it's just that compared to the other toddlers in the band, he stands out as more mature than he actually is. I mean, the guy still burps at every opportunity and uses his sleeve as a handkerchief, so he's not exactly a respectable adult just yet. He's well on his way though.

I'm responding to an email from Gabriella Reed's PA Ceska when the food arrives.

Finally!

I watch the waitress putting down our plates nonchalantly. The boys are talking amongst themselves about their schedule tomorrow when the waitress, who looks Norwegian, suddenly bursts into song.

All five of their faces drop, as they turn to look at her, not sure what's going on.

"Oh, did I not mention that everyone here is an opera singer?!" I bellow over the singing, and they look at me wide-eyed.

"What?!" Matteo and G wail.

I cackle under my breath and we turn our attention to the opera singer. She's bloody good, hitting notes so damn high it makes me 'wow' under my breath.

Sometimes I wish I could sing, properly, but I don't see myself being happy as a singer. Singing doesn't give me the same pleasure, the same connection to music that playing does.

The same goes for lyrics – when I was eight, I tried to write a song. It was called 'Forget the Past' and it was about an imaginary ex-boyfriend. I thought it was great, but my brother laughed at it and said he had never heard of anything more generic. I think that was probably the biggest favour he could have ever done me. I never tried to write a song again.

I watch the boys grinning in excitement as they listen. Suddenly Elliot gets up and joins her. I giggle as I watch them, the opera singer welcoming his participation.

They sound incredible together. I get out my phone to film it, shocked that Elliot can sing so well. I don't recognise the song as I know nothing about opera, but they're singing in Italian and it's sending shivers down my neck.

Once they finish, we stand up and applaud. Elliot takes a bow, and I whistle. Once the applause dies down and the opera singer goes back to waitressing, our table is buzzing with excitement in the aftermath of what was a pretty terrific operatic duet.

I look to Elliot for an explanation as the boys all blurt out things at the same time, talking over each other as they always do.

"I sang opera as a child."

Of course he did.

Once lunch is over, I invite them to Camden with me to get some new vinyl records, but they all decline. All except Elliot.

"Oh fuck yes, I'll come with you. I haven't seen Camden yet!"

Elliot and I hop on the tube to Camden, sharing headphones as we listen to American punk bands from the seventies, like Black Flags and Dead Kennedys.

I now know Elliot's taste in music inside out. I've continued to introduce him to good music, such as The Cure and Portishead, but so as he. He introduced me to some unknown John Mayer tracks, Italian act Motta, and Bring me the Horizon. Okay so I don't like Bring me the Horizon, as much I tried to, but I think he's forgiven me over it.

We get to Camden and I show him around – the stables, the markets, the pubs. We have a blast visiting old record shops and asking the owners about their adventures in the music business (they're mostly previous musicians who have incredible stories to share).

Elliot's energy is always contagious; he tells stories with such light in his eyes and magic in his voice, you feel like you are always the less energetic one, no matter how much vivacity you bring to the table.

I forget that I'm carrying my old polaroid camera under my jacket (I take a camera with me everywhere now – I have four in total, and today felt like a polaroid kind of day). It's only as the owner of the third record shop we visit starts eyeing my coat that I remember I have it with me, and that I look like I'm shoplifting.

"Oh! No, wait, this isn't a record – it's a camera!" I tell the owner, Alfie, from California. Once I show him the camera and we joke about it, he starts to tell us his life story.

He has lived in London for the past twenty years, and he's had his record shop for thirteen of those years. He's mixed race, in his fifties, and loves everything rock. We get on with him straight away purely based on our mutual love for music, for *good* music.

We talk about the industry, how it's falling apart, how London isn't how it used to be.

We talk about music itself, punk in particular, both British and American, we talk about rock over the ages. All three of us are engaged, and happy, because music is our mutual love, and we will never grow tired of discussing it.

Eventually, we get onto the topic of the Foo Fighters.

"Oh, do you like them?" asks Alfie, and Elliot snorts.

"*Like* them? If she could have sex with an entire band…"

"Hey!" It's weird to hear Elliot talk about sex in any way, as even if I see him as older than the rest of the band, I still see him as younger than me.

"Well you're in luck then," Alfie tells us, "I have one of their original records here somewhere."

My eyes widen. *"WHERE? WHICH ONE?"*

It takes some searching but Alfie manages to find it – it's Medium Rare and I cannot believe my eyes. I've been searching for this for years.

"I'll take it, I'll take it, I'll take it!" I bellow, with people in the store looking at me. "No one make eye contact with this record, it's *mine!*"

Elliot laughs, shaking his head. "She loves the Foos, in case you didn't get that," he says to anyone who will listen.

We walk over to the counter and just as I dig my hand into my purse, Elliots blocks me.

"I'm getting it," he announces and I frown. It's a nice gesture, but I wouldn't allow him to for two main reasons: 1) he's younger than me and my responsibility, even if I don't help manage the band anymore, 2) Elliot grew up poor, this much I know. He doesn't talk about his childhood, but I know it – there are certain signs.

Like his mum was holding down three jobs, and he once mentioned he never got presents for Christmas one year. Elliot is far from materialistic, but I know that that must have hurt him as a kid. I've also seen him budget for the month back in Milano, he's the accountant for the band, which tells you everything you need to know.

I stifle a laugh. "What? No," I say.

"Yes."

"Elliot, I have a paying job-"

"So do I."

I stare. "Since when? Where?"

"Since yesterday. At a pub down the street from where we're living."

I cock up an eyebrow, realising he's being serious. "Ell, you've been in London forty-eight hours and you've already got yourself a job?"

He nods, and I'm impressed. I allow him to pay for Medium Rare, and we walk out, pulling out the record and my eyes turning into heart shapes.

"Okay, okay, enough of that. You can stare at the record when you get home. I want to see more of Camden."

I playfully roll my eyes and put the record in my backpack, linking arms with Elliot as I take him through Camden.

When I hear that there is a male singer in the office with the exact same voice as Morrisey's, I am looking everywhere for him like an excited child trying to find Father Christmas. I am marching down the office peeking into all the meeting rooms when I hear Gavin call my name.

"Alexis!"

Gavin has this insane way of calling your name without even being visible to you. I scan the office, and find him popping his head out of the kitchen. His facial expression is, as always, blunt. You cannot read him at all, unless he's furious with you. "Meet me in my office in two? Just going to make myself a tea."

My heart sinks at the thought of missing Morrisey Version Two, but I hide it behind a smile and nod. I go into Gavin's office and park myself in the leather chair opposite his desk.

His office is always creepily empty and cold – no pictures other than one of his kids on the desk on a ski trip somewhere in Austria. Other than that, there is absolutely nothing in his office that gives anything away about his life or his personality. It's depressing. It's as if he sold all of it for his position at Ruby.

He walks in with a cup of tea in hand, and shows me a smile, with teeth and all. Unsure how to respond as he's never smiled at me before when we are alone, I try to smile back, with teeth, but it feels awkward.

"So, Alexis," he sits down in his chair and is still smiling. I try to prepare myself for absolutely anything, but I'm a bit nervous. "You've been with us four months now."

"Yes," I manage to say.

"And in these four months, we had a bit of a rocky start in Milan. But I admit that perhaps that was my fault by sending you out to Italy as your first assignment," he tells me.

"But even if it was a rocky start, since you've been working here in the office, you've been amazing. You've been handling everything I've thrown your way, you're amazing with Gabriella, with Mind Spin, with Dazza. They all love you, and have absolutely no complaints.

Apart from Gaby when you messed up her smoothie order that first week," he chuckles to himself as if her prima donna ways are cute, and then snaps out of it. "Anyway, we all love you and would like to make you an employee here at Ruby."

My eyes light up.

What. The. Fuck?

"Now, you will start in an entry role position of course, so I'm afraid it doesn't pay very well."

Pay?
Money?
Be paid to work at Ruby?
In music?
Is this really happening?

"But hopefully, knowing you, you'll work hard to get promoted, and then the higher you get and the more senior you get, you obviously get paid more as you get rewarded more responsibility."

I cannot believe what I'm hearing, and it's hard to react as fast as I probably should. Gavin is looking at me, waiting for me to say something. "Wow, Gavin. What a privilege."

"Your role will be as an exec. You will work under me."

"Like an assistant artist manager?"

"Uh, sort of, yes, I suppose."

I beam at him.

"So, you accept?"

"Of course I accept!"

"Great. I'll get HR to sort out your paperwork – just go and see Jo when we've finished."

I nod, and he narrows his eyes at me as I get up with a big smile on my face.

"Oh, and there's something else."

I sit back down.

"I want to touch base on something – the Devilled Eggs have moved to London." Before I can say anything, he continues. "I only ask that you leave them alone, Alexis. They're not one of my clients anymore – they're Matt's. He's overseeing all their music, the album, the tour-"

"Tour?" I interrupt.

"Yes, they're going to be supporting G-lorious on their European tour dates."

G-lorious are a hip-hop duo from Brixton and one of our biggest clients. Just hearing the word 'tour' gets me excited for them. Their careers are going to take off here, I can feel it. I must have hearts for eyes because Gavin is looking at me funny.

"But like I said Alexis, Matt is their manager now, not me. And I want you to focus on my clients, okay?"

I'm trying to listen to Gavin, but I notice something in the window behind him. It's the Devilled Eggs walking past, and I hope to God they don't notice us, but they do.

Matteo is the first to notice, and he stops in his tracks, tapping Elliot and G to have a look. They all stop in front of the window, and wave. I cannot wave back so I try to ignore them, but realising the opportunity, they begin making faces at me – sticking out their tongues, cross-eyes, pretending to choke each other, and, Gavin.

I gulp, and snap out of it as I focus on Gavin.

"Good. I don't want you to worry about them; they're being well looked after."

They only continue to pull faces, and now G is pretending to walk up some stairs. God, I haven't seen someone do that in years. They're such children!

I want to laugh but resist. "Of course," I reply to Gavin with a serious face.

"And Matt knows what he's doing – he's got three Grammies under his belt, for goodness sake."

"Right."

Do. Not. Laugh.

Gavin stands up, and I'm relieved. I follow as he leads me out of his office as if I don't know the way. He smiles again, and it puts me at unease once again. It's just not something I'm used to seeing.

"Congratulations, Alexis."

"Thank you," I reply, just as I spot the Devilled Eggs hiding in the meeting room adjacent to Gavin's office.

"Well I'm going to go get a coffee before our meet with what's-her-name again. See you in there?"

I nod and watch him disappear into the kitchen before I turn around and scurry into the meeting room, chasing the band with a folder in my hand, playfully slapping their backs with it.

"Animals! You're all animals!" I hiss with a smile.

I don't mention what Gavin said to me to the boys, as I'm not really sure myself what I'm going to do with this information. How am I supposed to leave them alone, anyway? It's not like I'm giving them career advice anymore. Do I not talk to them at the office? Do I not hang out with them, during office hours but also outside of work hours?

I leave the band to get to my big meeting – today is the day I'm finally introducing Gavin to Anastasia. I've been planning this meeting for two weeks, as Gavin hasn't had time to fit it in, but today is finally the day. He accepted the invite five days ago, he's in the office, he's making a tea, and then he's making this meeting.

I get a call from reception that Ana has arrived and so I go and pick her up. When I arrive at reception, she's wearing the coolest black dungarees with a white shirt I've ever seen, or perhaps it's more that everything looks the coolest when Ana is wearing it.

Her hair is up in a messy bun and I am envious of her and all women on this planet who are able to pull off the messy bun look. I only look like I have the face of a hedgehog when I do it.

"Hey stranger," I say, as I watch her reading her book – The Music Management Bible. She looks at me and gives me a relaxed smile before putting her book away in her bag and following me out into the office.

"Thinking of managing yourself?" I ask, and she seems embarrassed that I spotted her book.

"Well you never know. This industry is full of too many snakes."

"We're not all like that," I say, feeling the obligation to defend Ruby. Especially now that I'll soon officially be an employee, and well, I'm walking down the corridor of their offices.

"Well *you're* not, but I'm sure there's a few snakes lurking in this place."

I want to reply but Twat Intern Jacob appears, introducing himself to Ana with that sly smile of his. I guess there are a couple of snakes in this place. But isn't that the same anywhere you work?

Ana doesn't take much interest in Jacob, seeing through him in a nanosecond. When we slip away and arrive at the meeting room, she makes a hissing snake noise as if to call Jacob one.

I give her a small smile but choose not to say anything. The more time I spend with Ana, the more I really like her. She's one of those girls that if she sees another girl succeed as a singer, she's not going to be jealous, she's not going to be angry, she's going to be happy for her. And for this I completely love her. We need more women like this in this world.

Women who go through life thinking 'this is a man's world and we can't do anything about it' are the people who are keeping this world this way. If more women actually *helped* each other, *supported* each other, *cheered each other on,* I swear to God, we would have already been able to conquer the world.

Maybe someday.

But until then, I will continue to support inspiring women, cheer them on, and be happy for them and their success, as if it is my own. Because that's the way it's supposed to be.

In typical Gavin style, he strolls in fifteen minutes late with yet another tea in hand. I introduce him to Ana, and they talk about her music, her upbringing, her views on life.

Gavin then tells her he listened to her demo and liked a couple of the songs. He says that we could do a lot with her

293

voice and her face, but that he sees her music heading in the direction of leading a cool, all-female rock band.

"We do actually need one at Ruby," Gavin says, and the idea instantly excites me. Being the person to bring in an all-female rockband to Ruby would make my entire year.

Ana seems excited by the idea too, and we think about strategy for a good hour. Gavin doesn't mention signing her or anything – first we would need to find the rest of the band members, and then record another demo. Then, I guess, we would see what would happen next. Yet the idea of being able to bring in a new client, managing that client, doing everything that an artist manager does, that is getting me beyond excited!

I imagine myself standing by Anna's side before she debuts at Brixton Academy, and giving her a proud hug before she strolls onstage in Anna-style.

I imagine guys like Twit Intern Jacob looking on in envy, shocked at the possibility of succeeding in music through using your brain, and developing real skills, other than *who you know*.

We spend the next two hours listening to Anna's music and chatting as if we are all old friends at the pub. Gavin even asks me to go and get some beers. Since we've been in the meeting for three hours, once I leave to get beers, I also take a quick two minutes to check my emails.

Nothing major, and so I grab the beer and go back to the meeting room. I shake off visions of me hugging Anna at Wembley before she hits the stage. I shake off the screams of thousands of fans, who, if they had a chance, would reward me with limitless tiramisu, because it was me who got Anna her big break.

Excited to return to strategising, my smile fades when I re-enter the meeting room to find Gavin is sitting alone, checking his e-mails.

"Has she gone for a bathroom break?"

He looks up at me with blunt eyes. "Huh? No, she actually had to go."

I frown. "What? That was abrupt."

"Hmm?" he says, looking back down at his phone. I put down the beers slowly, trying to understand what is going on here. Why Anna would leave, why she wouldn't say goodbye, and why there is a tense atmosphere in here that Gavin is trying so hard to pretend isn't present.

I don't know why, but I casually walk out of the room. I don't say a word to Gavin, but once I am out and he can no longer see me, I run down the corridor and into the lift.

Something feels weird. She didn't wait for me to come back, she didn't text me, nothing.

When I reach the ground floor, I spot Anastasia exiting the building in the distance. I run after her, calling her name, and it only takes me half a minute to reach her. She is now out on the busy high street.

"Ana!" I reach her, and she turns around with anguish in her eyes. I am taken aback, and I freeze in front of her, out of breath.

"What…happened?" I ask her. "I thought…we were making progress?"

"Yes we were Alexis, until your jackass boss hit on me."

My eyes widen, and I even force a laugh. "*Gavin?* What? No."

"Yes, Alexis. And you shouldn't be so naïve about who you work for," she points to the Ruby Records building. "All snakes, I fucking told you. This was such a bad idea, I knew it. I trusted you, not them-"

"He hit on you?" Imagining Gavin hitting on Ana is weird for me. He has never made any advances on me or anyone I know or work with, that I know of. I have always known that yes, okay, he's a bit of a dog, but not at work? Surely not in a professional environment?

"Yes, Alexis! He hit on me, he put a hand on my leg and insinuated I would be signed if I fucked him, okay?"

I gulp, having flashbacks of my job interview just a few hours before the London Paolo Petrinelli gig. It seems like such a long time ago, but I never forgot it.

The anger, so much anger, towards that jackass. The way he had unzipped his trousers, the way he had smiled at me. I can see his grey boxers in my mind as clear as day, the smell of his office – of coffee, his shiny black shoes that sat on his desk when I first walked in.

These types of incidents stay with you forever. How they made you feel, how there are men (or women) who walk around thinking they can do things like that.

They are serious things that happen to women every single day, and no one is doing a damn thing about it.

"I'm sorry, Ana. I'm so sorry. I had no idea."

"Don't worry about me, Alexis. I'm a tough chick, and I've gone through worse. That's why I stay away from corporations like Ruby. Women are treated like shit," she tells me, "but it's you I'm worried about."

I frown. "Me? What do you mean? Gavin wouldn't dare try-"

"You haven't been listening to me, Alexis. That place you call your workplace? It's a snake pit. Get out whilst you can." And from that, she walks off down the street, and I watch her.

I watch her purple hair glisten in the sun, and as I do so, I wonder if I'll ever see her again.

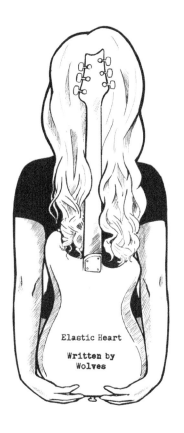

19

When I was seventeen, I went to a music event doing research for the college magazine. It was a relatively dull event with less than 2% talent, and so I got talking to the guy sitting next to me. He was wearing a backwards cap, blue tracksuit bottoms and a matching sporty, blue jacket. He asked me if I knew what time it was, as he had lost his phone. I told him, and we got talking about the event itself.

He told me he was from Turkey, as if it wasn't abundantly clear from the Turkish flag pendant that dangled around his neck. He told me he had been in London two years and that he hated it; he missed Turkey and he missed his family, but he was determined to make something of himself in London.

He had scary eyes, as if he wasn't completely there, but he was interesting. We began judging every act that took the stage, and I found that despite the craziness in his eyes, he had a warmth to him that I took to. I always find people with a little crazy far more interesting than the tortuously dull.

Just as I was about to ask him what he does in London, the stage goes quiet, and a presenter suddenly calls 'Harim Kaman' to the stage.

"Oh, that's me. See you in a bit."

Wait, what? I thought to myself. *He's an artist?*

I watched him curiously, as he took to the stage. He introduced himself, the beat kicked in, and he began to rap. I had always admired rap from a distance, which is why when he began I knew straight away that he was by far the most amazing rapper I had ever heard in my entire life.

I was taken aback, hardly breathing, as I watched him spit out bars not only at an impressive speed but with incredible lines too! I watched on in intrigue, a grin appearing on my face as I bopped my head to the beat.

Once he was done, I was on my feet, clapping like his biggest groupie. We went for a coffee afterwards, finding out that Harim was a famous Turkish rapper trying to make it in London. He had sold out two albums in Turkey already, in only two years.

"English rap is a much tougher market to crack, you know? Especially because back home I had connections; here it's starting from scratch."

Harim also had a troubled past though that prevented him from fully focusing on his career – he was out on bail with a court case pending for grievous bodily harm. He was dangerous, scary, and a little bit mad. But I was so in awe with his talent that I did something crazy – I offered to be his manager.

We wrote down our contract on a napkin, and we were off. I started contacting record labels to set up meetings, at the same time encouraging him to work on an English album.

We were making great progress, but his temper poisoned all our plans when he beat up some guy who wouldn't give him correct change at the supermarket. He was soon deported, and I never heard from him again.

But that contract hangs on my wall, no matter where I live. And sometimes, I go online and listen to one of his Turkish albums. He was my first ever client, and I like to remember this period of my life; when I had no idea what I wanted to be, but had a simple hunger to help talented artists get heard.

It's always been a part of me. And the contract hanging on my wall reminds me of exactly this.

I scroll through the NLP courses available in London, as I sit at my desk at Ruby, nodding my head slightly to the indie music playing in the background. The good thing about the Ruby office is that they never play anything on loop – there's always fresh demos to play, bands and artists *begging* to be noticed by Ruby.

It's like a constant reminder of how wanted we are. That being said, the music itself can vary. Sometimes I'll be pleasantly surprised, and other times I'll wonder how the hell actual humans paid money to make what is currently playing.

I'm desperate to go on an NLP course. I bought three NLP textbooks since Ric first brought it up in conversation in Milano last summer. The more I read, the more I became interested in it. NLP helps out with lots of different situations, from building confidence, to making you overcome tragedy in your life.

299

I'm using it to a), build up my confidence in meetings and presentations, and b) develop better ways to communicate with the people around me through the power of both verbal and body language.

I find one that catches my eye, but it's *really* expensive. Since becoming a permanent employee at Ruby, I still haven't been able to make rent without having a second job on the weekends and evenings. I did however quit my cleaning job in order to start something new – photo shoots.

I've always had a knack for taking good profile pictures of people, and so I've started my own sessions for budding entrepreneurs, interns, and execs just starting out. Right now it's mostly just people at Ruby, but they're starting to spread the word, and charging £50 a session, I'm doing okay.

It's enough for me to quit my cleaning job, stick to just Ruby Records during the week, and photo shoots on the weekends.

I switch tab to one of my favourite new bands – Wolf Alice, they're playing at the 100 Club this week. I buy my ticket and smile to myself, excited to see them live. I've been listening to their music the past month and even had them added to the playlist in the office after hours.

As I bop my head to the music, I suddenly freeze. The sonf sounds very familiar, and I turn my head to glance at the speakers hanging from the ceiling.

I definitely know this song.

It suddenly dawns on me – who is playing. My eyes widen, and I walk over to Gavin's office in a daze. I stand by his open door, as he sits at his desk, glancing at something intensely on his laptop screen.

It cannot be.

It can't.

Gavin is going to tell me that I'm wrong, that this isn't what I think it is.

"Is this the Devilled Eggs?" I ask, pointing at the ceiling. He doesn't look at me, nor does he change expression.

"Yes."

It can't be. It just can't. How could Gavin do this? Has there been a mistake?

I fidget awkwardly. "Isn't this, uh, one of the tracks that they wrote…post-recording?"

The songs you banned from being recorded.

The songs that cost me the remainder of my time in Milano.

I recall that very special afternoon when they had demo'd the track to me; the day that I had seen them as musicians for the very first time.

That was a good afternoon.

"Yes. We made them re-record with the new tracks," he tells me nonchalantly, as if he hadn't yelled at me for days on end when I had suggested exactly that. As if it hadn't been my idea but Gavin's. As if I hadn't been punished for a good two months with shitty, brainless tasks as consequence for trying to push those songs to the EP.

"Right."

"Anything else, Alexis?" he asks me.

An apology would be nice.

Or a thank you for making them fucking create good music.

"No," I say, and he asks me to close his door as I leave.

I do so but I'm so angry that I march back to my desk in a huff. I'm happy that the boys will be releasing good music, this will help them, but I'm annoyed, in fact, I'm *angry,* at how Gavin treated me over something he went ahead and did anyway.

Once I sit back down, I wonder where the hell Gavin gets off not telling me something like that. After all the lectures, the yelling, the backlash I got for educating the boys and encouraging them to create new music, he goes and makes a master of those songs without even telling me!

So he thought they were good, too.

So I wasn't imagining it.

So it *was* worth re-recording.

I scowl to myself, and shake my head.

What an asshole.

I take a deep breath in, get out my phone, and ring Elliot.

If Gavin is going to treat me this way, to take my ideas and make them his, whilst also punishing me for those exact ideas, then I'm not going to listen to him.

I'm not going to stay away from the boys, I'm not going to avoid them or abandon them when they ask me for my help.

They've already asked me eight times to visit them in the studio and I have declined, time and time again, every excuse worse than the last, to keep my distance, to respect Gavin's wishes.

Well, not anymore.

When I arrive at Church Studios, I have to take a moment to take in the beautiful venue in front of me. If you live in London and work in music, you have heard of Church Studios and fantasised about entering this beautiful building a thousand times over.

It is only used by the elite musicians – the ones who can afford it. Why? Because A) it's beautiful, B) the production is out of this world, and C) did I mention it used to be a church?!

The Devilled Eggs are recording here for one very obvious reason – Damiano's father. From what I've heard from the boys, Brett Gardner doesn't give a shit about his son's band, but I guess it's about keeping up appearances.

I buzz the studio, and the receptionist lets me in, as I gasp at the beauty of the church from the inside. As a teenager, I'd sit and stare at pictures of their studios on the website and just smile. And now here I am – walking in, seeing it all with my very own eyes.

Before I can have a proper look at my surroundings, the receptionist pulls me into a room that I quickly realise is the rehearsal room. I've never been in the rehearsal room at a recording studio before, mostly because they usually don't tend to exist! You have to be earning a *buckload* to be able to rent out both a studio *and* a recording room, and to find a studio with both too.

I cannot imagine how much the fees are in a studio like this, in London, but the word *astronomical* comes to mind.

There are black leather sofas everywhere, a fireplace (*a fireplace!*), and instruments everywhere – they belong to the boys, I can tell by how badly they are maintained, but I've noticed that they've upgraded since Milano.

The space is massive, and just as I take in all the details of the room, the receptionist disappears and I hear shouting.

The voices sound aggressive and so I power walk across the room to find the recording studio door ajar.

I am about to stroll in with a smile when I am grinded to a halt by what I see in the distance.

Elliot and Damiano look as if they are going to kill each other; Matteo and Lino are holding Elliot back, and G is doing the same for Damiano.

My eyes widen.

"You're such a fucking asshole!" Elliot yells.

"Go snort some cocaine to forget your life, you loser!" Damiano shouts back. I cannot believe how hostile they are being with each other. I realise that I never really paid attention to the relationship between Elliot and Damiano and how they interact. Retrospectively, it doesn't appear as if they like each other very much.

Well, I can see why Elliot doesn't like Damiano, but why does Damiano not like Elliot?

"I cannot believe we are related, I will *never* call you my brother!" Damiano wails, and my eyes are about to jump out of their sockets.

What.
The.
Fuck.

"You're a fucking dick," Elliot says, slightly calmer. He storms off in my direction, and suddenly all the boys notice me. Elliot gulps, realising what I have just overheard, and I follow him down the corridor as he marches off.

I call after him, but I know he's not going to acknowledge me. Not until he has a cigarette in his mouth. And so I follow him out into the car park, and I watch him light up.

Did I hear right?
Elliot and Damiano are brothers?
This has to be some sort of joke?
Right?

I try to relive every memory I can of any interaction they may have had in front of me, and honestly, I start to notice that they avoid each other like the plague.

Why didn't I pick up on that? Or did I just simply assume that as the two most handsome of the band (Elliot leading), that they probably have a clash of egos?

There is silence as we stand underneath some shelter, watching the pitter patter of the softest rain. I don't know what to say or how to say it, and so I keep my eyes fixed on the grey clouds above us.

We stay like this a while. I continue to relive my memories of Damiano and Elliot being in the same room, and try to figure out if they are half brothers from Brett Gardner's side – I've read he is quite the man whore.

But all this time - my interpretation of the dynamics of the band have been inaccurate. There are actually two *brothers* in this band, and this changes everything.

"You two are brothers," I eventually say, as if I need him to confirm it, as if what I overheard wasn't enough. That it doesn't make it real enough. I need to hear it confirmed.

"Yep," he replies, and my heart sinks. I like Elliot so much, and it makes me sad to think he's related to the douche prima donna in there. I watch him blow out a smoke ring; they're not as good as Ric's but they're close enough.

"That sucks," I say, matter-of-factly.

"Yep."

We stand there, looking out at the rain as if we are both in shock, as if Elliot can't quite believe it himself, like he has never really been able to believe it.

"Brett Gardner is my father," he tells me.

I knew it, that shagging bastard.

"He was seeing my mother when he was looking after an Italian band. They had an affair, one of his many, he treated my mother like shit, even more so when he learnt she was pregnant. Left her without so much as a goodbye. My mum raised me alone, and we'll be damned if we ever need a *dime* from that family."

Elliot is trying his best to look unphased by the story he is telling me, as if it has happened to someone else, that he is nonchalantly passing on the details of that person's life, and, it's a good performance. If I had met him yesterday I would have believed it, I would have gobbled it all up.

But I don't, because I know Elliot now. I see the pain in his eyes, from the abandonment, from the rejection of his brother. It affects him, just as it would anyone.

I realise as I look at Elliot that he reminds me of cocky wrestlers before they enter the ring; they put out their chest, beating it, as they cheer themselves on with fierce, confident faces. Elliot does that all day long, everyday.

But not today.

He tells me how he grew up in a shit neighbourhood in Pisa, whilst stalking Damiano's life online. He said he was obsessed with him, with the life he never had. Damiano was born just two years after Elliot, and he couldn't fathom how one son could get everything, whilst the other could get nothing.

"But then once I moved to Milano to attend the same music academy as him (under a scholarship of course), I saw that my life is a lot richer than his. I am so, so glad for my mum, for the way she raised me. I have so much more than Damiano has ever had." He looks at me, as he blows out smoke. "That guy gets it *hard* from Brett Gardner."

"I've heard."

"No, no, you have yet to witness his rath."

I ask him what happened when he saw Damiano for the first time, and he tells me the story: he paid him a visit at his villa, revealed his true identity, and Damiano laughed in his face, the way I can imagine him doing, and they didn't speak for months following that.

"Then I discovered we were both mutual friends with G and Matteo, and even if Milano is the music city of Italy, there are not a lot of teenage Italian rock musicians willing to start a band, so we formed the Devilled Eggs," he tells me. His eyes are morose, and I can't tell if he truly regrets the entire thing or not.

I stare at his face as he tells his story, searching for resemblances with Damiano and finding none. Once he finishes, we stare out at the rain.

"Knowing he's your brother, I'm now sorry for all the times I was rude to Damiano."

He forces a laugh. "Don't be. He's an asshole."

"Yeah, but he's your brother."

Elliot doesn't say anything, and it's because he knows it's true.

Brothers.
They're brothers.
Family.
Blood related.

"I really do just feel sorry for him, you know? Can you imagine having a father that sees through you? I would rather have no father than one that looks right through me," he tells me, and I can see that he almost believes his own words.

Almost.

I relive finding them ready to pounce each other. "What were you fighting over?"

"I don't even know. He suddenly, out of nowhere, starts a fight with me. We have never physically fought, but I feel like we are not far from it. He wants a fight. As if it's going to help him or something."

"How does Brett act around you?"

"Well, the first time he was a bit taken aback when he saw me. But from there, he avoids visiting Damiano where I am obviously going to be there. He has never seen us play a gig. And thank fuck for that – I would probably throw something at him."

I recall in Milano how Brett had been downstairs at the studio and Elliot had been the only one to refuse to go.

It's crazy, but I know that every sentence that Elliot is saying out of anger is a lie. He would never hurt Brett or Damiano. He may have grown up rough, he may have not had everything he had ever wanted as a child, and he may have grown up without a father, but Elliot is actually the most decent, caring human being in the band. And probably one of the most caring humans I have met in a long time.

He hides behind drugs and his incredibly disgusting burps, but underneath, he has a pure heart. And you can tell because the pure of heart are always trying to hide that fact.

I want to ask him, 'what now?' but I already know the answer. He will head back into the studio and continue like normal. Because there is an album to record. Because he will put aside Damiano's shitty personality and concentrate on the music.

We stand outside whilst Elliot finishes his cigarette, and then, as predicted, we head inside as if nothing happened. Damiano is nowhere in sight, but the other boys are watching something on G's laptop.

"Guys, ready?" Elliot asks.
For what?
"Yep! I've got it."

Got what?

The boys suddenly gather around me and I become apprehensive. I look at all of them, and feel like something is definitely going on. Elliot smiles, and it's a new smile, one I haven't seen before – one of pure joy. In fact, it's only now that I see the boy in him.

"We, uh, we wanted to tell you that we appreciate all the help you have given us, all the advice, all the music lessons, and for renting out our space for us in Milano last summer. You're really badass, and we know you're going to make such a fantastic manager someday."

"And, we uh, we wanted to show you our appreciation with a little something." Elliot nods at Matteo, who in turn hands me a bottle of Disaronno.

I gasp, and just as I think these boys couldn't have given me a better present, I see that they have printed a selfie I took with them at Bell Canto on the label.

"Wha…? How did you..?"

"Damiano's father knew someone who could sort it out for us. Do you like it?" asks G.

"*Do I like it?!* I love it! This is such a beautiful, beautiful gift. Thank you so much, I don't know what to say," I tell them.

It's a nice feeling, when someone acknowledges your help. And I didn't help them to get gratitude in return, I helped them because I wanted to, because I simply want to see them succeed, but it is nice to be acknowledged for it.

"We know how much you love Disaronno."

We group hug and I want to squeeze all of their cheeks but I can't because we're in Church studios and we're too rock n'roll for all that.

"Great, now that we've got that out of the way…" Elliot says, and they all quickly disperse. They grab their instruments, take their places, and suddenly music starts.

It's all happened so fast that I'm a bit taken aback, but I nod to the catchy and well crafted song, sitting down on one of the leather sofas as I watch and listen to them with a smile. Elliot and Matteo play but also fill in on Damiano's vocals.

It doesn't even sound anything like the boys I first met in Milano. They sound good, really good. They need a bit of a push still, but they're well on their way. If they were playing at a gig right now and I didn't know them, my bra would be flying on stage right about now.

Joking. I don't do that shit. But, imagine if I did.

I give them feedback on all five of their songs on the EP, on their performance, on their 'stage presence'.

We hang out, eat pizza, listen to music (Black Honey, Until the Ribbon Breaks, Alt-J) and tell stories. Elliot tells us about the time he got robbed at gunpoint in Milano near San Siro stadium, and G tells us about the time he dumped one chick just to get with another, and then got back together with his ex 'because she was the best in bed'.

Their stories vary, with no real topic of inspiration, and I like that they feel they can share this stuff with me. I, in turn, tell them about the time I went on a date on a guy I met on a dating app and he was half my size, and the time in south Italy a man on a motorbike approached me begging me to hop on the back 'for a quick slice of apple pie at his house''.

Music wise, I ask them how it's going at Ruby, and they immediately tell me that they hate Matt. He apparently doesn't know how to manage them, how to look after them, and how to book them gigs. He doesn't understand their music, nor their inspiration behind the music. He simply only cares about making a name for himself at the label as he's only been there a year, and he's still quite young. I listen to them and their complaints, but I don't contribute.

Who am I to say anything about Matt? I don't even know him. All I do is encourage the boys to focus on their music and be inspired by what they're doing – because what they're doing, and how far they have come in only four months, is something to be extremely proud of.

And then comes a request I had not been anticipating.

"Play something for us," Lino asks, and I frown.

"Yeah go on!"

"Play!"

It appears to be a popular request, and before I can even react to it, Elliot has pulled his Strat out and is passing me it. "Play something," he tells me, and it's only when Elliot says it to me that I listen.

I'm suddenly on my feet, fiddling with the pedal, thinking of what to play. It takes about twenty seconds for me to think of the right song, and I smile as I tune up.

I know all five pairs of eyes are on me as I begin. It takes them a while to get who it is that I'm playing, but once they do, I can hear them whispering excitedly to each other.

I don't dare look up, but continue playing a guitar version of Sia's 'Elastic Heart'. I can feel them move around on the sofa as they take in the great version I learned in class a couple of weeks ago. Yes, I'm going to class twice a week now. It's my favourite time of the week.

As the playing gets more intense, more complicating, more enticing, the energy in the room electrifies, and I can't help smiling.

I do really love playing. The more I learn, the more I love it. It takes me to another world, relaxes me, inspires me, soothes me.

Once I finish, I look up and just as I do all four of them have leapt off the sofa and are surrounding me.

"Holy shit! That was *so good*!"

"You're a natural!"

"Where did you learn that song?!"

I beam. "Thanks guys, I've been taking lessons."

"That was amazing!"

I beam and thank them, just as they get up.

"Right, Lino, you ready to finish the drum parts?" Matteo asks, as they step out of the rehearsal room and into the studio. Damiano and G follow, complimenting me once again before they slip out.

It's Elliot and I left in the rehearsal room, and he picks up his packet of cigarettes. "Be right back," he tells me and I nod.

I am still beaming, and I start playing Chandelier, slowly, and at my own pace. I feel Elliot approach slowly by my side. "Look up when you play."

Taken aback by his words, I look at him as I stop playing. His eyes are serious, the most serious I have ever seen them.

He no longer looks like a boy, but a fully grown adult. "Being a female guitarist is something completely badass and awesome. Nothing else. Look up when you play."

Before I can say anything, he turns on his heel and walks out with his packet of cigarettes. I smile to myself, and go back to playing, wondering what song I'm going to learn next. Knowing that perhaps Elliot does indeed make a good point. One that I hadn't even noticed before.

I stand in the lobby of the Hilton hotel, unable to enter the hall. Nerves are holding me back – really big ones. Along with paranoia. And self doubt.

But it's okay – I know exactly what to do. I take a deep breath in, and step to the side, even though there is nobody around at present. I put down my handbag, press my dark blue elegant dress, and imagine a square on the floor in front of me. I fill it with bright purple – my colour of confidence, and I step into the square. I immediately feel stronger, more confident, and more *me*.

I'm ready.

I open my eyes, grab my handbag, and head inside. As soon as the double doors fling open, I am hit with bright lights, loud commercial music, and people talking. It's the Weeknd's 'Starboy' that's playing and I smile – I do love him and his genius music. He's probably one of the very few commercial acts I not only like but respect too. He makes great music.

I walk in with confidence and beaming with joy at the realisation that I am now part of Ruby Records. I am finally a part of the music business (officially), and I deserve to be at this party. It's only 9pm but people are already tipsy, some are smoking weed, and some are snorting cocaine.

Welcome to the music business.

I am at the TGI Records Christmas party. Since we are one of five labels under TGI, it was decided that there would be a joint Christmas party.

I hardly know anyone in the room. This used to scare me, but since taking on NLP exercises, understanding my weaknesses better and working on them, I am no longer afraid. In fact, looking around this huge hall of strangers only makes me hungry to approach them all.

Behind the group of coke users, I spot the Devilled Eggs. They're chatting amongst each other as they check out the buffet, and I smile to myself as I watch them. Before I can head over and say hi to them however, I am distracted by a familiar face. It's Gareth Jones – the co-founder of Ruby Records.

Gareth is in his mid-forties, short and well built. He is one hell of a powerful man in this business. Prior to becoming half of Ruby Records, he was a DJ. Gareth, or as he was previously known as, DJ G, started his own techno label – Jenga, when he was fifteen and toured the world as a famous DJ on the techno scene shortly after that.

Yes, that's right – Gareth is not just a co-founder of a big label like Ruby, he is also an artist. It's a very rare sight – co-founders and board members are usually financially driven and logical, as opposed to artistic and emotional. And trust me, there is a lot of emotion to DJ G's music; he is the only techno artist I willingly listen to. I've been following him for a while now on social media, ever since I heard about his past. I've never been in the same room as him though, and I know what I have to do.

A waitress approaches me with a tray of white wine glasses, and I take one as I thank her. I walk over to him as he looks around the hall, taking a sip from his white wine. I do the same before I reach him.

"Really great wine," I tell him.

He turns and gives me a look of intrigue.

"And my parents are Italian, so I really ought to know."

He slowly smiles, as he relaxes. "I guess I need to trust you then." He puts out his hand. "Gareth Jones."

"Alexis Brunetti – I work for Gavin Heath. The indie artists section."

He frowns. "An artist manager."

I am close to correcting him, to telling him I am only an assistant, but I know better now. I know that it's tempting to undersell yourself, but it will never work in your favour.

"Have you been scouting much?" he asks me.

"I have. And I've met and seen some great artists. But no one has stood out so far."

I want to mention Anastasia but I hold back. I have flashbacks of her hurt, fragile expression as she had yelled at me outside the Ruby building, and I don't want to ever put a woman through that again.

No, I will be more careful this time.

"Well it takes a hell of a lot of digging around and attending gigs."

"Do you think you'll ever return to touring yourself?" I ask. He's thrown off by the question, about how I could possibly know about his past, and he hesitates a moment before responding. But then a spark appears in his eyes, a spark that tells me that nobody has asked him this in a very long time.

Bingo.

"I wish. My life is too busy for a tour now."

Gavin and I talk for a long time, like two old friends that haven't seen each other in years. To my surprise, I find Gareth both down-to-Earth and genuine, two characteristics I find rare in board members of a label.

He tells me about how he grew up in a small town in Cornwall, where neither of his parents were artistic, and his brother is a mildly famous former rugby player. You can tell that when he was younger he was handsome, though now he has a bit of a pot belly and some wrinkles under his eyes.

I've seen footage of him as a DJ on tour online, and he was very attractive – maybe it was his six pack, or maybe it was his tan, but I swear I had heart shapes for eyes when I watched these videos. He could still pass for a silver fox though, if only he went back to the gym.

We get on so well that he asks me to send him over links of live concerts from Oliver Heldens I referenced three or four times in our conversation – he loves him, and I've watched a ton of interesting live concert footage. I make a note to do so first thing on Monday, and when we eventually part ways (and only because someone pulls him away to join another conversation), I walk away pleased.

I did a good job. I am learning. I am improving. The introvert in me is crying, but the extrovert in me is doing a happy dance. Yes, you can be both.

I continue to explore the party with a big smile on my face, and I am ready to meet more people. I walk around feeling excited, confident, about who I could meet, about the opportunities I have in front of me, and about how far I've come in less than a year. I am happy, I am beaming, I am a better version of myself today than I was yesterday, and I will continue this growth.

And then I see him. In the distance. And it instantly wipes the smile off of my face. I freeze in my spot, my jaw dropping, and I realise that is in indeed who I think it is.

Before me in the distance, stands Riccardo D'Angelo.

He is talking to one of the board members of TGI. He is dressed in tight black jeans, a black buttoned up shirt and his toned arms flex as he talks. His tan has disappeared, yet he's still as handsome as ever. In fact, even more so.

His eyes have a glint, as always, and his smile reaches them in a way that has always made the hairs on the back of my neck stand up. He's talking passionately to the board member, who in turn, looks hooked. Well of course he is – Ric is a terrific storyteller.

He looks sexier than I remembered, and I never thought I'd see him dressed in tight, black jeans. They make his toned legs stand out impeccably, and I am suddenly outraged, for those are legs that I used to know so well, and now, there they stand, on a body I once knew, and a face I once used to kiss, as if we had never even met.

I stare, wondering what the hell he's doing at the Christmas party of TGI Records. Did he know I'd be here?

Oh please, Alex – does he even remember who you are, four months later?

I remember his ignoring of both my texts, and a pang of hurt hits my stomach. He does not want to know me. Not anymore. And I have to be okay with this.

I decide to walk over to him. I don't know what I'm going to say, how I'm going to say it, or any of the other things I should probably take into consideration, but I am walking over to him.

He is in mid-conversation with the board member when he spots me. He has to double take, just as I had done. He tries to remain cool and charming Ric, but I can tell he's taken off guard.

His eyes always give him away.

"Hi," I say, and the board member disappears, probably picking up on the tension suddenly present; you could cut it with a knife.

"Hello," Ric says to me, looking me up and down as he takes a swig from his beer. "You look nice."

That voice. I haven't heard it in so long. I deleted him on all social media, to avoid it at all costs. For hearing his voice reminds me of Milano.

"Thank you," I hesitate, debating whether what I'm about to say is rude, but deciding to say it anyway. "What are you doing here?"

"TGI might be signing me. Going solo," he takes another swig.

"Oh wow. Great," I manage to say, and I am happy for him. He deserves it, I told him from the beginning that he is supposed to be a solo artist. The tension continues to build, as does the awkwardness. I know the person in front of me, and yet at the same time he feels like a complete stranger.

He does not care how I'm doing, he does not think it's cool we have bumped into each other here. So what the hell am I doing standing here? I find myself annoyed at the fact that he is here right now, in *my* country, in *my* city, without even so much as a heads up about it.

"Don't you want to launch in Italy though? I mean, why the UK?"

Why my country, my city, my label?

"I'm not here for you, Alex," he says, as if reading my mind.

"Good," I immediately say. I have flashbacks of us having sex in his kitchen, that first time. The multiple times we did it on his desk, his bed, his bathtub, his sink. And those couple of times backstage in the green room after hours.

I'll admit that I do miss it; the sex. But I will never show it.

"Great. Glad we cleared that up," he tells me, and I've never seen Ric act cold before. It stings, and he no longer even feels like someone I used to know, but a complete and utter stranger.

Before I can say anything else, the Devilled eggs are surrounding us, wailing Ric's name.

"Wow! Who *are* you boys and what have you done to The Devilled Eggs?!" he says to them, switching from Cold Ric to Warm Ric in a nanosecond.

"Ric!"

"What are you doing here, Ric?!"

"Our manager Matt gave us a re-branding!"

"Oh yeah?" Ric tells them, "is this Matt also going to change your band name? No offence but The Devilled Eggs *has to go.*"

The boys tell him everything about their meeting with Matt that morning, and though I am no longer on good terms with Ric, though I no longer like him or want to know him, there's something nice about seeing the band looking up to him and having that relationship with him.

"Ric, are you going to come to our first gig in London next week? You have to come," Matteo pleads, and the others chime in with 'yes, you must!'

Ric's 'of course I will' is easy and loyal, and I expect nothing less from him.

Once they leave us alone again, Ric's face changes, it goes back to being cold, but his tone is slightly different this time. "Look, I may be here a while. We may bump into each other. Let's be friendly, okay?"

And before I can reply, he has disappeared back into the crowd.

"Sure," I say to myself, watching the back of his head until I can no longer spot it amongst all the other heads in the crowd.

"You know you want me. You know you do," Mauro says in my ear, and I am nauseous. *"I've seen you looking at me, I've seen you walking around in those cute little clothes, you were telling me you want me. I am simply making your dreams come true. I can have you whenever I want, don't you get that, Alexis? You are a piece of meat at my disposal, and a body that I can enter whenever the fuck I want. Never forget that."*

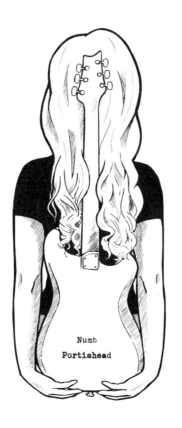

20

It took me a long time to understand that I'm an introvert at heart. There's a lot of people who seem to misunderstand what the term actually means, so here's my definition: When you are shy at a party, you are not an introvert - you are shy.

An introvert is someone who gets energy from being by themselves, from taking the time to embrace and take in their own thoughts without any interruptions. It's unfortunate but introverts are quite often frowned upon. I mean, you couldn't possibly be okay spending time *all by yourself?*

The concept is quite commonly seen as 'weird' by extroverts, thus my desire to mask it or change it or tweak it as a teenager. But I realised, as I grew, that there's absolutely nothing wrong with getting excited about going on holiday alone, or eating alone, or spending weekends alone. It does not mean you cannot socialise, when you want to.

It does not mean you cannot hold a conversation, when you want to. And it does not mean you cannot express your ideas, when you want to.

It simply means that in order to socialise effectively, communicate effectively, express your ideas effectively, it just takes a little bit more effort. And if you're not putting in the effort to do that, then the question should really be: How badly do you actually want to?

When I arrive at Brixton Pub, I am beaming from ear-to-ear. I am practically dancing as I enter and follow Elliot to his tables.

"Hey, hey, hey! I have a surprise for you!"

"I think this gorgeous bird wants a quickie in the bathroom," chirps a rather large, tattooed man in the corner, sitting alone. We both turn to look at him with bewildered looks.

"Is it a six-foot blonde model?" Elliot asks me, as we ignore the man, who goes back to eating his late breakfast.

"Yes! But she said she'd rather die than go on a date with you, so…"

"Ha*ha*," he tells me, as he walks over to the next table and I follow.

"You and I are going out tonight."

"Okay, where? Please say Shoreditch, I cannot get enough of that place."

"Nope. But we can go afterwards if you want."

"After? After what?" I can no longer hold back and so I pull out the tickets, waving them in his face.

"Royal Blood! Tonight! Standing tickets!"

"No fucking way," he puts the plates back down on the table, as the customers stare in confusion.

"You know what that means – first row, baby!" We start jumping up and down like idiots, all eyes on us.

When we arrive at the Electric Ballroom, there is already a long queue, despite it being a good three hours before doors open.

I call a promoter I know and can get him to put us on the list. In just fifteen minutes, we're on the list and skipping the queue, walking straight into the empty venue. This is the beauty of working in the music industry – contacts everywhere who will do favours for you, hoping they can one day ask the same of you.

We order drinks at the bar and some snacks as we chat. I ask him how it's going with Matt, to which Elliot tells me it's okay. Though he struggles to tell me why he's only okay.

"He's a twat," he suddenly tells me.

"Is he not doing a good job with you guys?"

"He's lazy, careless, selfish – he doesn't care about us, he just wants his damn promotion. He eats everyone's ass."

"But he got rid of your emo looks – I thought that was a good move." I would love more than anything to be the one helping to manage the boys, to have an official part to their journey, but I know that's not possible, and I know I can't say bad things about Matt. Even though he *is* a twat.

The Devilled Eggs deserve a manager who will care about their music, and their development as musicians.

"Yes, but seriously Alex, anyone could have done that. It was only a matter of time." He pauses, not sure if he should proceed. "I wish you were our manager. We all do."

I scoff. "Even Damiano?"

"Well, maybe not Damiano, but he doesn't know what's good for him," he tells me.

"I do too Elliot, but you have Matt, and he's good." It's bullshit and Elliot knows it, but he nods anyway. He knows I can't say anything to the contrary, not if I want to stay at Ruby. Elliot orders shots and gulps his down immediately.

"Slow down!" I tell him, laughing.

"Nope, can't. I'm seventeen; this is the time to be living life in the fast lane."

I give him a baffled look. "Hey, I'm young too, but I don't 'live life in the fast lane'."

"If I slow down at twenty-three I want you to shoot me, okay Alex?"

I hit his shoulder playfully, as he breaks into a smile. "How's it going with Damiano?" I ask, changing the subject.

He shrugs. "As per usual. Pretends we're not related, I pretend not to care."

"Maybe you should talk to him? Maybe he doesn't see what a shitty thing he's doing by-"

"He knows, Alex. He sees it." Elliot's tone is serious the way it is only serious when the topic is Damiano, and so I decide to let it be. Maybe down the road they will both find a way to get along, to be brothers.

Three hours fly by and it's soon time for Royal Blood to take to the stage. We're in first row and have been standing here a good couple of hours. The downside to standing in front row is that you get pushed into the barriers by the entire crowd, but we don't care.

Through the screams and the heat and the speakers blasting our favourite music of the moment, we are happy. Ecstatic. We are at a Royal Blood gig, and nothing is going to bring us down.

As we mosh to their songs, grinning at one another, I remind myself to go to more gigs. It's ironic but since joining Ruby, I have been to *less* gigs than when I was not doing anything in music. We put our arms in the air and grin at each other as we sing along, knowing we won't have our voices tomorrow, but not giving a fuck.

This is Royal Blood, and this is what good music is about.

I'm assigned to help out on the next album for Mind Spin, so I make a whole presentation on it – slides, and slides, and slides of information commenting on the guitar technique of their demo, vocals, lyrics, and for the other instruments I sit down with musicians I know at Ruby. It excites me, to think I could have a view on what direction a nationally well-known band could take their music next.

Mind Spin are a five-piece indie rock band who remind me of the likes of Blur and Oasis. They've got that nineties vibes to them that brings nostalgia back to you, in a good way. Their new album is ok-ish, but sounds a lot like their previous three albums. I am daring them to take a new path, combining their old stuff with a new, modern sound - think a cross between Blur and Royal Blood.

I stride into the packed meeting room with excitement, and I nod at Gavin as I pass him. I look over at the band, who are sitting at the table, talking loudly with each other. And as always, they stink of weed.

It takes me a few seconds to notice that there is also a girl with them. I do not recognise her as I study her; blonde, blue eyes, and wearing a sleeveless, summery dress.

I shiver just looking at her bare skin. I have never understood women who can dress like it's summer in the middle of winter. The amount of them that I see in London on a Saturday night bare legged in heels in sub zero weather is limitless. I am one of those people who are always cold, even in summer, so I simply cannot relate at all.

I watch the girl as she laughs with them, all eyes fixed on her as she clearly holds all of their attention. I approach, and I suddenly feel very ugly and unfeminine in my black jeans, old school Vans shoes, and Foo Fighters t-shirt.

I'm not wearing any make-up as I chose instead to use that time to sleep some more this morning, as I do most other mornings. This girl's face however is perfectly groomed with foundation, baby blue eyeliner and rosy pink lipstick. I find myself wishing I had at least brushed my hair this morning.

"Hey, guys!" I say. They all turn to me, but the girl instead gets out her phone, immediately reminding me of Damiano.

"Hey, hey Alexis!"

"All good, Alexis? I'm excited for your presentation!"

I small talk with the band about music news, upcoming tour dates, and David Bowie (somehow Bowie always find his way into my conversations with musicians).

The girl, I notice, does not look at me once. She does not acknowledge me, nor does she interact with me, and I find it a little odd. I don't take it too personally – I'm probably not feminine enough or 'cool' enough for her standards.

I'm guessing she's probably a girlfriend of one of the bandmates, but I can't figure out which, as they all seem to interact with her fairly equally (and by that, I mean that they are staring at her push up bra the entire time). I don't understand why she is at this meeting, but shrug it off as typical music business behaviour – Gabriella Reed's boyfriend Todd has sat in many of her meetings before and nobody has ever said a thing.

Though, he is extremely famous, and I've noticed that this appears to give you a free pass to most things 'normal humans' wouldn't be able to do. I squint at the blonde - *is she a famous model I haven't heard of?*

I really can't tell.

I make sure everything is ready for the meeting; beverages, snacks, whiteboard, etc. I'm ready to go, but Gavin has disappeared to take a call and we are now waiting on him to return.

"I'll go find him," Eric, the drummer, announces, though we all know he's lying and actually stepping out to smoke weed.

"I'll join you," the lead singer, Derek, chimes in, and I roll my eyes as the entire band walks out of the meeting room to smoke weed.

Suddenly it's just the girl and I in the room, and I notice a weird tension present. She's still not making eye contact with me, instead choosing to fixate her eyes on her phone. I watch her as she scrolls with one hand and runs her fingers through her hair with the other.

It is fascinating to watch her ignore me. To observe people like this as they poison the rest of society, and make us lose faith in humanity.

Okay, I'm being a tad dramatic. But I really don't like her. She looks so up herself that I want to throw cake in her face. The fat kind – with double whipped cream and something sticky, like jam, or toffee. I'd get it to stick to her face so I have enough time to take a picture of it and post it on the Internet. Because girls like this die of embarrassment at shit like that.

I quickly realise that throwing cake at every conceited blonde's face would make my career in the music business very short lived, and so I decide to instead focus on setting up for my meeting.

I notice the remote control for the screen is near her. "Could you please pass me the control?" I ask her, politely. She sighs, as if I have asked her to import a herd of camels illegally from Dubai, before she reluctantly pushes it over to me. And all of this without looking me in the eye.

The audacity, the sheer rudeness of this person. *How do people like this exist? How? Where do they even come from?*

Before I can burst into flames, before I can swear at her, attack her, tell her where to shove her fake eyelashes and future fake boobs, I take a deep breath in.

I ignore.

And I move on.

I decide not to care. For I am an adult, a sensible one at that, and I do not have time for pettiness from female brats. I will not allow that. I will not survive in this industry if I let these fake tanned weirdos get to me.

It's only a couple of minutes later that Gavin strolls in, and he's got a big smile on his face. He's in a good mood. "Ah! I see you two have met. Alexis, this is our new intern - Natalie."

INTERN?
THIS MONSTER?
AN INTERN?
ARE YOU JOKING?

"She is your replacement, so I was hoping you could show her the ropes."

I'll show her THE rope alright. I look over at her expecting her to be giving me her bitch mode look, but instead she's beaming at me in utter (fake) joy.

"Oh I'd *love* that! You are *so* inspiring! I've heard about everything you've done at Ruby so far and it is *so*

323

impressive! I want to be the exact same way. It would be an *honour* if you'd teach me a thing or two!"

Okay, what the fuck is wrong with this chick? I'm a girl, I've encountered plenty of bitches in my lifetime, *believe me*, but she is on another level of crazy. She can't be any older than eighteen; her face looks as young as a baby's bottom.

Does she really think she's going to be able to fool me? Or trick me? Or be inferior in some way? I have something better than her - a brain. My integrity. I work hard, I'm sharp, I come in early, I love this place, I love music, and I understand bands. I take the *time* to understand bands. She is not going to be able to use her cray-cray manipulation to beat that - hard work trumps a basic bitch.

The band walk back in, bringing their loud energy and strong smell of weed with them. Just as they do so, with Gavin's back to us, the girl drops her pencil, squeaks "whoops!" and bends down to pick it up.

I force a laugh at the sheer level of pathetic this girl is demonstrating, but the band, plus Gavin, are all focused on taking a peak at her bright baby blue thong.

This is outrageous. Disgusting. Despicable. And yet, this is reality. And I know it. And I cannot be emotional in order to get what I want. I would love to pull her up by the hair, throw cake in her face, and then…

Make her wear a grandma jumper. She would, again, *die* of embarrassment. But I know I can't. Not if I want to succeed.

And so I instead take a deep breath in, smile, and ask everyone if they are ready for my presentation.

A song I never tire of is The Verve's 'Bittersweet Symphony'. I first heard it in the film Cruel Intentions and it became my favourite movie ending for the rest of my teens. The story is both well told and powerful, but I have always known that it's the Verve's song that really took that ending to another level. It was one of the first times I really began to notice the impact of music on our emotions.

Advertising.

Films.

Music videos.

Music makes a huge difference and has a supreme impact. It's one of the reasons I love it so much.

I then of course got to know The Verve separately to Cruel Intentions, and came to love many of their songs. I even saw them live in concert at the Forum (and they weren't half bad).

Yet I never separated the song from the visual ending of Cruel Intentions, and this always just reminds me of the potency that music possesses, of the influence it can have on you.

I walk into Church Studios with a smile on my face, as if I am Reese Witherspoon.

Damn, I wish I had Ryan Philippe appearing out of nowhere and seducing me.

Ryan Phillipe from 1999. Yum.

I had a good day; my presentation with Mind Spin went well, they loved my ideas, and they want to proceed with my musical direction. It's terrific news, and even Gavin looked pleased - he mentioned three times that he was the one to hire me as an intern, already spinning the fact that I *used* to be an intern, and look how far I have come.

Yeah okay Gavin, I have yet to get my first paycheck though, could we wait for that before we start spinning my history at Ruby as if I've been there for nine years and brought it millions of pounds?

Though I must admit, it does feel good to hear Gavin say 'she *used* to be an intern." Damn right. I'm now a paid employee in the music business, and I'm never letting go.

I don't have my foot in the door now, I have my entire body now!

Just as I'm about to open the door to studio one, it flings open and G greets me with his usual grin, his tongue piercing glistening. "Hey! Come in!"

"Hey G, how's it going?" I walk in to find the band spread out – Elliot and Matteo have their respective guitar and bass hanging from them, as they chat. Damiano is sitting on the sofa with Lino, watching a commercial music contest on a laptop. G goes over to them, and dives onto the sofa.

Argh. Reality shows. I despise them, all of them. Especially music related ones.

I watch the video as a man attempts to sing a Bowie song and fail miserably.

"He's made it to the finals, can you believe it?" G tells me, Elliot and Lino glancing at me.

"Hey Alex," they say to me and I nod at them, my eyes trailing back to the video as I cringe.

"Are you seriously watching this stuff?"

"It's funny."

"Sure, but is it still funny knowing that this shit is killing the music industry? All those shitty musicians making it big because of how *crap* they are, blocking the pathway for the actual *good, talented, hardworking* singers and artists out there who are trying to get even a slither of the exposure they get? Artists much like yourselves."

There is silence in the room. "Shit, she's right," Matteo says in a semi-whisper.

"Anyway, guys, can I get your attention for a second – I have a surprise for you."

All heads turn to me, and Matteo slams the laptop shut.

"Alright, come in," I yell, and the boys look confused as the door clicks open. In walks Parker, in his usual black top hat, tight black jeans, and black shirt.

"Parker May," Elliot says, his mouth open.

"Who is Parker May?" G asks, confused.

"Lead guitarist of Luminous, idiot," Matteo tells him.

"Precisely," Parker replies. He walks in with swagger and that extra dollop of confidence he saves for the artists in the music business. Much like the first time we met.

"Parker has just dropped by to have a listen to your tracks, jam a bit, hope that's okay?"

If anyone says no I will kick them in the head.

"Oh hell yes," Elliot says instantly, walking over to us. He looks like an excited child about to meet the Queen. "Hi, I'm Elliot – lead guitarist of the Devilled Eggs."

I watch them shake hands with glee.

"This is bullshit!" Damiano blurts out, all eyes turning to him. "Why does Elliot get someone he can get help from but the rest of us don't? Just because Alexis is best buddies with him and they both love guitar or whatever, this isn't right!"

"Thought you might say that," I reply, nonchalantly.

"Come in!" I yell, and I hear the door click open once again. Four people walk in – three women and one man. "Dean Hatt, lead singer of Somerset Nights – here to sing with you, Damiano."

His eyes widen.

"G, rhythm guitarist of Status No, to jam you with. She's awesome!" G grins from ear-to-ear.

"Matteo, meet one of the finest bassists in Britain – Natalia Gella. She's a session bassist now and toured all over Europe."

"Oh, the pleasure of mine!" Matteo squeals, as he shakes his hands with her.

"Lastly, Lino, meet-"

"Gina Di Mario, holy shit," Lino interrupts me, and I beam.

I watch them all with their assigned mentor for the next two hours. This is definitely another highlight of the contacts you get in this business. You just get to meet and become friends with many, many cool artists.

I look over at Parker and Elliot as they chat in the corner, both of them already with guitars around their necks. They're grinning as they talk and play, and it makes me smile. I'll admit, out of everyone, I wanted these two to meet, for Elliot to be inspired by Parker. He could learn a lot from him as a guitarist. There's something really nice about seeing them together in the same frame – the two main guitarists of my life.

I let them all get on with their sessions and sit in the corner, finalising some stuff for Dazza's debut album release.

Hours fly by, and one by one, the mentors start leaving. It's just past 10pm when the only ones left in the room are the Devilled Eggs and Parker. I take off my headphones, saving the rest of Florence and the Machine's latest album for later.

"Alex, I'm off," Parker announces, and he rushes over. "Bea is having some sort of meltdown in the studio."

I cock up an eyebrow. "She okay?"

"Yeah, yeah, I'd just better be there."

"Okay."

He leans in and pecks me on the cheek.

"Thanks for tonight."

"Anytime. Elliot is one fine guitarist," he winks at him. "You have my number, kid." And from that, Parker disappears.

I yawn and get up, plopping myself down on the leather sofa, next to G and Lino.

"That was *insane*," Elliot says, coming over to me and leaning over the arm of the sofa. "Oh my God, he is *so good*. Thanks, Alex."

"Yeah thanks!" the others chime in, except for Damiano. We all turn to him, as he sits in the armchair, reading something on his phone. He feels all eyes on him and looks up. "Thank you," he manages to say, and I am shocked.

"You are welcome, boys."

"Back to recording we go. Shall we go get cigarettes?"

"Let's." The band, except Elliot, get up and tell us they will be back in five. Elliot crashes in the seat next to me on the sofa, and we stare out at the fire place.

"Crazy day."

"I really like Parker. Like *really* like him."

"Well good – you could learn a thing or two from him. He's been playing since he was eight."

"Wow."

We suddenly hear a loud voice scream "CIAO!" in the building, and turn around to see Ric through the glass, giving a bear hug to an Italian-looking man in his forties.

He has a huge grin on his face in the corridor of Church Studios as they throw their arms around each other. Seeing Ric happy, in his element, makes me so proud of him. To see him doing what he's always supposed to have been doing – being a solo artist.

It however also comes with an incredibly huge amount of sadness, to watch all of it from the outside. From the outskirts of the bubble that is his life.

I didn't want to be romantically involved with him, sure, but it would have been nice if we could have been friends.

Sometimes I really regret ever having slept with him. Things would have been very different if sex hadn't been a factor in our friendship, and I know this.

"Yeah, he got signed by TGI."

I look at Elliot. "Really? Which label?"

"Simple Records."

I don't say anything, but I feel Elliot's eyes on me. "What happened between you two, anyway?"

I shrug. "Nothing."

"You two were banging, right?"

I nod, seeing no reason to lie, and he rolls his eyes as he smiles. "Yeah, sex ruins everything."

"It sucks. I miss him sometimes." *Or maybe, all the time.* "We were friends before all of that, and I liked our friendship."

"Well," Elliot begins as he rolls up a cigarette, "maybe you two will still be able to salvage your friendship."

"Sure," I scoff, as we get up and head out. We pass Ric and the older Italian man in the corridor as they catch up loudly in Italian, and neither of them look at us.

I'm in a meeting at Ruby, and I've just signed my first client! Gavin is pleased, in fact he's getting out the champagne!

We clink our glasses with smiles, when the door opens. It's Mauro. He's the singer's father and he's here to celebrate. He grabs my wrists and drags me across the room.

I scream for him to let me go, I feel the pain of his grip on my wrists, I scream for someone to help, but nobody does. Mauro tells me to shut up, again and again, until he gets out a gun.

"I'm going to have you whether you are dead or alive, got it?"

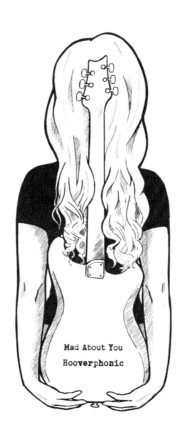

21

It's crazy, but before I started working at Ruby, the perks of working in the music business were just one: *I'd get to work in the music business.* It was based solely on my burning desire to be near the creation of music, that's all it was.

Once I however started working at Ruby, I began to realise, yes there are plenty of cons, but there are also plenty of pros too. Like getting backstage passes to the most prestigious music venues in the country. Like getting an entire suite at festivals like Glastonbury.

And, like getting free tickets to the top music award ceremonies in the UK.

I stand outside the venue for the GMA's wearing a ridiculously expensive red, sparkling dress, accompanied with red high heels I can barely walk in, and I've left my hair naturally curly. My lipstick is a strong shade of red, and I have a pin on the left side of my hair holding it up.

Now, I don't particularly care to get *this* dressed up, but I've been ordered by Gavin (exactly seven times) to make 'a huge effort to look good' tonight. I represent Ruby and I shouldn't disappoint them.

I mentally rolled my eyes every time Gavin gave me this lecture but honestly, now that I'm all dolled up I feel *really* good. It was actually kind of fun - I put on Placebo as I got ready, bopping my head to the soothing voice that is Brian Molko. He has such a sexy voice it's unreal.

But this is definitely not something I'd do more than once every, well, once every awards ceremony. How many of them do we have to attend in a year, anyway?

"Well hello beautiful," says a voice, and I turn around to find Parker approaching with his usual confident swagger. He walks as if he's stepping onto the catwalk; this is Parker's walk.

I eye him up and down as he approaches – he looks very sharp in a tux, and for the first time ever, he is without his black top hat. This is the first time I have ever seen him without a hat, and I look at his wavy hair, all perfectly aligned to match his elegant attire. He is one attractive man.

"Well look who scrubs up well," I tell him, and he pulls me into an affectionate hug, as he always does. It lasts at least five seconds, and I always smell his coconut shampoo. The man washes his hair every damn day of the week – fun fact.

"I look like a dog next to you. You look absolutely stunning, Alexis."

I blush unintentionally. "Thank you, Parker."

"You ready to lose your music awards virginity?" He offers me his arm and I link it with mine, as we walk down the stairs to the venue. "I bet you were one of those feisty virgins, saying *'just fucking take it already! I was ready ten years ago, okay?!'*"

I laugh, as I remember my first time. "Yep. It was with a sweet bassist who had plenty of experience, and he guided me through it thinking he had to be gentle."

'Poor, clueless kid."

We both laugh, as we enter the hall. Parker and I are always making dirty jokes and neither of us ever gets uncomfortable or awkward. We act as if we have done it with each other, but whenever I really stop to think about it, I'm always a little surprised when I remember that Parker has never seen me naked.

The venue is huge, filled with bright lights, dinner tables with expensive silverware, elegant table spreads, and the smell of chicken. We are greeted by a waitress holding a tray of expensive red wine; we take a glass each and thank her, before making our way through the venue.

The GMAs are the second biggest awards ceremony in the UK. There are quite a few nominations for Ruby: Gabriella is up for best female act, Mind Spin is up for best album, and a couple of acts from other managers have also been nominated. Parker's band, Luminous, is up for best international act.

Parker and I decided to go together, even though we're sitting in completely different spots during the ceremony. I guess we just wanted to walk in together, and it's assumed we will hang out afterwards.

He's probably one of my closest friends now – Bailey and I hardly hang out anymore, and Blake is busy in

Indonesia still. He said he doesn't want to return as he finds London too expensive, and I can definitely relate to that – I am returning this ridiculously expensive dress tomorrow; the tag has been stuffed under my dress. There's no way I have money to splurge on such superficial things.

We walk around, and talk to people Parker mostly knows, and he knows *everyone*. One person asks him if he's ready to start a new band yet and he laughs it off. When we walk away however I question him about it.

"Ah, I don't know. I've been playing with Luminous a good five years; I'm getting a bit bored. But let's see."

"But Luminous is just starting to get recognised?"

"Success isn't everything, Alexis."

I try to take in his words but the wine is already getting to me. I made the silly mistake of not eating before I left the house, but I was lured in by the free dinner that awaits. I just probably shouldn't have drunk first, being the lightweight that I am.

Parker is so smooth when he talks to people; he just has such an elegance to him that people are taken in by it, all wanting to talk to him, to see how he is, to see his thoughts on the latest scandal in music.

I chime in, but I also enjoy just watching him in action. He sometimes squeezes my arm when someone we're talking about says the biggest horeshit lie in the world, and I nod, as if we both have the same horseshit radar.

It's not long until the ceremony starts, and we go to our respective tables. I sit in-between Gavin and the Devilled Egg's manager, Matt, who keeps telling terrible dad jokes to anyone who will listen.

I try to imagine him managing the band, and it's hard to do. The boys need a manager, but is it Matt? Can he look after them, can he understand them and their music? Can he navigate them through their first album launch and tour?

"Hey Alexis, the lead singer of Slay must be slaying it, am I right, or am I right?!" he laughs at his own joke before anyone else can, and I watch him in intrigue. Somehow, I don't see him as the Devilled Egg's manager.

Each award has me at the edge of my seat, curious to see who will win. I get most of them right, except for Mind Spin, who lose to a crappy Scottish band called Milkshake for

Best Album. Gabriella, as predicted, wins best female act, and our entire table stands up and claps aggressively, especially Gavin who whistles using his fingers like a nutty groupie at a Justin Timberlake concert.

Most of our table is completely and utterly drunk by the interval. I have been sensible and waited to drink again until after I ate. But I'm getting tipsy too now; it feels as if if you don't join in you will be left out. It annoys me, but it doesn't look like I have much of a choice.

The performances in-between the awards are pretty poppy and crappy, so I don't take much notice of them or their strange costumes. I instead talk to the people on our table – mostly drunk senior heads at Ruby.

They're speaking very loudly and are spitting too, but this is the perfect opportunity to build rapport with people who don't even *look* at me at the office. They mostly tell silly jokes and talk trash about our rival labels, nothing of actual substance.

I get bored quite quickly, secretly waiting for the second half to begin again so I can pretend nodding along to the idiotic, sexist jokes that I'm listening to.

Eventually, my prayers are answered, and the second half goes a lot quicker than the first half. As soon as the awards are over, everyone is on their feet, rushing to God knows where. I meet Parker halfway across the venue, making my way through crowds and crowds of people to reach him.

"*Heeeeeeeey*!" he says, and I laugh loudly.

"That's the longest *heeeeeeeeeeeeeeey* ever!"

"How dare you, attacking my heys!" he replies, in a posh British accent that makes us both burst into laughter. He pokes me in the stomach, as we look at each other and know that we are both equally tipsy.

This is going to be an interesting night.

We head over to the after party, waving at strangers on the walk to our taxi with big grins on our faces. What is it about saying hi to strangers when you're tipsy?

We talk to our taxi driver about pasta, spicy food, and doughnuts with smiles on them. We ask him where he's from (India), how he finds London ('little bit grey but okay'), and if he's ever travelled to space (his answer was no).

By the time we arrive at the after party, it appears most people have beaten us to it, with crowds of people standing outside, smoking and drinking and laughing loudly. Though to be fair, we did stop to buy cheese balls.

Yes, cheese balls.

That's little balls of cheese.

They're yummy!

We bid our taxi driver a lovely evening and head inside, arm-in-arm. We tell jokes that make no sense, sing to one another, and play air guitar. It is safe to say, we are wasted. I don't think I have ever been this wasted in my life, and yet people keep offering me things to drink.

Argh, why do I have to be such a lightweight?

At this rate I'm going to end up throwing up on someone, and I shudder at the thought. I decide to grab a glass of water at the bar, and Dazza appears next to me.

"Having fun, old chum?" he says, in a fake British accent. He looks just as tipsy as me, and I giggle.

"I am indeed!"

"Alexis wasted - I like this!"

"Right back at you, what are you drinking?" I ask him, as the bartender comes over to us.

"Red wine please," Dazza tells the bartender.

"Ooh, didn't know that was your buzz," I tell him.

"And it's not my only one," he pulls out a small see-through bag with white powder in it. I gulp at the sight of cocaine. This is the first time I have ever seen cocaine in the flesh, and it's a weird feeling. It looks the same as anything else white, and yet, it's drugs. In Dazza's hands.

"Want some?" he asks me. It's funny, Dazza is such a handsome, young man - a semi-talented singer with a charming personality, and yet, no one has ever been less attractive to me in this moment than the man standing in front of me.

I want to tell him to throw it away, to give it up, to find a new addiction - one that doesn't harm your body. But I know I can't do that - I work in the music business, and if I want to continue to do so, I need to keep my mouth shut. I need to keep my 'grandma ways' to myself.

"No thanks - maybe later," I tell him, with a wink.

Smooth, Alexis.

"Suit yourself," he tells me, and I watch him snort cocaine right there on that bar stand. He does so in front of an entire room of people, as if he is alone. He knows nobody is going to call the police. I look around the room, and realise that every single person around me is doing drugs. *Every single person.*

Cocaine.

Weed.

Some are getting out syringes.

All whilst Lady Gaga blasts from the speakers, and they speak to each other about their weeks, what they're up to on the weekend, or Britney Spears' new single.

There is suddenly a darkness that consumes me, as I look around at everyone. Parker is nowhere in sight, but I recognise some others - Gavin, Matt, marketing from Ruby, some senior heads.

They're all here, and they're all doing drugs, nonchalantly.

I look around at the political madness of this industry that surrounds me. And I am at the heart of it. I am at the centre of the chaos. The feeling is troubling. Never have I felt less part of something, less comfortable by my surroundings. I do not do drugs. I do not blend in. I look after myself and my body. I do not see the beauty in becoming submissive to a chemical.

I find myself immediately consumed by sadness, though I'm not entirely sure why. And I am suddenly sober again; the only sober person in the room.

I shake it off, determined to not let in ruin my night. I re-join Parker who has three girls listening intently to him story tell about that one time he ended up in Bono's dressing room, eating apple pie. It's a great story, but I've heard it one too many times.

I instead watch Dazza in the distance, talking loudly with some guys I don't recognise. They're all high together. Gavin is off his head too – you can hear his laugh from across the room.

He only talks to seniors though, even when he's drunk.

Gabriella left early as she has to go back on tour tomorrow, and Mind Spin are in the corner smoking weed. I recognise some of our other clients at the party, but I don't work directly with them. Nevertheless, I make conversation, I ask them how it's going, but, as expected for a conversation between drunks, nothing we say makes sense, and we laugh it off with shots. Yes, I've decided to ease myself into the crowd by continuing to drink.

Definitely a bad idea. And it wipes out all the water I drank an hour earlier. It's okay though because I've decided to leave, and Parker has decided to leave too.

We end up in a taxi to his hotel, and we stop for champagne on the way. We buy bottles and bottles of it, and the taxi driver helps us take it to his hotel room. He doesn't judge us, or look at us funny, his eyes only read 'hey, whatever floats your boat - just give me five stars, please'.

Once he's left us, we think it's an excellent idea to put on Rolling Stones, and fill the bathtub with champagne. We do so giggling uncontrollably, as 'You Got Me Rockin' blasts from the speakers at what is probably 4 or 5am.

"This is so much fun!" I scream at the top of my lungs, and Parker covers his ears with his hands.

"That was loud, *Alexis!*"

We laugh, and accidentally bump heads as we reach for another bottle at the same time.

"Ow!" we say in synch, and we take sips from our respective bottles of champagne before going back to pouring it into the tub. Once we run out of alcohol, we look down at the bathtub, our hands on our hips. It's 3/4 of the way filled.

"Now what?" I ask.

"Boh. Isn't that what you guys say? Italian 'I don't know', *right? RIGHT? RIIIIIGHT?*"

"Yes, yes, you're fucking Italian now, well done." I tell him, patting his back. I suddenly stumble and it looks like I am going to fall into the tub, but Parker pulls me back.

"Hey, hey! No swimming!" he tells me, and we burst into laughter.

"Hey, aren't you a fucking rockstar? You should know what to do next," I tell him.

"I don't know. I just play guitar, okay?" he pauses, and it's the longest pause in the history of long pauses. "Maybe we should make out," he says to me.

"Okay."

"Okay." we turn to one another, and I want to kiss him, simply because it feels like this moment was bound to happen. Also, we are very drunk.

However, before either of us can lean in to kiss, Parker stumbles and looks a bit queasy, "just let me sit down first."

"Me too." We drop to the floor, leaning against the bathtub. "Oh my God, this is going to hurt in the morning."

Parker laughs, as he puts his arm around me. "Welcome to the music business, Alexis."

We clink empty champagne bottles together in-between giggles, and as our drunken laughter fades away, I rest my head on his shoulder, he rests his head on top of mine, and we instantly fall asleep.

Dreams are the map to our subconscious, I have always believed this. They tell us things that our conscious mind isn't ready to hear yet, for our subconscious can take anything. It is a bull. It fights our corner with every ounce of strength it has.

So when I awake in the middle of the night, sweating and scared, I am longer surprised. This is now the norm. For I know I have demons I carry with me. But what is different this rainy Tuesday evening is that I don't try to go straight back to sleep this time.

I stare at the ceiling a good half an hour, counting the cracks. I then pull out a black biro pen from my nightstand, and I start drawing shapes on my forearms. I do so with a determination one probably shouldn't possess at five in the morning. I stare at the shapes for a good hour with no particular expression, before I decide to go back to sleep.

When I awake, I spend another half an hour staring at the shapes before I get up. I shower, get dressed, have cereal, and head out. Work starts at nine, but I'm making a little detour first.

I arrive at Suntoast Cafe, and spot Anastasia through the life-sized windows. She is serving a couple their breakfasts, and is giving them her gentle smile. She probably knows them or they're regulars. The sight of her makes me smile, and I walk in.

She notices me straight away, and frowns. She doesn't look angry though, and I expected this. Our last conversation may have been heated, and she has every right to be frosty with me, but Ana isn't someone to be petty. You can tell that she's just a hothead who forgives the following day.

"Hey," I say to her.

"Hi…" she looks around, "can I get you a table?"

Or, maybe not.

She's being a little frostier than I expected.

"I actually came to see you," I tell her, and she's off onto another table. I follow.

"Look Alex, I have no interest in being signed by Ruby. I told you, I don't work for snakes like that. If it's the choice between waiting tables and becoming a famous singer who is managed by a snake, I choose waiting tables. I know it's crazy to some, but it's logical to me."

She's saying all of this without turning around, and as I respond it feels as if I am talking to her back.

"No, I… Look, I'm not here to convince you of anything, I'm here to apologise."

She turns around, and I have at least half of her attention now.

"I'm sorry, Ana. I had no idea who I was leading you to - he's never been like that with me, I've never seen that in him, but it was stupid of me not to take that into consideration. I had no idea, honestly - I had no idea, Ana."

I think she sees the sincerity in my eyes, as she's looking really closely into them. She then takes a deep breath in and nods. "Okay, thank you." She picks up some dirty plates and heads to the kitchen. I follow.

"That's not all I came here for though," I tell her and she forces a laugh.

"Ah! Funny that, isn't it?"

"There's something I've been thinking about from that day - something that seemed to stand out to me, and it was the way you reacted, the look in your eyes, the fear in your tone. It felt exactly the same as mine would in that situation, given our mutual history."

She immediately turns around, and I hold up my graffitied wrists. "The map to mine," I tell her, and the way her face drops tells me that I have her full attention now.

We agree to meet after work that cold winter's evening, and we do so at a bar in Soho. We talk about our days, we make a few light hearted jokes, but it's not long until we become deadly serious.

Ana decides to go first. She tells me about her experience - she was learning how to produce from a guy called Graham Oldings, he's apparently rather well known in the music business. She would go to his studio on Sunday afternoons, and these were paid sessions. One hot Sunday afternoon, he said he was feeling a little warm, and he took off his shirt. Ana thought it odd but didn't say anything. He then sat down next to her, and put a hand on her thigh, supposedly playfully.

She smiled but moved it away, to which he pounced at her, pushing her up against the studio desk, fondling her and telling her he wanted her, that this was 'bound to happen', and that she was fighting it because it was sexier that way.

"It was only as the pizza delivery guy rang the doorbell that I was able to escape. He had no idea that I had previously ordered a pizza whilst waiting on him - it was going to be my treat for him teaching me everything he had." She forces a laugh, keeping her eyes on the table as she continues. "What a joke."

"They think they can get away with it, that they can do what they want because they're successful," I say.

"I know. And it's not *everyone*, it's just…" she looks up at me. "There's too many of them. I mean, one is too many, but there's a hell of a lot more than one."

I think back to our first encounter, how we had told each other stories of men inappropriately hitting on us, how we had been outraged by the stories, but how neither of us had been okay talking about our cases of sexual harassment or attempted rape. And it's because we feel as if it is our faults, like we will be judged for sharing them, that somehow we will be the Bad Guy. I wonder just how many women keep quiet about experiences such as this in their lifetimes, and it makes me sad.

Ana doesn't say anything more, and I know it's my turn. I'm anxious, as I've never told anyone this story out loud before, other than Ric and most of it he understood from my expression; I hadn't really needed to do much explaining.

I tell Ana what happened last autumn in Mantova with Mauro, I tell her every detail I can of the experience; the regret of having walked into that room, how he had been smiling the entire time, how I had felt a lump on my leg, how he had smelled like dog biscuits.

I tell her about the nightmares every night, and the fact that whenever I see him on the Paolo Petrinelli social media pages I shudder. I tell her everything and she listens, and it feels so good to tell someone all of this, to have them listen, to have them nod at the parts where I go off on a feminist rant, and shake their heads in disgust at the parts where I admit, out loud, how despicable people can be.

I begin trembling as I tell the story, and by the end, I have tears in my eyes. I am shocked by then, as I have perhaps cried only twice in my adult life - once when my cat died, and the second the night after the Mauro incident. Multiple times.

Ana doesn't grab a napkin, she leans right across the table, and wipes my tear as it tries to trickle down my cheek.

I continue with my story, despite the trembling, and despite the tear. By the end of it, we are choosing to sit in silence, to take in each other's stories, to be sad at the world we live in.

To accept, as we do everyday, just how strong we must be as women in this industry, or any industry for that matter.

We continue to sit in silence, as Frank Ocean's 'Nights' plays in the background.

Ana suddenly reaches out across the table, and puts her hand on top of mine. We give each other half smiles, and it's probably the most heartfelt smile I have ever given anyone. She gives my hand a squeeze, and I squeeze back.

It's funny - I'd say I'm a pretty good lone wolf, but, fuck, sometimes the world sure is lonely.

I'm at a music networking event, I'm happy to be where I am, doing what I'm doing. But I bump into someone to find Mauro in front of me. He smiles and shows me his yellow teeth, as he grabs my wrists, and slams me up against the door.

I feel nauseous as I smell his dog biscuits breath, and I scream for someone to help me, but no one does. He tells me how much he wants me, how much I deserve to be treated this way, and I beg him to stop. To leave me alone. To get out of my life.

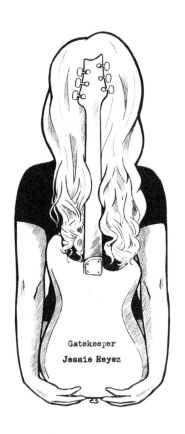

22

When I was eleven, I moved school. I didn't know anyone at this new place, and I hated it. I had no friends, which was fine with me, but I was actually actively disliked by the people in my class. They would look at me like I was a freak for knowing who Black Flags and Descendents were.

I was used to being a part lone wolf, as I had had only two friends at my previous school who were both in different classes, but this was taking on the entire definition, and it was proving difficult.

In one way, I was fine. I liked it. I guess the issue was that the rest of society didn't see it as fine, and this made me question whether I should be okay with it myself.

I struggled for the most part of that year, but there was one wonderful thing about this new school that made all the difference: it was five minutes from my house. This meant I could go home for lunch, and this meant that after that Christmas, I could go home to *play guitar.*

I begged and begged my parents from ages eight to eleven to buy me a guitar, and for my eleventh Christmas, they finally gave in. So that year, whilst everyone at middle school hated my guts, I was running home at lunch to play guitar. It was my escapism from reality, my therapy.

I would sit in class and daydream about it, what I would learn this week, what I would play this lunchtime. I would imagine myself onstage with Pearl Jam, laughing with Eddie Vedder as I played with McCreedy - yes, I was allowed to call him McCreedy; we were close that way.

I was in love with good guitar riffs and unique voices; it took me away from the shittiness of my life at the time. Everyday there was a girl trying to start a fight with me for no reason, and there I was, imagining myself playing my white Yahama guitar; having my own voice in music - a part of my life where I had total control. Where the world was mine.

At eleven, my guitar was my only saviour from reality. In some ways, it still is.

When I get to the Devilled Eggs gig, I am incognito. I don't want anyone from Ruby to spot me and rat me out to

Gavin, whom I'm guessing wouldn't want me here, but this is the Devilled Eggs' debut gig in London – I wouldn't miss it for the world.

They're playing at The Dublin Castle in Camden; my favourite of the intimate gig venues in London. I grab a drink and pay to get to the back room where they are set to play.

There's a band onstage and I look on with a smile at the stage that has hosted Travis, Blur and Arctic Monkeys, to name but a few. The venue is pretty tiny, the stage too – I calculate about thirty people in the audience and already it's starting to feel claustrophobic. But it's a venue that always gives me a buzz and always has a really good energy to it.

I feel ridiculous; I'm dressed in a long, blonde wig, black shades, a black motorcycle jacket and ripped black jeans. I order one more red wine at the bar before I throw myself into the crowd.

I stumble as I make my way through, feeling a little silly as I do so but knowing I have to if I want to avoid the wrath of Gavin Heath.

I manage to spot a couple of colleagues and push past them as fast as I can before they can recognise me. I settle for third row, and there I wait.

I'm at least half an hour early and some crappy trip hop band is performing. I suddenly hear "hey, Alex!" and turn around to find Elliot, Matteo and G beaming back at me.

"Hey, guys! Not so loud, please - I'm in disguise!" I hiss at them, playfully.

"Oh sorry, Alex! Oops…"

"You ready?" I ask them with a smile, all three of them grinning back at me.

"Oh, hell yeah!"

"Ready as ever!"

"We were *born* ready!"

"Excellent," I tell them.

"We are still buzzing from the gig! Heath text Damiano earlier and wished him and us good luck tonight!" G tells me and I beam.

A few days ago, I took the band to see Décor Kind, an emerging punk band. They were playing at the 100 Club, and since I have been friends with the band from before they even hit the scene, I took the Devilled Eggs to the gig and then backstage to meet the band afterwards.

We spent the evening altogether, drinking beer and discussing music. The boys were immediately inspired by Decor Kind, especially Damiano with lead singer, Matt. They seemed to hit it off pretty well. The band had loved their music too, moshing away with the crowd.

Elliot even pulled me up onto his shoulders at one point, and we all had a blast rocking out together. I always love introducing them to good music.

"That's great! Heath is pretty cool," I tell them. "Go and get ready! And don't tell anyone I'm here, okay?!"

Once I'm alone again, I'm so excited for the night that I find myself dancing to the crappy music. Tonight is a big night, and it's an exciting one. The boys aren't even on stage yet and I'm already ecstatic for them, for how far they have come. Tonight is a big night for all of us.

As I happy dance, I smile to myself. I bop my head to the trip hop music with the girl next to me. She has no idea that I actually detest the music but that I am dancing to it because I am simply happy at where I am right now. The boys are about to debut in London!

I spot Ric standing near me - he's alone, bopping his head to the music in the middle of the crowd. He looks cool and collected, as he always does. Most people would feel awkward standing in the middle of a moshing crowd, but not Ric.

I wish I could go over to him, I wish I could casually ask him how it's going, say congratulations for getting signed, ask him if he's enjoying London. But I know I can't. Too much time has passed, and Elliot was wrong - there is no friendship left to salvage after sex.

I suddenly spot a woman appear next to him, and whoever it is, it makes Ric grin from ear-to-ear. They hug, affectionately, and Ric's arm remains around the woman's shoulder.

Jealousy fills my soul in only a nanosecond, like a sharp punch to the stomach. She's pretty, with perfect white teeth and friendly eyes.

I see their future instantly - marriage, kids, grandkids. Ric will get the woman he so deserves, not crappy, fucked up, temperamental Alex Brunetti.

I nod to myself, as I accept it. And I go back to dancing, closing my eyes this time, in fear of accidentally eyeing Ric and the woman again.

The band finish their set, and the wait for the Devilled Eggs to get onstage feels like a lifetime, though in reality it's only twenty minutes.

I text Parker a selfie of me in the crowd, and he sends one back of him backstage at a venue in Memphis. It's open roof and it's still day there. The caption reads "Luminous go live in FIVE hours! Wish the boys luck from me, let me know how it goes!'

I smile, and send him a kiss.

You'd think things would be awkward between us, given that last time we saw each other we had fallen asleep in his hotel bathroom next to a tub full of champagne. But what you think would make it even more awkward was that we had nearly made out. And we both know that would have led to sex in a nanosecond.

I'm glad we didn't kiss, and I'm glad the Parker-Alex friendship dynamic is stronger than that. We're fine, we're closer than ever, and I've made a note to myself to never agree to that in future. If it ever comes up again, that is.

Once the boys hit the stage, I am *woo*ing like crazy, so loudly that the woman next to me covers her ears with her hands and gives me a dirty look.

"Don't look at me, look at the band – they're amazing!" I tell her, and she obeys. Damiano confidently introduces the band, and I am *woo*ing my heart out.

These are *my* boys, in *my* city, performing live here for the very first time!

I am emotional already and they haven't even begun. I find myself having flashbacks of them in Milano the very first time I saw them. How I had been distraught at having been assigned such a crappy band. How much I had wanted to cut off my own ears when I had heard them play.

How much has changed in just six months.

Lino is first; he leads on the drums, followed by Matteo, G and finally, Elliot. This is so exciting, and I am so proud of them. Yes, even Damiano. I watch them, happily, as they perform as real musicians for the first time. They look so good, and they *sound* so good.

Damiano is moving around the stage like he's supposed (it looks like he may have taken some training), Matteo is not looking as awkward as he used to, and Lino is his usual, pudgy happy-go-lucky drummer at the back. G is playing and looking cool, though I quite miss the emo look on him as it suited him rather well; he was, after all, the only *real* emo in the band.

And lastly, Elliot. Lovely Elliot. The first person in the band to take a chance on me, to welcome me with open arms when Damiano pulled out my headphones and Joy Division blasted in the studio. The same person who shares his pizzas with me, and sends all his guitar riff ideas to me first.

He has grown too, despite having been the only person onstage that was semi-decent that first time I saw them live. He's only added to his onstage presence, his playing has improved, and he writes much better guitar riffs and solos now.

He's looking great out there, even if a little sweaty. Argh. A little *too* sweaty actually, I wonder if someone can hand him a towel? There's sexy sweaty and then there's *ew* sweaty.

He's definitely very energetic, which is normal for Elliot and he's probably excited to be playing here tonight but, slow down Elliot!

He's jumping around all over the place, and I laugh.

The crazy animal!

I watch him as he runs across the stage and back – three, four, five times!

You energetic boy, you!

He then starts clapping, and getting the crowd to clap, before pulling apples out of his pocket and juggling them. Yes, he *stops* playing, and pulls out these apples. It's the most bizarre thing, and at first I'm smiling at it, but then, slowly, my smile begins to fade.

I narrow my eyes at him, and begin to push my way through the crowd. I push and push, ignoring all the swearing and mean looks I'm getting, and I make my way to front row.

My heart is thumping fast now, and fear invades every part of my body.

Once I make it to first row, there are people yelling at me and calling me names, but my eyes are fixed on Elliot. I glare at him as he juggles onstage, squinting my eyes as much as I damn can without my glasses present, and in only a few seconds, I see what I had prayed was just a figment of my imagination, a ridiculous notion that simply could not be reality.

Elliot's pupils are dilated.

I gasp, my eyes widening as I watch him juggle.

Elliot is high.

My world becomes instantly dark. Everything good about this night fades away, evaporates, as I watch him onstage. I take in what is happening, as I see the immature, naive little boy in him unfold.

I knew that the band did drugs, of course I did, but I had never asked them about it. I had never lectured them, or told them it's bad, or told them to stop. I thought it wasn't my place, and I still don't, but if I had any idea that Elliot would decide to take something right before his debut gig like this, I sure as hell would have warned him.

I look on in disgrace, not recognising the person onstage right now. He is another person; he is not my sweet, lovable Elliot. He is a pale, sweaty stranger. He is someone I do not understand.

He is a stranger.

He throws the apples into the crowd, winks at me, and starts playing out of tune. I cover my mouth with my hand, trying to understand what is happening right now.

Damiano begins the second verse, and even he looks confused, as if he doesn't understand the situation. I glance at the others - they are puzzled too, unable to comprehend or know how to react to Elliot's personality transplant.

I am frozen in my spot, my eyes fixed on Elliot. He stops playing altogether, not even twenty seconds in, and he scratches his head as his right eye twitches.

He leans into the mic. "I really need some water," he tells the crowd, and he runs offstage. The others in the band exchange bewildered looks, and I am no longer frozen.

I instantly leap onto the stage, and gallop after Elliot. I throw off my wig and sunglasses and follow Elliot into the kitchen. He is pouring water from a bottle over his head in the kitchen sink.

"What the hell is going on?!" I yell, as the band follow me in.

"He, uh, kind of took some cocaine and is having a bit of a weird trip," Matteo tells me.

Cocaine.

You seem to be following me everywhere lately.

"Elliot, you shouldn't be taking drugs before a gig!" I shout, and I look at the boys. "Where did he get them?"

Before any of them can answer, I hear a thud. We all look to see Elliot has fainted. I rush over, and gently lift him, resting his head on my lap.

"Elliot?!"

"Give him some room," I hear a familiar voice say, and I look to find Ric kneeling beside me, ordering the band to stand back. There is a certain comfort in seeing him here that helps me.

I slap Elliot's cheek lightly. "Come on, Elliot."

Ric grabs a newspaper and starts fanning his face.

"Is he okay?!" Matteo asks.

"He's fine, cocaine is his best friend," G states.

"He needs some water," adds Lino.

"Enough!" I snap, as I look at the boys surrounding us. "Move back!" I order, and they do so. "More! Give him room!"

They obey, but are moving at snail's pace, and it is irritating me. We hear the crowd outside yelling and demanding their presence back onstage.

"Go back on and continue playing!" I tell them.

"Are you serious?"

"We can't do that!"

I get up. "I am not joking here, get back onstage and play till your fucking hearts sing! We are going to get Elliot back to consciousness but you need to handle the crowd."

They look blankly at me, wondering if this is a test.

"Now!" I yell, very loudly, and they are off. I quickly go and lock the door before running back over. Ric now has Elliot's head on his lap and he asks me to pass him some cold

351

water. I obey as he turns Elliot's body to one side. "In case he vomits," he tells me, "he doesn't choke on it."

I nod and we watch as Ric pours some over his forehead. The silence in the room is killing me. We hear the band outside start playing again, and the crowd go wild.

"He's boiling hot," Ric tells me.

I wave the newspaper in his face. "Come on, Elliot. Come on."

"He's going to be okay," Ric tells me, "he just needs to come back to consciousness."

I know Ric knows this because he was once a drug addict too, and a part of me despises him right now – in fact, I despise all drug addicts right now, but there is another part of me, a bigger part, that is really glad Ric is here with me.

When I see there is no reaction, I'm on my feet. "I'm calling an ambulance," I announce, and just as I grab my phone out of my back pocket, there is thumping at the door.

"Alexis! Let me in! What the fuck is happening in there?!"

It's Gavin and I run over to let him in. Both Matt and Gavin are standing at the door with exasperated looks on their faces. "What the *fuck* is going on in here?" Gavin repeats, before pushing passed me and rushing over to Elliot.

I am panicking, and scared, and confused at the turn of events, but I sure am glad Gavin is here. He will know what to do.

"He's having a bad trip; he fainted and now we're trying to bring him back but nothing's happening so I'm calling an ambulance-"

"An ambulance?!" roars Gavin, turning to me. "There will be no fucking ambulance, he is just having a bad trip, Alexis!"

I expected Gavin to shout and swear, I did, but never in a million years did I expect him to refuse I call an ambulance. It makes no sense.

"*A bad trip?!* He's unconscious backstage at the Dublin Castle – we are two police officers away from a seventies Hollywood film about the music business, he needs to go to a hospital-"

"You're overreacting in your typical grandma fashion, you don't do drugs so you don't know how these things work,

Alexis. You're panicking for nothing." Gavin tells me, and I'm taken aback. Gavin is being particularly brutal right now and I am taking it very personally.

"Gavin's right Alexis, Elliot is just having a bad trip-"

"I'm sorry, was I talking to you?" I blurt out, my pent up frustration toward Matt finally rearing its ugly head.

Who is this twat that follows Gavin around like a lost puppy? And where were you when Elliot was snorting dodgy powder up his nose? Who are YOU to look after the Devilled Eggs?!

Gavin forces a laugh. "Mate, she's jealous because you manage her Dream Band."

"What?" I say, and before we can continue, Ric interrupts us.

"Alex, he's awake."

All three of us rush over, as Elliot slowly sits up, confused. Ric gives him a sip of water and he gulps it down. He looks around, with a dazed expression. "What happened?" he asks, and the way he asks the question reminds me of my grandpa in Biella; so old and fragile and confused.

"How are you feeling?" I ask, but I get no response. "Elliot?" Still no response.

Ric gives him another sip of water, and we watch him slowly take in his surroundings. "What happened?" he repeats.

"You fainted," Ric explains. "Keep drinking."

Elliot obeys, and I sigh. "I'm calling an ambulance-"

Gavin grabs my phone and throws it into a pint of beer on the kitchen top. I shriek in pure and utter disbelief.

"I told you no fucking ambulance, Alexis," Gavin barks, and Matt starts laughing very loudly.

Did he just...?
Did he just throw my phone into beer?
I have no phone.
I am without a phone.
My boss just threw my phone into a pint of beer.
What the fuck is happening right now?

"What did you just do?!" I scream at him. "What did you just do?!"

"How do you feel?" Ric asks Elliot, and when I look back over I see that the colour is slowly returning to Elliot's face. He gives Ric a half smile and nurses his back.

"Ow, my back hurts a bit, but I'm okay. I feel okay."

"You fainted, and I think you might have hurt your back a bit when you fell," Ric tells him.

"And I have a bit of a headache, too. But other than that, I'm okay."

"Come on mate, up you get!" Gavin says to Elliot, and I watch him in disgust as he pulls Elliot up from under the shoulders. Realising he's too heavy, he orders Matt to help him. They take one arm each and pull him to his feet.

"Hey, hey, hey, he's not going anywhere," I say.

Gavin laughs so hard his cheeks are red in seconds. He shakes his head at me and looks at Matt. "This girl. She thinks she's his guardian or something!" he turns back to me. "Remember they're a client, Alexis. *My* client, not yours." He turns to Matt.

"Jesus, why did you let him take drugs before a gig?"

"I can't babysit them twenty-four hours a day, they take a *lot* of drugs!" Matt replies.

I grab Elliot's arm. "He's not going anywhere with you."

"He has a gig to play. His fans are waiting."

My face drops. "You can't seriously think he is going back out there to perform?"

"Excuse me?" Gavin says to me. "*Excuse me?* I would strongly suggest you remember who you're talking to, Alexis." He turns to Elliot. "You're okay to perform, aren't you, Elliot?"

Elliot does seem to have perked up, and he gives them a strong yes.

"Of course," he adds. "I'm ready."

"Elliot, you don't have to do this," I tell him, putting my hands on his shoulders and looking him in the eye. And though he's looking right at me, it feels like he doesn't see me at all. Elliot is not currently present in the person standing before me.

Cocaine, you are nothing but poison.

"Alex, sometimes you've got to *chill*," he tells me, before he walks out with Gavin and Matt. I leap after them, about to attack Gavin in pure fury, but Ric pulls me back.

"You can't stop them," he says to me, and I gulp, knowing he is right. I will only lose my job. If Gavin wants to do something, he's going to do it. I cannot stop it. I am powerless.

Once they are gone, I cover my face with both my palms, trying to take in what has just happened. I am not only powerless, I am phoneless too.

When I take my hands away, I see Ric fishing out my phone from the pint. I walk over, knowing it is completely dead.

"He'll replace it tomorrow," he tells me. "He has to or you'll sue. He knows this. He was just trying to be dramatic."

I don't reply. I simply go over to one of the cabinets and pull out a glass and a bottle of red wine. I pour myself a drink, feeling Ric's eyes on me.

"Drinking quite a lot these days," he tells me. "Since when did you become a heavy drinker?"

I can hear the band onstage playing, I can hear Elliot's guitar riff kick in, and I wish so damn hard that I had earplugs with me.

"Since today," I say, bluntly. But it's not true. Alcohol has in recent months become my company in times of stress.

"If you allow alcohol to be your go-to solution in this business, it will eat you up. The music business will eat you up and spit you out. You'll be done by thirty."

I hate to admit it, I want so badly to prove Ric wrong, but he's right. If I count just this past week's alcohol intake, hell, even just the past couple of days alone has been too much. I am using alcohol as my escapism, and it is going to eat me alive.

I don't want to be an alcoholic.

That is just as powerless as being a drug addict.

The glass is already poured, and so I slide it over to Ric without looking at him.

"Oh why *thank you* Alex, that's very kind of you," he says, and I smile at the sound of him calling me Alex after such a long time.

"Why didn't you respond to my texts?" I blurt out, and I know it's the wine talking but I've been dying to ask him since I first saw him at the Christmas party. He appears a little taken aback, but he coolly takes a sip from his glass before answering.

"You left Italy without even so much as a goodbye. As if I were just another hook up. What do you want from me? To chase you, to text you and see how you are?"

"No, but you could at least have replied."

"Why, to ease your guilt? No, sorry. I didn't want to talk to you, and you have to respect that decision if you've treated someone like shit."

There's silence between us, and I feel pangs of guilt resurface. "I'm sorry. For doing that." I say, softly.

"It's fine, it's in the past."

"I see you've moved on anyway, so I'm sure you're fine. I'm glad you're fine."

There is silence for a while before Ric speaks again. "Go light on the alcohol, don't worry about Elliot, and, maybe give the boys a lecture on drugs tomorrow."

I nod, too afraid to use my voice box in case he detects the disappointment in my voice at his lack of response regarding the woman I had seen him with. He makes his way out of the green room.

"Hey," I call, just as he gets to the door. He turns to me with curious eyes. "I have no phone, and I don't want to stick around to see this. Do you mind calling me a taxi?"

He forces a half smile the way I knew he would. "Sure."

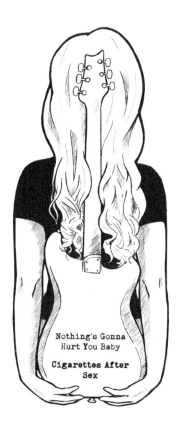

23

As we make our way through the venue to the exit, I can hear the Devilled Eggs playing onstage. I stop in the middle of the crowd, and turn to have a peak.

Elliot's energy has returned, and he's driving the crowd wild with his performance. He is indeed playing in tune now, and if you didn't know him, you'd think he was just an enthusiastic guitarist. But I do know him, and all I see onstage is a stranger. The rest of the band look so good out there however, so talented, and I am so proud.

But watching Elliot perform is breaking my heart, and I cannot stick around for this.

I shake off the sadness, quickly catch up to Ric and we burst through the double doors to the high street. I take a deep breath in of the cold, winter air, and sigh in relief. I am glad to be out of there, to be on the other side of that venue, of that pub. But I know instantly that this place will forever be tainted with this horrible memory.

"Right, Gus is four minutes away," Ric tells me, and I nod as I put on my coat and scarf. There is suddenly an incredibly awkward silence between us, and I cannot for the life of me remember why we thought it was a good idea to come and stand on the high street like two twats. It's cold and there is tension and oh, right - I wanted to get away from the band.

I can hear the sound of Linkin Park's 'Faint' playing in the pub part of the venue and I laugh to myself. Ric looks at me, bewildered, as I continue to laugh. I laugh so hard my stomach hurts. He demands an explanation with his eyes and it takes me a while to recover enough to explain.

"Faint is playing in there. *Faint.* By Linkin' Park. My favourite Linkin' Park song. *Faint!*" I go back to laughing, and Ric continues to watch me.

I laugh, and laugh, and laugh, until I am suddenly silent. The shock, the disgust, the horror of the night's events, of events that happened just ten minutes ago, have shaken me to the core.

I look out into nowhere, lost in thought. Too many thoughts. Thoughts I have to forget. Thoughts I have to push to the back of my mind for tonight or I'll drive myself crazy. I'll sort out everything tomorrow. Tomorrow everything will be better; I will have a solution for everything in the morning.

I remember that I am standing next to Ric, and realise that this might be the last opportunity I ever get to talk to him one-on-one, especially if he has a girlfriend now.

"Congratulations on getting signed by the way," I say, and he looks up from the taxi app.

"Thank you."

"It must feel great."

"It does."

"And you deserve it, truly," I tell him, and he knows I mean it. That I have always meant it.

"Thank you, Alex."

We hear the double doors open and out strolls the woman from earlier; the one Ric had had his arm around. I can see now that she is most definitely Italian; my radar is blinking like crazy. She looks at me and then Ric, and I instantly tense.

"*Ma sei sparito?*" *Did you disappear?*

I watch her approach us with her five-inch heels click-clacking with every step. It reminds me of the time that I met Ric's ex, Valentina, and the jealousy that I had felt in her presence.

He always has such beautiful girlfriends.

I look down at my jeans and manly motorbike jacket, feeling extremely embarrassed. I want to scream: this is not me, this is a disguise! I do not dress like this normally! I can look half decent when I try!

But I know I can't say any of that.

Damn disguise. And I didn't even need it.

"Yes, just helping Alexis here get home - her phone went in a pint of beer," Ric explains to her.

Don't kiss in front of me.

Don't you dare.

I don't want to see that.

"Oh wow, what? How did that happen?" she asks me with a thick Italian accent.

Ric looks at me and then back at the woman. "Tiziana, this is Alexis - she works for Ruby Records."

We shake hands, politely.

"Alex, this is my cousin - Tiziana."

I want to scowl at him, hurt him, throw food at him. He could have mentioned it was his cousin earlier! I relax, remembering that he had mentioned he had a cousin living in London. She has a husband, two kids, and a mortgage.

"Probably the most structured cousin in our family," he had told me. I try to see if they bare any resemblances but fail miserably.

"So how did your phone go into a glass of beer?" she asks me, curiously.

"Uh, I drank too much and, uh, it went flying." It would take too much time and effort to explain I have a crazy, mean boss who threw it in to prevent me from calling an ambulance for the guitarist of the band currently playing onstage who was experiencing a seriously bad trip.

"Is it water resistant? Maybe you can save it? Though I'm not sure it would be beer-resistant," she tells me, looking at Ric for confirmation.

"It's not," he says. "I checked. It's not working."

My beautiful phone. I don't remember the last time I backed it up, so I have probably lost all my pictures, and my contacts, and my messages. All the pictures Elliot had sent me of the band, or Ric had sent me of gigs back in Milano, one he took of Vinnie and I, of me on the beach that one Sunday we had gotten up early to go. I've lost so many sacred memories.

But I can't think about this now, or I may march back in there and throw beer in Gavin's face.

"Ah, there's my taxi!" she tells us. "Lovely to meet you Alexis," she turns to Ric, "see you Sunday, cous." He nods and we watch her get into the car. Once it has driven off, there is silence between us and Ric quickly looks down at the taxi app again.

"You wanna get a drink?" I ask him, and he turns to me. "Mine will be non-alcoholic, I promise."

I know he could say no, that there is a huge likeliness that he *will* say no, but this feels like an opportunity to make amends, and I want to try my hardest to take it.

"I, uh, I have to be up early tomorrow-"

I lean into his phone and glance at the time. "It's 9:30pm on a Saturday night - live a little."

The words sound familiar, and it takes Ric all of two seconds to realise that these were the exact words he had said to me the night we met.

Flashbacks of that warm night last May come rushing back to both of us, and obliterates all the negative memories we have shared since then in a heartbeat.

"Okay smartass, one drink."

I manage to convince Ric to go to the Roadhouse in Covent Garden, and we use the taxi he ordered me for us to get there.

On the journey there we are a little awkward, and so I start up a conversation with our driver. I make it an open conversation for all three of us to participate in, and we are suddenly lost in banter about winter nights in London and how this city can't handle the cold nor the hot.

We talk about the taxi driver's job, and how long he's been in London. He likes it here, but misses South America. Ric contributes by agreeing with all the cons of London that the taxi driver lists, but then chimes in with some pros - such as the music, and the job opportunities, and the fascinating history of this country.

We seem to relax when it's the three of us, and I wonder how we will be once it's just Ric and I alone again.

I love the Roadhouse, and the music they play is always perfect; it's as if they dig into my brain and pick out playlists put together by yours truly.

The place is packed already, and the heat hits our faces instantly as we enter. My nostrils fill with a mixture of the smell of sweat and beer. I'm leading the way, and I turn to give Ric a quick smile as we find a free couple of seats at the bar.

There are tons of people waiting to be served, and only three bartenders. Two are barmen, and I watch Ric fail at getting any of their attention, even the girl. I guess I've only ever seen him order in a packed bar in Milano. London bars are a different ball game.

"Hey handsome," I call, and Ric turns to me, taken aback. Both of the barmen turn to me, and I smile flirtatiously at the more good-looking one. "Yeah you, handsome. Can we get two Jack Daniels? On the rocks."

He nods, as he shakes a drink. I feel Ric's eyes on me, and I glance at him, coolly.

"Did you just order for me?"

"I did indeed. Problem?"

"Impressed."

I do love a man who is also a feminist.

And I suddenly remember how he didn't mind at all when I was dominant with him in the bedroom. In fact, he seemed to enjoy it quite a lot.

"What happened to your non-alcoholic quest?" Ric asks me, and I shake off our sexual history.

"Oh!" I look back at the bartender. "Hey handsome, make that one Jack Daniels, and one lemonade!"

I turn back to Ric, only to remember something else and look back at the bartender. "Oh, and one tequila shot, and one shot of...lemonade. Thanks!"

Ric gives me a confused look. "Trying to get me drunk?"

"We're celebrating you getting signed!" I pause. "And it takes a hell of a lot more than that to get you drunk."

I want to add 'and even then you're amazing in bed' but I hold back. We haven't reached that level of comfortable yet, though I hope we do. It would be fun to make dirty jokes together again. We used to be so good at it, both of us just as perverted as the other.

Our shots arrive and we gulp them down. I am emanating pride for Ric, for I know how talented he is and how much he deserves this. Once he's signed, there will be an album, a tour, and well, world domination.

I suddenly remember everything I like about Ric, and have flashbacks of us having sex, of him saving me from the crowd at the Paolo gig, and that one time I fell asleep with his head resting on my chest.

We study each other with smiles, and I feel as if he is sharing the same flashbacks as me. The stare, like it always has been, is hypnotising. And it takes a few seconds for us to react when the barman slams our drinks down in front of us.

"Now let's forget this shitty night!" I wail.

I don't know if it's the venue setting or the alcohol on Ric's part, but Ric and I ease into our old rapport pretty quickly. We're laughing and telling stories and sharing experiences in no time.

Ric tells me what he's been up to since we last properly spoke or saw each other. It turns out Paolo himself fired Ric, a day after punching Mauro. Paolo then released a statement, saying that it was time to change guitarist.

Ric, in the meantime, though temporarily sad at the outcome, started to become very inspired by his solo career and began to really focus on it. So instead of finding another job as a guitarist in a band (and there were plenty of offers coming in), he decided to sit down and try to write some new songs.

Within a few weeks, he had enough to make not just an EP, but an entire album. Nine tracks, all his, and just his.

He booked in time at the studio, found himself a studio band, and within another two weeks, had an album. Just like that. He then started reaching out to labels, but since he sang in English and his music has a nice Brit-pop sound to it, no one was interested.

It didn't take him long to realise he needed a label that would be interested in his music and his sound, and so he started reaching out to labels in London. Lots of rejections came through, month after month. Until finally, someone at TGI gave him a call and asked him to fly to London to discuss further.

Following this, Ric hired himself a manager, to ensure he doesn't get screwed over. "I know how they like to screw artists over all too well, so I wanted someone street-smart with this stuff to cover me when I can't see a hustle coming my way," he tells me, and I can't help but stare at his handsome face and that smile that, for me, is the most beautiful smile I have ever seen. Ric, in some ways, is the most sincere person I have ever met, and I am glad we still have a rapport.

Maybe Elliot had been right.

Ric has been in London six weeks, and it gives me such a sad feeling in my stomach to know he's been in my city all this time and I've not known about it. But I know I treated him badly, that I didn't deserve to know, and I don't blame him.

I catch him up on my side of things, and tell him about the various artists I help look after. He laughs so loud when I tell him about when I first met Gabriella and accidentally spilled coffee on myself in fear, and the time I was stuck in the studio with Mind Spin, who did nothing but smoke weed for the entire six-hour session.

I tell him about how I'm now an employee at Ruby, and he promptly orders another two shots to celebrate *my* achievement. Yes, actual shots this time.

"To the woman who is going to absolutely smash the music business!" he shouts, and a few people turn to look at us, but we don't care. In fact, we raise our glasses to them.

I am telling him about my challenges looking after Dazza when we are interrupted by a presenter on stage. The entire venue pipes down.

"Good evening, everyone! I hope you're all having a great Saturday night so far – we will soon be starting our karaoke night."

Ric turns to me, eyes wide as he realises why I chose this venue.

"As you may know already, here at the Roadhouse we do karaoke every Saturday night, and we have a live band that plays the song you choose, live!

Only *one* person is allowed on stage at a time, unfortunately, but don't be scared off - this is your chance to sing in front of people like you're in a band! We've all had that dream, don't even try to deny it. So please sign up by approaching me, as I make my way around the venue to each table."

The music returns and it's Arctic Monkeys' 'Arabella'. I bop my head to the song, as I feel Ric's eyes on me.

"Alex," he says, calmly.

"Yes, Ric?"

"What are we doing here?"

I turn to him with excited eyes. "This is going to be your debut gig in London!"

I've never seen Ric's eyes widen this much before, and he's on his feet in seconds. I pull him back by the arm before he can bolt.

"Come on, it'll be fun!"

"No, Alex! No way! Plus I'm signed now, I need to get approval from the label-"

"You sign tomorrow! You said so yourself – you're a free man until then! It's *one* song, and it's not of yours! We can pick from this huge book of song options. It's like a catalogue of the world's best songs!"

I've never performed at the Roadhouse, but I've always wanted to. Maybe someday I will, when I get the guts to. But I spent most of my Saturday nights from aged eighteen to twenty here, and loved every moment of it.

Fun fact: it's been the same man presenting it since I was eighteen.

Ric admits defeat, and sits back down. He won't admit it to me just yet, but it's not a bad idea. He hasn't sung in London in a very long time, and this is the perfect opportunity.

I explain how it works: you choose a song from the songbook, get a number on the list, and then you wait until it's your turn. Once the presenter reaches us, Ric chooses Red Hot Chili Peppers' 'Scar Tissue' and is told he's number fifteen on the list.

We're left waiting a long while before it's Ric's turn, and so we chat and share more stories, watching others perform and though they're mostly awful, we clap ferociously at the end of every performance, even standing up and whistling.

We judge every act, as if we are on some sort of panel. The energy between us is vibrant, and I realise just how much I've missed this – simply hanging out with Ric. I'm having a lot of fun, as if we have never been apart, and he soothes the pain of not being with the Devilled Eggs for their first ever gig in London.

Every now and again, I ask Ric to check social media for live footage of the band – Matteo's friend is recording the whole thing live, and from the videos it looks as if they're going from strength-to-strength.

I look longingly at the screen, but seeing Elliot jumping around is making me sad. Ric puts a hand on my forearm and it gives me shivers.

"Lecture on drugs tomorrow."

I nod, and Ric puts his phone away.

For tonight, we are not a part of the music business, and we vow not to check again.

When number fourteen takes to the stage it's a guy in his fifties, and he's singing Boy George. We watch him as we '*woo*' rather loudly every thirty seconds.

"Not half bad."

"Yeah, except he chose Boy George," I remark. I've never been a fan.

Ric suddenly sprints out of his seat and grabs my hand. "I have an idea!" he pulls me through the venue and the adrenaline rush I feel as we run through the venue brings out drunk giggles after only one shot.

I'm giggling and excited and happy that our rapport is back and stronger than ever. I hope it stays this time.

We reach the side of the stage, and in front of us stands the general manager, Rob, with a clipboard in hand as he bops his head to Boy George.

"Hey," Ric says to him, "would it be alright if my sister Gwen here joined me onstage? As the guitarist?"

I feel instantly violently nauseous. "What?! No, Ric-"

"I'm sorry mate, that's not allowed – we have a live band for a reason-"

But Ric is uninterested in Rob's response, and just as the Boy George wannabee finishes his song, Ric is hopping onstage and dragging me with him. He goes straight up to the lead guitarist, a shy man in his late thirties with curly hair and a calming smile.

"Hey there! Terrific playing by the way," Ric is getting out his words so quick, as if the world is about to end and he needs us to perform together on this very stage before that happens. He tugs me forward by the arm. "This is my sister, Gwen. She would *really* love to play guitar on this next track as I sing-"

"Uuuh, thanks guys, but I'm not sure that's allowed-" he looks over at Rob, who has been distracted by a rather overweight stoner. They seem deep in very serious conversation.

Ric blocks the guitarists' view of him. "What's your name?"

"Steve, but-"

"Steve, listen, let's be honest - the music business is a man's world. It always has been, and until we do something about it, it always will be," he points to me with his nose.

"Gwen here is a fantastic guitarist, but she never gets a chance to play onstage. Sure, she doesn't push for it, and even when asked, she is terrified. She doesn't want to take a chance, she doesn't want to show everyone that she can play. But that's because she's been taught not to.

I would like to show her how incredible a feeling it is, to play onstage. To not make her afraid ever again, to play in front of men, or tell a man that she is a guitarist, and a damn good one at that.

To make her push herself to get better, because, there *is* a point, it's not all for nothing. Can you help us, and the future of feminism in the music business, by allowing her to play this one very song with me?"

I am moved by Ric's words, and am overwhelmed with emotion in my stomach, so much so that I feel it swirling around at the back of my throat. And I realise, he is my favourite human on this planet. He has been since the moment we met.

We look at Steve, anxiously awaiting his reaction. There's a 90% chance he's going to laugh in our faces. There's a 90% chance that he doesn't give a fuck about feminism in the music business – after all, he is a man; he'll always be okay. And there's a 90% chance that Rob is going to storm onstage and drag us off by the ears before Steve can even decide.

Luckily for us though, Steve is a feminist. Luckily for us, Steve tunes his guitar for me, and then passes his beautiful 1962 Sunburst Fender Stratocaster over my head.

I clutch the neck with an overwhelming smile, and Steve looks back at me with what feels like the exactly the same smile. He doesn't say anything as he steps offstage, and the Boy George wannabee hands Ric his mic before stepping off too.

And just like that, Ric and I are onstage together. He opens his mouth to say something, to which I'm pretty sure it's 'you can do this', but then he smiles, and holds back. He does not need to tell me I can do this, for I *know* I can.

Right?

Right.

I take a deep breath, as the venue remains silent. Someone coughs in the audience, and I breathe out.

Let's do this.
Do I remember the chords?
Of course I do.
I've played this song a thousand times over.
And it's exactly why Ric had chosen it.

There is silence in the venue, and all eyes are on us. I know I need to start before Rob spots us and boots us off, but I also want to take a moment to take this all in. That magical, perfect moment before a song.

And just like that, I begin playing the main riff to 'Scar Tissue' in front of about a hundred people. I play well, and I play with confidence. Passion takes over as soon as I start, and excitement, for I love to play.

I fucking love to play.

I suddenly hear Elliot's voice in my head, ordering me to lift my head, to look up at the audience, to be proud of the fact that I am a female guitarist.

I instantly obey, and smile at the audience. They smile back, and I relax. The buzz that I am receiving from playing onstage is incredible.

There are no words to describe how amazing a feeling it is to be playing with the spotlight on us, to have everyone's attention. Ric's voice helps to sooth me, and it feels so good to hear it again after such a long time.

I had forgotten just how beautiful a singing voice he has: deep, sexy, profound. He sings with emotion and depth, connecting with my soul the way it always has been able to.

I mess up on a couple of chords in the chorus, but I doubt anybody notices except perhaps the rest of the band and Ric. I look at the band a few times, and we exchange smiles, even though they're wondering who the hell I am.

The audience love our song, and I think they love me too, for when it's time for my two solos, they're clapping and *woo*ing, and I'm really infused in the music, taking it in, closing my eyes as it takes over my body, giving me goose bumps.

Ric looks on with immense pride as I deliver the solos. I look down whilst I play them in fear of messing up, but once

I'm done and the audience is applauding, I look up to meet Ric's happy eyes. He's clapping too, he's clapping as if he has waited an eternity to witness this moment.

I make zero mistakes on the solos and I'm relieved; I am surprised at just how well I had managed to deliver them. I sigh in relief as I go back to playing the main riff, just as Ric sings and approaches me with the mic. We share the chorus together, and I beam at Ric as he beams back at me as we sing along.

Playing onstage is the most amazing feeling in the world. There is nothing, absolutely nothing, that can beat it. It is better than sex, which says a lot coming from me.

You are creating music, and you are creating it in front of an audience that is connecting with what you're playing – changing their mood, influencing their feelings, sending something to their minds and to their souls. You are giving them a piece of you.

Ric and I exchange grins, just as the song ends and the audience is clapping. It's all over in what feels like a nanosecond, and I feel as if I have swum across the ocean. I breathe out, relieved, but also sad that it's over.

I want to play another one!

The audience is roaring with applause, and as Ric and I beam at one another with pride, Steve is the first onstage.

"That was amazing! You're really good!" he says.

"Thank you, Steve!" I wail, my heart pounding out of my chest and my hands trembling. The audience is still roaring with applause for us. "I messed up on some chords but-"

"Easily fixable with some practice," he hands me a card with his name on it and 'advanced guitar teacher' written underneath with his contact details. "If you want a couple of lessons let me know – on the house," he smiles as I pass him his Fender Strat.

"Oh my God, thank you! But you'll need to let me pay for the lessons – gender equality and that."

He nods, and I pass him back his guitar. The audience is still going nuts, and Ric and I turn to one another with the biggest Cheshire cat smiles.

Ric puts a hand on my cheek with pure pride in his eyes, and we instantly hug. It's a tight hug, filled with love, affection and joy.

The audience go even wilder, and I am overwhelmed with emotion.

"Thank you," I whisper in Ric's ear. He doesn't respond, but I know without seeing his face that he's smiling with pride.

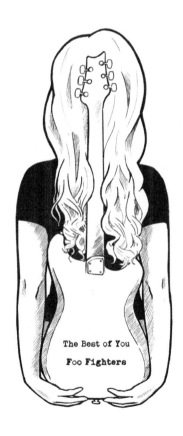

24

David Lloyd George once said, "don't be afraid to take a big step. You can't cross a chasm in two small jumps." Choosing to take a big step in life involves risk, there's no doubt about it. It takes courage, faith in yourself, and just the right amount of crazy.

It can be the best decision of your life, or the worst. For this, I cannot stress enough how important it is to avoid making decisions founded on impulse, emotions, or as a reaction to a negative feeling or incident. Every decision needs to be carefully thought out, using your logical side to help you discover what is top priority to YOU.

Accept that you won't know the consequences (good or bad) until much later, because this too is essential to remember: you cannot predict the future.

But here's the thing – if you choose to not take a risk at all, play it safe at the cost of your happiness, then you'll forever remain exactly where you are. And is that not the same as failing?

You would think it would be awkward as fuck to wake up on a former hook up's shoulder on a hotel bathroom floor. But it's not. Because it's Ric, and with Ric it's always been natural.

I'm the first to wake up, and it's to the sound of cars beeping outside in Monday morning traffic. I remember the events of the previous evening, and spot dribble on Ric's collar. I quickly wipe it off and as I do so, I freeze to look at Ric sleep.

He looks so peaceful, and being at such close perimeters with his face after such a long time gives me flashbacks of nights at his flat in Milano – his place always smelling of sun dried tomatoes, and how there were always healthy snacks in his fridge. To this day, I can't look at chopped celery and not think of him.

I remember his flat, the desk spread with guitar plucks, and the way his room would turn a mud yellow at sunset. I think of his Pink Floyd posters and how they had got to witness some Grade A porn sex.

*Our sex was **so good.***

He suddenly moves and I look away, nonchalantly standing up.

"Hmmm," he says as he yawns. "Oh God, did we sleep here?"

I put out my hand to help him up and he takes it. "Afraid so."

"Who the hell pays two hundred quid for a hotel room and then sleeps on the bathroom floor?"

Probably former hook ups who are unsure sharing a king-sized bed is appropriate.

After our moment of glory at the Roadhouse, people from the audience had bought us and chatted to us about their pending careers in the music business.

When they learnt that Ric is a solo artist, they seeked musical advice from him. When they learnt I am an assistant manager at Ruby, they pressed me for a meeting. We stayed a while and chatted, but once it turned into too much of an involuntary sales pitch, we bolted.

Since we were by then completely comfortable with one another, we found it a great idea to head back to Ric's hotel room and 'hang out'. We knew neither of us would try anything, that our sexual chemistry (though still admittedly present) was something futile; we are better off as friends.

And so we watched a film, drank too much (yes, I broke my non-alcohol rule or I'd be the only one sober - but promised to not drink for at least a month starting from today), and ended up rocking out to the Ramones in his bathroom.

Yes, I do realise that this is the second time in less than a month that I have fallen asleep on hotel bathroom floors with guitarists, I'm not trying to start a trend, and I assure you my back is not very happy with me.

I glance at Ric's watch and swear under my breath in Italian. "Shit, it's 8:45! I have a meeting with Gavin and Gabriella in *fifteen minutes!*"

"Isn't Gabriella on tour?" Ric asks me, nursing his back.

"Yes, but she's back for a couple of days to sort out this radio competition – long story, will explain later! I gotta go."

I am about to rush out when I turn around, his eyes on me. "Thanks, uh, for a memorable night. Let's do it again soon?"

He smiles warmly at me. "Sure."

By the time I get to the office it's 9:10am and I'm scolding Drunk Me for deciding to stay at Ric's hotel - it's so far away from the Ruby office!

The taxi driver lends me his phone to use as a mirror as I take off last night's make-up and put on a fresh batch.

"You look beautiful!" he tells me, in-between his story about how he once met Bill Murray.

"Thank you! Does it look like I didn't go home last night?"

The taxi driver falls silent and I sigh.

Shit. Shit. Shit.

I run into the building before the taxi has even fully grinded to a halt, zoom past the revolving doors, and squeeze into a jam-packed lift. "Sorry, sorry," I whisper, out of breath as they all shoot me dirty looks.

Once I arrive at level 37, I rush out and head straight to Gavin's office. As I do so, I notice that though the office is busy, it is eerily quiet.

A few people look at me as I rush past them, and I wonder if I have lipstick on my teeth. I contemplate getting out my phone to check when I remember, once again, that it does not work!

I have a flashback of Gavin throwing it into a pint of beer and tell myself to not give Gavin any attitude about it. He is still my boss.

Remain professional.

I stop by my desk, leave my stuff, and rush off to Gavin's office. Once I arrive there however, to my utmost surprise, there is no one inside. The lights are off; a sight I have never seen before in my three months at the label.

Perplexed, I am wondering what to do next when I hear his voice behind me.

"Alexis."

I turn around to face Gavin, and he looks at me with a quick smile and tired eyes.

"*Wow*, late to the office?" I tease, as we walk in and I shut the door behind me.

"Well I had some stuff to take care of, didn't I?" he takes off his jacket and hangs it on the back of his chair.

"Where's Gabriella? Don't we have a 9am with her?"

"Uh-huh. I cancelled it," he yawns and licks his lips, looking up at me as he feels my gaze, waiting for an explanation. "I mean, after last night and all. It was a long night, *believe me*."

Argh, Gavin and his wild drunken nights on the town. Hung over Gavin is so moody it's scary. Does he even remember what he did to my phone last night?

"Brett was not a happy bunny, as you can imagine. And the way it all happened – it puts Ruby in such a bad light. Argh, the press are having a field day with it. I tell you Alexis, sometimes I just want to quit the music business and be done with it! Become a duvet salesman or something."

I snort. "Well that I *definitely* have to see," I tell him and he rolls his eyes with a smug smile. "But what happened yesterday? You mean Elliot's breakdown backstage?"

Gavin's smug smile disappears instantly. "What do you mean what happened yesterday, Alexis? Elliot dying right there on bloody stage, for fuck's sake! It's a bloody mess, I tell you!"

As soon as I hear the words 'Elliot dying' I am somewhere else. My soul has left my body, and I am feeling violently sick. Darkness harnesses the core of me, and I am a trembling, shocked, nauseous mess in only a second.

How two words can turn my entire world upside at the drop of a hat.

Gavin continues to ramble but I no longer hear him. I cannot make direct eye contact with him either, in fear that if his smug smile returns I may push him through the window.

The words 'Elliot dying' repeat themselves in my head, again and again and again, echoing and forming a knot at the pit of my stomach that keeps getting tighter and tighter.

I am dizzy and the wine from last night suddenly wants very much to escape my mouth from my throat, and I try not to imagine a cold, dead version of Elliot's body, but I can't. And maybe I don't want to.

I throw up on the floor of Gavin's office, red spilling over his white carpet, and as disgusting as it is, I wish I have more to give.

"Alexis! What the fuck?! What the...Jesus, have you gone *insane*?! What the fuck is wrong with you?! I just got this carpet cleaned last week! Jesus!"

I bolt out of his office as fast as I can, my heart pounding as I hear Gavin yelling after me, demanding for me to return. People in the office look at me as I run past them, last night's wine dripping from my mouth. I wipe it clean as I grab my stuff and rush to the lifts.

I'm trembling hard, in complete and utter shock – my legs are jelly, my teeth clattering. I cannot control my body or its reaction.

Just as the empty lift arrives, I bolt and decide to take the stairs. I need to be moving, I need to be doing something to get out of this office as fast as I can. I skip down the stairs two or three at a time despite how badly I'm trembling, and I try not to think about it. I try damn hard but it's proving a challenge.

It can't be true.
It can't be true.
It can't be true.
It's not possible.

And yet I know that it damn well can be.

I burst through the staircase exit door, and crash straight into someone.

"Sorry!" says a voice I recognise, and I look up to find Ric standing before me, worry and anguish in his eyes. He is broken too, I see it straight away. He knows. "Alex!"

I break down instantly in a flood of tears, and I fall to the floor in pain, in guilt, in shock, and he falls down with me. I scream in the pain, in the confirmation in Ric's eyes that it's true.

All I can say is 'no' again and again and again, I scream it from the top of my lungs, as if in some way it is going to bring him back, it is going to make time rewind so that the loss of his life could have been prevented.

I dive my head into his chest and soak Ric's shirt in only a matter of seconds. He holds me tight, and close, and he does not say a word. For he knows that there is nothing he can say.

He cannot tell me that everything is going to be okay, because he does not know this. He does not know this, and Ric is the last person to make a fake promise.

I hail a taxi to the nearest hospital, but Matteo tells me that Elliot isn't at the hospital, he's at the morgue. The fucking morgue. I've been rushing to work like it's the end of the world, whilst Elliot, dearest, sweetest, seventeen-year-old Elliot, has been lying in a morgue. His body cold, dead, and no longer a part of the living.

I hang up on Matteo and hand Ric back his phone. He rubs my thigh as we sit in silence. A silence I cannot bear. Because it gives me the chance to hear my inner thoughts, and I am afraid of them.

"Stop! Please stop! Please stop!" I open the taxi door as he slows down in confusion, and I jump out whilst the car is still moving.

"Alex!" Ric calls after me, but I'm not listening. I bolt through Monday morning traffic, knowing it's not less than a fifteen-minute walk, that I will get tired, that a taxi is smarter.

But I don't care.

"Alex!"

I don't even turn around to acknowledge Ric, but I know he's catching up to me.

"Take a taxi! I'll meet you there!" I tell him.

But he doesn't say anything. He instead runs by my side in silence. All that can be heard is our breathing in synch as we do so.

We run the rest of the way in silence, but it's okay because the noises of London are keeping my dark thoughts at bay. Also, not collapsing from exhaustion is keeping me pretty distracted.

We arrive out of breath and burst through the double doors to find the boys huddled in a corner of the empty, white room. They quickly turn to us and they're in my arms in an instant.

They have red eyes and runny noses and a tremendous sadness to them that equals mine. Nobody says anything and we remain there, hugging each other, holding on for dear life, crying, for what seems like an eternity. They have surrounded me and all that can be heard are sniffles every now and again.

Ric is to the side, sitting on a wooden chair, looking solemnly down at the white floor. We remain like this, and nobody moves.

I love these boys so much, and I have only just realised how much. That I have always loved them, each and every one of them, with all of my heart. I may not have shown it as affectionately as others, but I love them. I would always help them as much as I could, to see them succeed, be happy, be healthy, be alive.

And now one of them is dead.

I have flashbacks of moments shared with Elliot: the first time we spoke back at that studio in Milano, the first time we shared a pizza, the first time he played me a guitar riff.

His smile.

His laughter.

His voice.

You don't know just how much you love these things about a person until they're gone. Until you'll never see or hear them again.

I have a flashback of when we reunited in London, running into his arms. The way his rough, unshaven cheek had felt against mine.

All I can think is that I will never be able to feel that again.

He was seventeen years old. He had his whole life ahead of him. He was the sweetest, most honest, most beautiful soul I had ever come across. He had had a rough upbringing, but he was using that to make something of his life.

And now, he won't be able to do that.

We slowly and eventually let go of each other, and it's only now that I notice we are missing another member: Damiano.

"He went to the bathroom an hour ago and never came back," Matteo tells me, as if reading my mind.

I nod and walk out, telling them I'll be right back. When I turn to look back at them, Ric is now hugging the boys, and I have never been more grateful to have him here with me.

When I walk into the mens' toilets, I give zero fucks about entering a forbidden domain or seeing something I shouldn't. Thankfully, the place is empty though, except for a sixteen-year old boy curled up in the corner, looking straight into nothing.

His expression is blank, as if he is a million miles away, and he does not look up to meet my eyes when I approach.

I am not sure what to say to him, not because we have never been close or because we have never really liked each other, but because what the hell do you say to someone who has just lost their brother?

I go over and sit down next to him on the reasonably clean floor of the mens' toilets.

"I'm so sorry," I say, very softly. They are the only words that find their way to my tongue.

"What do *you* need to be sorry about? He liked you. He *loved* you," Damiano replies. Tears surface on my cheeks and I wipe them away.

"He loved you too, Damiano."

"Bullshit!" he wails, turning to look at me with tormented eyes. I am not sure what to say in response, and I am too afraid to argue with him. There is silence again and all we can hear is a loose tap dripping at the sinks.

How did we get here? How did life change in an instant? Just like that. Someone is here, and then they're gone. You think you're on your way to work, happy to be friends with someone again, excited for your day, ready to lecture a band on drugs, to fix your phone and go and see your friend who had not had a good experience last night, only to find out, life has bigger plans for him.

Never did I imagine when I woke up this morning that in two hours I would sitting on the floor of the mens' toilets of a morgue, crying with Damiano over the fact that Elliot is *dead*.

Dead.

I will never see him again.

Or hug him.

Or listen to him play a song to me.

"How did he…? What happened when I left?" I manage to say. But Damiano doesn't answer, and I feel immediately guilty for asking. It is not relevant, not right now.

He's gone. He's dead. And we will never see him again.

"I didn't once call him my brother," Damiano suddenly says. "I didn't once acknowledge that he was my brother. Or that I loved him. Or that he was family. My real family."

He starts blubbering as tears flood his eyes, and mine flood too. I put my arms around him, and to my surprise, Damiano dives his head onto my lap, and cries.

Loudly.

Painfully.

Unbearably.

I cry uncontrollably too, and there we sit, two people that have never gotten along, united in the pain of someone we have lost.

And God, how much we love him.

Loved him.

"I'm looking for my son!" an angry male voice wails from the other side of the toilets. I know it's Brett Gardner, and Damiano shoots up instantly, wiping his tears and splashing water on his face.

He hasn't finished crying though; I know it and he knows it, but we both say nothing.

The door bursts open and in walks Brett Gardner, looking pristine and clean cut. As if he has had a perfectly normal night's sleep. As if today is just another day.

He looks at us both, before settling his eyes on his son. "We're going. You have a singing lesson at noon."

They walk out together and Damiano doesn't even look back at me as he does so. They leave me alone in the mens' toilets with nothing but the sound of the dripping tap.

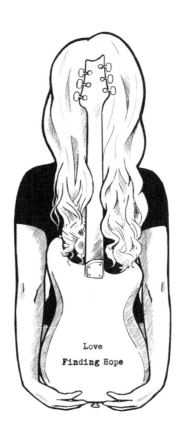

25

Laurell K. Hamilton once wrote, 'you cannot die of grief, though it feels as if you can'. For most of my life, I had believed her. But then, what the hell had I known about grief?

Nothing.

Absolutely nothing.

Ten days have passed since I got the news that broke me into tiny, little pieces. Once Damiano left with his dad, I remained in the mens' toilets a good half an hour before Ric found me. When he did, I broke down into tears again, crying and shouting in the pain that was slowly and truly hitting me.

Ric held me close, as I let out the pain in the realisation that I have lost Elliot forever. That he is no longer breathing, no longer a part of the living. That we would never again share a John Mayer song, or a pizza, or any sort of moment together. His smile, his presence, his voice, it's all gone now.

In the flicker of an eye.

We stayed there, on the floor of the morgue's mens' toilets a good hour, before eventually getting up and going home. But the thing is, once I got up off that floor, something changed in me.

I much preferred it when I was shouting in the pain, letting my heart ache for the news, because what has followed is a pain so deep and so dark, it swallows me up and spits me out, every single day. It is as if it hurts so much there is no energy to shout or scream or wail anymore. Because this is a new level of darkness, and I can feel myself falling, further and further down a black hole; no rope to get me out, no light to switch me on; the darkness is infinite. It is consuming me and I am letting it. I have no energy to try and fight back.

It's crazy, if I think about it. I've read a lot of stories about celebrities dying of drug overdoses and just always assumed it was more prone to happen to rich people who took ridiculous amounts of drugs. To the elite. To the spoilt rotten who don't know how to limit their intake. But I couldn't have been further from the truth.

Elliot died onstage at the Dublin Castle at 9:57pm. He simply collapsed onstage, and died soon after from an overdose. The audience thought it was part of the act, but the boys knew it was no joke. Gavin called an ambulance, but it was of no use – he was dead before they even arrived.

All the senior heads at the label arrived and took interviews for the press, trying their best to shed some good light on Ruby, Gavin standing by Brett's side the entire time. Nobody looked after the boys or asked how they were doing. The only thing they did was make sure they were *nowhere near the press*.

Elliot was portrayed in the media as a druggie who grew up poor and had nothing going for him but his band. The label had told him multiple times that he should clean himself up and even offered to pay for rehab treatment, but he had always declined and said he was in control.

I read nothing about him being Brett's son, as expected. Brett wouldn't want to taint his reputation by being associated to a poor, loser druggie.

Coroners reported Elliot's death an overdose on cocaine. He had only taken a line but that's all it took to kill you – one fucking line. I remember hanging out with some musicians backstage a few years ago whilst one of them snorted, and one of them said, 'you'd have to be a rich motherfucker to die of a cocaine overdose'.

I had believed it, because I had heard a druggie say it and had never really been a drug expert so I believed shit like that when it was said, but it was only when I heard that Elliot had died from a heart attack that I decided to research the effects of cocaine.

Did you know that you are twenty-four times more likely to have a heart attack when you snort cocaine? That's how Elliot had died – a heart attack. He was seventeen years old, he went to the gym, he was in the prime of his life, and yet he died from a line of cocaine.

Death is something you hear about from the second you're born; it's this terrible, inevitable thing that happens to us all and plagues our lives, turning our worlds black when it happens to someone we love. We see it in films, where actors and actresses lose someone they love and cry their eyes out, and maybe it reaches us sometimes, with the emotion they put into the loss, or the connection we had made with the fictional character. But that's all they are – fictional characters.

We subconsciously find comfort in the knowledge that they are in actual fact *not* dead but well and truly alive and sipping cocktails in Malibu as the money rolls in.

But you do not and cannot understand the entire weight of death until it happens to you; until someone *you* love and would never want to see any harm come to, dies, suddenly, with no way of trying to save that person, with no way of saying goodbye, with no way of seeing them again with a pulse and that smile you truly didn't understand how much you actually loved until it was too late. Until you wouldn't ever see it again.

I could tell you it turns your world black or that it drills a hole in the pit of your stomach or that you spend hours and hours and hours just being nothing but fucking sad, and not just any type of sad, but that really dark sad that consumes you like nothing else in the world can.

But you know that already. You've learnt that in films and in books. We all have.

Yet there's something that changes you when you literally watch somebody you love get buried underground. When you stand in front of their casket, knowing that he's inside, and watch people put that casket underground. When you watch people shovel dirt on top of that casket. And hear his mother's loud and painful cries as they do so; cries that haunt your dreams every night, cries that will stay with you forever. It's here, it's right here that you realise how dark and unfair and cruel this world is.

The silence that took place in the moments that Elliot was buried are something that will stay with me forever. I saw him in front of me as they buried him – the night we had hung out and played John Mayer songs at the shitty little rehearsal space in Milano, drinking Peroni and talking about music.

He had said I had a little tear in the back of my cardigan but I couldn't see it, and I didn't believe him, and so he took a picture of it with his phone and showed me, both of us laughing at the picture, he decided to stick a filter on it to make it look classier.

We had then proceeded to talk about one summer he had gone to camp and met all these phoney rich kids from Milano with more pink polo shirts than Italy could handle. His eyes were bright as he told the story and took gulps from his Peroni, burping every now and again and ignoring messages he was receiving from some hot girl at the music academy, because when Elliot told you a story, he gave you all his attention.

This is how I'll always remember you, Elliot. Exactly like this.

It was less than a week ago that I was at the Decor Kind gig with him and the others, Elliot picking me up and putting me on his shoulders. We had so much fun that night, we always seemed to when we were together. We had such an incredible bond, and now it's gone.

It's been ten days since I lost Elliot, and I am okay. I have to be. I went straight back to work following the funeral, dove headfirst into Dazza's album and Gabriella's radio competition.

Ric has been staying at mine, refusing to leave me alone in the evenings, and I keep telling him it's unnecessary. Though I have to admit, it has been nice to have him around. He sleeps on the sofa, and keeps his stuff in my bedroom.

We have dinner together late at night, catching up on each other's days. Ric's album is being mixed at the moment and so he's spending most of his time at the studio. He's getting a little frustrated with his producer, Marco, and I suggested I have a listen or pop in to give my input, but he's being very adamant about keeping his music to himself until it's finalised. Talk about being a pre-Madonna.

On my eleventh day without Elliot, I find myself waking up twenty minutes before my alarm. It's been happening a lot; I don't tend to sleep much nowadays, and that's fine with me. More time to spend building my career at Ruby, and more time building my photography business.

Ric suggested I also start freelancing as an artist. He thinks my drawing skills are impressive. I think he's feeling sorry for me because I just lost someone I cared about. But, I'll take it into consideration. I do love to draw.

It's the day of Dazza's final photo shoot (yes, he had to have one more - apparently five were not enough) and I'm fairly relaxed about it; he's been relatively well behaved recently. I arrive and he's already there, which is a first. He is dressed as a sailor for the shoot.

"Hello, gorgeous!" he pecks me on the cheek. "I bet you like a man in uniform," he wiggles his eyebrows at me and I can't help but laugh. "If you want, I can buy you this boat, you know," he whispers in my ear, and I roll my eyes playfully at him.

"Get ready for the shoot, you looney," I reply.

It's Cris, the moody photographer with permanent resting bitch face, who is running this shoot. He has run all six of Dazza's shoots, and I feel a little bit sorry for him. He must be so tired of directing Dazza by now, and so I make sure he is fully stocked on coffee to keep him happy. He goes nutty for good coffee.

We have a fun day on set for the final cut – this time Dazza's on a boat on the river Thames, pretending to navigate. Every time a shot is over, Dazza steps on the pedal and the boat *zooms* off down the Thames, everyone squealing for him to stop except me.

I know we can die in an instant, that life is random that way, that we could die walking down the street or stepping out of the shower, and so I'm no longer worried about Dazza speeding down the Thames without a licence.

If it happens, it happens.

Death can happen anytime, anywhere, to anyone.

The fact that we can die at any moment is always on my mind now. Life is fickle, and the sooner you learn this the better you can navigate your life.

Elliot is always on my mind too. I wonder how his mum is doing - I met her at the funeral, but I could not hug her. How do you hug a mother who has just lost their son?

A hug isn't going to bring them back, it isn't going to make them feel better. So I simply told her she had a very special son and that I had loved him very much.

Matteo came to see me at the flat a couple of days after the funeral. He had in his hands a box of some of his stuff, said he would have wanted me to have these things.

We sat down in silence in my living room, and we didn't say anything for a good hour. I then managed to find the courage to open the box, and I find: his polka dot gloves that I bought him as a belated Christmas present, his Joy Division albums, his dragon necklace, and a picture of us at the gig with him on his shoulders.

I burst into tears, as did Matteo, and there we sat, in my living room, crying, for a long while. And I remember thinking, I suppose I'm making up for the years I never cried over anything.

I look out longingly at the river and my city, rubbing the dragon pendant around my neck. I allow myself to feel the tortuous sadness for sixty seconds, and then I take a deep breath in, and I get back to my day.

Dazza's shoot takes up most of the day, and it's only at 5:15pm that I remember I have to meet Gavin at The Sebright Arms to do some scouting – a supposedly super talented DJ, whose name I don't even know, is playing.

We're going to scout him together, which is something new – Gavin usually never tags along. He usually has something better to do.

Gavin hasn't been talking to me much since I returned to work. He avoids eye contact when he can, and ignores my important emails about clients. He hasn't brought up me throwing up on his carpet, though.

When I returned to work, the carpet was clean, and he asked me for my phone so that he could get it fixed. By the end of the day, I had a new one. I found it by my desk after returning from a client meeting. I thanked him and that was the last reminder between Gavin and I that that night and that morning had ever happened.

Nobody at work talks about the Devilled Eggs to me directly, but you can hear them being discussed in the kitchen, at the printers, at the lifts. It's the talk of the office.

Did you know them? Did you work with them? How old was he? What drugs did he overdose on?

The poor employees of Ruby Records contemplate *just how many drugs* they can take to have fun, to get ahead in their careers, but not die from an overdose. To not end up like Elliot.

It hasn't occurred to anyone that perhaps *no drugs* is the way forward. Why? Because people die in the music business every other day from an overdose. It is not something new, and it is unfortunately not something that will stop because a seventeen-year-old overdosed and died from it.

It is seen as *his* fault, it is seen as foolishness on the part of Elliot. Nobody stops to think about the fact that he died from *one line of cocaine.*

No, people die in this industry and everyone is shocked, but they do not change their ways to prevent themselves from taking the same path. They simply carry on.

Because today is just another day of opportunity for the music business. Get involved, or get out.

Dazza is happy following the shoot and so I invite him along with me to The Sebright Arms. We laugh and joke on the way, and when we arrive at the venue I'm surprised to find Gavin already there. He's usually late, unbothered, and tired.

He's sitting at the bar however, talking to an important-looking man in a suit, and he looks rather perky. I think the stranger with him is a board member at Ruby.

The crowd are starting to warm up for the DJ set, and it's pretty packed already. We approach and Gavin has to look twice when he spots Dazza with me. With all the power he can muster, he keeps his smile.

"Well hello there! What are *you* doing here?" he asks Dazza, not even looking at me. It's funny how something changes in your rapport with someone once you vomit on their carpet.

"I thought I'd come along and scout with you! See what it takes to be an employee at Ruby," Dazza turns to me, "what would you like to drink?"

"Lemonade?"

He nods and walks over to the other side of the bar to order. Gavin's eyes remain on Dazza for a good twenty seconds before they dot to me. He's smiling, but his eyes are not happy.

"Bringing clients to our scouting nights too? Brilliant money-making idea that is," he tells me, sarcastically. I can tell that Gavin is already tipsy, but there's a maliciousness in his voice that is intangible.

I find it hard to work out if it's always been there and I've never noticed, or if it developed after the night at the Dublin Castle.

The board member stifles a laugh, and my phone buzzes in my pocket before I can reply.

Ric:
How did the shoot go?
I should be done in the studio in a couple of hours.
A FULL ALBUM DONE!

I smile in pride, and am about to type back when Dazza returns with our drinks. "Here you go, babygirl," he hands me my drink and I thank him, putting my phone away.

"Dazza, how did the shoot go? Are you all done?"

"Yes! We finished today, thanks to Alexis here," Dazza winks at me, but Gavin ignores the statement as if he didn't hear it.

"When did the photographer say they would be ready?"

"Uuuh, end of this week I think?"

Gavin gives him a nod of approval and takes another gulp from his beer.

"So, who are we seeing?" Dazza asks, his eyes dotting back and forth from me to Gavin. I shrug.

"DJ Tango."

"What a *shit* name!" Dazza says, cackling.

"Well, we can always change that. The point is, we need a new and hot client to come in and undo the mess that fucking band did."

I gulp.

The Devilled Eggs.

He's talking about the Devilled Eggs.

"Oh, you mean the overdose?" Dazza asks, naively.

"Yes, and now that we're out a client, we need another one desperately. So he better fucking be good!"

My eyes widen, but before I can ask the question, Dazza does it for me.

"What, that band, The Eggs or whatever, are out?"

"Well of course. We dropped them the second that fucking punk dropped dead."

I am finding it hard to stand, and I gulp, trying to act as unphased as I possibly can.

The band are out. They are no longer a part of Ruby. They are no longer signed.

I feel dizzy as I try to take it all in.

There will be no album, there will be no tour, everything is gone. Everything that they worked for.

Dazza laughs. "Bit harsh, ain't it? Literally the night their bandmate dropped dead right there in the venue?"

"No of course not you plonker, we left it a week or so. Told them yesterday. But they knew it already; they're not stupid."

"From how they used to dress, I couldn't be too sure," the board member chips in. I am suddenly very nauseous and I cannot stand listening to this conversation anymore.

I walk away from them, slowly, and without saying a word, I drift into the crowd. I do so just as the venue goes dark, there is applause, and DJ Tango steps onstage.

I tell myself that I'm fine. I tell myself that I have a job to do and I must concentrate, I must focus, because if I take my eye off the ball, even for a second, it's going to ruin me.

If I remember his face or his laugh or his voice or his touch, it's going to break me into tiny little pieces.

And I may not be able to survive it.

But it's too late. For when DJ Tango starts his set, the deep house music is connecting with my emotions, the way only music can connect to my soul.

It opens me up, making everything surface to the top, making me vulnerable to all of it. I remember all of it. I feel the pain all of it. It's incredible the power music can have on you – to slice your heart open to the pain in a nanosecond.

And it's horrendous.

Unbearable.

To the point that I find it hard to breathe. The sadness is too much, it tears me to pieces, and I begin shaking.

Tears floods my eyes as it consumes me, and I know that I no longer belong here.

This is not my place.
This is not my place.
This is not my place.
Not anymore.

My heart is so filled with sadness I can hardly take it, and I wish so badly I could switch off the music, but it's too late now. It's entered. All the pain has entered.

I push my way through the jumping crowd to get back to the bar.

"I quit!" I announce to Gavin. I don't say it in anger, or sadness, or even happiness. I say it simply matter-of-factly. This is the end of the road for me here.

Goodbye.

All three of them look at me with shocked eyes, and with that, I rush out of the club as if my life depends on it. As if if I stay still too long, the pain is going to eat me alive and spit me out.

I hail a taxi to the one person I trust with my entire life, and it's a good fifteen minutes later that I arrive outside Church Studios. I pay the taxi driver in floods of tears, but he's not phased – I've been crying for the entire journey, and he did not dare to ask me if I'm okay. For this I'm grateful.

I buzz into the building and run up the stairs three steps at a time. He is the only person I want to see in this moment.

I burst into the studio as he's standing there, alone, daydreaming about something with his arms crossed. When he spots me, his eyes widen. "Alex?"

I am standing there, in floods of tears, and I throw my arms around him.

"I can't do it, I've been trying to be okay but I'm not and I miss him, Ric – I miss him so much and I'm not okay and I quit Ruby and I'm not okay and I just left everything and I'm not okay, Ric-"

"It's okay, it's okay," he holds me close to his chest, resting his chin on top of my head as he does so. It feels so damn good as he rubs my back, and this only unleashes more tears. "I can't do this. I need to get away. It hurts so much. It hurts so much, Ric. I need to get away-"

"Ssh, it's okay, it's okay. I know exactly the place to take you. We're gonna get you away from London, okay?"

"It hurts so much, it hurts so much, it hurts so much."

I continue saying it, over and over, and every time I say it, it hurts just that little bit more.

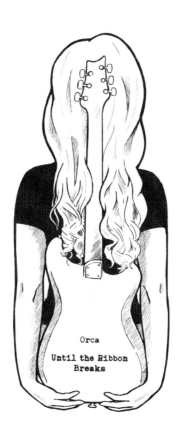

26

All my life, all I had wanted was to work in the music business. I had dreamed of the moment I would be around the creation of music, somehow, and the moment someone would offer me employment. To be *paid* in the music business always seemed so far away from me.

And then it happened. All of it. I got what I wanted, I got what I put in work to get, and it wasn't perfect, but I was happy. At least for a while. I liked, no, I *loved* what I was doing. But one of the biggest lessons I have learnt in recent months is that it takes a nanosecond for your life to turn completely upside down. For a job to become a living hell.

For you to lose someone you love.

I had it all, and I could have gone places. If I had sucked it up and just continued to ignore the monsters I was working with, I would have made something of myself. But what would I have become in return?

I had had it all at my fingertips, and I had given it all up. To save myself. To do what was right for me.

So why does it feel so shit?

I scroll down the taxi window and pop my head out, taking in the view of suburban Siena. The greenery reminds me of England, but the sun is unfamiliar to me after such a harsh British winter that back in London has still not ended.

It is clear that in Siena spring has already emerged; there is a warmness in the air that I find unnatural and a blue sky that seems straight out of a painting.

A cheesy Italian pop song plays on the radio and the taxi driver, an Italian in his forties with dark eyes and a breath that stinks of tobacco, nods his head and hums along to the song, one hand on the steering wheel whilst the other holds his fourth cigarette.

We flew to Pisa, from there taking a train to Empoli, and then another to Siena. Only in Italy can two main cities in the same region not have a direct train.

Welcome 'home', Alex.

The train station at Siena is smaller than I imagined. We had then crossed the road and walked into a shopping mall to take six or seven escalators.

I became a little weary at the fifth escalator, wondering if this was really the right way but not daring to question Ric's choice of route. This is, after all, his city.

I paid attention to as much detail as I could, as if a shop window or a crack in the ceiling could tell me something about Ric that I don't already know. Something that I have yet to unearth.

At the end of the final escalator we reached the exit and found ourselves on a high street. Siena sits on top of what seems like the end of the planet. It's now one plane, two trains later, and one taxi later, and we still have yet to reach Ric's parents' villa.

I glance at Ric, who is sitting all the way on the other side of the taxi's backseat, reading a copy of Siena News – the politics section.

It was only last night that I quit Ruby, that I burst into Church Studios in floods of tears. We booked flights out to Pisa straight away, to stay at the villa where Ric grew up in suburban Siena. The idea of leaving London temporarily seemed to soothe me, and so I said yes.

If I slow down at twenty-three I want you to shoot me, okay Alex?

I shiver and scroll up the window just as Ric's phone begins to ring and he picks up, smiling.

"Mamma, ciao!"

When Ric had suggested we go to Siena for a few days and stay at his parents' villa, I had assumed that they wouldn't be there. It was a mere thirty seconds after we booked our tickets that Ric declared he would ring his parents and let them know we were coming.

It was only then that I realised that I would be meeting his parents. I'm not sure what I'm getting myself into, after all, I am not Ric's girlfriend and they're going to think that I am, but, we've booked our tickets now, so let's just see what happens. With no job and nothing on the horizon, I cannot afford to be spending money right, left and centre.

But is this really going to help you with your pain, Alex?

Elliot's smile flashes in my mind, just as Ric's voice snaps me out of my thoughts and I am grateful. I don't want to think about Elliot.

"Si, okay, va bene…ciao. Ciao, mamma." He hangs up and catches my glance. "She's making pasta…i pici!" he smiles and goes back to reading his newspaper.

Yeah, this is going to be terrible.

Come on Alex, make an effort, it's just for a few days.

Once we arrive at his parents' place I have nodded off.

"Alex…we're here," Ric gently shakes me, and I awake to find him leaning over from his side of the car and I rub my eyes, remembering our trip and where we are heading, nerves hitting me as I spot the villa in front of us.

Oh God. I am not ready for this. I want to be back in my bed.

The big wooden door suddenly flings open and out steps a woman in her fifties with straight, dark brown hair just reaching her neck. She is rather slim, wearing typical 'mother' clothes – loose trousers and a flowery top, and she walks over to the car in a sincere and homely manner. She does the Mum Walk.

She smiles at her son through the window, who smiles back and opens the car door like an excited child stepping out to be greeted by a big bear hug.

"Mamma, ciao!"

"You're here! Finally! What happened? Flight delayed?" she says to him in Italian, and I know full well it will be non-stop Italian for the next few days. They peck on the cheeks enthusiastically and I realise I am trembling.

Shit, can't I just go back to the airport? Get on the next flight home?

I glance at the taxi driver, who hasn't moved from his seat either, probably on his eighth cigarette by now. He hums along to Robbie Williams' Millennium.

Italians love Robbie Williams way too much.

Get out of the car, Alex.

I open my car door and step out, my whole body trembling now.

"…so in the end we were delayed by half an hour," Ric glances at me, as I peer over at them, hands on each other's arms as if they are about to waltz. "Mamma, this is my friend, Alexis."

Ric's mum looks over at me with curious yet friendly eyes as I approach. Her eyes are the same as Ric's; big, brown and friendly. Her olive skin shines in the sunlight beaming down straight onto her face, and she gives me such a homely, sincere smile it is hard not to smile back.

"Oh, *Alexis*, it's a pleasure to meet you!"

"You too, Mrs D'Angelo," I reply politely, as we peck on the cheeks.

"Oh please, call me Elena. Did you have a nice trip?"

"Apart from the delay it was fine thanks, it's so lovely out here."

"Oh, you haven't seen the garden yet!"

Ric smiles at the sight of his mother and I in the same picture frame.

"Riccardo! Sei arrivato!" says a deep, manly voice. At the wooden door stands a man in his late fifties with grey hair, and a slightly mischievous smile. He has green eyes, a crooked nose and he looks nothing like Ric. He walks over to us.

"Ciao, papa! Si, si, tutto bene?" Ric asks him as they exchange pecks and half a man hug.

"Yes, I'm loving retirement, it suits me," his eyes move to me. "And who is this beautiful young woman?"

I blush.

"This is my friend, Alexis."

He frowns. "*Friend?* A woman like this should be nothing short of your girlfriend, Ric. Lovely to meet you, Alexis."

"You too."

His mother claps her hands together.

"Okay! Shall we go inside? Lunch is ready…"

"Sure mamma, we'll be right in."

As his parents walk back inside and I remain still, looking up at the magnificent villa, Ric opens the boot and pulls out our suitcases. He pays the driver as I remain in a daze, trying to imagine a young Ric growing up here.

This place is four, maybe even five times bigger than my parents' place in Enfield.

The stoned villa towering over me consists of three floors with terraces covered in green vines, Tuscan windows with blinds, the typical brown window doors and that homely, Italian feel to them. The balconies typically black steel, and the front door of this beautiful house wooden and antique.

If this is only the outside, how the hell is it inside?

"He always says what he's thinking," Ric says, appearing next to me with our luggage, the taxi driver reversing down the hilly driveway, ninth cigarette in hand.

I look at Ric, a little confused.

"My dad – he always says what he's thinking."

I give him a weak smile and attempt to take my suitcase from him, but he pulls it away before I can take it.

"It's fine, I'll take them both. Come on..."

I scurry after him as he power walks through the foyer, and passes his mother who is stood with her head popping out of what I guess is the kitchen, where the smell of tomato sauce and prosciutto seems to be coming from.

Oh, prosciutto. How I have missed you.

But before I can let my heart melt to the smell of Italian food, I find myself stopping in awe at the beauty surrounding me. The foyer of Ric's house is incredible.

The walls bright white, the pillars tall and gallant, there are a couple of Renaissance paintings hung on the wall, a little iron table in the middle with a plant on it and a glass angel statue, and a sparkling white, silver and black chandelier hanging from the ceiling.

Wow.

"Are you taking your stuff upstairs?" Ric's mum asks her son. "Then come down and eat, it's nearly ready."

"Okay."

"Do you remember which one is your room?" she jokes. Ric glances at her and shakes his head at the joke as we make our way up the white marble steps.

The staircase ends on the first floor and we walk down a corridor of rooms. Everything remains bright white, and I look around in awe at how big this place is.

"My parents sleep there," he points to the first door we pass. We continue down the corridor until we reach a second staircase and then Ric leads us down a second corridor full of rooms, where he finally comes to a halt outside a door with a Van Halen poster on it.

"You guys had a floor to yourselves?" I ask, bewildered. He looks at me as we reach the door.

"It's the countryside. And you know Italian houses are bigger than the ones in London. There are *countries* bigger than the houses in London."

I half-smile and he opens the door.

"Welcome to my room," he drags the suitcases in and I follow. We enter a rather spacious bedroom, where there is a bunk bed, a big, wooden desk, a wooden chair, a guitar case leaning against the wall, and in the far right a set of Tuscan windows that leads to a terrace.

I ask him why there is a bunk bed and Ric explains that his brother, Beppe, would get scared at night and come into this room to share with Ric. Apparently the countryside gets scary at night.

I look around at the posters on the wall – Flashdance, Rocky, Back to the Future, Pink Floyd's the Wall, and some Italian films I have never seen. Continuing to observe his room as Ric unpacks a few things, I notice a pin board of pictures and walk over, curious.

Ooh. His life as a teenager.

I move in closer and scan a few of them – Ric as a kid on his birthday with a funny, bright hat and a massive cake; as a teenager with floppy eighties hair and eighties blue jeans; a big grin on his face as he poses with some friends at around fifteen; as a late teenager smiling as two girls kissed his cheeks.

Ric fishing with a Juventus shirt; a picture with his parents at graduation; standing at the top of a mountain with a girl, both of them in their twenties. Big black eyes, jet black hair and a smile to die for.

His ex-girlfriend, Emma. Oh shit. She is pretty. She is gorgeous—

"Riccardo, hurry up!" yells his mother from downstairs.
She must need a speakerphone to do that.

"Okay!" he picks up his suitcase and looks at me as I stand there awkwardly with my arms folded. "Shall we? I'll just dump my stuff in my room and then we'll go eat."

It turns out Ric is giving me his room, claiming it is the best room on the floor. He will be sleeping next door.

So we dump Ric's stuff in the next room and I follow him downstairs, through to the kitchen where the heat hits our faces instantly. The kitchen is surprisingly small for such a villa, the tiling on the floor mosaic and beautiful.

Ric's dad is nowhere in sight but his mother is stirring one of four pots. She orders us to go through to the dining room and that the first course is nearly ready.

You know you're in Italy when there's more than one course.

My eyes widen and my stomach knots. I haven't eaten a proper meal in two weeks, how am I going to eat so little and not offend them?

"Mamma, you didn't have to go to so much trouble," he tells her, putting a hand on her shoulder.

I leave them to converse and walk through a door to the living room. His father sits at the already set dining table, reading a newspaper.

Like father like son. I bet you he's reading the politics section.

I spot a certificate hanging up on the wall and go over to have a closer look.

RICCARDO D'ANGELO – GRADE 10 IN PIANO

"Oooh, back in the piano days," I say to myself.

"Best in his class," says his father and I turn to him. "The teacher said he could have been a world class pianist."

I frown, walking over to him. "Really?"

"Yes. And if he hadn't run away from class he could have been," his dad says, just as Ric walks in.

I stare, baffled. "Run away?"

His dad laughs. "Don't you know Ric has a flare for drama? Instead of quitting he decided to run away from home and go to lo stadio d'Artemio Franchi."

A stadium?

I sit down at the table, completely enthralled by the information I am learning about his son.

Ric? Dramatic? I thought I was the dramatic one between us both?

"Why did he go there?"

"Papa…" Ric interjects, getting uncomfortable.

"Whaaat, Riccardo? Not telling her what isn't true, come on," he turns back to me as Ric sighs and sits down at the dinner table next to me. "So…he went to lo stadio d'Artemio Franchi because Maradona was playing that day. He was planning to find him and ask him to adopt him."

I burst out laughing, turning to Ric who is tremendously embarrassed. He rolls his eyes and picks at the olive bowl.

"Hey, hey! Wait for your mother."

Woah, this is weird.

I suddenly have images of Ric as a kid sitting at this very table, being told to sit up straight and eat his vegetables. Up until now I guess I never imagined Ric as a kid. To me he had been born thirty-three years old.

"So Alexis, what do you do in London?"

"I, uh, I worked for a record label, Ruby Records. They weren't huge but they were getting there."

"I see, that sounds good. Where in Italy are you from?"

"Uh, actually, I was born in London but my parents are Italian – from Piemonte."

He frowns. "But your accent is perfect!"

"It really is, I find it hard to believe it myself that you were born in London!" says Ric's mother, walking into the room holding a massive bowl and placing it in the centre of the table.

I blush.

"Her mum taught her Italian and then she learnt English at school," Ric tells them.

"Ooh, smart woman your mother!"

I smile.

"That's what I always say. Mamma, sit down, come on, let's eat."

She takes her place opposite me with one free chair next to her.

Are we missing someone?

399

"Piemonte is a lovely region, I spent a summer there," Ric's mum tells me.

"It is, I find the place amazing, so different from London, such an enticing region. The fresh air, the great views...much like Siena."

Ric's mother lifts the bowl and steam bursts out. "Well it's good to know you're not too much of a Londoner, I love London but the smog and the rain and the no beaches nearby..." she says.

"Tell me about it."

"Anybody home?" bellows a male voice from what I assume is the foyer.

Ric and his mother exchange excited glances.

"Beppe," Ric says softly. "Beppe, we're in here!" he shouts.

Suddenly a good-looking Italian man dressed in an expensive black suit bursts into the kitchen with a huge grin.

"Hey!" he wails, narrowing his eyes at Ric. "Big bro!"

Ric leaps out of his chair to hug his brother and I smile, as I watch them.

"Mamma said your flight was delayed so I stopped by the bank before driving out here," his eyes move to me and I slowly get up, uncomfortable at the way he is studying me.

They have the same cheekbones!

"Well, well, well...and who may I ask is this beautiful young lady?"

"Alexis," I say with a smile. He takes my hand and kneels a little as he kisses the knuckles.

I blush and Ric rubs the back of his neck.

"Piacere, Alexis."

He rises but still holds onto my hand. "And what, may I ask, are you doing with my troll of a brother?"

Ric puts him in a playful headlock instantly, as if he knew the line was coming. Beppe lets go of my hand to try and wriggle out of it but is failing miserably.

"Do you have a mental illness?" he asks me and I grin, watching the two brothers play fight. "Perhaps he paid you?"

"*Boys*...stop it." their mother hisses, no different than a mother would do to six-year-old boys play fighting at the supermarket. Ric slowly lets him lose and they smile at one another, Ric messing up his kid brother's hair playfully.

Beppe cleans up and joins us at the table where Ric's mother has put pasta on everyone's plates, and we begin eating in silence, the clinking of forks on the plates and sips of wine from glasses the only noises heard.

"So Alexis," Beppe suddenly starts and I pick up my glass of wine nervously, "you're the reason Ric has been spending so much time in London."

My hand freezes in mid-air with the glass, taken back by his brother's statement. Ric fidgets next to me in his wooden chair, making it squeak.

"Beppe, don't be an idiot," he says.

His brother looks from Ric to me from across the table. "What? No, no, I mean it in a good way. Lots of opportunities in London, your career has more prospects there, and with your love for Pink Floyd you probably spend all your time outside historical points in their career," he narrows his eyes at me as he puts a large amount of picci in his mouth, grinning. "Big lover of Pink Floyd, my brother."

"She knows that already, idiot."

"Well I don't know, do I? It's been a good five plus years since you brought a girl home."

"Everyone knows Riccardo likes Pink Floyd, Beppe," their dad interjects. "And anyway, that's better than all the girls you've brought home every other week."

Beppe's jaw drops.

"Maria, ti amo!" mocks Ric in a high-pitched voice, playfully. "Sara, ti amo!" he punches the air. "Nadia, oh Nadia, ti amo!"

I nudge him and he looks at me.

"Don't tease," I say.

"Yeah *Ric*, don't tease. I am awful lonely."

"Oh *please*, you're just a manwhore. You love every second of it."

"Shut up, idiot."

"Asshole."

Their dad glances at me as he takes a fork of picci into his mouth and rolls his eyes.

"Basta!" their mother turns to me. "Alex, I love your hair, it's really very beautiful."

It's a mess!

"Thanks."

401

"She's always re-dying it," Ric tells his mother as he cleans the tomato sauce off his plate with a piece of bread.

"It's a beautiful colour... cherry, is it?"

I nod.

"Yeah, dark cherry. It was a bit lighter before, but I went a shade darker at Christmas." I look at Ric who is wiping his mouth with a napkin. "And I am not always re-dying it."

"Yeah, you are!"

"I love how it's curly too, is it natural?"

I glance back at Ric's mother and nod.

"I've told her time and time again that it looks better curly but she just doesn't listen to me," he looks at me with a playful smile.

"But they're curly right now," Beppe states.

"Yeah but that's just 'cause she can't be bothered to straighten them..." his voice dies away.

You mean because she's not bothered about anything anymore.

Because Elliot's dead.

Elliot.

I gulp, and I know as Ric looks at me that he can read what I'm thinking, of who I have been reminded of.

I glance down at the picci that remain in my plate; there are too many, I am already full from my five forks full, but I don't want to seem strange, and I don't want to be known as that girl that eats the same quantity of food as a bird.

"Well I have to agree with Riccardo on this one – your hair looks lovely curly, I wish I had curly hair like yours!"

I force a smile at his mother and take a sip of wine.

Elliot.

"See, I told you," Ric tells me, as he casually scoops more than half of the picci left on my plate onto his. It feels like a huge weight has been lifted off my shoulders.

I stare at him as he puts down my plate and he gives me a quick smile.

How is he always able to read my mind?

"So how's it going in London with your solo work? Album finished?" Beppe asks his brother.

Once Ric has taken the food from my plate, I relax a little. We talk about Ric's career, Italy, and summer holiday destinations for Ric's parents.

As his mother talks, I study her face and the more I study it the more I see Ric in it. Her eyes darken when the subject turns to Italy's economic crisis the same way Ric's does, and she has a charismatic way of telling stories that I recognise all too well.

His mother is a retired private nurse, his father a high school history teacher and physicist. I know, I too was puzzled at the two career choices, but Ric's father says he has two passions in life: the history of the world, and the future of the world. He seems a pretty intelligent man, in fact they both are, and it is clear to see Ric had had a pretty middle class upbringing.

His mother is warm and down-to-Earth, not an ounce of snobbiness in her, which makes me understand instantly that homeliness in Ric that drew me to him from practically the first second I had met him.

You could tell that growing up Ric had probably been checked regularly for everything, taught everything about medicine that he would need to know.

Ric's father is more the political influence. He only speaks about it for five minutes at the dinner table before his wife shushes him, but it's clear to see he has that same flare and passion for Italian politics that Ric has.

They're a lovely family, and it makes me miss my own, yet I do not get out my phone and text them. For I am beginning to like this Siena bubble that I'm in and I feel it's important I stay here a while.

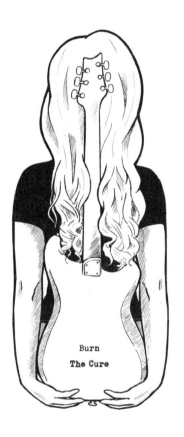

27

You must have thought about why we're put on this planet at least once in your life, right? I mean, we're pretty good at avoiding that question, since we don't have a tangible answer, but it must have crossed your mind.

I've had it happen to me twice. Once when I was eight years old, I was drawing by myself in the living room of my parents' house, when I suddenly stopped and was instantly sad at the realisation that I didn't have a clue as to why I existed. Why I was on the planet, why I had been given life. It lasted only a few moments, but I swear I was a different kid after that experience.

The second was three days after Elliot's death. I was at home on Monday night alone, I put on Jeff Buckley's 'Grace' and it happened. I began to wonder why I existed, why I was given life, and what I was supposed to do with it, if anything. Because if life meant nothing, that was the saddest, most morbid of all the explanations I had.

Once the song ended, so did my experience with this question. But I swear, again, I was a different person to before I had asked the question at the start of the song.

After lunch with Ric's parents, and once Beppe leaves, Ric takes me into town to show me Siena. As a city, Siena is magnificent. I have always wanted to visit it, it's always been on my list, but I've just never had a chance to make it happen.

He takes me to see the Cathedral, the Torre Del Mangia (we climb all the way to the top, which by the way, has the narrowest staircase I have ever come across in my life, at one point I felt as if I was going to fall out the window), and end in my favourite place so far – Piazza del Campo.

It's even more stunning than it seemed in pictures, and there is an atmosphere to the piazza that hits you right in the soul and sets it on fire. I cannot explain it, but standing in that piazza, the sun hitting my face, I am suddenly smiling. For the first time in two weeks, I am smiling.

There is warmth to Siena that goes way beyond the weather. The people, the smiles, the atmosphere. It makes you feel right at home, and it makes you feel instantly at ease.

Piazza del Campo is swarming with tourists, some are standing, and some are sitting, even sunbathing. The floor is clean, the whole city is ridiculously clean in fact, and we begin walking across it. Ric smiles at the fact that I'm smiling, and he begins.

"So Piazza del Campo was originally a marketplace, back in the twelfth century. Over *there* we have the bell tower, i.e. Torre del Mangia, the tower we just climbed," he points and I look. "FYI, the second tallest bell tower in Italy. Siena has maintained its medieval integrity because about half the population died in the plague in 1348. In consequence, the republic's economy was destroyed and Siena's development stagnated, which meant it did not develop during the Renaissance."

I frown as he talks, and he pauses. "What?"

You're just even more handsome when you feed me knowledge, that's all.

"Nothing."

"No come on, what?"

"Nothing, just taking in Nerdy Tourist Guide Riccardo D'Angelo!" I tease.

"*Haha*, you're so funny, Alex!" he puts his arm around me and squeezes me tight. "*So* funny, you should become a comedian, you know that?"

"Well I do get told that quite often!"

"Okay back to the serious stuff, down here we have-"

"Riccardo?" bellows a manly voice suddenly, and we both turn. A tall, Italian man with cool sunglasses and a ton of grocery bags in hand approaches. "*Sei tornato?*" *You've returned?*

Ric's eyes instantly become serious, his face tenses, and I wonder who this person is to have such an effect on him.

"Ciao Marco. Yes, I'm back just for a few days."

The stranger's expression is blunt, he is trying hard to smile but doesn't seem capable. Ric, in turn, reflects the exact same challenge.

"Have you gone to see Luca?" the stranger asks.

Who's Luca?

"Um, no."

There is silence between them, and it is a cold, awkward, almost resentful silence.

The stranger looks at me, as if debating introducing himself, but then hesitates. "I'll see you around." he instead says.

"Yeah, see you around Marco." We watch the stranger walk away, and once he is halfway across the piazza, I turn to Ric for an explanation as his eyes remain on the stranger.

I see a cloud of darkness infiltrating him, entering his soul. I'm quite sure he's sweating through his winter coat.

"Who was that?" I dare to ask, as nonchalantly as humanly possible. But Ric is not making eye contact with me, he is looking anywhere but at me. He begins walking in the opposite direction to the stranger, expecting me to follow.

"Come on, let's go."

"Ric?!" I scurry after him. "Ric?! Who was that guy?"

But Ric is only getting worse, anxiety turning into panic, panic turning into some sort of episode. Suddenly it doesn't matter who the guy is, it only matters that Ric is okay.

"Hey. Hey! Look at me."

But he doesn't listen. He starts walking faster, so fast that it's hard to keep up.

"Ric!"

"I'm fine, Alex!" he barks, and I've never heard him bark before. A little taken aback, I continue to chase him as he powerwalks across the piazza.

"Will you tell me who that was?! You're acting strange!"

"An old friend, that's all."

"Yes - Marco, I heard. But *who* is he?" I ask, but Ric is no longer responding. "Ric?"

I pull him back by the arm and when he turns around, his face is in complete turmoil. For a moment, I can hardly breathe as I watch him.

His forehead is covered in sweat, and there is a sadness to him that makes me instantly want to cry. It consumes me, takes me over, as if there is a third person with us, as if the sadness has a life of its own and its currently possessing Ric.

There is a pain to Ric that I had never been able to spot before. And for the first time since I met him, I see the vulnerable side to Ric, even if he's trying his damn hardest to hide it.

There is a torment in Ric's eyes that I had never seen before. I wonder if it's always been there or if this is new. Something tells me it's the former and I just never noticed.

"Come here," I pull him down on a free bit of ground in the middle of the piazza, some people around us looking on in intrigue. He follows, and this is when I know it must be bad.

Normal Ric would remain stubborn, he would keep walking, he would find strength to pretend that everything is fine. But everything is not, and he can't seem to fight it.

I put my hands on his cheeks and look him in the eye. "Hey, it's okay. You're okay."

He nods as he breathes heavily. He is having a panic attack, unable to take deep breaths in. I put one hand on his arm, and another on his cheek, looking him in the eye.

"Look at me, everything is okay. You hear me? Everything is okay," I tell him. I see darkness in his eyes, darkness that I have never seen before. Pain has surfaced for Ric, pain that has been triggered by that man, and I have no idea how to stop it, to bring him back to the surface, when I have no idea what it is that has had this effect on him.

I don't know what to do, and so I throw my arms around him. To feel close to him. To tell him I'm here. I hug him tightly, and I keep hugging him, even though he is not hugging me back. His arms remain slumped to his sides, but I keep hugging him.

"Everything is okay, please believe me," I whisper in his ear, and I don't let go. My back hurts after a while but I don't care – I will not let go, not until he is okay. Not until he has stopped trembling.

It takes him a good while, but he suddenly, very slowly, hugs me back, cheek-to-cheek. He hugs me just as tightly, and I am relieved.

"Everything is okay," I repeat. And there we sit, for the rest of the afternoon, in the middle of Piazza del Campo, in what feels like a permanent embrace.

Once we get back to his parents' villa, we are hit instantly with the smell of dinner – lasagne, my favourite.

"It's like she knows!" I whisper with a huge grin.

"Well, she *may* have asked me what your favourite dish is, and I *may* have told her."

I give him a playfully mean look and he shakes his eyebrows at me. I've never seen Ric shake his eyebrows at me, and it's almost a peak into his childhood. It feels as if whenever we enter his parents' villa he enters a different version of himself, one I haven't seen before but want to get to know better.

I wish so much I could somehow see him as a kid, how his life had been like then, and what friends he had had. I realise now that though I have known Ric a while, I haven't really ever asked him much about his past, and in order to truly understand a person, you *must* ask them about their past.

Ric seems much better than he was just a few hours ago. He calmed down, stopped trembling, and the panic in his eyes disappeared. As time passed, he slowly slipped back into the Ric I knew – the calm, collective, relaxed and wise Ric that I had met that night at the Forum, and the Ric I have known ever since.

When we let go of each other, the sun had gone down and it was evening. I wanted to ask him right there what had happened, who that guy was, but I knew it was better to respect his privacy. If he wants to tell me, he will. I'm just glad that he's okay now. To see Ric in pain had really hurt to see; I just want to see and know that Ric is happy. Always.

We eat dinner, and discuss the best moments of today with his parents – his dad agrees with me that Piazza del Campo is the most beautiful part of Siena, whereas Ric and his mum say nothing beats the view from the top of Torre del Mangia.

We eat, and we tell stories, and I realise just how much I like Ric's parents. That whoever gets to return as his girlfriend someday will be very lucky. They are so welcoming and genuinely warm people.

Ric again scoops up half my plate of food whilst nonchalantly chatting about Siena, and I am always grateful for the way he is able to read my mind.

It's been an eventful day, and though stressful in parts, by the end of the evening Ric and I are the happiest we have been all day. That's why I am so frustrated when, as soon as my head hits the pillow, I am overcome with sadness. That, no matter what I try to do to stop it, all I see is Elliot's face. And it can't stop making me cry.

It takes a lot of effort to cry in silence, in fear that Ric next door will hear me, but I manage to, only taking deep breaths in when completely necessary.

I remember his mother's wails at the funeral. I remember the looks on the boys' faces. I remember that Gavin has sacked them off harsher and with less relevance than an old tuna sandwich.

I get out my phone and text Matteo.

Alex:
Hey, all good?

I check the time and realise it's 3:03am. *Damn it you idiot, he's sleeping.*

Alex:
Just wanted to check in and see how you guys are doing. I miss you all, video chat tomorrow? X

The tears are still streaming down my face uncontrollably, and so I put my phone away and dig my head into my pillow.

I remember the first time Elliot and I played together, I remember us sitting down in the loft to listen to John Mayer and Elliot playing Free Fallin' on acoustic. I remember him video calling me from the studio and telling me 'this riff was inspired by you'. I remember him being the first one I hugged when they arrived in London.

"Alex," I hear a voice whisper, and I realise it's Ric. I slowly remove my face from my pillow to see that there, at the side of the top bunk bed, hovers Ric. He's dressed in a grey t-shirt, and he's looking bluntly at me.

"Come on, let's go. I want to show you something."

"Wha…? Huh?" I say, but he's gone.

I assume it's only to go downstairs or into the garden, so I don't change into normal clothes, and step outside in my pyjama shorts and cat t-shirt (the cat is licking its paw rather adorably). Ric is waiting outside the room with a backpack, and he looks me up and down.

"Alex, warmer clothes, and shoes."

I want to ask him where the hell we're going but something tells me he won't be letting me know anytime soon.

Once I've changed into jeans, my favourite Arctic Monkeys hoodie (the AM album) and put on Vans shoes, I follow Ric to the garage. I assume we're taking the car, but he walks over to the bikes. One is a mountain bike – dark green and rather cool. The other is a small, pink bike with a bell and a basket.

I cock up an eyebrow at Ric.

"Yeah sorry, we only have these two bikes - it's my niece's. You gonna be okay with the pink?"

"Where are we going?" I ask, in a huff. I don't like not knowing, but Ric doesn't respond. He instead checks the tyres on both bikes, and we head out.

We walk down the driveway with our bikes, and I look around the deserted and beautiful suburbs of Siena. Ric hops on his bike first, I follow, and we begin cycling down the empty roads of Siena in silence.

I forgot how much I like to cycle, it's been a decade or so since I last was on a bike. There's just no opportunity for it in London – you either rent one to cycle around the roads in London, which is dangerous and life-threatening, or you cycle through the parks, even though most of their paths are prohibited and you risk getting caught and yelled at by police (not that that happened to me or anything). I can safely say that these two options made sure I was put off cycling in London for good.

But man, I do love cycling in the right city. Siena is perfect for it, and I take in the slightly cool air for it, pulling up my hoodie so I don't catch a cold. We soon enter the hillier parts of Siena, and before long, are completely and utterly surrounded by countryside.

The view is beyond incredible, taking my breath away in an instant. On our left there are huge vineyards, and on our right is a view of Siena beneath us.

We continue to cycle in silence; all that can be heard is our peddling, and our breathing in synch. There is also the typical countryside sounds you would hear at 4am that accompany us – owls hooting, rustling in the woods of God knows what animal, and a slight breeze.

It's magical, and freeing, and beautiful. I don't know why, but David Bowie's 'Ashes to Ashes' starts playing in my head, as Ric and I accelerate beside one another. We smile at each other as we begin to race uphill.

We huff and puff in happiness, and it looks as if nothing can beat us as we cycle in synch. The roads are so empty and the lights off the lampposts bounce off of them so beautifully.

I am at one with nature, and I feel connected to planet Earth much more than I ever have done so in my life. It feels important, to have this connection, to feel this in touch with nature, and I am happy.

There is a calm in my soul that hasn't been there a while, one that I needed badly, and I am glad to be here, in Siena. To be away from London, to have left Ruby, and to be away from all chaos. This is what I need, this is my therapy, and Ric knew it.

He knew it like he always knows it, because he knows me. I don't know him, but he knows me. He took the time to know me, and I never took the time to know him. That is the difference between us.

I look up at the crescent moon and smile, for this is now my happy place. The Siena countryside has become my happy place.

As we continue to race however, I go from feeling happy and at peace with myself, to sudden flashbacks of Elliot. I see the last words I said to him, I see me leaving him at the venue to go and get drunk with Ric. I remember his hugs, his touch, his smile.

The memories encompass me, plague me, and I slow down. Ric races off into the distance ahead of me, and I begin to lose control of the bike. I let the bike drive me, I *allow* it to drive me, and it goes in whichever direction it wants.

I struggle, as my feet let go of the pedals and find it hard to find their way back. Ric, who is now far ahead of me, turns around as he hears the struggles.

"Alex?"

Yet I have lost control, and the bike crashes straight into a tree. I fall forward in an instant, and graze my knee when it bashes into the trunk. Ric brakes, jumps off and runs over.

"You okay? What happened?!"

I'm in tears, yet again. And I'm mad at myself for crying again. I can't seem to stop, ever. And I'm getting tired of it, of feeling weak and useless and fragile, all day long, every day.

I am a fighter, I am not weak!

But all I see is me leaving the Dublin Castle, leaving Elliot in the venue to die. I abandoned him. I am shit. I am useless. I am careless. And it's my fault he is dead.

"It's all my fault, I shouldn't have left him, I shouldn't have left him, I shouldn't have-"

"*Hey*, this is not your fault, what happened to Elliot is not your fault-" he puts a hand on my shoulder but I shake it off. I have buried my face in my hands so he doesn't see me crying. I wipe my tears and get off the bike in an instant.

*I am not this girl. I am not weak and pathetic and I sure as shit do not need a man to **save** me, for fuck's sake.*

"Don't do that," I tell him.

"Do what?"

"Comfort me. I can look after myself. What are you doing, anyway? What are you doing bringing me here at 4AM, what are you doing sleeping at my flat, what are you doing bringing me to your parents? I am not your girlfriend, Ric."

Ric forces a small laugh and shakes his head. "I was expecting this at some point."

"Expecting what?"

"The 'I can look after myself' timeless classic from Alexis Brunetti.

What am I doing, Alex? I am being here for you, because guess what? Every single human needs someone. Someone they can turn to, someone who will be there for them, someone who will tell them everything will be okay.

And I don't know what sort of past you have, what sort of people you've had in your life before me, but there is no motive behind me being here other than wanting to be here for you. I want to help."

"And how the fuck are you going to help me? How can you possibly know what it feels like to have this happen?" I pick up the broken pink bike and storm off back in the direction of his villa with a broken bike in hand.

"There you go - being a spoiled brat again. Running in the opposite direction. You can't run from grief, Alex. Trust me."

It's my turn to force a laugh. "How the hell would you know?" I mutter, thinking he can't hear me. "You cannot possibly understand this pain."

"Believe me, I understand it better than you know," he shouts to my back, but I continue walking. "You want to know who Marco is? He's the little brother of my best friend, Luca, who… died three years ago."

I immediately stop, and turn around. Ric is standing in the middle of the empty road, that torture in his eyes having returned. The same pain in his eyes from this afternoon, the way we had hugged as if we understood each other. I just didn't know it. "Drug overdose - heroine. We did coke together, and he decided to take it a step further. He tried to convince me to join him, and I told him, 'you go first and maybe then I'll try.'"

I freeze, hardly believing what I'm hearing. I have flashbacks of us sitting up on the stage of San Siro last summer, Ric telling me he used to be a drug addict. I remember asking how he had stopped, and his response being, 'I just did'.

How odd, I remember thinking. *To stop a drug addict it usually takes something pretty big to sway him.* And though he said his girlfriend left him and he sobered up because of it, I always felt like there was more to the story than that.

"I never went to the funeral, and I've never been to visit his grave," he tells me, with shame in his voice.

"Why not?" I ask, softly.

He gulps. "I felt too guilty. I could have stopped it, prevented it, I could have told him not to. But I didn't. I just told him to go ahead."

"You couldn't have saved him."

He looks at me. "And neither could you have saved Elliot."

There's silence between us, as I realise I cannot argue with him. He has just told me possibly the most vulnerable, darkest pain that exists inside of him, and one that I had no idea existed. That it had existed from way before we met, and every second we had shared together.

The concept completely eludes me; how behind a smile, or a joke, or a normal conversation, someone can be holding onto so much pain. He looks surprised that he has told me, as if he hasn't discussed the topic for three years, and I am grateful, honoured, that he has decided to share with me. I remember his pain from this afternoon, from seeing that stranger who had asked him if he had seen Luca.

He meant his grave – if he had gone to see his grave.

"I'm so sorry about Luca," I say. "And…I'm sorry for being a bitch."

He stifles a laugh as he looks anywhere but at me, hitching his hands in his jeans pockets. "I'm getting used to it."

I slowly approach, and we stand opposite one another.

"Now what?"

"Now we walk the rest of the way."

We do so in silence, and I listen in content to the owls hooting and the breeze hitting our backs.

Once we get to the top of the hill, I spot a tennis court, and know before Ric takes off his backpack that there are rackets and tennis balls inside.

"I used to love to play here as a teenager."

"Never pegged you as a tennis player," I retort, and he cocks an eyebrow up at me. "I mean, you know – you love your beer and hanging out with Vinnie and stuff."

"And how do you think I stop myself from getting a beer belly?"

I guess I hadn't ever thought about it. I guess I hadn't ever thought about a lot of things when it comes to Ric. Perhaps if I had paid more attention I would have seen more. Perhaps if I had paid more attention, I would have been able to see the pain in his eyes that I see now.

"Can you play?" he asks me, curiously.

"Can I play?!" I repeat back to him, his eyes remaining on me. "No. Tennis balls are hard to hit."

"I'll show you." As he fishes out two rackets and a tennis ball, I hover next to him with something I know I have to say. I have to say it before it's too late, before the moment has passed. For I may never get this chance again.

"You should go see his grave," he looks up at me, and I find the courage to finish the sentence, "whilst we're here. You should go see him."

He looks back down at the rackets as if he hasn't heard me.

"You chose this place for a reason, Ric. Elliot's death triggered something. You should go see him."

That's all I say on the subject before I put out my hand for the tennis ball. He hands it to me, along with the racket, and we play tennis at 4AM on top of a hill in Siena.

Tennis is much harder than it looks. I have flashbacks from school, which was the last time I played. I hadn't been able to hit the balls back then and I still can't now.

Luckily for me though, Ric is a pro and he teaches me a few moves. The chemistry between us is, as always, as strong as ever, but I try my best to ignore it. Every time he touches me though it sends shivers down my neck, and I fear that after this trip we may not be able to be friends. For if this chemistry remains between us, how can we ever have a friendship?

I don't remember how shit I am at tennis until we begin. I miss ball, after ball, after ball. I try really hard, putting so much into energy into it, and getting nowhere.

Soon I'm sweating as I try, but I keep failing. My irritation grows, wondering why I've agreed to this, and the more balls I miss, the more I hate being here. I just want my bed, so that I can cry into my pillow.

I eventually break. I throw my racket to the floor and storm off the court. "Why the hell am I here?! I'm shit at tennis, I'm going home!"

Ric doesn't change expression, as if he had expected this. "So that's it? You're just going to give up? Every time it gets hard?"

"If I know I suck at something – yes! Why waste my time?!"

"See, that's the problem with you – you claim to be ambitious, and driven, and competitive, and yet you give up the moment it gets hard."

"Actually, I gave it my all for a good half an hour or so before giving up!" I wail, as I pick up my broken pink bike.

"And you think that's enough? You think that's going to be enough to make you a champion, in anything you choose to be?

That's not how life works, Alex. You want to go back to the villa, and be sad, and continue to drown yourself in the evil that exists in this life – go ahead. Find your own way.

I'm staying here, to fight against it. Because I am a survivor. I will take all the bad shit that happens, and I will turn it into good, Goddammit."

I feel a surge inside me take over. One I had felt when I first met Gavin at that pub, the same one I felt when Damiano nearly beat me in Milano when I first arrived. A surge that has continued to grow, and show itself to me, from the books I read, and the inspiring people I have met.

Ric doesn't look at me, the same way he didn't look at me the first time I played guitar backstage at the Forum. He doesn't want to put pressure on me, to make my decisions for me, but allow me to be me, whoever that person is.

I slowly put down the bike, and nonchalantly walk back over to my racket, picking it up. Ric doesn't change expression but I know he's happy.

We play a few matches, Ric at first beating me, but I eventually manage to hit the ball, and it's such a good feeling.

Once I manage to hit one, I am able to hit more. In fact, I soon catch up to him. Every time that I score a point, I jump up and down in joy as Ric laughs. My excited jumps soon turn into victory dances, and then laps. All of course, with Bowie's 'Heroes' song as the theme tune to these victory dances.

Ric of course, then decides it's time to step up his game and completely destroys me. But it's okay. For I know that with time and hard work, I can win the next one.

And the next one.

And the one after that.

Once the sun rises, we realise it's time to head home. We make our way on Ric's mountain bike, Ric at the front and I hop on at the back, carefully holding onto his waist.

I forgot how toned it is, and for a brief second, my body screams out for his, but I hold back thinking any dirty thoughts. I am exhausted.

I am in fact so exhausted, that when we arrive home, say good night and retreat to our separate rooms, my head hits the pillow straight away. I am too tired to lose myself in thoughts of Elliot, and I fall instantly into a beautiful and relaxing sleep.

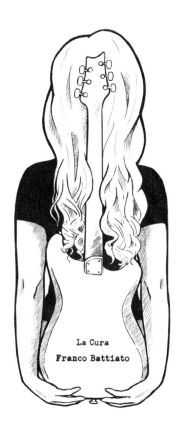

28

I don't know how it's like for everyone else, but I find it so hard to trust other people. I find them liars, disloyal, selfish twits.

But the thing is, what if we're all like that? How many times have I witnessed someone call someone else mean when they are terribly mean themselves?

Perhaps we are all assholes, to some extent.

I used to think I was a good person, but if we look at how I treated Ric we see that some may disagree. Some may call me obnoxious, cold-hearted, mean.

I know I've been called that in the past by hook ups, but those same hook ups all had something malicious inside of them - one was a cheater, another was a liar, so was my cold-heartedness towards them not a reaction to who they were? Because the one thing I am sure of in life is that intuition is my best friend. No one else can and ever will be. Except family. Family may drive me crazy, but they love me unconditionally, as I do them, and for this they have my trust.

But others? I always find it wild how people meet, fall in love, and just trust each other because it's what you're 'supposed to do'. I can't do that. I trust no one. Trusting only burns me.

It's the same with friends. I can have people close to me, but it doesn't mean I trust them. And yet I trusted Elliot. I don't know why or when it happened or even how, but it did. I trusted him when he said nice things, when he played me songs, when he called me just to see who I was. He was the very definition of genuine, and now he's gone. As if life is playing a cruel joke, showing me how only the truly genuine disappear from your life.

When I awake, it's past 1pm. But I don't care – I feel so refreshed. It's the best sleep I've had in over two weeks. I yawn, as I catch a glimpse of the beautiful countryside through my window. I smile and say a good morning to the immense beauty of Siena.

I have a shower and put on a spring dress with cute knee-high boots. Well, the sun is shining outside – it deserves a nice summer dress.

I head downstairs and there is no sign of Ric. I instead find his mum in the kitchen, cooking something that smells delicious.

"Buongiorno," I say with a smile.

"Buongiorno! How are you? Would you like some breakfast?"

"Sure," I say, just about to add that I can find the cereal when she brings me out an omelette.

How can I say no to an omelette?

It's just been made, and I wonder how the hell she knew how to time that. I ask her if she's seen Ric, and she tells me that he headed out pretty early this morning. I ask where his dad is, and she explains to me that he's outside setting up the barbecue – that's when I learn that it's a long standing tradition in the D'Angelo family to have a barbecue the first Sunday spring hits Siena.

They invite their family and friends, eat lots, drink wine, and enjoy the sunshine. Honestly, I thought only Brits were crazy enough to host barbeques when it's still ten degrees outside, but who am I to complain? Especially once I see the meat his dad is cooking.

And so I help his mum with setting the table, and then his dad with the cooking. I learned how to barbecue from my uncle in Biella, who always does the most incredible barbecues every summer. Being in Siena, I begin to realise how much I miss Biella, and promise myself to go back this summer.

Guests start arriving, and I meet some of Ric's cousins, aunts, uncles, and neighbours. People from Siena are so lovely, so warm and grounded; before Ric I had never met someone from Siena, but now I know where he gets it from.

They explain to me some of the traditions of the city, such as the annual horse racing in Piazza del Campo, and the celebrations that take place if the horse rider is from Siena. As a city they are very united, in both their wins and their losses, and I love this.

Ric's dad tells me that his own father was a horse racer, and though he never won, he made the D'Angelo name very well established in town. That, and one of Ric's great uncles was a famous photographer. How much I didn't know about Ric, all because, I had never asked.

I think back to Luca quite a bit as the day progresses, and worry that after opening up to me about it, Ric has now flipped or is consumed by the sadness. I text him a couple of times, but get no response. I shake off my worry and focus on learning more about his family.

Two of his friends from school turn up and of course are the two grungey-looking guys sitting and playing guitar in the corner. One of them asks me who I am, and when I say that I'm a friend of Ric's, they tell me that Ric doesn't have friends.

"Except for some chubby asshole in Milano about ten years his senior."

Vinnie.

They tell me stories about Ric from school – they all used to be in a band together! Pink Slippers.

I laugh. "Wait, so who played what instrument?" I ask them, curiously.

"Well I was on bass," Paolo – the blonde, tells me, and he does rather look like a bassist.

"And I was on drums," adds Claudio, the meatier of the two. "Ricco was on rhythm, and Luca was on lead guitar, and the singer."

Sadness hits me as I hear the name. "Luca?"

The two of them tense, and look solemnly at the ground. "Yes. He was the singer."

I imagine a teenage Ric, happy and go-lucky, playing in a band with his best friend. I then envision him in his late twenties, losing his best friend, and it's too sad to bear.

I shake it off and focus back on the guys. They tell me about Ric's weird phases - when he was thirteen, he went through a phase of playing guitar naked. Wherever he rehearsed or performed, he had to be naked. He came to be known as 'il pazzo nudo' (*'the crazy naked guy'*).

It gets worse. At the time, he was going out with a girl called Lucia from his class, and he thought it an excellent idea to turn up at her house naked when she was home alone and play her a song.

Only, her parents were home and Lucia's mum chased him down the drive with a wooden spoon.

I love hearing these stories from Ric's past, as if putting together pieces of his life from before I knew him. They make me smile.

By the time early evening comes around, I am an anxious wreck, even if I am enjoying my time with his family and friends. He's been gone for a good eight hours and knowing he is fragile at being back in Siena, my worry is reaching breaking point.

It's 8pm and fairly dark when Ric walks into the garden, nonchalantly. I secretly sigh in relief.

"There he is!" booms his dad.

"*Where* have you been?" his mum asks.

"Ciao tutti! Sorry, sorry, got caught up in town with some errands. I'm here now! Did I miss the entire barbecue?"

He comes over to me, and I am sat in-between Paolo and Claudio.

"Hey," he puts a hand on my shoulder and I look up at him, curiously. "Had a good day?"

"Yes, thanks. You? Where have you been?" I try not to sound worried, but I was, and I can't seem to find a valid reason to hide it.

"I, uh…" he eyes the entire table staring at us, and gulps. "I saw some old friends. Sorry, time just flew by. Hope my family has been treating you okay?"

"No, we kidnapped her and hid her in the basement," his mum jokes, who is sitting opposite us, and the entire table roars with that typically friendly and loud Italian laughter.

"Don't suppose I could get any leftovers?" Ric asks his mum with puppy dog eyes, and she's up in an instant to collect some for him from all the trays.

We shuffle down so that Ric can sit next to me, and we look at one another in intrigue as everyone else goes back to their own conversations.

I stare with a slight smile, waiting for an explanation. "Had a good day?"

"Yes, you could say that," he pauses, as if making sure nobody else can hear us first. "I went to see Luca."

My eyes widen. "What? You mean…?"

He nods with a smile. "Yes. At the cemetery." Ric seems calmer, as if his soul has been soothed. "It was amazing, Alex. I spoke to him, I told him about my life, I told him what I'm doing. I told him everything I had wanted to since it happened. About our friendship, about his last words to me. It was good."

"Wow, Ric, that's amazing."

"Yeah, it was. And then I went to see his brother, Marco. The guy you saw yesterday in piazza. We went to get a beer. I mean, it was okay, I needed to clear the air.

He's married now, with a kid. Which is weird, as he's Luca's little brother – we used to catch him masturbating in the bathroom and stuff, to think of him married is crazy, but…yeah."

My heart warms, and I'm glad that he made the decision to go, that he's okay. He's going to be okay. We stare at one another for a long moment before his mum hands him a plate of goodies.

"Grazie, mamma!" he exclaims, happily. He looks around at Paolo and Claudio. "Have these twits been keeping you company?"

"Oh yes!" I say.

"We've been telling her your adventures from school."

"Oh *God*, what have you heard?!"

"Oh I've been loving it! I especially love the naked guitar playing to your ex-girlfriend," I tell him, Paolo and Claudio instantly laughing like school chidren.

"Oh geez! 'Ex-girlfriend' - hardly! I was a kid."

"And yet you felt obliged to play to her naked - that means something, Ric. You are bound together for life now," I tease and he shows me the finger as he takes a huge bite of salame into his mouth.

"We have plenty more where that came from!" Paolo tells me.

"That's what she said!" Ric and I say in synch, and we high-five the way only Ric and I can high-five.

As Paolo tells me more embarrassing stories from Ric's past, I realise how glad I am that we came out here, that I'm glad Ric chose this place for me to find a sanctuary for my pain, as if he knew this would be the only place that could truly help me.

I'm not healed, far from it – but there's hope, and hope is what I need right now. Grief is not something that can be cured, but it's learning how to deal with it.

It's deep into the night when all the guests have left. Ric's dad has gone up to bed, and Ric stepped out about half an hour to take a call from the label and never came back.

It's only his mum and I, clearing away the last plates and bringing them into the house and to the dishwasher. I'm stacking the last glasses out in the garden as his mum pulls off the table cloth, and she suddenly smiles at me.

"I'm glad you're here, Alexis."

Her kind words reach my soul in an instant. "Me too."

"I see how happy you make my son. I haven't seen him this happy in a very long time."

The words hit me with a sudden happiness, a joy I haven't ever felt before. I am proud, proud that I am able to make Ric happy.

"He makes me happy too," I find myself saying, and I realise that it's true.

I suddenly have an intensely urgent desire to go upstairs, to see Ric. To be around him. To see if he's okay. To laugh. To talk. To be in each other's presence.

The feeling is very urgent, and so I help bring the glasses inside the house, lock up, and then I excuse myself upstairs to bed.

Each step I take I become more excited, and more nervous, but I'm not sure why. The nearer I get to his room, the faster my heart is beating. I don't know what I'm doing, but I'm following this thrill, this desire to be where Ric is.

By the time I reach his room I see that it is empty. Confused, I make my way to my room like an excited child, and I get ready to turn the door knob when I see it is already open.

The door is ajar, and Ric is standing, leaning over his pinboard of photographs. I can see that he is staring at a photograph in particular – one of whom I assume is Luca – he has his arm around Ric, they are about eighteen years old and at a school dance of some sort. They look happy, and possibly a little intoxicated.

I slowly walk over, and turn him to look at me by the chin. His eyes have sadness in them again.

I guess this grief thing is more complicated than we thought.

"You couldn't have done anything."

He nods. "I just miss him, that's all."

"I'm so proud of you for going to his grave, to facing all your fears."

"Thank you, Alex. For making me go."

I know it's hard for him to say, to show this side to him, and I feel such a strong wave of emotion hit me. Emotion that has been building up over time, trying to surface but I kept beating it down, and beating it down.

Maybe, it's time to let it all go.

Maybe, there is much more to this than the lies I have continued to tell myself.

"*Me? You're* thanking *me?* I should be thanking you. I've never known anyone like you Ric; you are kind, and considerate, honourable, talented, a feminist – your soul is humble, despite the impressive career, the guitar skills…"

Ric narrows his eyes at me, in curiosity. He's studying every inch of my face, and my God, I am sure he is reading me and what I'm thinking, the way he has always been able to. From the Goddamn first moment we met.

He slowly reaches out and caresses my cheek with one hand, and I am slightly distracted by his touch but continue nonetheless.

"…and you're always willing to help others, even when they're utter bitches to you, even when they push you away with all the effort they can muster. Even when they lie to themselves."

Ric's hand continues to caress my cheek affectionately, and I know he's looking me in the eye but I am afraid to do the same. Yet I know I have to.

When I do so, he is looking at me with such warmth in his eyes that it makes it easier to continue. "I'm so sorry, Ric. I'm so sorry for pushing you away, for pretending I don't care - I *do* care, I have *always* cared, I have always felt…connected to you."

My voice dies away, as he leans in, slowly, and I follow. We kiss slowly, savouring it, after such a long time.

No matter how much I had denied it to myself, my desire for him has always been there, even when I was mad at him, even when I was distracting myself with other things. There is a connection here that I simply cannot deny, and, I no longer want to.

Tenderness quickly turns to aggression, the way it always has with us. We kiss passionately, tongues colliding and ecstatic to be reunited, though it feels as if we have never left each other.

We crash into the table as we take off each other's clothes, kissing fiercely and groping as we do so. Our skin-on-skin feels so good, so natural.

I wrap my legs around him, he lifts me up, and continues kissing me as he carries me over to the door so he can shut it and lock it. He then throws me onto the bed, and we reunite our bodies the best way we know how.

And yet it's different now, even better, with feelings involved. Who knew? If I had known this before, perhaps I would have allowed myself to get emotionally attached to people more often. But when you both care about each other, know each other, trust each other, sex can be on a completely different level of amazing.

The way he looks at me, the way I look at him, it's…different. I feel connected to him in a way I have never felt before. But perhaps, previously to Ric, I had never connected to anyone.

Don't get me wrong though, we still fuck like porn stars.

Once we're two rounds in, we take a break. And I find myself lying on his chest, running my fingers through his hair as I look down at him with a smile. He is smiling up at me too, and, we are happy.

"Well, I have missed this," he tells me, caressing my cheek.

I kiss his hand before I rest my head on his chest, relaxing. He strokes my hair softly, as we dive into blissful silence. He kisses the top of my head and I beam.

But I soon remember Ric's sadness when I had entered the room. "It's not your fault," I tell him, and he knows exactly what I'm talking about. "Please don't blame yourself."

"And you don't blame yourself for Elliot."

Even just hearing his name stings, and sadness hits me like a ton of bricks, out of nowhere. "I could have stopped it, Ric. I could have stayed. I could have taken him home. I didn't go against Gavin's wishes because I was afraid of losing my job." Tears have invaded my eyes and there's no way to stop them.

"Hey," Ric says, and I look up at him. "You had no idea what was going to happen. If you did, you would have stayed, you would have done everything you could have," he wipes away my tears. "I'll stop blaming myself if you do. Deal?"

I nod.

"And I tell you what, we'll create a grief jar, and whenever one of us starts blaming ourselves, we have to put in a five-pound note. By the end of the month, we buy ourselves some apple pie with the cash."

I laugh through fresh tears, and again Ric wipes them away. "You don't even like apple pie."

"No, but you do, and I *may* have grown to like it through your influence."

"Because it rocks," I say, and Ric puts out his hand.

"Deal?"

"Deal." We shake on it, and kiss, before I resume my place resting on his chest.

"You know, Elliot figured out I liked you before I did," Ric tells me, and I frown.

"Really?"

"Oh yeah, we were in Milano, and I came to see you at rehearsals, and you had gone somewhere with the others, it was just Elliot and I and he said, 'so we'll see you in London, right?' and I asked him what he was talking about and he said, 'come on man, you're totally going to come to London to visit her – it's written all over your face.

You like her, big time.' I, of course, denied it at the time, but began to think about his words. And then he added, 'you hurt her, I've got connections in the mafia.'"

I laugh, and it's a laugh mixed with pain and joy. I miss him so much, and I know it will never leave me. But I will find a way to deal with this pain, to live with it.

"I wish Lucio could have met you. He would have loved you," Ric tells me.

"Yeah?"

"Oh yeah. He had the *best* taste in music; we used to jam together, he was a guitarist too."

"Oh wow."

"Yeah, he was good. Though he was more of a heavy metal fan; he introduced me to so many of the classics out there."

"How did you two meet?"

"Funnily enough, when I was getting bullied."

"Who the hell had the audacity to bully *Riccardo D'Angelo*?"

Ric tells me stories about Luca, and I listen in content, as he strokes my hair, affectionately. I am comfortable with Ric the way I always have been, from the very first moment we met.

Except now we understand each other even more, and are able to exchange stories on the people we have lost. We celebrate the happy memories they gave to us; the memories that will live on in us, through us, for us.

And I'm slowly learning that to be at one with someone and to connect with someone is possible. It's rare, but it's possible. And I have decided that it has to be worth it, for it to feel this incredible.

I am learning that in life, it's good to let at least one person in. Just one person will do. Because sure, they can always turn around and hurt you, but that's a risk you're just going to have to take, if you want to let in all the good.

Ric and I stay a couple more days before heading back to London; Siena is exactly what we both need, and we soak it in, sharing in both the happiness and sadness of where we are in our lives.

I get to know Ric's family better, and we go out exploring Siena alone together, sharing stories, and basking in time alone with Ric.

Being by myself is incredible, and I will always need that time and space, but being with Ric is also incredible, I have to say. Time just flies when we are together, and with a level of comfort as if I am alone.

The flight back to London is long and tiring, even though it's only two hours. I've always been a thinker on planes; I'll stare into nothing and think about life. I guess my thoughts are heavier than usual, given Elliot is on my mind, and the fact that I have no idea what I'm going to do with my life now.

Do I want to stay in the music business? Do I still want to be an artist manager? If I give up, does that mean I never belonged in this industry? If I continue despite everything that has happened, am I an idiot? A masochist?

I don't know the answer to any of these questions, but I'm okay with that. I am willing to take my time to discover what path best suits me, and what I want to do next.

Ric reads the entire trip; a book on how to promote an album by yourself. Every time I look over at him reading it makes me smile, and without looking up at me he says, "stop staring," in a playfully annoyed tone.

Once we land and pass passport control, I am rambling on about trying to get Ric's mum to reveal the secret ingredient to her lasagne as we make our way through the exit doors.

I stop, mid-sentence, as I recognise the two people I see waiting for us. I cover my mouth with my hand in shock, as I see Bailey and Blake standing at the barriers with flowers, Disaronno and tiramisu.

I turn to Ric, who is beaming at me. "I thought you might want your support system."

I grin as I look at him, having flashbacks of the night we met – shaking hands backstage at the Forum, deciding to accompany Kyle and him to Stansted airport, the night on the stage of San Siro, saving me from that gig, and the feeling of comfort I have felt when I had caught his hand.

I am so very grateful for having met him, for having him in my life, for always challenging me, for never being afraid of telling me when I'm wrong or being foolish, and for always being so damn patient with my monster of a personality.

"Thank you," I say softly, before running over to my friends, and jumping into their arms, one arm swinging around each of them. We giggle, and we scream, and we kiss each other, for we haven't seen each other in what feels like a lifetime.

"No, no, no – no Disaronno for Alex, she's been having *way* too much alcohol recently," Ric swipes the bottle of amaretto as he approaches, and my friends stare at him.

"Quick Alex, he's going to drink your Amaretto!" Blake exclaims.

Ric forces a laugh. "Trust me, this is the absolute *last* alcohol on the face of the planet that I would ever drink, argh. But it's not for Alex!"

"What, are you now owned by this stranger, who is this?" Blake asks, half-joking.

"Hey Ric," Bailey says and they exchange a quick hug, as Blake stares.

"Oh my God, you're the guitarist at that gig… the Italian gig!" Blake wails, but nobody else is reacting. "Alex! What?!" he shakes Bailey. "It's the guitarist from a gig we went to last summer-"

"Yes Blake I know – it was he who called me to see if we could come to the airport, you twit," Bailey rolls her eyes at us playfully, and I cackle.

"Well I'm sorry if I've been AWOL in Indonesia all this time, what else has been happening? Become best friends with Pablo what's-his-face? Maybe was a bridesmaid at his wedding?"

"*Paolo* Petrinelli," I correct Blake, as he takes my luggage from me.

Bailey and Blake lead the way to the taxis, and I pull Ric back and kiss him. I don't say anything, for I have always spoken with my eyes.

And he has always been able to read them.

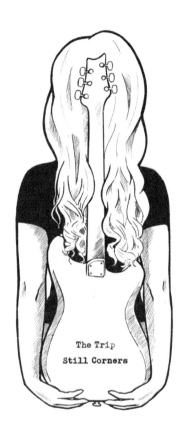

29

"Mr Miller is ready to see you," says the receptionist, who is wearing a blue flannel shirt, black jeans and red Old School Vans.

I really need to get myself a pair in red.

I thank the receptionist and follow her instructions. First I knock, and when I hear 'come in!' I enter. Sitting at his desk is a man in his forties wearing an expensive suit and shiny shoes.

His hair is slicked back with gel and he has a rather fake smile on his face. He gets up to greet me as we introduce ourselves, and we shake hands.

My handshake is firm, confident. My smile and eyes are confident, too.

"Please, Alexis – sit down." I do so, as he takes his place on the other side of his desk. As he sits down, he holds onto his blazer, as if terrified of creases.

Looking into his eyes, it's clear he has six thousand other things on his mind, that he doesn't want to be here. His body language is telling me he could care less about me or why I'm here, and the way he takes big pauses tells me he has not planned any questions.

This means that I can greatly take advantage of what questions he asks, and so I steer each answer into a subject that can benefit me, make me look good, and highlight everything I've done.

I sit still in my seat, back straight and looking him in the eye. I answer to the point, I do not faff, I do not bullshit, I do not skirt around the facts.

I'm doing well. I'm doing really well. He at at one point however asks me what my three main strengths are, and I take a moment to respond as his mind remains elsewhere.

I open my mouth to spit out the pre-planned answer that I wrote myself last night, when I hesitate, and he waits. I relax. "You know what Mr Miller, I could give you a whole set of generic answers, things I planned to say last night as I listened to some of your clients' music, which by the way, some of which truly *sucks*, I mean what do Moon Beans think they're doing? Their music is so poppy it made my ears cry for me to turn it off, and their name? It feels as if someone doesn't change it soon the name itself will go ahead and commit suicide.

I could tell you all the things you want to hear, run on cue with the structure set out for job interviews like this, smile when I'm supposed to, and act completely different to how I actually would if you hired me. Or," I tell him, "I could tell you that I worked at Ruby for the better part of a year, I dealt with every kind of artist imaginable, I grew in ways that normal humans take five years to do (I had to or I wouldn't survive), and I am responsible for this entire campaign."

I get out my phone and show him Dazza's debut music video, "from the music, to the lyrics, to how he sings the song. Not to mention re-branding him (he used to wear blue jeans and t-shirts his grandmother bought him)." I put my phone away. "I didn't know what I was good at until six months ago. Some are good at accounting, some are good at gardening, and I, I am a born artist manager."

I watch Ben Miller, as he looks curiously at me. I caught his attention, as soon as I started the speech, and he's now looking at me with all the concentration he can muster. His eyes are full of life. He is interested, I have sparked interest. But the question now is, is it going to get me the job?

He leans back in his chair, putting his hands behind his head, as if he is not thrown off by my speech. But he is. I can tell. He liked it. He did.

"You know, you passed the first two rounds of the interviews with flying colours. Our HR lady loved you, so did your potential boss. And Bernie never likes anyone. I thought, what is it about this girl that they like so much, when she doesn't even have a year's experience in artist management?

Some people go from internship to internship year after year, and yet here you are, applying to work at LOK Records, the second biggest label in the UK at present."

"I guess there must be something likeable about me," I reply, sharply.

"Indeed there must be." He pauses for effect, and then without hesitation, he proceeds. "We would like to offer your job."

Fireworks go off in my head. Every upbeat Prince song starts playing, and it takes all the resistance possible to not get up and do a victory dance in front of him.

"That is fantastic news, thank you Mr Miller." We both get up at the same time. "I will need twenty-four hours to think about it."

He freezes, mid-handshake, and a confused look appears on his face. "Erm, sure. Of course."

We small talk a little more, and then he escorts me out of the office. I remain cool and collected until I am out of the building, but once I am on the high street, I dance around in a circle like a crazy person. I grin from ear-to-ear as people stare at me in disbelief, but I don't care.

This is a big step for me. Huge, in fact.

Once I've stopped dancing around, I scurry off to get the tube. I get to the photography studio with only ten minutes to set up, but I'm used to rushing around now.

"Ah, finally!" says Fernando, Elsie's manager. "I thought the artists are the ones who like to be late," he hisses. "Elsie is ready!"

"So am I! I just need to grab my camera."

"Darling, you make it sound like you're just grabbing your phone."

I roll my eyes as I head over to my locker to get my gear. It's hard to believe that I rent out this studio, that it's technically mine to use.

I share it with some other photographers I met on a photography course – it turns out there's a lot of us out there who just need somewhere to take shots that doesn't cost an entire lifetime of money. And so eight of us decided to put our cash together and share a very cool space in Shoreditch.

It's tiny, and we run on a fixed rota, but it's pretty damn cool. I spent a lot of time studying different marketing methods, putting the word out there, even promoting it on my blog, and the clients have slowly started getting in touch.

Sure, I only get about a few clients a week, but everyday the number keeps going up, and I'll continue to push until it's a viable career option.

Of course, this doesn't cover the rent, and so I work two days a week at the record shop in Camden where Elliot and I bought that Foo Fighters record. It feels like home, as if I can see Elliot smiling at me when I'm there.

That's not all, though. Whilst playing on Ric's Fender Strat in his bedroom one day, I turned to him and said, 'I think I'd like to be a guitarist.'

He simply smiled at me, the same way he did when I asked him to get me an interview with Paolo Petrinelli – that sort of knowing smile, as if he had been waiting for this moment a while. As if he knew before me that this was what I was supposed to be doing.

Yes, I want to be a guitarist. I don't think I've ever *not* wanted to be a guitarist; I just took a while to realise.

And so I called that teacher we met at The Roadhouse the night Elliot died, and booked in a couple of sessions. Steve is a great teacher, and a few lessons in he started telling me about people he knows who might be looking for a guitarist, and I've been going to a few auditions.

Not only that, but I called up every single person I know in music and told them I am now a guitarist. I've had some interesting leads so far, but nothing that has really taken my breath away.

Not until I got a call from Parker May. He told me he is starting his own band, and that he'd love to have me audition as guitarist. They already have a bassist and drummer, Parker is lead singer and rhythm guitarist, and so the lead guitarist needs to have approval from everyone in the band. He asked if I'll audition, and I said I sure as fuck will.

Oh, and it turns out I also want to be an artist manager, but in my own name, and in my own right. I don't want to work for a label or an artist management company.

So when I called everyone I knew in music to tell them I'm now a guitarist looking for a band, I also told them I'm an artist manager looking for an act.

"Jesus Alex, is there anything you're not doing at the moment?" was the response from most.

Some interesting leads have come through, but nothing gripping enough that I've taken anyone on yet. But I'm sure it'll happen, if I continue to fight for it with every fibre of my being.

I love being a photographer too, though. It turns out though that freelancing isn't all that difficult; I have the self-discipline and drive to make it work, to make it coincide with my career in the music business.

I spend the next hour shooting pictures of a weird singer called Elsie, chatting to her about her life and her music prior to shooting her. She tells me about how she likes to eat wood and once knocked on Christian Slater's door.

I take it all as if it's normal conversation, concentrating more on making sure she becomes comfortable with me. I think it's important before you do a photo shoot to make the subject trust you. It helps to capture their soul, as people often say I do well, which is really the highest compliment I could ask for as a photographer.

She seems to relax with me quite quickly, and I remember that Ric tells me quite often that I'm very good at making people feel comfortable.

The shoot lasts just over an hour, and I enjoy every moment of it. I really do love to photograph strangers, even when they are actually strange. I'm hoping that the more clients I get and the more I grow my brand, the less strange my clients will be.

I'm packing up when fellow photographer James, the most hipster person I have ever met, approaches me.

"That looked like a fun shoot," he tells me, as he pulls out a pack of chewing gum from his back pocket.

"She's very beautiful," I reply, as I close my locker.

"True. Hey, there is someone here to see you."

My eyes up light in delight, but when I turn around I am taken aback with who I see in the distance.

Standing awkwardly next to the black spiral staircase is Damiano. His hair is longer, flopping down over his forehead like in the days of Milano. But his face looks different to every other time I have ever seen it, though I'm not entirely sure why.

I haven't seen any of the boys for a while, and seeing Damiano brings back instant memories. I suddenly am reminded of how much I miss all of them.

Matteo text me back in Siena and told me that he and the rest of them are staying in Milano, except for Damiano, who Ruby offered a separate record deal, right after they dropped the Devilled Eggs. Typical Brett-Gavin behaviour to be honest, and a move I saw coming a mile away.

If I ever start my own label, I swear to God, it *will* be different to all this bullshit.

I talk only to Matteo now, who is back attending the music academy in Milano, and is also taking a course in art – he wants to be an illustrator. We speak maybe once or twice a week, and it's always great to hear about what's he doing.

He still chats to the others, and through him I have learnt that G got a job as a waiter and gave up guitar. Lino has become a songwriter, and Damiano, well he remained in London to take on his contract as a solo artist.

I'm a little nervous to see him, but I'm not sure why. He spots me, gives me a very awkward motionless wave, and I approach him just as he gives me a smile I've never quite seen before.

That's because he's never actually smiled at you before, Alex.

"Hey," he says, with the friendliest tone he has ever used on me, and I decide to mirror it.

"Hey. How are you?"

"Good, you?"

"Yeah." Awkward silence hits us, and I wonder what he is doing *here*, of all places.

Did something happen to one of the others?

"I left Ruby," he announces, with a grin. "I left Ruby, and my dad, and the fucking record deal. I left it all."

My eyes widen in a mix of joy and surprise at the news. "Oh wow! Good for you, Damiano."

"Yeah. I work at a café down the road from the label now, was the first place that would hire me. Pay is *really* shit – fuck, how do people in London survive on minimum wage? Geez, had to get a second job at *another* café, just to pay the rent. Anyway! It feels good. To get rid of everything toxic to me."

I am overwhelmed with happiness for Damiano. To be honest, I hadn't thought he had it in him, so this is really great to see. It's hard for a spoiled rich kid to let all of that go; they are brought up a certain way.

"Good, I'm proud of you Damiano." Again silence, and again I wonder why he's come to *me*, the girl he's never liked or even respected, to tell this news to.

"We created a spot in Elliot's hometown for people to remember him by," he tells me, and you can tell that it stings for the both of us to hear his name. I see it in his eyes, and we wince at the same time, recovering at the same time.

"Oh, that sounds nice – Ric and I created an Elliot Day, on the day of his death, every year we will celebrate his life – I'll invite you to the first one.

Ric is doing one for his friend Luca, too. There will be a gig and a gathering afterwards and everything." I realise I can't stop talking and I go quiet.

"That sounds nice. I'll be there for sure. Listen, Alex. I actually came here to ask you something."

I look at him in intrigue; for the first time ever, Damiano looks nervous.

"I want to ask you if you'll be my manager."

I frown.

What?

Did I hear that right?

If ever I had to guess what the most unlikely thing Damiano could ever possibly say to me, this would surely be it.

"I heard you left Ruby too, I heard you're looking for artists. I cannot think of anyone better to manage me as a solo artist; frankly, you are the only person that has ever been honest with me in my life. Except for Elliot."

"So, what do you say?"

I think back to how I met Damiano, all the awful things he had said to me along the way, and all the names I had called him under my breath. And yet, I have never wanted to be someone's manager more than I do the person standing in front of me now.

"Yes, Damiano. I would love to."

He grins. "Okay! Great! Great! Oh, this is going to be fantastic! And I promise not to be an asshole!"

"Oh I'm sure you still will be, but I'll be an asshole right back," I wink at him and he laughs nervously.

"Okay. I have to get to work! I guess I'll text you later and sort out our first meeting?"

"Sure."

"Okay!"

439

I watch him walk out with a huge, excited grin on his face. Somehow, it also feels nice to hold onto a part of Elliot. Other than the part that will forever remain in my heart.

Just as Damiano walks out, Parker May comes gliding through with his usual I'm-too-cool walk, holding a guitar case in his hand. He turns to look at Damiano, perplexed, and then back at me as he approaches with that Parker smile of his.

"Good morning, sunshine! Did I just see who I thought I saw?"

"Yeah, I've just become his manager I think," I tell him.

"*Oooh*, the plot thickens! Congratulations on your first client."

"Thank you."

We hear footsteps up the stairs again and turn to find Ana gliding towards us in a similar way to Parker. She's dragging her luggage behind her and holds her passport in her hand with a cunning smirk on her face.

"You ready to smash Mauro Fucking Fontana?" she asks me, putting both her arms in the air with that infectiously unique energy that Ana encompasses.

"Oh hell yes, let me just pack up," I tell her, as we exchange pecks on the cheek.

"Oh hello manwhore," she says to Parker.

"Hey Ana, how you doing?"

"You coming with us to Milan?" she asks him.

"I am indeed. But first…" We both turn to look at him, as his tone is now serious. He puts down the guitar case in front of me, unzipping it with his I-mean-business look. "Shall we go over the details of the US tour?"

I smile. *"Bring. It. On."*

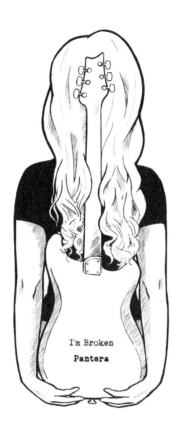

"I don't know, I've never liked punk," Matteo says. "I've just never been into the whole genre, even when I was a kid."

I smile as Matteo continues to ramble on; this is the longest he has ever spoken to me for, and he can't seem to shut up. I suppose this is my fault; I bought him a beer even though he still has a year until his eighteenth birthday.

"Shut up burger-face," Elliot tells him, playfully pushing him backwards by the forehead. I cock up an eyebrow at Elliot.

"Don't be mean to burger face-uh-I mean Matteo."

Everyone apart from Matteo roars into laughter, and I scruff up his hair affectionately as my way to apologise.

"Who are this band, anyway?" G asks me, almost as a groan. I know he's missing the latest episode of his favourite reality show for this gig, but I honestly see it as killing two birds with one stone.

"Décor Kind are an awesome punk band, just trust me, G."

He gives me a weak smile, but I know that the only one excited for this gig is Elliot. He doesn't know them but he trusts my taste in music. He always seems to trust my taste in music.

The venue suddenly goes dark, and the crowd 'woo' in excitement.

We have an amazing view in front row, and we 'woo' with the rest of the crowd. In true punk style, the band don't introduce themselves, they just start playing, and we start bouncing around to the song. The Devilled Eggs are instantly taken in by the song, all of it - the cool guitar riff, the deep vocals, the addictive drum beat.

I had forgotten just how much I love this band, and it looks as if the Devilled Eggs love them too. They grin at me, as we mosh with the crowd.

I realise as I mosh arm-to-arm with Elliot and Matteo that these boys have long surpassed being a client to me. They are now friends of mine; people I like to hang out with, and share funny stories with.

Especially Elliot. Sometimes I swear, it feels as if he is my age. As if our love for good music could never divide us.

He suddenly lifts me up and I squeal as he puts me on his shoulders. The view from Elliot's shoulders is incredible, and I find myself wondering why I've never had someone put me on their shoulders during a gig before!

I 'woo' harder and louder than ever before, and Elliot laughs beneath me as he dances around. I beam, feeling completely in my element, as I take in the good music. As it seeps right through to my soul, connects with my skin, my bones, my soul. It electrifies me, bringing me to life in a way that absolutely nothing else in the world can.

I know that Elliot is feeling it too, losing himself in the incredible music the same way I am.

I close my eyes, as I smile.

This right here, I think to myself, is most definitely one of life's greatest gifts.

Read *Canned Tuna* from the same author!

Canned Tuna is the story of Skye, a twenty-something Londoner, and what happens when she meets an arrogant and troubled man called 'the Shark'.

Told through snippets of her life, Skye makes comical observations about modern dating, from her own perspective and as an outsider looking in, to create a perplexing illustration that reminds us of what falling in love is really like…

Lisa Sa grew up in north west London, and has been writing since she was seven years old.
In September 2017, she published her first book, *Canned Tuna*. Drawn in by the music business from an early age, Lisa has met and worked with many honorable bands and artists.
She then moved over to the advertising industry, and is currently a strategist for a reputable marketing agency in London, where she gets to do what she loves best – storytell.

Printed in Great Britain
by Amazon